HAWAIIAN ESCAPE

By

Debbie Flint

ISBN 978-1-909785-14-4

Amazing front cover illustration by Angela Oltmann
www.angieocreations.com

Published by Flintproductions
www.debbieflint.com
@debbieflint

FOREWORD

This book 'Hawaiian Escape,' is Book 1, and the prequel to 'Hawaiian Affair.'

If you are new to my work, do read this first.

'Hawaiian Affair – Sadie's Story,' is book 2 in the trilogy.

'Hawaiian Retreat – Helen's Story', book 3 in the series, is out June 2014.

Why a prequel?

I had so many requests for more from Sadie Turner, PhD, that I began a short story to show what happened *before* her Hawaiian adventure began. But as I wrote it something strange happened – Helen came tumbling out.

Helen is Sadie's sister and here in **'Hawaiian Escape'** you'll read a tale of intrigue as Helen and Sadie each face a crisis – in love, in career and in life. But it's what Helen does to try to solve it – and the secrets that she keeps – that form the foundation of this tale: a tangled love life, and her attempts to escape it.

Read Hawaiian Affair already?

For those who have read Hawaiian Affair first, I hope Helen's shenanigans fulfil your hopes for this book. The feedback so far has been great, and I look forward to your thoughts. You can always email me Debbie@debbieflint.com. Do kindly leave a review on Amazon.

Caution – PLEASE don't buy this if you've read '*Hawaiian Affair*' already and you DON'T like 'knowing what happens at the end...' Seems obvious, but I thought I'd point it out – I don't want you to waste your money! : –)

And for those avid readers who have long awaited the 'next one', I hope I've done you proud with this carefully crafted PREQUEL of Hawaiian Affair. Enjoy.

Other titles by Debbie Flint

<u>Hawaiian Affair</u> is the follow up story to this book.

Published first, it's the story of Sadie and Mac and their race against time, taking them around the world from a luxury yacht in Monaco to the magic of Hawaii. It was my first ever finished novel, and a step into the unknown for me. At first it was released Charles Dickens-style, in serialised instalments, but I also did something a little unusual.

There is either a PG or a Steamy version available.

And what sold best in Hawaiian Affair? Across eBook and paperback, the Steamy outsold the PG by around 8 to 1. There's a message in there somewhere!

The third book, '**Hawaiian Retreat**' will follow Helen's story, and is the SEQUEL to Hawaiian Affair.   Coming to Amazon, summer 2014.

For more info on my other titles, search 'Debbie Flint' on Amazon, or go here http://www.amazon.co.uk/Debbie-Flint/e/B00C02VYAG/

Dedication

Thank you so much to all my lovely beta-readers on our fabulous Facebook group, particularly Sharon Harvey who continues to be the most supportive pal an author could wish for, proof reader extraordinaire Caz Jones, and talented illustrator Angela Oltmann, who put up with my little requests to tweak things a bit like the Golden Shot – 'up a bit, down a bit...' Another stunning cover, thank you for being so in tune with what I was trying to achieve.

And to everyone who loved Hawaiian Affair – I'm still amazed at the proportion of top marks on Amazon! And whatever your opinion, thank you if you've taken the time to review it, it means a lot.

Now on to Hawaiian Retreat!

Keeping in touch –

Go to www.debbieflint.com where you can –

- Sign up for updates and get my regular newsletter
- Plus news of free downloads and short stories
- A full list of my novels
- Follow my weekly QVC UK blog
- Find *RiWiSi* – Read It Write It Sell It – my weekly look at all things book.

Or keep in touch via Twitter @debbieflint

Or Facebook – search DebbieFlintQVC

Hawaiian

Escape

By

Debbie Flint

Steamy version also available on Amazon in paperback or eBook

PROLOGUE

To be honest, a marketing conference in Tuscany with her sister in tow hadn't exactly had 'find a naked hot guy' at the top of the agenda. But here he was in her hotel room, dominating the doorway of the bathroom in nothing more than a towel. A little towel.

'You can't guess, then?' he was saying. 'Ok, I will tell you – I think I should take you up on your challenge.'

What challenge?

Oh-oh. All the way back to her hotel, he'd been paying more attention to her face than to the road ahead. His voice had been low, seductive. The way he'd helped her adjust the seat, leaning a little too close. The way he'd brushed his fingers against her leg several times as he changed gear. Even the way he'd opened the door for her and taken her hand as she stepped out of the low, luxurious car – it wasn't her usual experience of a ride home. But then he wasn't her usual experience of men.

But there was a problem – he was exactly her type. Well, the type of man she *would* have chosen if life hadn't got in the way.

Tall – tick.

Brooding – tick.

Broad – oh yeah, BIG tick.

Tantalisingly sexy, with his movie star good looks and his thick, dark hair falling over intense deep brown eyes. And that Mediterranean charm... the accent which had made her quiver when he'd introduced himself three days earlier. A quiver that reached from her neatly manicured, scarlet fingernails right down to the tips of her toes inside the towering 'I'm making a statement' Manolo Blahnik's.

They were still on her feet, resting on the edge of the plush hotel bed with all its crisp, white linen and dozens of designer cushions, even though her jacket was off, and her shirt was slightly open... Well, it *was* hot.

'Challenge?' she replied.

'Yes,' he went on, walking towards her. His towel was so small, he had to hold it together with his fingers, and she could see the top of his thigh, slightly whiter than the rest of his tanned skin. His chest was pin-up perfect and still moist from the shower – it rippled slightly as he moved. She snapped her eyes back up to his face as he replied.

'You said to me, did you not, that no man was capable of breaking down the barrier in your… defences – and that right now you are too closed-down, too hurt…'

I did?

'…And I told *you* – have faith, because one day a *very* special man would open your mind again…*Tesoro mia*, what if that time has come?'

CHAPTER ONE

Ten months earlier...

Helen sat writing at her computer, in the kid's room she always stayed in when she retreated to Sadie's. In between jobs, in between countries, in between men...

She got up to open the window slightly and fresh air rushed in. She breathed it in deeply and stared out at her sister's pretty English country garden – it was the back garden, so was a bit less tidy than the front. The bird table was full to the brim with fat, happy, bluebirds fighting with sparrows over suet balls and seeds. The cherry blossom tree had decorated the lawn with a carpet of pink petals, and the ivy on the summer house was a lot more overgrown than the last time she'd been here. Had it really been a year? Must be a record – a year. With one man. She'd had such high hopes this time... but in the end it didn't last. *They never do.* Helen steeled herself, took another deep breath, smelling the faint honeysuckle fragrance in the air, then stretched her arms and sat back down in a slightly-too-small purple chair to continue her typing. She felt like Goldilocks.

But it didn't matter whose chair she was sat in, it was obviously just right – for inspiration to strike. 'Cos strike it had. And it was a genius idea. One of Helen's best.

Sadie's store was in trouble. And maybe the publicity from this piece would save it. And with a bit of luck, it might even mean a fabulous trip abroad. Maybe even together – like when they were kids. And if this didn't help her sister, then nothing would.

Helen banged away enthusiastically for a few more minutes at the keyboard. It was propped up on a typical youngster's dressing table, surrounded by nail varnish and nick-knacks, magazine clippings of boy bands taped to the mirror, and an assortment of purple gonks of different sizes – some of which looked older than Helen.

And some of which looked better than Helen.

She paused and frowned at her reflection in the mirror – then made a face like one of the gonks. *Yuk.* Too many sleepless nights – well what could anyone expect after losing her job, her future and her man – all in one go? It hadn't been a good month. For her sister neither, it seemed. Because today whilst Sadie was out at the store, Helen had accidentally opened a bank statement, then 'accidentally' picked up her sister's business folder which had – 'quite by coincidence' – opened on the right page showing that Sadie was soon to be in financial shit. Deep shit.

It had snapped Helen out of her stupor. She'd cancelled that evening's pity party and jumped into action. Now she was once again doing what she did best – bringing in the cavalry. Rescuing people. A quick brainstorming session on the internet using all of her resources had led to one of those eureka turning points – and an offer that could put Sadie's health shop in the spotlight. It was last minute, but if Helen could pull this off, she may just rescue herself, too. She already felt miles better. Even if the mirror disagreed.

So far, her article was going well. A work of art, even if she did say so herself. A personality piece, with a powerful message. Sadie would be proud... wouldn't she? Let's see...

Attention grabbing opener – Emotional impact – Sob-story... well let's see how this sounds. She read it back to herself in the mirror.

"Everyone has a dream, right? The sort of dream you never tell anyone – you just swat it away like a mosquito, but it keeps coming back.

It's as if the child in you has big plans, big hopes, big dreams. But somehow life gets in the way, and those plans get put on hold – next year, or the year after, or the year after that – then we'll have time for our dream.

We've all got one, haven't we, so what's yours? No, seriously – what is it?

Career or Kids?

Home or Travel?

Independence or Relationship?

Climb a mountain, learn to ski, become a wine expert, get slim... one day? Bucket list stuff. Don't you admire the people that DO do it – even the smug gits?

And now you're a bit older and time's slipping by, but it's still right there on your list of 'to-do's', hanging around at the top – waiting for the right time to come. Then suddenly it's like the universe has finally heard you, and you know it's now or never. Keep focussing on it and focussing on it and expanding it – as if it's real? (That's what 'The Secret' says anyway – and books like it – all that Law of Attraction bullshit, right?)

But the one thing it's NOT is 'just luck' – unless you're one of those people who make your own luck. And we all know someone like that, don't we?

My sister Sadie, for instance. And me – on a good day...

Sadie Turner did something she'd never done before – something she'd had in her heart and soul since cooking her first nut cutlet and tasting her first camomile tea. Turned out to be the steepest learning curve she'd ever ridden. But this could be it – the making of her. Yes Sadie Turner was about to get all grow'ed up."

'Auntie Helen, Auntie Helen!' There came a loud banging on the bedroom door. Helen jolted out of her concentration. 'Mum says do you want organic oat cream with your pudding? Or just the apple and cinnamon compote on its own?'

'Georgia!' Helen said and stopped typing. She called out to her niece, who was still hammering loudly on the other side of the locked door. 'I told you I'm on a deadline for America. Just the fruit – your mother knows I can't stand bloody oat cream! And cover up the plate for me will you? Put it with my mungo bean salad? I'll be a while yet, tell your mum I'm really in flow and I don't want to stop – I've got a deadline of ...' she looked at her watch and counted on her fingers, 'ten pm – it's got to be sent over tonight before they close for the day. I'm checking it back.'

The hammering stopped and there was no reply.

'Now, where was I?' Helen resumed reading out loud.

"That health food store she'd always wanted? Well it's all about location – get that right and it's half the battle. ...BLAH BLAH... If she's facing a barrier, and conventional wisdom lets her down, she'll just use her Mensa brain to find a way round it. ..YADDA YADDA... That dilapidated shop didn't know what hit it and neither did the picturesque Surrey village ... ETC ETC... If they hadn't heard before about the benefits

of adzuki beans and quenwa... kwinowa... kinwoo," (oh whatever it's called*)*, *"they certainly did after she hit town."*

'It's "keen-waah",' came a childish voice through the door. 'Like couscous only it's a whole grain instead of a pasta. Keeeeen-waaaah!'

'Thank you Georgia. Now go away and let me concentrate. I told you I promise I'll read it to you later.'

'Does mum know you're writing about her for your new column?'

Helen was reminded it's sometimes best *not* to make children your confidantes. Even when they *have* supplied you with endless Hello Kitty tissues *'for when you start grizzling again, Auntie.'*

'Don't tell her – it's a surprise!' Helen called. 'And it's not my column yet. Nor will it be, unless you let me finish this! Now, go!' There was a thumping of footsteps away from the door and Helen listened carefully. Then she got up, opened the door suddenly, and caught the youngster bending her ear to the keyhole. Georgia squealed in delight and ran away laughing as Helen trotted a couple of steps, chasing her up the landing. Satisfied her niece wasn't coming back, Helen returned to continue the article. She smiled and scanned her work, tapping her chin with a pencil.

It was important, this.

In fact, it was inspirational.

The best idea she'd had in months... actually, the only idea she'd had in months – her brain had gone a bit numb since the troubles began. Thank god for friends in international magazines tipping the wink about urgently needed new features. The fact that her best pal believed wholeheartedly that Helen could pull this off had been a real confidence booster, sorely needed since she'd been made redundant.

Hah! Redundant? *Got rid of* more likely.

Now THAT was another story – maybe it could even be Helen's next article – if she won this commission. It would make her feel better to spill the beans publically even if publishing it was wholly inappropriate. She could see the headline now...

"Marketing High Flyer Sacked after Being Hit-on by Boss's Husband..."

Should have fended him off a bit harder, perhaps. But Victor had been persistent, as well as warm, kind, and in need of love. Oh and rather good in bed. One thing led to another and it all got out of hand – or rather, *'in-hand'*. Then it got deeper and it had all seemed so genuine. So welcome, after all those transient years, history making Helen run a mile at the first sign of meaningful. In any case, she'd long since given up hope of finding a replacement for her first love – the man who had become just a distant figment of her imagination. The only man who…

Enough.

She shook herself.

Anyway, was it any wonder after years of being a go-getter, holding all the cards, cherry-picking the roles and excelling at everything she did – work-wise anyhow – that Helen Parker-Todd had finally broken down having suffered the ignominious humiliation of being given her marching orders. Publically. The shrill tones of her 'ex' boss were still ringing in her ears two months later.

'No head-hunters chasing me down this time,' she said aloud to the gonks, then paused as if waiting for their reply. 'Pah. You don't care,' she said to them, and flicked one on the nose then pouted at herself in the mirror.

Word travels fast in the marketing world and now Helen was finding that her calls were no longer being returned, so she guessed that some serious dirt was being dished around the industry. Shame 'cos Helen had been at the top of her game – and she'd liked working for Winston, Winston & Grant Marketing in New York. She missed her luxury condo on the top floor of 560 Park Avenue. Her cold Clapham flat was stark by comparison. So after a couple of weeks moping, she'd given in and gone to stay at Sadie's to mope there instead and eat flapjacks. Now the only contact with her old firm was the continued negotiation for her so-called 'redundancy payment'.

'Get-the-Hell-Away-from-my Husband payment', more like, thought Helen.

Just then a ping came from her computer. An email. She pressed Alt-Tab, saw it swap to her inbox and spotted the new arrival. Seeing who it was from, she made a face and shook her head – *talk of the Devil*. She opened it, scanned it, then growled under her breath. She deleted it with a flourish and turned back to her article. *It was HIS fault. Broken promises, leaving me high and dry.* Just her bad luck it had happened right after she'd taken his advice to invest in some long term bonds that couldn't be undone.

This genius idea had better pay-off soon. Helen wasn't used to being skint. Or being let down by men.

Unable to resist, she switched to her photo album and opened a folder marked 'Victor'. The chief gonk was staring at her as if it knew what she was up to, so she picked it up and turned it round the other way so it couldn't 'see'. Then she took a breath and clicked some buttons.

Helen allowed herself precisely sixty seconds of wallowing. She gazed at the pictures of herself and a smart guy in a suit at the office party where they first met – dazzling, vivacious – charisma oozing from every pore – that's how she used to be. Seeing herself back then made her feel as though she'd been kicked in the nuts. And she used to have nuts, did Helen.

Yes, hers would make a good story.

She was usually the one who did the kicking, and the walking off, not the other way round. Escaping before the relationship got too serious and before the talk turned to babies and futures and 'his and hers sinks' in the bathroom and weekends at the parents and… no, Helen always found it best to flee, as she'd done with every single man whose name graced a folder on her cloud files. Yep – it had got to be a routine – flee, see Sadie and the gang for a week or two and wait for the head-hunters to come calling once they all heard she was back on the job market again. Then, deal done, home visit over, and galvanized with that 'first day of a new term' feeling, off she'd go to start all over again.

But this last time had been different. *He'd* been different, or so she'd thought. A painful feeling filled the back of her eyes and her throat hurt and she fought off yet another bout of tears – in any case, the Hello Kitty box was nearly empty. No, enough was enough. Helen had never been much for self-pity, but this last time it had taken her by surprise, and after all, it was so very public.

Helen reached for a tissue, took the last remaining one, blew her nose violently and loudly and then scrunched the tissue up to throw it away. She looked down – the bin was full. Seeing all the cried-on tissues started

some sort of Pavlov's dogs reaction and her ey/
so she lifted her head to the ceiling to blink !
threatening to brim over her eyelids. Perhaps t

Maybe it was time for a change – hence this article. Ana y↙
her own fall from grace was also just as Sadie needed help like ɴ↙.
before. *So enough*, she sniffed. There are two careers at stake here.

Perhaps she'd feel better soon. Like last time.

Last time, when Helen had returned, it was just as Sadie got the keys
to the dusty shop and Helen had swept in like the knight in shining
armour to help out. Helen was in her element, organising everyone,
creating an impressive 'schedule of duties' chart – which Sadie had
typically copied onto Excel and laminated.

They'd all got stuck in and worked long hours on the big clean up – all
hands on deck. Well, nearly all – all except one person – conspicuous by
his absence. Helen's eyes narrowed as she thought of her soon-to-be-ex
brother in law.

Despite the venture directly affecting his two children, Turncoat
Turner – as Helen called Stuart – had not got his hands dirty. Not once.
Too busy sorting out his own dirty linen, Helen suspected. Then she
smiled as a thought crossed her mind. She began typing away again
furiously, paused, deleted the lot, then shook her head and typed it all
back again, then wrote some more.

Helen's article described feeling so proud of her little sis, making the
break for independence. Sadie had finally got shot of him, proving she
wasn't the 'useless co-dependent little wifey' he'd claimed she was. Yes
she'd finally walked away from her one-sided marriage to Stuart.

Helen stopped typing and chewed her cheek. She hated Stuart. She
decided not to include that bit. Instead, she described that early
transformation. People love reading about a makeover story – *so let's
make this a good one.*

Helen tapped her fingernails on the table top. She pondered whether
to mention herself much in this piece, as it was supposed to be Sadie's
story. But if it was going to become a regular column – a personality piece
– maybe she could make an exception – or would it be too indulgent...?
Hmm... Then she gave in and included the bit where she, Helen, had

.ted the new sign for the store. She stopped typing for a few minutes
ıd sketched a little mock up as an illustration for the article – and it
didn't look half bad. "Turner's Health Foods." *Maybe I could be a sign-
writer, if this journalism lark doesn't work out,* Helen thought as she
stretched her arms out. Then she began the part she was looking forward
to writing most. The part that would never have happened if Helen
wasn't around to give Sadie a kick and tell her she COULD be a serious
business woman and take no notice of damned Stuart.

And so the crusade had begun.

Helen described Sadie's excitement – at filling the store with all the
things she knew would make people healthy, making use of her passion –
all the geek stuff Sadie had been studying for years in her previous job at
the university research lab.

She wrote about those early months when every regular customer
was greeted by name and slowly the news started spreading. The local
paper quite liked this quirky, colourful new retail outlet in the sleepy
Surrey backwater, and the local residents liked Sadie, with her local,
organic 'Punch-with-a-punch' tastings, and the 'Arthritis-free tasty-
treats', the 'Dairy-and-wheat-substitute cookie giveaways'.

"Sadie did build it, and they did come," Helen continued reading to
herself. *"But it was for the freebies and advice more than the stock she
was selling. Sadie's was the most talked-about health store in Surrey, but
the sales didn't match. And then out of nowhere the monthly rates
changed, the new lease kicked in, and the cash flow problems began. She
worked long hours, gave too much of herself away, and didn't relax
enough. All that effort in making other people better? Well, it kind of
made Sadie sick."*

Helen pondered whether to include the bit where Sadie's ex, Stuart
used to say, *'Sadie, sweetie, it won't be long and you'll need me to pick up
the pieces like I always do, you'll see.'* And the bail-out. He could see she
was vulnerable, but against Helen's advice, Sadie had accepted his offer
of an 'early divorce advance' – in the form of an off-the-record monthly
payment. Why did he offer it? Not because he was caring, although that's
what he claimed. But because it kept her reliant upon him.

Damn him.

Helen shook her head, thinking about how her sister had refused financial help when Helen had offered it, saying she preferred to 'make her ex-husband pay'. What she hadn't realised is that it kept her right where he wanted her. Keeping her stuck. Yes, this had to go in.

"Stuck in the way that horrible husbands like you to be, you know?" typed Helen. *"For instance, when they pretend it's because they care about you but all they really want is be proved right. Helping just enough to keep her out of a hole, but not quite enough to stop her lurching straight into the next one. Not quite enough to break free…"*

Ain't that the truth, thought Helen. Yes this would resonate with a lot of readers. She hoped. It wouldn't harm for this article to say how unhelpful the ex had been, people could relate to that. It was for a hard-hitting women's magazine after all. And anyway, it *was* partly his fault, thought Helen – *too flaming controlling by half, he was – still is*. Stuart always knew better than anyone else. Trouble is with Sadie, she'd got into the habit of believing him. And anyway, the rules in the US were different about what you could print about people, so it would serve him right.

She carried on reading the rest of the article.

"It was a crucial time. You're a step away from being successful – from finally proving yourself to everyone who doubted you – then something happens to interrupt all that. Left field, out of nowhere. So what do you do? When that dream finally comes within reach and something gets in the way? I'll tell you what Sadie did."

And then Helen paused. She was taking a big gamble here. 'Cos Sadie hadn't actually *done* it yet. But she was going to – wasn't she? If Helen had anything to do with it, she would. And what no one knew was that Helen was going to have more to do with it than anyone – especially Sadie – realised…

CHAPTER TWO.

Mrs Sadie Turner, meanwhile, was downstairs holding an envelope in one hand and a piece of paper in the other. She looked at the well-thumbed letter one last time. *Not more bad news. As if last week's bombshell wasn't enough.* Then with relish, she tore it in half, in half again, and with a bit of effort, in half once more, and dangled the tattered strips in front of her. Her eyes were staring at them but her mind was somewhere else.

'Why don't you just do what you told *me* to do with Phyllis's nasty hate mail, darling?' said Sadie's mum. Grace Parker was over for her regular visit, which included making some dinner, making some mischief, and getting a pedicure from the granddaughter who wanted to be a beauty therapist – or a hairdresser – or a marine biologist. And judging by the look in Grace's eye, the mischief would begin a little earlier than usual. 'You know, that anonymous letter I got in my pigeonhole at the bowls club – from Phyllis.'

'You don't know it was Phyllis, mother.'

'Oh I know it was Phyllis all right. Fountain pen? That letter had her hallmarks all over it. It even smelt of her. Seriously, you should do what I did – you can imagine her face when she read my reply. What was that Wayne Dyer bloke's clever phrase? Oh, yes – "I'm sitting here in the smallest room of my house with your letter of complaint before me. Very soon, it will be behind me." Is that the one?'

'Yes, mother, that's the one.'

'Worked a treat for me, I can tell you, put Phyllis right in her place. Especially when I adjusted my knickers as I passed her, the very next time I stepped onto the green to bowl.' Grace Parker laughed out loud and patted Sadie on the shoulder.

There was life in the old bird yet.

Sometimes Sadie wondered who was the mother and who was the daughter. And whoever it was, how did older sister Helen fit in? The grandmother probably, thought Sadie – always taking charge and issuing orders. Except on this occasion when she'd come home in uncharacteristic pieces and had spent all day, every day moping around upstairs.

'Go on,' Grace continued, pointing at the decimated paper in Sadie's hands, 'don't tell me you weren't thinking about it – you've even torn it into strips! Although with *your* backside you should have made them a bit wider...'

'Ignore Nana, girls,' Sadie replied, but Georgia, the youngest, had just come flying down the stairs and was hovering.

'Mum, Auntie Helen says just the fruit. And what are you talking about, Nana? "Very soon it'll be behind me?" What do you mean?'

'It means you've used it to wipe your ar...'

'Mother! I'm trying to teach these two reprobates decorum!'

'Decorum? But the place has only just *been* painted.'

'You're not funny,' said Sadie, smiling and shaking her head as she scrunched the paper strips into a big ball.

'Yes she is. I think you're *very* funny, Nana,' said the wiry eleven year old with her coppery hair in Ga-Ga like stiff bunches and a twinkle in her big, dark brown eyes. So much like her father. In looks only, thank god, Sadie thought. *Which reminds me...* Sadie opened the next letter, which came apart very easily in her hands – another bank statement – looking suspiciously as though it had already been opened – and searched to see if the maintenance payment had come in yet... Nothing. Still in the red. He was late again – and he *knew* she'd needed it. *Plus ça change* – once a control freak always a control freak. Sadie sighed.

A very loud roaring noise from outside sent Georgia rushing to the window to peek out.

'Mum! Don't look now but there's some flash guy in a Ferrari just parked outside our house! OMG, he's coming in here!'

'Get away from the window Georgia, you're not Nana. That'll be Mr Hugh. From my evening class.'

He still looks flash though, thought Sadie as she caught sight of him and his designer glasses and his slightly-too-hot designer jacket for this warm late spring evening. *Maybe this was a mistake.*

"Oo − "Mr Hugh" − does that make you "*Mistress* Sadie?"' asked Grace, a twinkle in her eye.

'Don't be daft, Hugh is his surname. Georgia, come away from the window.' Sadie ushered her youngest aside, but Grace just stepped in her place.

'Let me see this MISTER Hugh. Shove over Georgia,' said Grace, as she vied for position with the eleven year old.

'OMG mum. You're going out with him in THAT? Abiiii!' she called, 'Mum's going out in a gas-guzzler!' A slightly older teenager started coming down the stairs with a face like thunder.

'I heard it! The whole street heard it!' she said, 'Mr Wilson opposite has already come out for a nose. Ugh. Mum! Think of the carbon footprint! Just because you've had to go back to school, doesn't mean you have to sell out your principles to the devil.' Abi snorted at her sister and Nana at the curtains.

'I'm not selling out. And it's not just 'school', it's Surrey Business School − part of the uni. He's an expert at marketing and he's going to teach me how to be a better businesswoman. And anyway if your Auntie Helen says he's the best,' she said, with a shrug, 'then who am I to argue. He'll help me become an International Marketing whizz kid apparently. And that means I'll be rich, like she... is.' Sadie corrected herself on the last word just in time.

'I don't know why you won't let *me* help you,' argued Abi. 'You're always telling us to think outside the box, and I just came top again in eBusiness. See, what you have to do is, you just have to build a social media profile first and − OMG mother! Him?' she said, as she too started peering. '*Really*?!' She made a face as she turned away from the window.

'Don't give me grief, it's NOT a date. Now go and get on with your geography, both of you.'

'It's German,' said both girls with a huff, both back at the window, both pulling the curtains even further apart. Sadie couldn't resist, and stood behind them. The thick-set guy with the broadest shoulders was hiding something behind his back, carefully side-stepping around the bluebells and greenery on his way up the meandering path. Sadie's heart missed a beat. He stopped to mop his brow slightly, caught sight of the girls, and waved his hanky.

'Eurgh!' said Abi. The teenager made a face and turned to her mother. 'I'm going upstairs to talk to Auntie Helen. At least *she* isn't dating a Boy Racer.'

'Not this month anyway. In fact, my first-born isn't dating anybody – ever again, apparently,' chipped in Grace, elbowing Sadie and winking. 'Nor does she want to...to... what did she text me earlier? Oh yes, "...speak to anyone about anything, anytime, ever". Which going on her last break up probably means till about tomorrow tea time.'

Poor Helen. But Grace was right. Helen retreated to Sadie's so often in between bad relationships, she even stored her precious shoe collection here. Not that Sadie had ever seen her this bad before...

'Oh for God's sake. It's like having four kids in the house. Yes, my poor sister is suffering and unusually isn't bouncing straight back. So – Abi, make sure you take Auntie Helen a cup of camomile tea – it'll help her nerves. Mum – don't eat her pudding. AND behave yourself – don't embarrass me in front of Mr Hugh. Georgia – get AWAY from the window, tidy up this pedicure stuff and go and do your homework,' Sadie said, making for the kitchen with the ball of crumpled paper and other post still in her hand, picking up clothing and school bags along the way.

Grace stopped her and ushered Sadie towards the door, straightening her up and taking the items back out of her hands. 'We'll be fine – don't you worry about a thing. Just you go on your date, love, with "Mr Hugh". Mr Hugh eh? Kinky date!'

'Mother! I keep telling you, he's not a date! I've asked him to meet with me so I can get him to go over my homework, that's all. And girls, I won't be out late – so I promise I'll help you with yours when I get back.'

'Oh-h-h,' Grace whispered, in a sing-song voice, 'Well I might just get Tom to "go over *my* homework" too, if I stop by his place on my way home tonight. Hahahaaa!' The cackle was infamous at the bowls club and it resounded down the panelled hall of Sadie's cottage. 'Go over *my* homework, hahaaaa.'

Sadie made a face – *gross*. The glamorous, slightly bohemian, red-haired older lady waved the look aside. 'Now go answer the door. Oh, hang on... here.' She looked admiringly at her daughter, and brushed a tendril off her cheek, back into the hair grip which was keeping the unruly brunette mop off Sadie's stressed face. 'Bit more lippy maybe?' Grace added.

'No, no lippy. It's NOT a DATE!' said Sadie, but her heart disagreed – it began pounding as soon as she saw the large figure looming closer. Through the small opaque glass window in the front door of her old 1850's cottage, she could see the silhouette lift an arm, but the loud bang of the ancient doorknocker still made her jump. *He doesn't know his own strength.* A brief flashback of his bare arms in a t-shirt in the hot classroom last Tuesday night made her tingle slightly, as did the memory of his aftershave wafting on the air as he strutted past her desk and his smart, military-like hairstyle and the small wrinkles at the corners of his eyes when he smiled – at her...

Well maybe this evening wasn't such a bad idea after all.

She hesitated then popped a lip gloss into her pocket from the window sill, then opened the door and the man-mountain reached forward.

'Sadie!' He beamed, and stooped to kiss her. Sadie offered her cheek. Then he clumsily thrust a large, messy bunch of daffodils and tulips towards her. 'I picked them myself from the... from my garden this morning – just for you!' He looked pleased with himself, almost embarrassed. Sadie took them and smiled.

'Thanks Damian. You shouldn't have – it's me who should be getting flowers for *you*.'

He looked at her quizzically.

'For helping me out... by going over my... oh never mind. Come and say hi to the family.'

Damian hesitated, then plastered on a smile again and followed Sadie into the kitchen. There, Grace and daughter Georgia were arguing whether to make Auntie Helen a 'camomile and elderflower' or a 'green tea and pomegranate' herbal brew. Grace's face immediately brightened, in the way the child-catcher's did in *Chitty Chitty Bang Bang* upon spying a new victim. Then she walked straight over, looked him squarely in the eye and shook his big hand with both of hers. Rigorously. And didn't let go.

'Oh how lovely to meet you. I'm Grace, Sadie's mother. Mr Hugh, isn't it? Yes? Well, Sadie's told me *naff-all* about you.'

'Oh, hasn't she? Oh, ok then. Well, she's *warned* me all about *you*… haha.' The hand-shaking didn't stop. 'Ha… Ahem. Well, it's a pleasure to meet you,' he said, trying to let go. Grace just beamed at him and carried on shaking − tightly. 'She's very talented, your daughter, actually,' Damian went on. Sadie intervened, thrusting the flowers at her mother who finally let go and took the bouquet. He flexed his fingers.

'Ooh, do tell me more,' Grace continued, 'perhaps you'd like a cup of tea before you leave? We're making gingergrass and snotflower − or something like that. Want some?'

'Er…' Damian looked to Sadie, his face unsure whether to laugh or throw up.

'Mum! Like I said, he's not stopping, we…'

'Hello, I'm Georgia. Why do you drive that car?' chimed in a voice from behind them all. Georgia appeared, and following her Nana's lead, stepped up to grab the man's hand and started shaking it − he bent down slightly and shook hers back, awkwardly.

'Well, I…'

'Now darling,' added Sadie. 'I'm sure Mr Hugh doesn't want to explain to us about his choice of car…'

'Not at all, Sadie, I don't mind. It's my pride and joy, actually, young lady. The achievement of a lifetime's ambition. What's yours, if you don't mind me asking?'

'My what? I don't have a car. I'm eleven.'

Sadie smiled, Grace smirked and Damian's brow furrowed. He shot Sadie a look of panic. *Oh-oh,* she thought, *obviously no good with kids. This one's a non-starter then.* Then she shook herself − *it's NOT a date!*

'Haha, no, er, Georgia,' Damian replied, wiping his brow. 'I mean, what's your life's ambition?'

'I don't know – I haven't had my life yet. I'm *eleven*.'

Enough was enough.

'Ok Georgia, thank you for that witty observation. Mr Hugh and I have to go now.'

Damian looked relieved. 'Nice to meet you all,' he said, then did a weird little salute to say goodbye and turned to face the hallway.

'Oh, but you *haven't* met us all yet,' Grace said, hurriedly leaving the flowers by the sink and stepping between him and his escape route, at the same time as Georgia slid behind Damian, imitating his salute whilst crossing her eyes and poking out her tongue. Sadie glared at the youngster then snapped a smile at Damian.

'Abi's upstairs,' added Grace, 'you don't want to miss her. ABIII!!' she yelled, making Damian jump. 'She's up there with our fifth musketeer, my elder daughter Helen – if she's not still on the phone to America.'

'Not again? I told her to Skype, it's...' began Sadie, but Grace carried on.

'... Helen's the one you saw in New York, apparently? Are you *sure* you wouldn't like that cup of tea? We can do a builder's brew if you don't like herbal – I make her keep some of the common stuff for when my gentlemen friends come and keep me company when I'm babysitting.'

'No, I'm ok. Thanks anyway. *Another time,* Mrs Turner...'

'Parker,' said Grace. 'I'm Mrs Parker. *She's* Mrs Turner. Or 'Ms' when she decides to finally cut the strings and let go of the holy matrimony stuff. What she's holding onto, goodness only knows. Load of old clap-trap if you ask me.'

'Not now, mother.'

'Well, it's been an experience meeting you all,' the big man said, taking Sadie's arm, 'but Sadie and I will be late if we don't depart shortly. I'll try the tea another time, Mrs *Parker* – yes, another time – that'd be lovely. Lovely.' He reversed down the hall, jumping as he nearly backed into Georgia who hopped out of the way. Damian grinned inanely and whispered under his breath, to Sadie, 'Yes another time – when the coast is clear...'

The interrogation posse weren't going to be shaken off that easily, and Georgia and Grace shuffled after them down the narrow hallway towards the big oak door. As they opened it, and Sadie bent to kiss her youngest on her mop of coppery frizz, an indignant voice piped up from half way up the staircase. Abi was back.

'Going already? Helen says to say hi,' Abi said, 'and that she's sorry she's not "visitor-friendly" – you'd know what that means. And – what was the other thing? Erm – yes, she says how long are you over here for and are you going to the big conference in Tuscany?'

Damian looked confused, 'Helen...?'

'She's not being rude,' Sadie covered for her sister, who was hurting badly considering the unprecedented events she'd been through in the last few weeks. 'She's probably got a headache.'

'I'm afraid my eldest has a perpetual headache nowadays – it's called being 41 and single.'

'Mum, don't rub it in, Helen will hear you,' said Sadie, leaning in to kiss her mother on the cheek, and glowering again at Georgia who was now trying to force Abi to take a turn to shake Damian's hand, as Abi backed away up the stairs. 'Play nice, mother. Girls. Better take Helen a camomile tea *and* a paracetamol – go.'

Grace narrowed her eyes shrewdly and kissed Sadie's cheek, whispering in her ear as she did so. 'Not too late for the lippy,' she hissed. Then Sadie and Damian exited before any more interrogation could begin, winding their way down the path past the overflowing flower beds and through the hedge which arched over the gate, overdue for a trim.

'Nice garden,' he said. 'Lovely smells. Or is that you?'

Sadie smiled. Damian gestured that he'd open the gate for her, and Sadie flushed slightly. She wasn't used to this. She was used to being independent nowadays, used to her freedom, used to being alone. Used to stating her opinion – like 'actually, why *do* you drive a gas guzzler, Mr

Hugh?' Or 'actually, you didn't need to "rescue" me from my own mother...'

Or did he?

Could I GET used to being treated like this? She wondered.

As she looked back at the house, Sadie saw her mother and Georgia and Abi all jostling for pole position in the doorway. She raised her hand as she stepped towards the car. As one, they grinned and waved. *Almost like a normal family*, which Sadie knew was impossible, as they were anything but. Thank the stars.

She lowered herself into the car trying to be as elegant as possible, given that Sir Galahad here was waiting to *close* the door for her too. She ended up twisting herself in at an awkward angle and gave him a sheepish grin. He closed the door reverently – hardly making a sound, plucked an invisible speck of something off the passenger window and strutted round to the driver's side. Sadie let go of a breath, and gave another little wave at the house. *Here we go then,* she said to herself. *And remember, it's not a date.*

Back at the house, Helen was coming down the stairs, having heard them leave. Grace and Abi were still smiling and waving, talking to each other through gritted teeth.

'How long do you give it, nana?' asked Abi.

'Judging from the look on my sister's face right now,' piped up Helen, 'about two hours...'

'Oh darling, there you are!' Grace replied, 'My goodness, you do look tired. Your eyes are rather red.'

'Cheers mum.' Helen yawned and wrapped her towelling robe around her body more tightly, rubbing her face. 'Yes, my eyes *are* red. About as red as that car. I've been bawling for two weeks solid. And as it's clearly the end of life as I know it, I might even top myself. But I thought I'd come down for some apple compote first. If you haven't eaten it.'

'Lovely darling. Yoo-Hoo, Mister Wilson! My daughter's friend!' she shouted to the neighbour whilst pointing at the car. Helen raised her eyebrows and made a 'she never listens' face at the girls, who giggled. Grace took no notice. She said,

'Isn't that a Ferrari Testes?'

'Well,' Helen replied, 'you know what they say about men who have big cars, so it could well be. But... who is that guy?'

'Don't you recognise him? Damian – from New York – the one Sadie asked you about, don't you remember darling? Perhaps it's time you gave in to glasses, lots of people do when they get as old as you...'

'DON'T say it!' Helen interrupted, holding up her hand. 'Don't use the 'O' word.' She huffed and held the dressing gown round her even more tightly. The engine fired up and Damian revved it once or twice. 'Ooo nice gas guzzler,' she said.

'Auntie Helen!' protested both her nieces at once.

'I'm just kidding, girls. He looks like he's enjoying the audience, though,' Helen added, indicating across the road where a sergeant major-type, silver-haired older man stood open-mouthed, watching the car as he watered his hanging baskets, the water overflowing and dribbling down his arm. The car revved louder, and Helen could see her sister's stony face inside it as she shrank down in her car seat. 'Yep, I give it a couple of hours. She'll be back early, you betcha.'

'Now, now, don't be jealous. Just because you're staying a spinster, doesn't mean your sister has to,' replied Grace, patting her daughter on the cheek. 'Sadie says it's not a date but we think it is. Maybe he's the one. Maybe this Damian Hugh is her oyster.'

'Haha! You are silly, Nana! If you mean like what Phoebe says on *Friends*, it's *lobster!*' chimed in Georgia. 'He's her *lobster!*' Just then, Sadie's 'not-a-date' leaned across Sadie to wave goodbye to them all, and Helen made a 'oh-oh' face.

'I hate to say this, oyster or lobster, that's NOT Damian.'

'Yes, yes it is – we just met him – Damian Hugh. Some marketing whizz kid, apparently – AKA her new tutor? Remember?'

Helen furrowed her brow. Grace went on.

'Runs the International Marketing department at Sadie's night school? Come on, Sausage, she only signed up for it because of your glowing recommendation about him … No? Oh dear. Remind me not to be in the room when *that* conversation kicks off. Ok my harem, want some cake? I can bring it out now that the food police have left the building. Come on girls, time for Big-Brother-on-demand.' Grace led her giggling granddaughters back into the house, leaving Helen standing awkwardly on the step, craning her neck to see the car disappearing up the road.

'Damian Hugh…. Oh dear. If that's her new tutor,' she said to herself, 'I may be in deep shit.'

CHAPTER THREE

In the Ferrari, the guttural roar was drowning out 'racer boy,' as he tried to regale Sadie with a ream of statistics about his pride and joy, revving up the engine to make a point. It didn't go down very well in the narrow main road through the leafy Surrey village. Two passers-by glared, and Sadie slunk down as low as she could in the seat, picking up a baseball cap and popping it over her head.

'So, time for some freedom! Shall I put my foot down?' said Damian, raising his voice above the throaty growl of the twelve cylinder engine.

'If you must,' she said. To herself, as it turned out – the wannabe Lewis Hamilton had already pulled out fast onto the dual carriageway. After a short while, they stopped at a lights and Sadie finally made herself heard. 'We're not going too far are we, Damian? You know I only have a couple of hours.'

'If we're not going too far, then I don't *need* a couple of hours. Not till I get to know you better,' he joked.

Sadie smiled back tentatively. 'Haha. Funny. No, it's just that I've had a bit of news today that means I need to get back and do some cash flow revisions. For my business.'

'Anything serious?'

'Serious? No, no nothing really... Plus, well, I like to get back to see the girls at bedtime.'

'Lucky kids,' Damian replied, 'all I got when I was growing up, was a cassette recorder with my mum's voice reading out stories for me.' Sadie made a 'poor you' face at him. He shrugged then carried on. 'She was always entertaining friends and the nannies were never that great at reading Shakespeare.' He looked at her out of the corner of her eye and she realised he was teasing.

'Oh. Haha. Well, I'm sorry to hear that. Stories are really important, we ... I always read to the girls,' Sadie replied, as suddenly they pulled away from the lights so fast she was pushed back against the seat. She raised her voice again. 'I guess, at least you heard some. What were your favourites?'

'Nought to sixty in five point two seconds,' Damian puffed. Sadie shut up. *Might as well just 'enjoy' the ride.* Fortunately a few minutes later they were turning onto a smart drive that led to the car park of a little country pub. Damian slowed to a crawl to painstakingly negotiate the speed bumps, which came within a whisker of his bumpers. He grinned sideways at her then opened his eyes and mouth wider and wider in concentration, as they rose up higher and higher, then narrower and narrower as inch by inch, they safely passed to the other side. *What a palaver*, Sadie thought about the totally impractical car.

'They're quite low, aren't they, the bumpers?'

'Spoilers. Spoilers at the front, and at the side they're called skirts,' he replied. She opened her mouth to make a quip then changed her mind. He was totally lost in the thrum of his baby. Oh well, each to their own, said Sadie to herself as she thought of her no-nonsense six year old Nissan Micra – the last big present she'd ever got from Stuart. *If he could see me now.*

They parked up and he held up a finger, wanting her to wait so he could go round and open the door again. He took her hand as she extricated herself from the sleek machine, as elegantly as she could. She was glad of the hand. His touch was warm, there was an unexpected energy in his fingers as they curled around hers snugly... *nice to be touched*. She beamed at him, and he beamed right back.

The pub had a thatched roof and a whole array of hanging baskets filled with brightly coloured pansies. He ducked as they entered the low doorway, allowing Sadie to go in before him. She looked back and caught him checking out her bottom, no doubt swaying a bit too much in the tight blue jeans she always wore.

Damian chose a little nook next to an open fire, where a flame was gently flickering – more for mood than warmth. Sadie made herself comfortable on the bench seat, whilst he went to the bar. She looked around. This was unfamiliar territory for sure – long time since she'd been on a ... *Oh for the last time – it's NOT one!*

Checking out her reflection in the darkening window pane, she realised how pale her lips looked. She wondered if he might want to kiss them and her heart began to pound. *What did they used to say in the lab – deep breaths slow down the heart rate?* She counted her breathing in and out, and sure enough, began to calm. She brushed her hair and finally took out the tiny gloss – just as Damian returned to the table with their drinks – she quickly replaced it unopened back into the floppy rucksack-style canvas bag, which was full of folders.

'So what exactly were we going to be "late" for?' she asked as she gratefully took her tonic and lemon.

He took his jacket off and shuffled his chair a bit closer to Sadie's.

'Eh? Oh, I just said that – to get us out faster! I could see you needed a break. Got your hands full there, haven't you!'

Well that was true enough. 'Oh. Yes but I wouldn't have it any other way. Very considerate of you, though... I think,' said Sadie, considering what he'd just said.

'Now, "Mrs Turner", let's get down to business. What was it in particular that you wanted my help with? I can't believe you got me here just to talk about this week's assignment... did you?' He put his arm on the back of her chair.

'Well, actually, no. I didn't.'

A smile curved across Damian's face.

'Remember you said we could talk to you about anything?' Sadie went on, 'You know, when you gave out your number at the end of last week's class? Did you mean it?'

'Yes,' he said, smiling and moving ever so slightly closer.

'Well, there's an international marketing competition,' said Sadie, sitting herself up straight, and launching into the speech she'd been rehearsing in her mind, 'for newcomers – and I'm thinking of entering. The prize is a fabulous all-expenses paid holiday to pick up the award – in Hawaii – at the big industry conference – I don't know if you've heard of it. But it's the prize money and the business mentoring I'm specifically interested in.'

'Oh.' Damian removed his arm again and reached for his glass of Guinness. 'You mean the International Marketing Trends Congress next year. Yes, of course I know of it,' he said with a sniff. 'Who doesn't.'

'I just thought, given how you've been so encouraging and supportive so far – about my work and everything – that you might not mind if I asked you for some advice? I've brought the concept sketches along to show you and it'd be really great if you would have a look at them. Just an overview, you know...'

Damian was still sipping his drink.

'...That is,' Sadie added, starting to flush a little around the bottom of her neck, 'if you don't mind. Of course if it's too much of a cheek, then don't worry,' she added hastily when he didn't answer, '...or else, I've – I've brought this week's assignment too...'she said, looking up hopefully and meekly produced two neatly bound folders from her rucksack.

'You do realise, Sadie,' he said, putting his drink down and staring ahead without looking at her, 'that I charge top rates for consultancy.'

'Oh,' said Sadie, hesitating, then slid her file back onto the table.

'But you're not asking me for consultancy are you,' he said, turning to face her.

'No, not really. I'm really not in a position for that right now. Just a professional opinion, you being so good at it. An award winner, my sister said.'

Damian narrowed his eyes then replied. 'She's the one I'm supposed to have met before, right? What's her name again?'

'Helen. Helen Parker.'

He looked blank.

'Helen Todd?'

Still blank.

'Helen Parker-Todd?'

He shook his head.

'Helen Todd-Parker...'

'No, doesn't ring any bells.'

'Are you sure? Looks a bit like me, only blonde and skinnier? It's unusual not to remember meeting Helen. She's someone you don't usually forget.' *Not like me,* thought Sadie.

He seemed slightly irritated. Sadie squirmed a little in her seat. He looked at her, tight-lipped and shook his head – again.

'You sure? New York – last autumn?' she persisted in a quiet voice.

More head-shaking.

'Helen told me that you and her friend Kate spent all weekend looking for The Real Central Perk, like that coffee shop from the TV show *Friends*?'

'The *what?* From *where*?' Damian looked down his nose at her.

'The one where... oh, I... it doesn't matter anyway,' she whispered. He took another sip of his drink and looked over to the bar, raising his glass to the barmaid who was watching. His profile was annoyingly attractive, even if, out of the classroom, he didn't quite have that same air of authority, that power. The power Sadie had found so damn attractive in her twice weekly evening-class-haven. Attractive *and* successful. And big.

'Nope. Not a clue who your sister Helen is. Sorry.' He shrugged. 'I'm sorry it wasn't me who was in New York with her last autumn, 'cos if she's anything like you, I'm sure it would have been fun. If she's anything like your mother I'd have run a mile.'

'Haha. Oh, ok,' Sadie said, shrinking into her seat. *I'll kill Helen when I get home.* 'Actually she is fun – lots of fun. Usually. And she's much more well-travelled than me, and quite a whizz kid herself, in advertising mainly. She's the one who told me about the competition and inspired me to come on this course. She's convinced it will help my shop – help build an internet business, importing some key products and...'

'Well I'm glad she *did* persuade you to come on the course,' he butted in, 'otherwise tonight would never have happened, would it?' Giving her a little grin and a 'cheers' motion with his glass, he put it on the table then tapped her arm, then did a 'give it to me' gesture with his finger.

Surprised, Sadie wondered what he meant, until he pointed towards the folder. She pushed it towards him. 'Well since you brought it along to show me, how about I take a look anyway,' he added, 'unless you want to wait for whoEVER it was in New York with your sister.'

'Oh, no, I mean, yes, thanks so much,' Sadie said, 'that's very kind of you. You'll have to let me know what I can bring to class on Thursday – as a thank you. Maybe something from my store?'

'Yes – your store. Tell me more?' he asked as he opened the folder.

Sadie sat up straight and beamed. *Maybe he could suggest some ideas.* 'Do you know Turner's in the High Street? We do all sorts of health food goodies. Maybe I could bring in some flavoured liquorice? Some Marmite rice cakes? Dried banana in yogurt? Some organic dark chocolate?' Sadie's voice tailed off slightly at the distasteful look on his face, which had got more incredulous at each suggestion, and she realised how ridiculous her list sounded.

'Got any doughnuts?' he said.

She paused, then he laughed, so she smiled back, feeling a bit awkward.

'How about I make some… cookies?' His face brightened and he nodded, touched his nose and then pointed at her. 'Ok, you've got a deal, cookies it is,' she said. If this was flirting, Sadie had no idea. *God I'm out of practise at all this,* she thought, then stopped herself.

This.

Was.

NOT.

A.

DATE.

'I'm really quite a good cook,' she added. *As my hips can tell you.*

'Maybe I'll be the judge of that,' he teased. 'Yes, cookies would be nice,' he said, took another swig of his drink and turned to her work.

Sadie studied his body language as he had a quick zip through the folder full of preliminary sketches for the competition in silence. She couldn't tell from the way he raised his eyebrows every so often, from the angle of his head or from his occasional grunt whether he liked them or not. Sadie felt like she was in the headmaster's office – and not in a good way. He said nothing until he'd turned the very last page.

'Hmm. Yes, they are quite competent,' he said at last, 'of much better standard than the work I've seen from you in class – so far.'

Sadie didn't let on that the actual drawing had just been done by Helen, who had produced a much more professional version of Sadie's sketches just three hours after first discussing the concepts Sadie had had in mind. As usual Helen had turned it into her own project, stepping up to help out and suggest and recommend. She'd have insisted, as usual, but this time Sadie drew the line. But the drawings were ok, it was the concept that would count. And the concept was hers – all hers.

'But I'm impressed enough to say, well, maybe you *could* benefit from a consultation. So you prefer my opinion to your sister's then?' he puffed.

Sadie sat back in her chair. 'She's quite happy to help me, but I'd rather I got there off my own back this time. There's always someone helping me, and telling me what to do, and what not to do, and...' she tailed off. 'Well, you know what I mean.'

'But you're quite happy having *me* telling you...what to do?' he asked, with a look of mischief on his face.'

'Only feedback – on what I've already done. You're my tutor after all, and I'm here to learn and I...'

'Ok, Ok, I was only teasing. Tell you what – I *will* help you. And if the advice I give you turns out to be useful, well then, you'll be my star pupil. And maybe you *can* do me a favour back...' His look worried Sadie a little, and it must have shown on her face. '... when you're in the mood...' he teased, then fondly tapped the tip of her nose. 'Haha, I mean you could cook me a cake! How about a gluten-free carrot cake for my aunt's birthday next week? She has to watch what she eats too.'

Phew, a cake. THAT kind of favour.

He looked amused at his ability to catch her out, then turned back to inspect one of her sketches more closely. She relaxed a bit more.

He was teasing. She liked it. Maybe this one IS just a straight up kind of guy, she thought to herself, maybe they're not all like Stuart. *Surely there's someone out there who is not another Stuart.*

She watched him peruse her handiwork with a look of intense concentration on his face as he turned the pages and made notes on a scrap of spare paper. 'I'm going to jot down some observations,' he explained, and picked up a pencil.

Sadie breathed out. Then caught sight of herself in the window pane again – it was completely dark outside now, and her reflection was clearly visible in the glass. For a split second she didn't recognise herself – surely those weren't *her* eyes? Dark shadows under them, drawn, hollow. Must be the poor lighting. She sat herself up straighter, and wished she'd put on more make up. And lippy. Maybe next time. *If there was a next time.*

Damian got to a sketch he particularly liked, and began enthusiastically appraising various aspects of it, jotting down a little alternative diagram on a spare sheet, to illustrate his point. She looked up at him, feeling a warm glow inside, and he beamed right back, puffing out his chest as he slipped into 'teacher' mode.

Ten minutes later, the mood was definitely brighter. Half way through the explanations there had been a distinct uplift in Damian's manner. He suddenly seemed extremely jolly. He'd carefully examined Sadie's ideas for the competition – an outline for a launch campaign for the new product launch being developed by the sponsors of the Trends Conference next May in Hawaii.

Her work was detailed, clever and innovative, he'd said, and his praise – and his attention – made her feel good. Then he'd proceeded to carefully go through all the documentation, for her, including the terms and conditions. He was obviously meticulous – more meticulous than she'd expected. Part of his success, she supposed – yes this guy could teach her a lot. And god knows, she needed to be taught, especially if this stuff could help her. At last he sat back, and raised his nearly empty glass.

'I think we have a little star on our hands,' he said.

'Oh?!' Sadie said, feeling herself flush.

'There's a long way to go, of course. With a little bit of work, some of these ideas could be knocked into shape. Who knows, with a bit more experience – say, a couple of years – you'll be ready to unleash yourself on the international stage, like I did when I was straight out of college.'

'Oh,' Sadie said, 'a couple of years. Thanks.'

I think.

Damian was swallowing down more of his Guinness.

'So – big question,' she gulped. 'Do you think any of them are good enough to enter *this* competition? As they are? Or with a tweak or two?'

The million dollar question, and she'd asked it. Was she about to have her hopes dashed?

'Well definitely not *this* concept,' he said, picking up one sketch with a naked person kneeling up in the foreground, and a clever play on words about a temple. 'There's a rule that anything to do with religion should be avoided – don't want to piss off any would-be consumers. No telling what harm social media campaigns can do nowadays if someone gets a bee in their bonnet. But,' he went on, picking up a different one, 'I think this next one's not too bad. But instead of "Water, but Faster!" how about "Water, but Wetter?" – it's all in the question mark, do you see?'

'Oh. Well, I'm sure but the thing is, you can't really have *wetter* water,' she replied, 'according to the research document in the entry material – it's all to do with the number of molecules in the cluster of H_2O, it's...'

'Goodness me, Sadie. Are you a closet boffin? You sound like you've been watching too many Professor Brian Cox shows!' He laughed and looked at her with a mixture of mock envy and sympathy. Sadie frowned.

'Actually, I am – well, I was – a boffin. Out of the closet, too.'

Now it was Damian's turn to think she was joking. 'Haha! Funny girl.'

'Actually, it's true. I did a doctorate – worked at the uni – in the Microbiology Research Lab. Before I left to set up my store.'

He stopped laughing abruptly and stared.

'Sorry – but you asked.'

'Oh. Ahem, right then. No problem.' The sweat had begun to glow on his forehead again, and he produced the hanky to dab it away. Taking his jacket off, he revealed those muscly arms that had caught Sadie's attention from the back of the class. He continued. 'Well, whatever you are – or were – I think as your sister will probably agree, this business is not so much about stating all the facts. It's about twisting them. Good advertising, it's more about perceived image. What grabs the potential customer's attention and makes them curious. In any case, if you just add the question mark,' he said, actually writing on her sketch, 'you're asking. Not telling – therefore you can get away with it.'

'I see,' said Sadie. But she didn't 'see' at all. She was only too aware of how strict the advertising rules were, courtesy of a certain local official from the bane of her life – the CAP team – the Committee of Advertising Practise. Their rep had rapped her knuckles over a piece she'd put in the local paper and since then had made it his business to ensure she knew precisely how closely you had to adhere to the rules – *'his'* rules. But at least this was only for a competition, not a real ad campaign – maybe that's what Damian meant. But now wasn't the time to have that debate.

He drained his glass. Sadie sipped from hers, still half full.

'Listen, let's thrash through these ideas a bit longer, shall we? Your turn to buy the drinks next, isn't it?'

'Oh... my turn. Yes it must be. Of course.'

'Same again, please Mrs Turner.'

'Certainly Mr Hugh.'

Sadie smiled and left him at the table rifling through her work, scribbling some more, and went to queue at the bar. *Not a date, no, this was definitely not a date.* She was just glad she hadn't bothered with the full face paint.

At the end of the night, however, having kindly spoken to her at great length about the various alternative versions of her sketches, Mr Hugh had gone up even more in Sadie's estimation – and she'd enjoyed his company quite a lot. Even if he did talk about himself, and his own work, most of the time. He was a genius as far as she could tell. And he'd made her laugh. He was quite funny, when he wasn't trying too hard. Even if Helen *had* got him confused with someone else and made Sadie look and feel like a complete idiot. He'd brushed it aside, and continued unabashed, thank goodness, but Sadie would be having words with her sister when she got home. This course could have been a big mistake.

In any case the evening had turned out to be more than ok. By the end of the night when it was time to go, Sadie felt much more at ease, and very grateful to have spent the evening with this guy with the big arms, the posh red sports car and the interesting theories on marketing. And if she wasn't mistaken, he might even be a little bit interested in Sadie too.

Wasn't that what the glances were all about?

The wry smiles?

The leaning closer and the occasional brush of her arm when he was talking to her? He'd even taken a photo on his mobile, of one of her designs saying he wanted to show the class, which had pleased her no end, since she was conscious of being the oldest in the group and so far, had felt a little left out. Everyone else seemed so much better than she was. He'd liked her work. But did he like her?

Of course he didn't 'like' her in that way. Wishful thinking.

'How about we meet up again soon?' He asked.

'That would be quite nice,' she replied.

'Free tomorrow night?'

'Oh!' She was taken by surprise, then felt warmth flood through her body. 'Yes! Yes I'm free,' she said, almost saying 'squeeee' like her girls did in texts when they were excited about something. He looked rather pleased with himself, for some reason, so Sadie made a mental note to buy some new lipstick. And eye-shadow. And mascara. Just in case.

CHAPTER FOUR

'No kiss goodnight on the doorstep, I noticed? Shame,' said Helen, a lot later, over a late-night cuppa and sugar-free, gluten-free, dairy-free cookies on the big old pine table in Sadie's farmhouse style kitchen. This was sister bonding at its best.

'Nope. Not with MI5 behind the curtains watching. Maybe next time. He's asked to see me tomorrow night too.'

'Cool. This dissecting the date is fun. You do know the last time we did this – properly – like, swapping stories, not just me chewing your ear off over *my* man-troubles?' continued Helen, breaking another cookie in half and picking some dried fruit out of the middle. 'It must have been ages ago – back when ...when you were just finishing with Andy Redfern from the butcher's shop.'

'Yes! I'd forgotten about him,' Sadie said, '*and* his corned beef legs and his sausage fingers.'

'Chipolata?' Helen quipped and Sadie laughed.

'No, more like a salami.'

They reminisced for a few more minutes about Sadie's old flame.

'We used to spend many a night putting the world to rights over a soothing mug of something special. What did you used to make us, back then, before you cut out taste from your diet?'

Sadie rolled her eyes at the dig but answered anyway. 'Hot Chocolate – whipped and covered with Cadbury's Dairy Milk Chocolate shavings.' *Mmmmmm* they both went. 'Dad called them a funny name.' Helen ignored her. Sadie continued. 'Remember waiting up with me for the adults to come back in? When they'd been to one of their many social nights or yet another rally?' She looked at her sister who seemed far away.

'Yeh. Tough times for me. God, mum was always raising funds for this cause or that campaign. Always out, wasn't she?'

'You were a good babysitter, Helen. Perhaps you could take it up again, if you're stuck.' Helen stuck her tongue out at Sadie, who went on, 'I used to hate doing what you told me to, you know – I didn't think you were that much older than me.'

Helen nodded, looking wistful. Sadie touched her shoulder. Helen was five years her senior and had taken on the role of babysitter from the age of ten – which she'd never let their mother forget and which of course, Grace hotly denied.

'Probably scarred me for life, being in charge of the remote and the microwave at such an early age. Carer in Chief, that's what I was,' said Helen. 'God you were hard work – a real problem child,' she teased, making a dramatic gesture of wiping her brow. 'Sitting in the corner whilst I watched Dallas, with your nose stuck in a book all night.'

'Yeah, can you imagine that here? All hell would let loose if I insisted on Abi looking after Georgia when I'm out. At least the girls love having Nana over to do it – and she worships the ground they walk on.'

'Yes,' agreed Helen, 'Seems she's determined as a grandmother to make up for what she'd lacked as a mother.'

'Kind of – but...'

'Once a hippy always a hippy.' Helen seemed unmoving. Sadie detected the same undercurrent that was always there for this topic.

'It is nice having her around more often, though now she's retired. She's mellowed a bit,' Sadie added.

'She'll never retire,' laughed Helen. 'Go on, for old times' sake – do me a hot choc will you? Like you made me when we first went away in that yurt to the Isle of Wight.'

'I would but I don't have any more cows' milk – almond doesn't whip the same way. I meant to get some for you on the way back but Damian couldn't hear me above the roar of that bloody engine. Did you hear the kids reel off those statistics about carbon footprints when I got back in? At least it meant I didn't get the Spanish inquisition about tonight with Damian.'

'It's ok, they'll just ask me tomorrow.'

'What makes you think I'm going to tell *you* what happened?' Sadie replied.

'Because that's what we do. Don't you see – this is just like the old days! Even mum's dating again. She hot-footed it off to Tom's as soon as you came in the door!'

'Eurgh.'

'So was she the only one whose luck was in tonight?' Helen asked, in a sing-song voice. Sadie made a big deal of rifling through the papers in front of her. 'Oi! Put that down. You said you'd finished revising your cash-flow,' said Helen, 'and now the girls have been accupressured into dreamland, with Jane Eyre ringing in their ears, you can spill. Give me the juicy bits.'

'Not so juicy, in this instance.' Sadie said. She filled Helen in on the evening's 'non-date' but omitted the part where she'd discussed her competition ideas with Damian. *Helen will only get the hump that I'd asked for a second opinion* Sadie thought. Instead, she tackled the embarrassing matter of mistaken identity. Helen suddenly decided to ask about the garden.

'No you don't,' Sadie said. 'I'm trying to have a go at you for completely getting the wrong guy and making me look an idiot – I only signed up for his course because you said Damian Hugh was an award-winning marketing whizz kid!'

'Easy mistake to make. I realised what happened. I thought you said Damian Grant.'

'Damian Grant? How did you get that mixed up?'

'Der…!' Helen quipped, but still Sadie looked blank. 'Remember our favourite film?'

'Dirty Dancing?' Sadie said.

'No, the other one.'

'Pretty Woman?'

'No the… *tut*, I MEAN Bridget Jones Diary!'

Sadie looked blank and made a face at Helen as if to say *what the hell are you talking about?* Then the penny dropped. 'Helen – you're telling me I began a year of evening classes with this man, 'cos you got confused with the guy who beat up Colin Firth in a fountain?'

'It's turned out ok, hasn't it?'

Sadie was incredulous. '*Trust me*, she says. *Believe me*, she says. Hah!'

'Look – all you said was *had I heard of him* and I said yes and raved about him because he's amazing and very talented and works in marketing. In New York. Had you given me the extra info of what he looks like or the fact that he's not a company director based in the States but a uni lecturer based in Guildford, you'd have had a different answer.'

'You didn't ask me for more info, you just... Oh whatever. Serves me right for always doing what you tell me to do.'

'Not. Always.' There was something in Helen's voice, the way she spat the words out – it made Sadie look over. Helen didn't meet her sister's eyes. 'Stuart.'

'What?'

'You never took my advice about Stuart.'

'Don't start that again – it's been years since you brought that up! Anyway if I had, there wouldn't be a Georgia and there wouldn't be an Abi would there, so leave it. And we're talking about *your* cock-up, here!' Sadie stood up, shuffled her paperwork and shoved it in a folder in a huff.

'Look, I got the wrong person. I'm – sorry,' said Helen.

'You're what?'

'I'm... sorry.'

'*A-a-a-a-and* THERE it is,' said Sadie. 'That wasn't too hard was it? To admit you were wrong? For once?'

'Whatever.'

Sadie marched over to her sister and held her fist upwards. Helen reluctantly joined her in a funny little handshake routine from their youth. They had to laugh.

'Anyway it IS going well – isn't it?' Helen asked. Sadie shrugged. 'By the way if you'd have told me he was English and in his mid-thirties, I'd have known it was a different guy.' Before Sadie could protest, Helen continued. 'So, no goodnight-tongue-tennis with racer-boy? You're such a prude.'

'Huh. I'd rather be a prude than a slapper.'

'Really?' asked Helen, laughing. 'That all you've got? Seriously tho', *Sade*, you've been given a second chance – a new lease of life. Maybe it's time to start trying new experiences. It's what *I've* been doing.'

'Yeah, and that's how you got given your Jimmy Choos. Allegedly.'

'Haha. You know I buy my own.'

'So *that's* where all your money goes.'

'Nothing wrong in the world that can't be put right with five inch heels! You liked them once, too.'

'It'll be a long time till I can afford anything like that again, I can tell you,' Sadie said, patting the folder containing the new cash flow forecast on the table beside her.

Helen paused and looked at her sister. 'Listen. I've been meaning to tell you – I've been working on something. It's an article – for a thing Kate is sub-editor of. She just needs to get the idea past her Chief Editor and I could have a whole new career! Thing is, I'm using you as a success story. It's a… You're not listening are you?'

Sadie was toying with her calculator. 'Yes, yes it's fine, whatever you need to do – you don't usually ask me, so why start now?' She yawned.

Helen tilted her head, thought a bit, then shrugged in admission that it was true. 'OK, I'll tell you if it comes off.'

Sadie stretched and continued speaking. '*When* it comes off. Say it.'

'No, 'cos I…'

'*Say* it!'

'But that's just a...'

'*SAY* it! Say it with me.'

'*WHEN* it comes off...' they both said in unison.

'Better. Remember to always s*tand guard at the door of your mind,*' Sadie said, wagging her finger at her sister in mock rebuke. 'It better work out for you. Anything to get you back in the real world and out of Georgia's room. I'm sick of getting kicked in the ribs every night whenever I snore. But are you sure you need to give up on advertising? You're so good at it.'

'Nothing out there for me, sis. Not this time.'

Sadie reached out and touched her sister's hand. 'What actually happened? Do you feel ready to tell me now?'

Helen looked thoughtful, then replied. 'Nothing much more to tell. I left Winston's to a serenade of rowdy fishwife accusations ringing across the office. I just never thought it'd get round the industry so fast. It's left me in a bit of a... pickle. '

'Bloody twitter,' consoled Sadie.

'Powerful tool – you better learn it if you're going to maximise your international sales, sis. Too bad The Bastard escaped a mention.'

'Victor? But didn't *he* make all the running at first?'

'Yes, but his other half doesn't care about that! My name's mud because of this... Every head hunter I've contacted just says leave it six months, wait for the dust to settle.' Helen shook her head. 'So – new era, new career.'

'A new career?'

'Yes it's never too late to try things for the first time. Age doesn't matter, right?'

Sadie didn't answer her.

'Right?'

'Right,' Sadie begrudgingly replied.

Suddenly age did matter...a lot. Sadie was surprised at the stinging feeling coursing through her chest. *Seeing Stuart with a younger woman – he's trying 'something new' all right.* But maybe it was just innocent. *But so what if it wasn't?*

Sadie looked up, realising that her sister was watching her closely.

Helen narrowed her eyes. 'So... no kiss on the doorstep eh,' she said, changing the subject. 'You know why that is, don't you?'

Sadie sighed. 'Go on, surprise me.'

'You didn't have your lippy on!'

Sadie laughed, despite herself, mainly at the expense of their mother, who had gone completely *au naturelle* when she was younger, in her hippy heyday, but now with the ravages of time upon her, was availing herself of every anti-ageing aid known to woman. Which the granddaughters thought was hilarious, since just lately it included a full complement of uplift bras and chicken fillets, wrinkle-reduction creams and bum-lift leggings. Not least to keep up with all the perky pensioners at her bowls club.

'You'll have to take a leaf out of mum's book eventually. At least update that makeup bag of yours,' Helen went on. 'Go on – let me give you an overhaul with some of my stuff, or you'll never get a new man. Or an old one.'

'Oi! I don't want an old one. Or a young one, before you say it. I'm not even sure if I want *any* one. Tonight made me nervous enough – and that wasn't even a proper date.' Sadie paused, feeling a flash of nerves. 'I've got more important things to worry about than meeting men. But yes, ok, I will give my makeup bag an overhaul – just in case. I think there's stuff still in there from the Student Union gigs – god those were the days!'

'Well in that case, have a complete makeover – new smarter gear – you can even borrow a pair of my shoes.'

'I'd never stand in them, let alone walk in them.'

'Abi didn't have that problem earlier. I caught her prancing about in my snakeskin ones, going through my makeup bag, doing a GaGa in just her bra-bra.'

'Helen! Abi's 14, she doesn't need makeup yet.'

'Not what *she* said. Took to it like a… like a… '

'…duck to water?'

'No! Be more creative than that, if you're going to win that competition madam! Like a… Turner to Tofu,' Helen quipped.

Sadie made a face and shook her head. 'No wonder you're the advertising expert.'

'I was. I'll be Columnist Extraordinaire soon! *You'll* be the next family marketing whizz, believe me! I told you what I thought of your ideas. Some of them are excellent! Don't doubt yourself, now. Especially *when* you win. You'll soon be back to feisty Sadie – the person you used to be … *B.S.*'

'BullShit?'

'*Before Stuart* – amounts to the same thing though. With him gone, you can reinvent yourself! Complete with heels! Cut the strings – have some confidence, girl. You won't have any choice with me around.'

'Yeah, you say that, but he helped me out. It'll be completely different when you've gone off again on one of your jaunts or moved in with yet another man and I'm left here facing a pile of bloody red bills.'

'Stop sticking up for him. You told me you only let him help out 'cos it felt good to take his money away from him.'

'Well, that's partly true. Before that, I'd had to resort to drastic plastic. The only way I got another extension on the overdraft was by sending mother in to see her old pal, at the bank.'

'And that wasn't the only extension she got out of the bank manager, from what I hear,' quipped Helen.

'Least he's her boyfriend now. Anyway, don't talk like that, you sound more like her every day,' said Sadie.

'One of us has to. You're just like your Dad. And as no-one's got the foggiest idea who my father is, god knows if I take after mine.' Helen's attempt to make Sadie smile wasn't working. 'Aw come onnnn, Sadie! Anyway why did you tell me the shop was really busy the last time we Skyped? At least I thought that's what you said, your laptop is so slow,'

'Well we can't all afford the latest equipment,' moaned Sadie.

'Or did you say it just to not worry me? I felt better after that – thinking you were ticking along. I can't believe that you were just fibbing to me? *Sadie doesn't fib*, remember?' Helen teased. Sadie cringed. 'What did you used to say when you were little? Oh yes,' Helen mimicked a little girl voice, *'I'm a GOOD girl boys!* Haha!'

Sadie elbowed her big sis. 'At least I was only 5. What's your excuse? You're 41 and you're still saying it.'

'No, now it's just, *I'm good, boys!*' Helen laughed. 'Little girl lost act puts them off the scent for the domination to come… Anyway, don't do yourself down – the bank wouldn't have given you the extension if they didn't trust your big old business brain and your Excel formulas…'

'Formulae…' said Sadie.

Helen poked her tongue out. 'Whatever. You'd have got it no matter what mother said to Tom Rosebery. *Or* what she did.'

Then both girls stopped and sipped their drinks, then made a face at one another at the thought of it.

'Yes,' said Sadie, softly. 'But my cash flow calculations were based on what I thought would be coming in…' Sadie glanced sideways out of the corner of her eyes at her sister. '… before today's news.'

'Oh-oh, this sounds ominous. Don't say you're pregnant again.'

'If I was, I'd have to call it Jesus. Mind you, I'm not supposed to include anything religious, not according to Damian this evening,' Sadie continued.

'Really?' said Helen, 'Your temple idea? I thought that was the best of the bunch. Anyway what happened today? I thought your run of bad luck was over.'

'Got a disappointing letter.'

'From Turncoat?'

'Yes. How'd you know?'

'Your grey cloud is back.' Helen waved her hand above Sadie's head.

'Hmm. Well, you know I told you the one off divorce settlement was imminent? Due any day but somehow it never came? Hence my jumping at the chance to take his monthly payments, actually. Well, he kept reassuring me – even joked about it – "the big get-shot-of-Stuart payment" he called it. Promised me it would definitely still happen. So I factored it into my cash flow. Was relying on it.'

Helen nodded, slowly, her expression suddenly dark. 'And...'

'And now the big news is...' Sadie took a deep breath and bent down to fish a crumpled ball of shredded paper off the top of the recycling tub in the corner of the kitchen by her chair. 'Apparently, *circumstances* – his circumstances – have recently changed somewhat.' She offered it to Helen, who paused mid-sip and looked at the ball but didn't take it, looking up as if to say *well?*

'Now I ain't gonna get it.' Sadie finished. 'Ever.'

'Don't say "ain't",' hissed Helen, 'say *nasty, selfish, double-crossing, slimy shitbag.*' Helen's voice started to rise. 'What excuse did he give *this* time for mucking you about?'

'Shhh. He says the credit crunch is finally affecting his commission. Says *now* if I want the divorce over and done with soon, I have to agree to the new terms.' Sadie was still holding out the paper ball.

'After three years apart? You were about to sign. What the hell's he playing at Sadie?' She snatched the ball from Sadie's hand and threw it back on the recycling pile, scoring a direct hit. Sadie half-heartedly offered Helen a high-five but she didn't respond. 'And so the control continues. Oh my god, the crafty bastard,' Helen said, slamming her coffee cup down on the table just a little too hard. Brown liquid splashed over the pine surface and she jumped up to grab a cloth.

Sadie put her finger to her lips and pointed upstairs.

'Sorry, Sadie. You know he gets under my skin, he always has. I wish you'd listened to me and never married him.' With an angry flourish, Helen grabbed a cloth, wiped the table then threw the cloth into the sink full of washing up. It hit the crockery and a cup went clatter. But instead of objecting, Sadie ignored it, looking blank. Helen sat down and reached across the table to put her hand over Sadie's.

'I'm sorry Sis. But I always said the guy was a conniving knob-end.'

'So? So you were right. Makes all the difference that does. Not. I listened to you about Damian without a peep, and it was the wrong guy!'

'Yes, well that was a minor misdemeanour, your honour. Nothing in comparison to marrying someone. And mine was a misunderstanding 'cos I wasn't thinking straight. It's ok anyway isn't it? As long as your Damian doesn't screw you over…' Helen declared. 'Now if that *should* happen…'

'Hark at you! Don't talk about me being screwed over – what you focus on expands. You'll make it happen!' Sadie snapped. 'Like the way you keep saying "why do I always get bastards," and they're what keeps turning up for you. It's not a coincidence, it's quantum physics.'

Helen looked blank.

'It's all about positivity. Maybe it's time *you* gave positivity a go. I do.'

'Yes, and how's that working out for you?'

Sadie grimaced at Helen and didn't answer. She just turned to straighten up the washing up pile. Helen softened.

'Well, when I'm ready, maybe I will give it a try. You've sent me enough books about it, I've got the lot – *The Secret, The Power, The Attraction*, and of course that classic, *The Attraction of the Secret of The Power*…'

'You made the last one up.'

'Actually I didn't, it's a send-up book – mum sent me it last birthday.'

'You two trouble makers both laughing at me again? It really is just like old times – only without Dad to console me.'

'Yes, if your dad was here you could have sat huddled in the kitchen together like the old days, sipping vinegar, nettle and cat's-piss tea by the fire and talking about how to fix me and mum. I used to hear you, thinking you could change the world. Then he went and died.'

Sadie made a hurt face at Helen. Helen rolled her eyes.

'What?! He wasn't *my* Dad. "Water off a duck's ass", as mum always says.' Helen stood next to her sister at the sink. She saw that tears were threatening in Sadie's eyes. She put her hand on Sadie's shoulder. 'Come on, Sadie. Practise what you preach. Don't start getting all misery-guts on me – that's not like you is it? That's someone weak, someone silly, someone Stuart turns you into. And like I keep saying, you're well shot of *him*, believe me.'

Helen turned away, then changed her mind and bent over and kissed her sister on the top of her head, giving her a little hug. Sadie smiled.

'Well,' Sadie sniffed, 'maybe it is about time I smartened up my act, and took a leaf out of the smart *bizznizz* woman's diary, *Ms* Parker-Todd,' Sadie said, placing the emphasis on 'mizz'.

'That's my girl,' said Helen as she went over and flicked the kettle on again. But Sadie's clever eco-kettle, involving a choice of different boiling temperatures, got the better of Helen, who couldn't make it switch on at all.

Sadie stood amused, not helping, till finally Helen stopped jabbing at the buttons and turned to her sister, hands on her hips. *Well?*

Sadie cocked her head on one side, raised her eyebrows – *what?* Then she gave in and did it for her, before they both sat back down together again.

'Thanks...' The air was a bit lighter now, and Helen sighed deeply. 'So when *does* the D.I.V.O.R.C.E come through?'

'If I agree to his new terms... big IF... it could be very soon.'

'Well – sod it, just do it. Get rid, move on. Shed his control on you – gone are the days when he decided whether you're even allowed to feel good about yourself, sis. You're managing to overcome this lack of self confidence in all the other areas of your life, now it's time to do it with him as well.'

'I wish I could, but what about the girls – they need their Dad. A girl always needs her Dad.'

The words hung in the air and Sadie shuffled a little. Helen didn't. Helen had done without a Dad her whole life. Whereas Sadie's had conveniently come back and moved in with their mother when she was 7 and Helen was 12. Until just over a decade later. And now he was gone too. *A girl needs her Dad...*

Both sisters stared ahead briefly, before Helen broke the silence.

'So – what about this competition – tell me the latest! It could be your way out! When you and I discussed it before, you were all guns a-blazing. Then a day later, here you are, all down in the dumps.'

'I don't know, Hells, from what Damian said tonight I'm some way off being good enough for something this big just yet. I'd be wasting time and money. He said he'd coach me for the next one.'

Helen's eyes flashed with something Sadie couldn't quite work out. 'What?'

'Nothing.' Helen replied. 'I just it was inspired. Great spin on some clever wording. Can't you send that temple one off anyway?'

'Not with that hefty entry fee. I really think that without Stuart's lump sum now, I'm a bit stuffed – I'm going to have to let Crystal go and do my own book-keeping again. Put on another sampling programme, do some leafleting,' Sadie was talking to herself now. 'Find some way of making the extra shortfall each month. It'll be hard to keep attending the evening classes, even though I love the learning. I've missed it. And mum's paid half of the fees already.'

'Mum paid for them?'

'Er, yes, sorry. Said it was my inheritance – in advance. She'd do the same for you if you were ever desperate too, don't worry.'

Another pause. Helen said nothing but looked miffed and got up to make another drink as the kettle finished boiling.

'Helen – *you're* ok for money aren't you?' Sadie continued, 'You're always ok, right?' Still nothing from Helen. 'Look, if you're not… Mum's threatened to cash in some of her ISA's – she said it was just in case the shop needed it, but if you're desperate perhaps you could ask her help?'

'I'm not desperate… Not yet. Unless Kate's editor hates my article…'

'She won't – you're Helen Parker-Todd, remember? It's me who people keep telling I'm wasting my time, as usual…'

'Who's *people?* Who now?'

'Oh, it doesn't bother me, don't worry about it.' Sadie didn't need to say any more. Helen visibly bristled, puffing out her chest, *him again.* But Sadie interrupted her. 'Don't – I've heard it all before,' she said.

'Not this little nugget you haven't,' Helen snapped, pausing to get Sadie's attention. 'Listen to this. Mum found out from Phyllis at bowls that apparently "your Stuart" has definitely got himself a "Toy-girl."'

Sadie just blinked. So it was true. 'Mum didn't tell me.'

'Maybe she didn't want to spoil your night out. Sorry, Sadie, but his new squeeze is some legal secretary – apparently she was all over him. Phyllis told mum she'd overheard him giving it all the "never met anyone like you, my wife didn't understand me" bollocks. The bastard!'

'Shhhh!' said Sadie, smiling ruefully at her sister's bad language. Not that Helen cared.

'I'm sorry, sis, but you have to face facts – he didn't want you back and now he doesn't want anyone else to have you. Or be in the girls' lives. Serves him right if you *do* get another husband – if Stuart had wanted to be the only man in his daughters' lives, he should have kept his dick in his pants.'

'Ok, ok, you don't have to rub it in. Anyway, I've got news too. I think I'm finally over Stuart. As of today, in fact.'

'What do you mean? Why? Has Mister Testarossa-sterone made that much of an impression on you?'

'No… well, maybe a little dent. No, I like Damian for his brain.'

'Body no good, then?'

'He has got some fabulous pecs, that's for sure,' Sadie said dreamily.

'You sure they're not *moobs*? I couldn't tell in that jacket.'

Sadie gave Helen a 'don't be a bitch' look.

'Sorry,' Helen added. 'Well?'

'Well anyway, today when I got that letter from him – well if that wasn't the last straw, what you just said… It kind of seals the deal.'

'Glad to hear it. Get level. Get even. Get Shorty.'

'That's a film.'

'That's your ex-husband.'

'He's not that short.'

'I wasn't talking about his height.'

'How do you know about his…?'

'It's a metaphor. Listen, I've been waiting for years to see you stand up for yourself. Make sure you do it while I'm back this visit? Preferably within earshot?' Helen smiled and Sadie nodded, yawned, and looked at her watch. 'Anyway it's time you got to bed, Lady Sadie. You're up earlier than ever nowadays, aren't you?'

'Yes – probably just as you're going to sleep. So if you *do* start Skyping your mates in America, again, please do it in the back room this time, so you won't be heard.'

'Ok. Listen, sis,' Helen said, putting both hands on Sadie's shoulders. 'Thanks again – for putting me up. Seriously. My lonely little flat in Clapham isn't the best place to be when you're heartbroken. I do appreciate it.'

Sadie squeezed her sister's arm, then stood up on tiptoe and kissed the top of her blonde, tousled head.

'I do wish I could be more like you sometimes,' Sadie said fondly, 'Just to get out there and go for it, with men. You know – the way you always have – hang the consequences. By the way, if you need to wash your hair, feel free to use the new lavender and rosemary sulphate-free shampoo – it's in the downstairs shower.'

'You saying my hair's smelly, oh sister of mine?' asked Helen.

'It's the big purple bottle. New towels in the tumble dryer, and a fresh robe. Help yourself.'

Helen looked down at herself and shrugged. 'Ok I get it, I get it. I stink. I'll shower. Thank you. Tell you what, in return, leave that folder here, I'll look over your entry for you again if you like? Make some more notes?'

'Have a flick through if you want to, but I'm not sure about entering it now. Thanks for the offer. And for the chat. Like old times eh? Night.'

'Like old times. Night night,' Helen replied.

Sadie peeped in at her sleeping daughters – both were still in Abi's bed since story time earlier – probably 'cos the scary person in Jane Eyre's attic had put the frighteners on Georgia. She had a vivid imagination, that girl. Then Sadie retired to her own room – the smallest one with barely any wardrobe space. *One day when I'm rich, I'll have a walk-in closet*, she said to herself as she undressed. And, focussing on her own happy ending, dreaming of one day finding a dashing millionaire or winning the lottery, she fell fast asleep.

Which was fortunate for Sadie, because it meant she was oblivious to Helen's frantic Skype conversations downstairs – ones which did indeed go on until the wee small hours. And it was fortunate for Helen, because if Sadie *had* heard what she was talking about, Helen knew, her sister might have been none too pleased…

CHAPTER FIVE

'The issue with any new relationship is how long you give it – to get to know the person – isn't it? If you didn't know them before? If you kind of, like, just meet them off the internet or something and you don't know if you fancy them but you quite like the sound of their voice from the, you know, *de rigeur* phone call, and there's been a spark so it seems quite promising, but when you meet them you don't quite have that connection, that animal attraction. It's like, how long do you give it to see if anything develops – you know, to find out exactly how much animal is inside him... So what facings did you want of the special offer Manuka honey, Sadie-Sahib?'

Sadie was miles away. 'Sorry?'

Crystal, the ditsy, purple-haired shop assistant with the West Country accent, tartan trousers, a heart of gold and an invaluable knowledge about grains and roots and shoots, gleaned from her Grandma's Romany past, was regaling Sadie with her opinions about the potential of Sadie's latest 'non-date'.

'I even bought some of the drinks,' said Sadie, coming back to the present.

'That don't mean nuffin', not this day and age. Still couldabinna date.'

'Hmm. But it wasn't. Not really.'

'So?'

'So what?'

'Manuka – choice is four or six.'

'Make it six facings, they just came out with a new study on how it helps healing so that'll be my new window display I think. If I can tone down the wording. Don't want to get in trouble with the CAP team again – they're due for another visit. We'll have to do a BOGOF in the local paper too – see if I can cadge that special ad rate. And I'll update that leaflet from last month once I get home on the computer... so, yes, six.'

'No sooner said than done, Sadie-Sahib.' Oh and Crystal also had an Indian guru boyfriend. She went on, 'And you can always leave the leaflet to me – I need some PowerPoint practice. I'll get Abi to show me on my laptop next time she pops in, yours is too slow. And how about the Evening Prim… Oh, oh. Looks like you're about to have your hands full…' Crystal nodded in the direction of an officious looking man coming towards the shop entrance.

Sadie narrowed her eyes at him. *That's all I need.*

The door opened, the bell above it rang (old school, but part of the inherited fixtures, and Sadie liked it) and the man strode straight over to the counter and deposited a wodge of small amateurish looking leaflets on the table top with a loud *thwump,* for effect. Then he stood there tapping his fingers till Sadie joined him.

'Ahh, good afternoon, Mr Percy. Have you come about my email? I wasn't expecting CAP to respond that quickly!' she said.

'Good afternoon Mrs Turner. The purpose of this visit was indeed initiated by your request to the bureau,' said the visitor, checking inside his weathered-looking leather folder full of notes, 'but sadly we cannot "kindly sneak it in to the top of the pile," in fact, right at the back of our backlog, you will remain, I'm afraid. I'm sure when the appropriate time comes we will indeed examine the copy for your advert for Omega 3 EPA and determine in due course whether we will give the wording clearance.'

Oh god, it's going to be one of those visits. 'So you came to tell me you can't process it any sooner – that's exceptional service Mr Percy.'

'I had a meeting at the town hall, Mrs Turner, and on my travels past the village green, I appear to have been the recipient of a flash mob marketing effort, led by an errant teenager – one who looks very much like you.' He gesticulated towards the pile of cheaply-made leaflets on the counter top. *Abi. She's been at it again* thought Sadie. 'Witness Exhibit One. Exhibits one to seventy six, to be precise.'

'You counted them?'

He responded by raising an eyebrow.

'It's the first I've seen of them, Mr Percy, and I do apologise,' Sadie said. 'I will of course *initiate an in-depth investigation forthwith*.'

'I do hope so, Mrs Turner. Otherwise we will not be taking kindly to having to issue a formal warning. Tradition may *say* 'publish and be damned,' but catching you a *third* time will not look good in court.'

Oh shit.

'Like I said, apologies. That's why this time I submitted my copy to CAP first. Like a good girl.'

No reaction.

'I will of course also deal with the ... *creator* of the leaflet – forthwith.' Sadie was good at rising to the occasion when it came to battling authority, even though she preferred to coerce or talk them round. The latter usually worked. Perhaps not this time. 'I imagine the perpetrator isn't out on the green anymore?'

'You think correctly. Once I began questioning her about her mis-spelling of the word "eczema" she scarpered. Kids' education nowadays... I don't know. In my day it was a...'

Mr Percy's flow was cut off short, as a loud influx of customers entered the store all waving the leaflet, and Sadie spied Abi hovering just far enough behind them to see if the coast was clear. When she spotted her mum, she waved, but Sadie waved her away behind Mr Percy's back, and the teenager about-turned as fast as she could before breaking into a run. Sadie went to continue her conversation with the officious government rep from the Advertising Standards Agency, but the three ladies and one man waving the leaflets were already firing questions at Crystal. Sadie wanted to stop Mr Percy overhearing the blatantly illegal advice which her well-meaning assistant was about to start giving out. As he'd made blatantly clear last time, even if it *was* true, it still wasn't allowed unless he said so. *Ludicrous.* Time to get shot of him.

'Well I'd better deal with this rabble, Mr P. Thank you so much for your visit, and do kindly consider my proposed wording at your earliest convenience? Anything else before you go?' she asked, gesturing towards the door.

'Well, I... no, it can wait. There is another matter, but I have to do a little more research before I return. Make sure this is the last time,' he said, stabbing at the leaflets pointedly, then bidding Sadie goodbye.

Half an hour later, once Sadie had dealt with the flurry of sales, and given in-depth advice to a glamorous grandma about how supplements and oily fish can help skin, hair and nails, *and* put a shine on her Labrador's coat, she took a breather and a closer look at the offending leaflet. Produced crudely on a computer, it had all the finesse of a Scout Hall Car Boot Sale flyer. But according to a scientific journal Sadie had left on her table top at home, the gist of it was broadly right. And also broadly illegal.

'She's only trying to help, Mrs T,' said Crystal, bringing Sadie a hot mug of Green Tea and Jasmine.

'Of course, and she did help. But we're not in 1920 – you're not allowed to advertise stuff that way anymore. Not according to Mr flaming Percy anyway. Mind you, we took £184.20 in the last half hour. That's... £134.10 more than we took all morning.' Sadie looked up at Crystal, caught the concerned look in her assistant's eyes, and opened her mouth to talk, then closed it again.

'Things not looking up then?' the purple-haired one said. 'Shame you can't charge for advice, eh?'

'If only I was officially qualified. I'm not a nutritionist. Maybe that would have been a better course to take than international marketing.' Sadie sipped her tea, thoughtfully. 'Crystal, I've been meaning to talk to you...'

'I think I know what you're going to say, and I've been expecting it, to be frank.' The young trendy assistant with hobnail boots looked at Sadie with her big doe eyes. 'It's not rocket science – I see the takings. Not working, is it – this – me here? Not enough business. I have to look elsewhere for my part-time work, don't I?'

Sadie nodded. 'I'm sorry Crystal, really I am. I thought it would only mean reducing your hours, but according to my new cash flow forecast I did last night, well, it's going to mean tightening my belt much more than I thought – and for a long while to come.' Crystal just nodded, and looked downhearted. Sadie continued, 'But I'm sure there's a new light on the horizon – let's be positive, about all this, shall we?'

'Yep – you be positive and I'll be behind the counter in Boots again. And I so hate Guildford. So impersonal.' Crystal paused and Sadie reached out to touch her shoulder. 'Anyway, don't let me not being here upset you,' she went on, 'You know you'll miss me!' At that, Sadie reluctantly smiled. 'That's better. I'll be ok, I'm always ok. I'll find another way of supplementing my student loan, even if it's going door to door selling brushes and cloths or working for some huge corporate gargoyle in their charity fundraising department.' She took a breath. There was obviously a bit of history there. 'And you, Mrs Turner, you're always so good at telling other people to be positive. Time to do it to for yourself. And mean it this time. The universe knows, you know,' Crystal added cryptically, tapping the side of her nose. She wasn't Romany for nothing.

'I know, I know… I will… I'm sorry.' Sadie shrugged apologetically.

Crystal sipped her own mug of hot tea, which had a rather peculiar smell, and said with a far-away look in her eyes, 'Actually – you'll be ok – something's going to crop up. I can feel it. You know I get insights, right?' Sadie nodded, trying not to smile. 'Well,' continued the assistant, lowering her voice, 'some people may laugh, but I have a strong feeling about you – and your store. That's why I was drawn here in the first place. And I can tell you now, there's something just around the corner for the best little independent health food store in Surrey. You mark my words.'

'Let's hope you're right.'

'I am. I'm always right. To be honest, I already took in an application to the pharmacy. Told Indira I might be back with her soon.' She tapped the side of her temple. 'See? Now, how about I do the rest of the afternoon for free, just as my little leaving gift to you?'

'You don't have to…'

'I insist. Karma – goes around comes around, see.'

'Ok, thanks Crystal. Anything you want in return?'

'No, of course not! Working with you is payment enough… unless I can relieve you of that herbal tobacco that's nearing its sell by date? I can replace it with a new display of something else?'

Sadie smiled. 'Of course you can. I'm discontinuing it, I only got it because of something my ex-husband had said – brought back memories of our university days. So you might as well take the lot.'

Crystal beamed, 'Great! That stuff goes down a bundle in the black market on my estate,' and she trotted off happily and spent the rest of the afternoon singing. Badly.

By the end of the day, she had joyfully helped Sadie completely revamp that part of the store, said goodbye and promised to call back often, to see her, Georgia and Abi. One or other daughter was usually not far from the store – they liked to help out and Crystal had appreciated the extra hands. She left still singing. Then it all went quiet. Too quiet.

For a few moments Sadie's mind drifted off to the marketing competition – a huge cash prize and an all-expenses paid trip to Hawaii... If only she could win it. But what were the chances? Damian certainly hadn't been confident, unlike Helen. But that's what sisters were for wasn't it? No, Damian was probably right – more pragmatic. After all, there were several rounds to get through first, then a grand final. Sadie smiled ruefully, *be positive, be positive*. She sighed, still undecided. Maybe she was just tired – yes that was it – tired and weary. She looked at her reflection in the glass door. *Eurgh.*

The herbal tobacco wasn't the only thing nearing its sell-by date.

But as Sadie finally reached for the 'open' sign at the end of the day, the sight that came into view making its way speedily towards her door, suddenly made her feel ten times worse. Before she could turn the sign over to 'closed' and hide behind the counter, the visitor burst in.

'Hello Stuart.'

Breezing into the shop, bold as brass and twice as devious, was her *soon*-to-be-ex-husband. It couldn't be soon enough. He looked suspiciously tanned, as though he'd been on a sun-bed. *It had to be from a sun-bed, right*? He couldn't possibly have afforded to go abroad?

'Sadie, darling,' he schmoozed, 'how the devil are we today? Just popped by to make sure you got the letter? Only, my new solicitor says he hasn't heard back from you yet?' The shiny suit and shinier shoes shuffled closer to the counter and he reached over to kiss Sadie on the cheek. A whiff of his signature aftershave evoked the reaction it always did in Sadie – a tiny little flutter in the pit of her stomach. *Dammit.* Sadie looked forward to the day it evoked nausea.

'Haven't had a chance, Stuart. Needed to think it over, really.'

'Nothing much to think about, Sadie honey,' he said, helping himself to a small packet of yogurt-covered raisins from the *reduced* shelf by the till, and opening them, 'is there, now? Hmm? If you've read the letter *properly* you will know there is no alternative – I simply don't have the means to pay that lump sum anymore.'

'But it doesn't say *why* not? What happened to our deal?'

'The one you made me agree to, in front of your mother and sister? Well, my purchaser tried to undercut me last minute – the sale fell through. So now I'm going to rent out the flat, rather than sell it. So there we are.' He chomped on the raisins, smiling at her through what looked suspiciously like brand new, shiny white veneers. With bits of raisin in them.

'Well maybe we should revisit the whole "clean break" thing completely,' said Sadie, holding her hand out for some money for the raisins, and getting a shrug in reply. 'That flat was half mine.'

'No, the car was yours – it was new then. The flat was mine, remember? There was hardly any equity left in it.'

'With the emphasis on WAS, Stuart – the value's gone up considerably since then, hasn't it, whereas the car's value has gone right down – and you know it has. In fact, the more I think about it, the more I like the idea of a re-negotiation.'

'Another expensive legal session? Can you afford it?' he challenged. Sadie narrowed her eyes at him. 'If you *can* afford it, be my guest,' he said, as he brazenly reached for another small pack of raisins and opened them with gusto – Sadie *tutted* as several flew to the floor. He popped another handful into his mouth and stared Sadie out, whilst munching. 'Extortionate fees, these legal people, right?' he said eventually, 'that is, *if* you have to pay top whack.'

Which means he doesn't have to. That explains the latest turn of events.

Sadie just huffed and carried on counting the takings of the till. 'You know I can't afford any extra legal fees.'

'So you'll sign the agreement then? Soon? Cos, let's face it, we can all get on with our lives, then, can't we.'

'You already have, by the sound of it – even younger, this one, is she?'

'Oh, you heard already! Yes, trust me, eh? Must be the older man thing. You know, this one reminds me of you, a little bit – how you were a few years ago. Might be the brunette hair,' he said, reaching over and pushing a stray strand back from her face. For a split second she almost leaned against his hand. 'Always liked your brunette hair.'

Despite herself, Sadie's heart pumped a bit faster, but then she realised it wasn't quite as fast as last time. Which wasn't quite as fast as the time before that. *Progress.*

She stopped counting her takings and looked at him. His face was close now – closer than it should be. 'Actually,' he said, leaning towards her, 'her hair is *definitely* like yours.' Sadie bit her lip. He went on, 'Well, the way it used to be, before this little grey patch showed up.' He rapped a finger sharply on her scalp. She shook him off.

Just then Sadie's mobile rang. She grabbed it and answered before the second ring.

'Sadie, it's Damian.'

'Oh hi, so nice to hear a *friendly* voice,' she spoke into the phone, looking at Stuart as she said it, 'can't talk now, hon, can you call me back in ten? Just seeing someone *out* of the shop. Ok, bye.' Sadie smiled at the phone in her hand, then turned back to Stuart.

'Ok, Mister Lover-Lover, enough,' she said. 'Eighty eight pence for the raisins, please. Now is there anything else? Only I'm just locking up. I've got a teenage version of you to deal with when I get home.'

'Actually, Abi's been a right handful lately. What *have* you been doing to that girl?' he asked, making a show of hunting around in his pockets then shrugging when he couldn't find any change. 'Yvette says...' he stopped when saw the look on Sadie's face. '... Yvette's my new lady...'

Sadie winced – *she* used to be 'his lady' – that's what he used to call *her*.

He continued. 'Yvette says that it might be the constant "pillar and posting" of our current custody arrangement. Making the girls all antsy. So I was going to suggest a change. How's this for a solution? How about I have them two days on the trot – Sunday as well as Saturday? But once a fortnight instead of once a week? What do you think? That way they can stay with me overnight, and get some proper Daddy-and-daughters time, like I used to have, remember? I could even carry on reading the Homer books like I used to.   The Iliad and the Odyssey I mean, not the Simpsons... haha...'

Sadie ignored his pathetic attempt at humour. She used to laugh at it. Not anymore. 'You mean the stories that bore them to sleep quickly, rather than something they might actually like? Yeah, good move, hot shot. Mention that, and they'll probably turn you down flat.'

'Actually, *Sweetie*, I have mentioned it and they've already accepted.'

Sadie blinked.

'Yes, thought that'd surprise you. Well, I did tell them they could watch *Made in Chelsea* – Yvette also loves all that godforsaken reality rubbish you and your bloody mother have let our two get hooked on. So they can all stay up late together on a Friday night, and watch the *conviction* or whatever it is. When I mentioned that, they said *yes* straight away. I phoned them both just now.'

'Oh.'

'In fact they're happy to start from this weekend. If it's ok with *you* of course. I'd hate to do anything that you weren't happy with.' His words hung in the air. Sadie just shrugged and nodded a 'yes' in reply. He went on. 'Oh good. That means the weekend after, they'll be with you, and Yvette and I can get away to her Dad's apartment in Cyprus. It's near Paphos, funnily enough.'

Another dart shot into Sadie's chest. She played her best poker-face whilst he carried on undeterred. Under her breath, she started counting to ten, slowly.

'You remember that resort you had your heart set on buying a holiday villa in, you know, whenever we had a bit of money? Well Yvette's old man has got a place there – in exactly the same complex you and I went to see. Small world eh?'

Sadie was staring blankly ahead, fiddling with the cash in the register.

'It's how we hit it off, really, she and I – when I was attending a meeting with my previous solicitor, sorting out the property debacle. Funny story. Tearing the useless man a new asshole I was, really laying into him,' he said somewhat proudly, in between tossing more raisins into his mouth. Then he smiled knowingly at Sadie, and patted her hand. 'You'd have hated it. But Yvette loved it – she was about to quit her job that very evening because she'd had enough of him. So as luck would have it, there was I, like a kindred spirit, her hero. She asked me along to her leaving drinks bash immediately, and it all took off from there. Turns out her *new* boss – well he's now my new solicitor – he's a divorce specialist don't-cha know, and... well you know the rest.'

Sadie just looked at him, stony faced.

'You always said everything happens for a reason,' he added. Sadie finished her counting and ignored him. 'This new lady of mine believes in that, too. She's clever as well – not quite in your league, but let's face it, that means she's more in mine. Haha haaaa.'

With that, Stuart tossed a final raisin up in the air and tried to catch it in his mouth and missed. He made no attempt to pick it up from the floor. Sadie put her hands on her hips and pursed her mouth.

'Oh dear, the danger stance!' he said, backing away in mock terror. 'Better get going. It's been nice chatting to you, Lady Sadie.' He turned to go. 'And Georgia needs more credit, as she told me earlier in a text, By The Way. Or *'bee tee double yew?'* I think she put. Bloody abbreviations. Kids, eh?' He finished off the raisins and scrunched up the plastic bag with a flourish.

'Yes but actually they don't *say* it, you only *write* BTW. It's actually faster to say *by the...*'

'See you on Friday, then,' he interrupted. 'About 7 o'clock? Gives me time to pop out to the pub to see Geoff and the mountain bike gang for a

quick pint whilst the girls are all cosying up watching their TV. "Girls" –
haha!'

'So much for spending time with them, Stuart? First weekend and
you're already leaving them with your new woman? Prepare yourself for
an earful.'

'Ahh, see Sadie, that's where you underestimate me,' he said, putting
the empty scrunched up bag into Sadie's hand, pinching her cheek and
picking up his briefcase, 'I promised them all a takeaway. Yvette's local
Chinese does Quorn. Done deal. Ta-ta. Enjoy going out with the boy-racer
– second date tonight isn't it, the girls said? There probably won't be a
third from what I hear, so have fun.'

And with that he snatched another bag of raisins and left Sadie to
clear up the mess from the floor. As he got to the door, he stopped, lifted
up the *Open* sign hanging on the glass, and flicked it over to *Closed*. Then
he gave her a smirk and left.

With shoulders drooped, she walked to the door and watched him
trot jauntily out of sight, pausing as he went to eye up a twenty-
something girl walking by in skimpy shorts. Sadie picked up the 'closed'
sign and looked at it. Then locked the front door behind him and rested
her back against it. Another day over.

At least she had tonight with Damian to take her mind off things.

As Sadie was collecting her coat and bag from the staff room, he rang
back.

'Hi Damian. Listen, about tonight, I thought that we could…'

'Yes it's about tonight that I was calling. *Sugar-lips*, I'm so sorry – but
I've got to cry off. Can't talk now, but I'll tell you more on Thursday night,
ok? Catch you after class, for a drink in the bar? My treat? I'll shout the
peanuts too this time?'

'Oh.'

'*Oh*…what? "*Oh*-ok"? "*Oh*-you're never going to speak to me again" –
what? I can't tell – hate talking to women on the phone,' he said.

Women. Plural.

'Don't worry, Damian. What I mean is "*OH...* Of course that's ok". Of course. I've got plenty I can do, no problem. I'm quite busy, really. Not a problem at all, don't you be concerned.'

'But I do have some great news,' he went on, 'I just heard that my aunt, the one who tidies up the house a bit for me, is not going to be around at all this weekend – so I was going to ask you – if it's not too inappropriate – if I can cook for you this Friday night?'

'Oh!' Sadie said again, brightening.

'Do feel free to bring your overnight gear – and there's a spare bedroom before you say anything! I respect you too much to make assumptions so early into our relationship.'

'Wow,' said Sadie, before she could stop herself. She straightened her shoulders and felt herself beaming. 'I mean... sure. As it happens, I've just had a cancellation from my usual Friday night activities, so yes, I'd love to. Thank you, Damian, seriously, thanks so much – you've made my day.'

Our relationship, she thought.

'Hang on, you haven't tasted my food yet!' he said. 'Haha. Yes, I'm a man who cooks as well – that usually does the trick eh? Thought that might impress the women – I read a manual about it you see, haha.'

'Haha.'

'See you at class, then – I'll catch you after so we can discuss the foods you like and don't like, and tell you what, how about you choose the wine to bring? Always a good test for a woman, that is, getting the wine right! "LOLL"! Haha! See you in two days and counting, gotta go, bye.'

'Bye.'

Sadie stared down at the phone with a furrowed brow, then brushed it off, and packed up to go home.

'Did he really actually *say* "Loll", mum?' Georgia asked, later that evening, eavesdropping again. 'What a loser. It means 'laugh out loud' – you don't say it, you just, like, laugh. Out loud.'

'I *know* what it means, Georgia,' said Sadie, ushering her recalcitrant daughter back out of the kitchen. She refused to go, so Sadie got hold of Georgia from behind and holding her under her arms, 'helped' her out of the door, as her youngest deliberately leaned back into her mother and did a crab movement side to side. Sadie pursed her lips to keep from laughing but she wasn't giving in – not this time.

'The loser!' Georgia called, finally scurrying away.

'And remind your sister as soon as she's finished her homework, she's got some explaining to do,' Sadie called. Georgia then did a mock salute – similar to the one Damian had done in the kitchen the night before – poked her tongue out, and disappeared upstairs.

Sadie closed the door firmly and sat back down in the chair as Helen laughed. 'He might still spend half his life in a classroom but he seriously needs to stop trying to be *down wiv da kidz*,' Helen said.

'He's not the only one,' said Sadie. 'Well at least I know it's a proper date this time.'

Helen shrugged. Sadie made a worried face.

'It *is* a proper date isn't it?' Sadie asked. 'I'm so out of practise.'

'He asked you to stay over, didn't he?'

'In the spare room.'

'But he's cooking a meal?'

'And asked me to bring the wine.'

'Hmm, well he's still the one that called it a relationship so shave your legs anyway. Better see what the signals are when you see him next – in the classroom – teacher's pet!'

'Well it's not my assignment I have to worry about now, it's bloody wine. Think I could get away with an organic fruit punch from the shop?'

'No you can't! No – make an effort. And don't panic – all you need to do is find out what he's cooking, then google what goes with it – easy. It's amazing what you can find out online these days. Out of interest, have you tried googling *him*?'

'No, as soon as you gave him the thumbs up, that was enough for me. Why? Should I have? Not my fault you thought he was someone else.'

'Yes, well,' replied Helen, looking at her younger sister out of the corner of her eye, 'You should always look. I research all my new boyfriends on the internet.'

'Don't you mean "find" all your new boyfriends on the internet?' Sadie teased. 'I blame Kate. She's a bad influence on you. It feels like when we were at uni together, all over again.'

Helen laughed. 'You can talk – those were my proudest years – seeing my sister finally turn rebel. Even if it was only till Turncoat got you pregnant. Anyway, you're wrong. Kate's giving it up. So am I. No more dating sites.'

'And what's the *real* reason?'

'Ahh you know me well. Actually we were discussing this last night. Kate says you get past 40 and suddenly all you meet are old granddads, cheats, geeks, or ones who are single for a *reason*.' On the word 'reason' Helen tapped the side of her nose.

'Spare me the details. Anyway, how is Kate?'

'Her website's doing well but she's not any closer to finding a man. Plus her mum's moving into a *senior sunshine home* soon, as they call them in New York, so she's tied up with that. That and Lucy's shop.'

'Maybe I should swap my Health store for a vintage store, like her daughter's. Perhaps vintage is the future.'

'No, you keep going with the one you've already got! You're good at it. *Positivity*-blah-blah. Something will turn it around, you heard Crystal...' Helen said reassuringly, but peered over the top of her coffee mug at her sister. Sadie was staring into space. 'Did you bring any of those zero-calorie noodles home? Or some cardboard rice cakes?' Helen asked. Sadie indicated the counter top and an array of large containers.

Helen got up to rummage in the biscuit jar. She turned her back on Sadie – and began systematically trying each of the assorted offerings and putting them back in the jar with a bite missing. Sadie could see her in the reflection of the mirror on the wall nearby. 'Yes, mmm, you never know what's around the bend. Just like something might turn around for me,' Helen said, still munching and not turning around. Sadie shook her head, marched over to Helen and swung her round, as Helen tried to hide the half bitten cookie, behind her back. Sadie just raised her hand to Helen's mouth and swiped a crumb off her lip. Helen shrugged sheepishly, then turned her back and carried on 'sampling,' as Sadie reached up to open a cupboard. Several neatly arranged folders stood side by side. She took out a bulging box file, hefted it onto the table then began rifling through a stack of receipts.

'Well if you want to pay for your keep, and make yourself useful – now that Crystal's gone – can you do invoices? All these need inputting on the computer. I don't suppose with your IT prowess, that you'd be able to...' Sadie stopped mid-sentence, as she saw the horrified look on Helen's face. '...No, perhaps not,' added Sadie, flicking through the wad of invoices, perturbed. 'I wonder what would happen if I just didn't input all these – if I just lost them? Maybe I can pretend they just don't exist. Then I won't have to pay them...'

'With your accounts OCD? You'd never manage to. How long can you string it out for?' Helen asked, suddenly serious.

'Dunno. My shop's going to be history if sales don't turn around, but if I last six months or so, and Christmas is busy, like it was last year, then maybe... Hopefully...' Sadie frowned.

'Must be had if you're using words like "hopefully",' said Helen. 'Or maybe you can pull something else out of the bag,' said Helen. 'Like that competition.'

Sadie frowned some more.

'You wouldn't have had to worry at all if Stuart bloody Turner hadn't let you down,' Helen growled. 'Bloody men. Bloody ex-husbands... What's that look for? What's wrong?'

For the first time, Sadie noticed something was different in her belly at the mention of her ex-husband. Weirdly, she felt none of the instant pangs of longing and jabs of regret. *Good god,* she thought. 'Nothing. In fact, I've never felt better.' Sadie grabbed her sister's arm and made her jump. 'Hey, Helen – I've got a question for you. Has Kate got any tips on her Real Grown Ups Guide website about what to do if your ex-husband's a control freak, a womaniser and a reprobate?'

Helen looked at her in surprise, but before she could comment, there was a knock on the big oak kitchen door. It opened with a creak and a little face looked round with trepidation. 'Hold that thought,' Helen said to Sadie. 'Come in Abs,' Helen said, offering out the biscuit jar. 'Have a cookie? Er, half a cookie?'

Abi sat down next to her aunt, who shoved a coconut covered morsel in front of her and stood up. 'Sis – I'll go look. Tell you later if Kate's website can help in your… er,' she looked at Abi, '…dilemma. I'm due to speak to Kate again tonight. She might have some good news for me.'

'Say Hi from me. And don't call her, Skype her. Sit here.'

Helen went to sit down again. 'No, not you, numpty. Abi.' Sadie added. Helen and Abi exchanged *'you're in trouble'* glances and Abi moved towards the far chair. 'No, not over there. Here,' Sadie said, patting the seat next to her own with an extra hard thump.

'Ok, well I'm leaving the combat zone,' Helen said and walked past Abi ruffling her sleek brown hair. 'See you later munchkin.' Abi smiled and pushed her aunt's hand away playfully.

'I'm not a munchkin. Soon I'll be as tall as you.'

'No you won't – you take after your mother. Night.' Helen winked at Sadie then disappeared out the door.

'Night,' said Abi, as she moved across to sit in Helen's seat. Abi ignored the cookie – and her mother – and continued working on her i-Phone. 'Yep?' she said, without looking up.

'OK, so I've calmed down a bit since earlier,' Sadie muttered, after a brief silence, broken intermittently by Abi's tap-tapping on her phone.

'Whoop whoop,' said the teenager, eyes still down.

'Abi, I'm not going to bang on about it, 'cos I know you were only trying to help me. But you do realise, now, don't you? How much trouble I'll be in, if you do it again?'

'Yes mum. I do, mum.' Still the tap, tap of the keys. 'But someone's got to do something – otherwise I won't be able to go on the school trip, will I? Dad's going to be hard-up too, now, he says. And I don't want to be the only one stuck at home, like billy-no-mates sitting at school with the sixth form every day for two weeks whilst everyone else is in China.' Abi's big green eyes looked up into her mum's – a carbon copy of her own. Sadie said nothing, and pursed her lips in response. 'Well that face says it all,' sniffed Abi, 'I better not start buying my phrase books anytime soon, then. Great.' And she made a hurt face and looked down at her phone again. Without looking up, she spoke in a small voice. 'Anyway I double-checked the extra bits on the internet, before I printed it. The wording's not made up or anything. It's all true.'

'You never know what's true on the internet, though, hon.'

'Well this time you do – I got it straight from your uni research library.'

'Did you hack my account again?'

'No, silly. I used your login.' Then she put her phone on the table and sat up. 'It's so interesting mum, all that data. No wonder you set up a health food store, knowing that stuff. All those facts – and I thought, if only people knew. So I decided I'd tell them. I don't understand why you can't use those statistics – if they're true?'

'It's just the rules about foodstuffs darling. One of the mysteries of the universe. But I do appreciate the time and effort you put into it, really I do. But this is serious, Abi. So now you know, you won't do it again, right? I can't afford to be under the spotlight of the advertising authorities any more than I am already. That official could make my life very difficult. But to make it up to me, there is a little project I might need your help on.'

The youngster looked up expectantly.

'But I've got to work on it a bit longer before I let you know – seek first to understand and all that.'

'Is it like proper work? Maybe it can count for my IT project. Will you know before Friday, when we go to Dad's? I can work on it whilst we're watching the eviction with Yvette.'

Sadie winced a little. 'It's a bit early but I'll try.'

'Do or not do, there is no try,' said Abi in a 'Yoda' voice and got up to go. As she passed her mum, Sadie caught her hand and pulled her onto her lap to kiss her daughter's cheek.

'Get off mum, I'm not a kid anymore, I'm a teenager.'

'Oh, but you're *my* teenager, and I *made* these cheeks,' Sadie added, kissing them some more before letting Abi go. Abi leant back in to kiss her mum on the head, then looked her straight in the eye. 'You and Auntie Helen will sort the money thing out, though, mum, won't you? That's what you do, isn't it? Everyone knows that's what you both do. Even Dad.'

'Thank you darling,' Sadie said, and felt a warm glow in her heart. 'I certainly hope so. That is indeed *what we do.* '

Sadie sat in the kitchen working on her notes for a long time after Abi left, happy to have some quiet respite from both her children *and* her biscuit-eating temporary lodger who had retreated into the back room where the occasional low hum of voices could be heard.

Sadie tapped a pen on her lower lip and an idea suddenly occurred to her. Pushing all the paperwork out of the way she grabbed her laptop, booted it up and began clicking on the keys. On the screen, she typed in the name 'Damian Hugh' and initially saw all the usual links to Facebook, linked-in, and twitter, for various different Damian Hughs, so she scrolled down till she found one that wasn't an author or a motivational speaker or a chauffeur. Clicking on what looked promising, she read several pages of info about 'her' Damian's work at the college, all about his work setting up the course she was attending, a couple of references to old court cases that couldn't be accessed in full, and then finally found his twitter name. Her prowess at creating normal Office documents knew no bounds, but Sadie hadn't yet mastered social media. The likes of 'ats' and hashtags and trending were, 'TeeBeeAitch', the domain of the kids. Frowning, Sadie got up and called into the lounge.

'Abiii! Do you still do twitter?'

'Yes! Why?' the voice was curious.

'I need you to help me. There's something I want to find out...'

Meanwhile in the back room, Helen was Skyping New York. Again. Her old friend Kate had been a stalwart, as usual, having offered Helen a bedroom as soon as it had all happened. Then she'd put forward an idea for a temporary role for Helen, helping out with the publicity for her expanding website, the Real Grown Ups Guide. But Helen had politely refused, due to *'not wanting to be within a million miles of Boss-zilla and the fuckwit husband'*. Kate had just laughed, and promised her old pal that she was working on a dating idea that might just succeed, and spoke at length about her new concept. But – tellingly – she hadn't spoken at all about Kate getting the all-important new column.

'So no news yet, Kate? Your Editors really like to take their time don't they. First they rush me, then they dilly dally. *Dilly Dally, All the way*.'

'What's dilly dally?' asked the pretty blonde woman on Skype in a light New York accent. She was about the same age as Helen, but tomboyish, wearing no make-up and what looked like dungarees.

'Dilly dally – delay. It's an old music hall song, it's… oh, it doesn't matter. So when will I hear? Can you sniff around a bit? There's quite a lot resting on this, you know that.'

''Course I do – and I'm already sniffing. AND I keep hinting about how great you'd be – every opportunity I can, don't you worry. And being based over there shouldn't be a problem – for now – and…' Kate paused, her gaze going to the corner of the screen. 'Hang on a minute – an email's just popped up…' She read it, her eyes darting from side to side almost imperceptibly whilst Helen held her breath.

'Hells, do you think I should reply to a guy who emails me this – *"If I were to ask you out on a date, would your answer be the same as the answer to this question?"*… Hmmm.'

'What?! I…' Helen paused and made a confused face, trying to work out the meaning. 'I… I might have to go ask Sadie about that one,' she said, finally. 'And I thought you'd stopped all the internet dating.'

'Old membership – runs out end of the month,' she was reading it again. 'You know, I think that's actually quite clever. And clever's good, right? This is witty, for god's sake! Maybe I *should* say yes,' replied Kate, flicking back her hair.

'Well can you sort out your love life after you've sorted out saving my neck please? And Sadie's?'

'Sorry,' Kate said, and closed the window with a click, resuming her chat with Helen. 'Now where was that info you wanted...'

'Yes – the circulation of the column – is it really seven million?'

Kate tapped her keyboard then looked full screen at Helen once again. 'Worldwide. Sounds impressive till you realise a lot of it's in places like Gambia. And the Far East. Oh and quite a lot in Europe – that'd help your case.' More clicks. 'So, anyway, sounds like our little Sadie's still having a tough time over there?' Kate asked and Helen nodded in reply. 'It's a tough world, my old friend.' Helen just nodded. 'Your sister usually pulls through though doesn't she?'

'Yes,' said Helen, 'Especially with my help. But she's got a blind spot where her ex is concerned. He's dumped her in the doo doo again.'

'Thought she'd left all the doo doo behind? Stepped away from the doo doo. No divorce yet then?'

'Almost. She just needs a break. Like the attention she'd get from this first column. Please God I get the commission. Are they still aiming to tie in this new series of articles with the lunchtime syndicated shows?'

'Far as I know, that's still the plan. New magazine owner – weird guy – secretive. He's stepping up his drive to cross-promote across all of his platforms, hang on, let me find the email...' Helen watched Kate clicking away and felt her heart start pounding. '...Yeh, sponsors are all lined up – they're impressive too,' said Kate, 'Hmmm, some serious money here.'

'Sounds like they might be able to afford one of the big guns. I'm not even a little gun. I'm more of a water pistol, I'm a...'

'Helen stop rambling and don't worry. The Boss has got a deadline – he's gotta pin this down. But he was close to Maggie. Must be hard, trying to choose the replacement for his bosom buddy. Poor old Maggie. Funeral's Friday. I gotta find something black. Might look in that old trunk I found in mum's attic – told you about Grandma's trunk, right? And that funny old dating manual?'

Helen nodded. 'Next time I see you, you can show me it – sounds old school. Might be just what we need! We're certainly not cracking it, using all these hi-tech ways of finding a man, eh?'

'Right! Yeh let's do that. Sadie would love it – it's really vintage too – some crazy advice in there about men.* Ok, so I gotta get this work done before I leave for the night – he's still in his meeting with the board so I doubt there'll be any decision today.'

Helen bowed her head, and Kate tilted hers in sympathy. 'Come on, *HellForLeather*. It won't be long.'

Helen smiled at the old nickname. 'Thanks Katski.'

'And you're sending that other stuff over, right?'

Helen nodded. 'Soon as I finish Skyping you.'

'Well if it goes through ok, I'll email you immediately.'

'Thanks Kate – you're a star. Bye for now.'

Helen clicked off the computer and chuckled to herself, thinking about the nickname Kate had given her in college, when Helen had gone through her 'rock-chick' phase. *HellForLeather*. Good times.

Then Helen sat deliberating over what to do about Sadie's folder full of sketches which was still sitting open in front of her. She opened the files again, and started rifling through them, looking for something. *Where is it, where is it…* After a few more moments, she pulled out a document and a smile spread slowly across her face. Helen picked up a pencil then looked at the door. She got up, walked over, opened the door a tiny bit, and listened outside it. Then she closed it shut – tightly and silently.

*'New spin off Story – 'Grandma's How to Find a Husband Manual' (working title) by Debbie Flint – coming to Amazon end 2014.

Subscribe to email list at **http://www.debbieflint.com** for updates.

CHAPTER SIX

Sadie was daydreaming. Sat at the back of the class on Thursday night, she was watching Damian pace up and down, going over last lesson's topic again for the benefit of two foreign students. They'd missed it, didn't understand it, and from the looks on their faces, would probably soon be abandoning it, Sadie thought. But nothing would stop him in full flow. Puffing out his huge chest, animated, powerful, he looked nothing like the athletically built (now a bit scrawny, Sadie acknowledged), Stuart.

Sadie's mind wandered – she'd covered this work already. She'd covered most of the rest of the term, if truth be known – well, she needed something to help her sleep and the course reference materials stopped her thinking about other 'stuff' at bedtime. Plus in true geek style she liked to get ahead. She looked up at Damian, standing there mid-monologue, and found herself once more comparing the two men. And not just in looks.

If you gave Stuart an inch he'd not only take a mile, he'd borrow your car to do it, and not refill the tank. He'd been on the make ever since Sadie had first known him – every opportunity he got. She could see that now, looking back. She could see so many things now, looking back. Funny how a rude awakening can fracture your rose-tinted spectacles. But back then, he'd just turn on the charm and get away with it. So charming, they'd say. As did Sadie. In the early days, he'd had a really attractive energy about him – an active student, full of brash optimism and hopes for the future and a certainty you couldn't ignore. As a young college freshman, he'd entranced her, and she was blinded by the headlights.

This being back at 'school' thing was certainly bringing back some memories.

As Damian turned to another student, an attractive female one, Sadie felt a tiny pang of jealousy spring up. Ah yes, she was the girl Sadie sometimes saw Damian talking to confidentially. Including just before tonight's class. *Weird to feel envious about getting attention*. She'd never felt that about Stuart, not even at the start. Interesting.

Despite all the other transient flings Sadie had had at college – during her 'wild years' as Helen had called them – Stuart had been persistent, and somehow he'd kept enticing her back. If it wasn't for Abi coming along, would she have ever taken the plunge and moved in with him? Million dollar question. *Probably not* – it was a tiny bedsit, barely big enough for one, let alone two. Or three. But then life happened and whilst Stuart had furthered his career at an investment bank, Sadie had played mummy. Sadie looked around the room. Back then, she was little older than most of the students in this classroom. They'd managed, she and Stuart, when Abi had come along. But Stuart was soon AWOL – going missing regularly – sometimes several evenings per week. Sadie knew deep down, she just didn't want to admit to herself – he was cheating. Had to be. And so it began. Sadie wondered if Damian was also the cheating kind, and she caught his gaze just as he stood up at the front once more. He smiled ever so briefly and if she wasn't mistaken, he winked at her too. Sadie flushed a little and brought her mind back to the present.

Damian announced loudly that it was time for the case study of a big mobile phone brand – and began handing out notes. Sadie liked that he still used class hand-outs, instead of just emailing everything or having an app. She suspected it was simply because it allowed him to parade around the room and show off – 'peacocking,' her mother would have called it – although in Grace's world that probably had a double entendre Sadie preferred not to know about. And tonight, Damian's peacocking was even less pea, and even more cock, than usual.

But Sadie didn't mind. She had to admit, in her old school way, she quite liked it when Damian stopped by her desk, smiled down at her, and handed her the print out.

'Thank you, sir,' she whispered. He did a double take and she looked around to see if anyone had heard. Then she suppressed a smile as he brushed his hand over her arm and walked on by. She picked up the crisp sheets of the hand-out. Sadie loved the feel of solid paper documents in her hands, so she quite approved of his technique. In the classroom anyway. So far…

The mobile phone brand in this case study was exactly the same type she'd had for her first term in college – she was amongst the early adopters who had all had their own mobile – her Dad had made sure of that. It had been partly because Helen was working and had already bought herself one. Therefore he thought Sadie had a right to have one too – she knew that because she'd overheard her parents hotly debating it. One of the few times she remembered Grace sticking up for Helen. But even though she'd started in college, Sadie was still old enough – just – to remember the days before mobile phones were in every pocket in the country. 'Cos after that, everything changed and so did the excuses for not being tracked down. Assuming the person in question kept their mobile turned on. Which back then, Stuart frequently didn't.

Her thoughts went back to those early years together – at home with two toddlers, and the nights he'd stayed out late – the nights when mysteriously *his* mobile battery just happened to run flat. Funny that. Big sis Helen had hit the roof when Sadie had confided and shared her suspicions about what he was up to. But after questioning him endlessly over and again and getting the same throwaway reply, Sadie decided to believe his shallow promises. And why? Well that was easy. She just couldn't deprive her little girls of growing up with their Dad always around – she'd seen what that had done to Helen. And sometimes – just sometimes – Sadie had convinced herself that everything was going to turn out fine. It had been no mean feat though.

She already had a stack of self-help books, and they'd led to a growing awareness of another life beckoning her. Ayurveda, macrobiotics, alternative therapies. Before he'd fallen ill, Sadie had taken turns with her Dad in serving up new creative veggie recipes at dinner time – once he was sick it was lunch time and supper time too. Of course this had appalled Stuart, and delighted their mother, who didn't seem to notice or care, when Helen began visiting less and less, once she found there was no chicken or pork at every meal.

Sadie couldn't remember the last time she'd personally eaten chicken or pork and had been very grateful that Damian had seemed quite laid back when, before class, she'd presented him with the long list of everything she usually avoided. But it wasn't really the meal tomorrow she was worried about, it was the wine...

Sadie's far-away look snapped back to the plate of cookies in front of her, suddenly being lifted off her desk.

'Sadie, you seem miles away. So as a reward for bringing in these delectable treats for us all this evening, you can be the first to give us your assessment,' Damian boomed, picking up one of the cookies and nibbling the edge whilst he stared her straight in the eye.

Bugger. She hadn't even looked at it. Was he deliberately trying to catch her out? *Surely not.*

'Stand up and tell everyone about why you think this logo was selected for their launch campaign in Eastern Europe, and its implications in the international arena.' He nibbled a bit more cookie, and gave her a little look of encouragement. *No, he really thinks I can answer this.* Sadie swelled with pride as she did as she was asked, feeling her face flush, talking only to him, and he nodded, standing with his arms folded, eyes only for her. He was commanding, in control, and completely different from the slightly tentative man who had knocked on her door the other night. And tomorrow night, he'd be cooking for *her.* Plus he had such a high opinion of her. She felt proud. So proud.

'Thank you Sadie,' said Damian.

'No problem, Damian,' said Sadie. She was very conscious of the fact that not only was she the oldest student in the room, she was also the only one who called the 'teacher' by his first name. She made a mental note to go back to using 'Mr Hugh' in class. *But what about in the bedroom...*

'Oh,' he added, 'and I've got a marvellous piece of Sadie's work to show you all later too. We'll be debating the importance of good copy in advertising.'

As he continued to speak, Sadie's pride turned to curiosity as she became aware of one particularly nubile apparition sitting in the next row – glaring at Sadie. She was the girl who'd been talking to Damian in the classroom when Sadie had arrived that evening, half an hour before class was due to start. But if anything was interrupted, Damian had given no sign of it. He'd greeted her warmly, and turned his back on the other student, who was Scarlett Johansson-esque with a dash of rock-chick. The girl had spotted a friend outside the door and excused herself. By the time she and the other twelve attendees started filing through the door, Sadie and Damian had sorted out dinner the next night. He'd covered all of Sadie's preferences for starters, main meals and desserts, but hadn't given away one iota about exactly what he was going to cook, but he had arranged a time for Sadie to turn up at the house. He'd promised her a surprise, and from the little grin on his face, she wasn't at all sure if it was just the *meal* he was referring to.

The rest of the evening class passed quite quickly until break time, as Damian initiated a heated debate, in which Sadie had taken an active role, and so had the girl – with an opposing viewpoint. He'd wound it up with a summing up, fairly representing both sides of the argument, and dismissed them all for tea break, reminding everyone to pick up one of Sadie's 'delicious' cookies from his desk on the way out, which he then waxed lyrical about. It didn't lessen the disgruntled feeling stirring in Sadie's stomach.

In the break-out room, the glaring girl stood staring for a while, then came over to Sadie.

'So you're a veggie too, huh? These are 'spelt', not wheat, right? Agave or Brown rice syrup?' she said, nibbling on a cookie.

Sadie was surprised and a little impressed, thinking this was the girl's way of breaking the ice and offering a truce. Sadie responded with the full ingredients list and a couple of tips on how to avoid soggy bottoms. 'I'm Sadie,' she finished, 'and, sorry, I didn't catch your name earlier.'

'That's because Mr Hugh didn't give it,' she said with just the slightest air of disdain. 'I'm Delta.'

'As in Goodrum? The Ozzie singer?'

'As in Delta sodding Dawn, the poxy country song. Don't ask. Blame the parents, that's what I always say,' Delta replied with a shrug, obviously not the first time she'd had to explain.

'Don't get me started!' Sadie agreed enthusiastically, intending to try bonding with the girl by having a moan about mothers. Sadie's fellow student must have been in her mid-twenties and probably a post-grad from the uni. She fiddled with a huge pair of silver hoop earrings whilst she spoke to Sadie and she was wearing a studded leather jacket, a short tight skirt and ballet pumps, which emphasized her long, slim, purple-tights-covered legs. Sadie opened her mouth to speak.

'So are you seeing Damian or what?' Delta asked suddenly. Sadie stuttered in surprise.

'Erm, n-not really, no. We...'

'Which means "yes, but he hasn't shagged you yet". Well just watch out for the fall out, Sadie Turner. He's not the most reliable of blokes. Andreas! Andreas Papadopulous! Excuse me,' she called, and she was gone, chasing a shaggy-haired student about her own age out the door of the break room.

Sadie bristled, and pondered the exchange, not able to get it off her mind a full hour later – even when Damian picked up Sadie's competition sketch and proceeded to debate, with full input from the group, the importance of a carefully placed question mark.

Several times throughout the class, Sadie looked up and caught Damian staring at her. At one stage, she glared right back, and rather than snatching his glance away from hers, their eyes met for one long moment, across the scruffy heads and the combat-clad guys, and the bespectacled or mini-skirted girls. Sadie felt her heart flutter a little, and was the first to look away. She couldn't be sure that he was actually looking at *her,* right? Just in case it was someone in front of her. She looked round, sub-consciously seeking Delta, and found her – looking directly at Sadie and not smiling. Sadie creased a grin but Delta just made a look of distaste and turned back to her work.

Suit yourself, thought Sadie, realising that she was suddenly back in that student frame of mind when every other woman was a rival. Back then they were competing for Stuart's attention, but he'd given all of it to Sadie – wholesale. The other girls had had to work hard, Sadie didn't. In fact, the more she'd ignored him, the keener Stuart seemed. Typical. Time and again he kept trying to win her over. It had felt good, back then. To get the man. Sadie glowed a little, as those same determined feelings came coursing back from the depths of time into her body. Then she realised with a jolt that the attraction she felt for Damian – right here, right now – was without a doubt greater than her feelings for Stuart – or what remained of them. *Halle-bloody-lujah.* And with that, she shook all loser-ex-husband images right out of her mind. She had her eyes on a far bigger prize.

At the end of the class, Damian gave everyone their assignment for the week, and held a finger up to Sadie as if to say 'one moment'. The others filed out and Sadie waited, picking up the remaining crumbs from her table, popping a couple into her mouth, and tidying the lids back onto the cake containers, and her papers and files back into her heavy bag. Delta was last in class, and seemed to be having a very confidential-looking chat with Damian. As they spoke, Damian kept glancing over at Sadie every so often. If Sadie wasn't mistaken, Damian looked as though he was being given a dressing-down. Curious...Perhaps – perhaps Delta wasn't just his student.

They ended with Damian bobbing his head down towards the girl – maybe to kiss her on the cheek – and then changing his mind and just patting her arm. He then handed something to Delta, something small, and she put it in her pocket. Then she walked out of the room, paused at the doorway to look back at him, then across to Sadie, smiled a long smile – straight at her, in fact – and then left.

Sadie clumsily walked across to join Damian at his desk at the front, and dropped one of the plastic cake containers on the wooden classroom floor. Damian leapt up to help, and suddenly they were both kneeling on the floor to pick it up. Then they were almost nose to nose. Then he started to speak, and then hesitated. His eyes were focussed directly on her lips and she just hoped she didn't have any crumbs still around them. Sadie's body wanted to stand, but her mind had other ideas. She felt a little disconcerted about that odd comment from Delta. She'd already felt pressurised, a little out of place – a mid-thirties mother in a class full of vibrant twenty-somethings, closer to her kids' ages than her own. And then one of them had made her feel an element of doubt – doubt about this man she admired so much – someone she had the greatest of professional respect for. Maybe she was making a big mistake. Suddenly she felt stressed, because the teacher in this classroom may or may not want to get her naked – tomorrow night.

He was still looking at her lips.

Maybe he wanted to get her naked tonight. Here and now.

No, more likely it was a crumb? Oh god, was it a crumb?

She wiped her mouth just in case. He was still looking at it. *Dammit!* She lifted her fingers to check her lips again and there, right in the corner, she felt the tiniest little bit of cookie.

Oh good god, I can't even eat a biscuit like a grown up, she thought, and then he reached out and held her wrist.

'Let me,' he said, never once taking his eyes off her lips. He let go of her wrist and, as if in slow motion – at least that's how it felt to Sadie as her heart began to pound – he put his finger on her bottom lip and moved it slightly to the corner of her mouth, traced around it across the top and back down the other side, dwelling on the corner, and then taking his finger to the middle of her bottom lip before tapping it very gently.

'Gone,' he said. Then their eyes met and she felt like she was back in the Student Union bar when Johnny TooGood the hockey club captain had been about to kiss her at the end of the Summer Disco. There hadn't been many moments like this recently. Not in the last four years, in fact. And then all that slow motion suddenly speeded up because his thumb came up and rested just below her bottom lip, and he held her chin slightly, pulling her lip down provocatively, making her mouth open, and then he reached forward towards her, watching her intently. He closed his eyes when his lips met hers – properly – for the very first time. It was slow, languorous and delicious. And not a cookie crumb anywhere.

There was hardly any movement, just the luxury of touch. She took hardly a breath. He pressed harder on her lips, then more gently, before pulling back slightly.

He stayed there, just touching with his lips – his big, full, warm lips – on her mouth, and slowly breathed her in. She could smell a faint tinge of coffee and cake and aftershave and...him, and she opened her eyes a little, but his were still closed. *Should she react?* What was he expecting her to do? Should she drop all her stuff on the floor and push him backwards and throw herself on top of him there and then? Should she...

And then it was over.

'Come on,' he said, slowly standing up from kneeling and taking her heavy bag from her. 'I'll walk you back to the car park.'

He seemed a bit distracted, talking all the way about next week's assignment and the directions to his house, so Sadie decided it could wait till tomorrow to ask him what Delta had meant. She was damned if she was going to be needy. And having got to the car and only been given a peck on the cheek as he bid her goodbye, she drove herself home, arriving at her gate without the slightest idea of how she got there.

Inside, Helen was busying herself with something in the back room as she heard Sadie walk into the house followed by a loud call up to the girls. Helen quickly tidied up, conscious not to leave any tell-tale signs that she had been doing something she knew Sadie would disapprove of. The printer had been going full pelt and there were reams of ripped up sheets in one pile, and scribbled-on sheets in another pile. Sadie suddenly popped her head round the door and Helen stepped in front of the evidence.

'Want a brew?' she asked.

Helen nodded and smiled and Sadie disappeared again. Helen felt she was having palpitations. If this subterfuge didn't work out, Helen thought, she certainly wouldn't be becoming a secret agent any time soon.

Joining Sadie in the kitchen with the girls, Helen noticed her sister's mood was a lot less effervescent than when she'd left earlier carrying her barely-cooled-down coconut and raisin cookies in neat little containers for the class. The girls made a big noise about going upstairs to get ready for bed, for their nightly acupressure, and in order find out what happened after Mr Rochester's house burnt down. Afterwards, Helen asked her what was wrong.

'Oh, just the obvious – men,' said Sadie.

'Or man, to be precise – what's he done?' asked Helen. Sadie told her about the class and the curious incident of the girl in the break-time.

'Innocent until proven guilty, sure, but apparently my new would-be Jamie Oliver is "not the most reliable of blokes", according to one of his model-thin young students who cornered me at break-time this evening,' Sadie replied, sitting down at the table, and undoing the button of her jeans. She peeled off her socks and rubbed her red-varnished toes. 'And by "unreliable" I don't think she meant that he forgets to put the toilet seat back down.' Sadie sighed heavily. 'Am I doing it again, sis? Am I? Perhaps he's… Perhaps I should cancel.'

Helen felt for her sister – it must be hard being back on the dating game after so many years being totally faithful to one man. Helen didn't think she'd personally been totally faithful to any one man since… Well, since 1997. 'Listen – don't take any notice of one woman – one probably jealous woman.'

'Why would she be jealous of *me*? She's blonde, slim, legs to die for and a cover-girl face. And she's about ten years further away from 40 than I am.'

'Ok,' said Helen, pulling her maudlin younger sibling up by the arm, 'Upstairs – get the girls sorted. Then it's Makeover-A-Miserable-Sister night. Go!'

'But I...' Sadie complained.

'No! No refusing. This is it. Tomorrow is the first day of the rest of your life, as you're always telling me, and from now on, you're going to live it in makeup and sexy clothes. Even if they're mine. Get!'

'Oh alright then,' Sadie protested, but her shoulders were lifted again and there was already a brightness in her face that wasn't there five minutes ago. Whatever it took to drag Sadie out of the doldrums, Helen would do it. Sadie had done it enough times for Helen. That's what sisters were for, wasn't it?

'And remind me to tell you what happened at the *end* of the night...' Sadie said mysteriously as she went out of the door.

Helen took the cups to the sink and then nipped back into the back room. She scanned around, checking there was nothing left on show, and caught sight of the edge of a tell-tale piece of paper sticking out from her attaché case tucked behind the armchair. She looked furtively towards the door, and then picked up the case, opened it and removed the protruding document, which was a neatly written envelope with a foreign address on it. Helen looked at it, resolute. Then she looked towards the door, then back at the envelope. She nodded to herself, then tucked it snugly back inside the attaché case, flicked the combination lock, and put the bag back behind the armchair.

Tomorrow was going to be a big day for Sadie, for more reasons than one.

The next day, post-makeover, Sadie turned up at work for the very first time *not* wearing her trademark jeans, and flat pumps. Instead, she sported a smart business suit – albeit with a skirt very slightly too long – her legs were a few inches shorter than Helen's. And a very high pair of heels – Helen had insisted Sadie should wear them around the store to 'practise the sexy swagger' and get used to the way leopard print Louboutins made you feel. Plus the store was carpeted so it was more likely the shoes would remain intact during Sadie's initiation period.

The day went by pretty fast, with only a couple of regulars commenting on the new look sultry Sadie, plus a few who just looked at her slightly strangely then left without buying anything, and the rest paying not the slightest bit of attention to her new look.

Sadie checked her lipstick in the mirror in the little office out the back of the store several times after realising her teeth persistently had more 'permanent gloss lipstick' than her mouth. By mid-afternoon she was in bare feet (stiletto-fatigue), and she'd had enough. She wiped the remaining lippy off with an Aloe-Vera wet wipe and peered at the reflection in the harsh fluorescent strip-light above the mirror in the little bathroom. *Who is that?* The make-up was like a mask, a mask that Sadie wasn't used to hiding behind. And in the sanctity of her own little empire, it felt strange. Sure, it had been her regular attire at uni, when everything was still new and a brave new world was waiting to be confronted every day; when Sadie felt she needed all the help she could get. But now... not now. For now, off it comes. Helen was right about many things, but not about war paint in a health food store. Earth-mother was probably more appropriate, as everyone knew, right? When did you ever see a power-dresser behind the counter in a shop that sold adzuki beans and dried banana? Nope, *time and a place, Sadie, time and a place*.

And maybe that place would be tonight at Damian's... 'Cos if it was meant to be, then maybe that's precisely when those heels might come in handy.

Sadie smiled at her own presumptuousness, then went back to her chores. At least she hadn't had to do her nails – thank *heaven* for long lasting gels, another of Helen's life-savers and executive 'sister-makeover' secrets – it meant she could pick and poke and prod around at the shop to her heart's content and still not have to redo her new manicure that night. And today there had been a heck of a lot of picking, prodding and poking needed at the shop, as the latest deliveries had just arrived. With Crystal gone, Sadie had had to cope with unloading, unpacking, storing and stacking them all by herself, alone all day – apart from a brief respite when Abi popped by to make her mum a cup of tea, on her way back from school. The youngster was becoming more and more indispensable nowadays.

Like last night, when she'd helped Sadie with some research she'd been putting off, research which had suddenly become more pressing. Abi had fulfilled her penance for the leaflet debacle, by providing Sadie with a cross-referenced summary of any web mentions she could find about Damian Hugh the lecturer, along with a selection of some of his recent tweets. During her afternoon tea break, Sadie examined them on her laptop behind the counter, perplexed at some of the abbreviations used on Twitter. She decided to drag herself into the digital age one day soon and learn them all. But first she'd unpack some prunes. Whilst in the back room, she heard the door go, and popped her head out to see Abi returning again – this time with the smiling face of Crystal right behind her.

'Mum, Crystal's just going to show me how to do some mail merging – that ok? Can we use your work computer?'

'Yes but don't move anything. Or delete anything. Or...' Sadie called. Crystal waved 'hi' to Sadie and they disappeared into the little office out back. Sadie was glad her eldest was computer-savvy.

After all, the international marketing course placed strong emphasis on Communication in The Digital Age and Sadie was determined to keep up with the likes of Delta Dawn and Andreas Popadopoulous and co, with all their tablets and apps and QR codes and their dewy skin and their lack of lines and their... now, now Sadie. *Accept the grace to change what you can, and not worry about what you can't.*

Just after five o'clock, Sadie was barefoot in the shop window, rearranging the Acai and Pomegranate Juice display, conscious of not bending over too far in any direction. Partly to avoid knocking anything with her tight-skirted bottom and partly because she might not get back up again if she fell into the display. For one moment she seemed to have willed that very catastrophe into being, as she swivelled a label at the bottom of the pile of carefully balanced cartons, and teetered forwards ever so slightly too far. She did a little tiny windmill motion with her arms, and regained her balance, just as two faces came to a stop in front of the window.

Stuart and a woman.

Oh god.

As she scrambled back to vertical, the bell above the front door tinkled again and the dulcet tones of a right royal pain in the neck resounded round the store.

'You know you really should lay off all that booze, Sadie, sweetie, it's not helping your elegance and grace.'

'Don't start Stuart. And what would you know about elegance and grace anyway?' Sadie asked, just as a gorgeous, elegant, graceful brunette-haired late-twenty-something followed in behind him and started perusing the items on the shelf next to her.

Stuart just looked Sadie up and down, did the same to Yvette, and smirked.

'Now Sadie,' he said, 'I thought it would be an idea to bring Yvette along to touch base with you before tonight. She's looking forward to having the girls to stay for the first time, aren't you Yvette?' he said. Yvette just arched an eyebrow at him and thrust out a perfectly manicured hand with beautiful rings and a gorgeous diamond bracelet on, towards Sadie.

'Pleased to meet you – finally,' she said. She swished her long, shiny tresses back over her shoulder and hit Sadie with a full-beam grin. It virtually knocked Sadie backwards with its glow. Reaching awkwardly for her hand, Sadie concentrated with all her might not to lose her balance again amongst the cartons, and shook it – hard. Instantly she was surprised to feel the handshake tighten to equal her grip. *Ouch.* A knowing smile passed over Yvette's face. 'So this is the little store,' she continued. 'Do the girls like all this stuff?'

'Yes they insist on it – I can provide you with some ingredients if you want to stock up?'

'Oh that's ok, sweetie,' Stuart interjected. 'Yvette's going to swing by the supermarket later, it's cheaper there.'

Sadie bit her tongue. She was about to launch into a lecture about organic provenance but she reconsidered and just said, 'OK, no discount for you then.' He was trying to rub her up the wrong way and as usual it had nearly worked. 'So I hear you're a legal secretary?' Sadie said to

Yvette, stepping down from the ledge and picking up her heels, wishing she was in her jeans not a 'trying to hard' suit.

'Yes, but only until I get my property business up and running,' she said. 'Then I'll be able to do all my own conveyancing – save myself a fortune.'

'Oh?' said Sadie, 'Amazing what you can do yourself online nowadays isn't it? I've been looking into ways of getting a divorce cheaply too – perhaps we should save ourselves a fortune, Stuart, and just do that. Didn't realise how easy it is until last night. Online divorces are a pittance. Then maybe you can use the money you save to pay half towards Abi's school trip and Georgia's new uniform.' There was a pause, as he flashed a look towards Yvette. 'You could, couldn't you?' Sadie pushed.

Stuart shifted uncomfortably. 'Oh, let's not worry about that now, I just brought Yvette in to see what you looked … I mean what the shop looked like. Yvette wanted some seaweed coated peanuts or something didn't you Darling? They're over there I think,' he waved an arm across the room then took Sadie by the arm and led her up one of the aisles. 'Let's discuss that when I bring the girls back on Sunday, *sweetie,*' he pressed, giving her one of his 'don't start now' looks and lowering his voice slightly.

'Oh but surely now is as good a time as any,' said Sadie, shaking her arm free from his grip and straightening her dressy shirt and smoothing down the smart skirt. Then she slipped her feet back into the heels. When she stood back up again she felt taller – in confidence as well as height. Maybe she could make herself like stilettos after all. Her eyes were level with his, now, and he looked very slightly taken aback. A flash of something exciting coursed through her body at the look on his face – one she hadn't seen for many years. Yes, she was smart, she was in command. She didn't have to kowtow to his every whim, and she wasn't going to be walked over – not any more. Not in these shoes. 'Unless you make time to discuss things properly on Sunday night. Without fail.' She stood up even taller and gave him a withering 'I mean it' look.

'Yes, yes,' he said, as Yvette came up to him with a curious look on her face, glancing down at Sadie's heels and furrowing her brow slightly.

'How much are these?' she asked Sadie.

'Oh – take them, as a little "welcome to the family" present,' Sadie replied, spreading her grin back as far as it would go, aware that Stuart was looking at his watch and was about to scarper.

Maybe there was a lot to be said for this dressing for the part. Yes, maybe Helen was right after all. Perhaps today was the start of a whole new era.

Sadie waved goodbye to them both and checked the time. The countdown was on. She just had enough time to nip to the off licence on the corner to choose the wine for tonight before getting herself dressed up to meet Damian. And, still coasting on the thrill of Stuart's reaction to her new attire, she knew exactly what to wear tonight. And it was nothing to do with the fact that Stuart would also see her in it, when he came to collect the girls.

CHAPTER SEVEN

Seven o'clock.

'Mum what ARE you wearing?' asked Georgia who was sitting dolefully on the stairs with her weekend requirements crammed into the One Direction rucksack on her back.

Sadie was rushing around, tidying the hallway and putting the finishing touches to the outfit that Helen had provided – it was a loan from 'when she was large'. Still not quite big enough for cookie-loving Sadie, but with a pair of their mother's pull-you-in-pants, the red high heels, black pencil skirt and crisp white shirt nevertheless complemented her bright red nails and vivid red lips perfectly. She stopped and looked herself up and down as if to say 'what d'you mean?'

'You look like a waitress. From that Robert Palmer video on YouTube. Doesn't she Auntie Helen?'

'Leave it, Georgia-porgia, you sound like your Dad – I think your mum looks sophisticated,' said Helen, who had just walked back in the house from the garden, where she'd apparently been 'Skyping America' on her laptop again.

'Robert Palmer?' asked Sadie, 'Has your father been force-feeding you his 80's music again? Has he still got that old cassette tape?'

'What's a...' began the youngster.

'Your mother's going out tonight,' Helen said. 'On something strange called *a date*. Get used to it.'

'Eurgh, not with gas-guzzler 'LOLL' man?' Georgia asked.

'Yes, with Damian,' said Sadie, trying not to laugh, 'but don't worry, I'm driving myself in my Nissan so a few less trees will be carbon-emissioned into smithereens tonight.'

'That's not even a verb,' said Abi, joining them.

'Not yet but maybe your mum will make it one – she's going to be a marketing whizz you know. Aren't you *Sade*?' Helen said.

Sadie stopped tidying, and made a 'you're a nut-job' face at Helen, as the girls waited for her reply.

'Yes you are! Visualise, Sadie, visualise,' Helen teased. 'Anyway, you kids are just jealous 'cos you have to ride around in your Dad's company Yaris.'

'At least it's green,' said Georgia.

'Green'ish,' corrected Abi.

Sadie wished fervently that Damian *had* been picking her up, especially if he could have pulled up outside in his Ferrari just as Stuart was leaving – in his Yaris. Downgraded from his Range Rover when he'd had to tighten his belt, Stuart had never stopped moaning about it.

At least his new car was one the girls approved of, and Sadie felt a sudden pang at the thought of them being driven away from her, gone till Sunday evening. Then she caught sight of herself in the mirror, and the pang of angst was replaced by the thrill of first-proper-date nerves. She didn't recognise the face in the mirror. In place of her usual played-down, no-nonsense persona, all she could see was the lippy.

And the mascara. And the eye shadow, *and* blusher – applied much more expertly than this morning's effort. Plus an expression of blind terror at the thought of staying overnight with a new man.

That session on the computer had turned up some interesting info about Damian, Sadie thought as she picked up six pairs of Helen's lacy knickers drying on the radiator. Nothing too juicy, but they'd betrayed his penchant for Merlot, revealed in a tweet where he'd joked that 9.30 *every* evening should be National 'Wine o'Clock'. It was lucky she'd found it, since after class on Thursday he'd refused to let on to Sadie exactly what he was cooking for her, leaving the choice of wine a complete shot in the dark. Abi had also found Sadie a string of replies to his tweets, mostly from females, whom Sadie assumed were just students or colleagues from the uni. Even though they mostly ended with kisses. That's how everyone signed off on social media nowadays, wasn't it? Wasn't it? *Blowed if I know,* thought Sadie.

Maybe tonight would end with kisses.

Or more.

Suddenly Sadie felt a rush of panic at the thought of being stark-bollock naked within the next five hours.

Maybe. Then... she couldn't help it and a string of doubts filled her brain. *Unless it wasn't really a date, maybe he meant it, about the spare room... maybe he just wants to talk about work... maybe...*

A loud honk outside snapped her out of the cannon-fire in her head and she looked around the hallway. Even though she was totally over him, Sadie couldn't help but make sure the place was tidy. Helen was watching her with a weird expression on her face.

'What?' asked Sadie, 'I'm tidying up in case Stuart comes inside,' she explained indignantly. Helen cocked her head to one side. '*What?!*' Sadie asked again. 'Have I got more lipstick on my teeth or something?' Sadie began rubbing them with her finger.

'No, sis,' said Helen, in a voice which made Sadie look up. 'You look... beautiful.' Helen walked over and kissed her on the cheek. 'Have a lovely time. And remember...' Helen paused as if she was about to deliver some precious gem of insider information. 'If he serves you corn-on-the-cob, just nibble it, don't take big bites or you'll be picking it out of your front teeth for the rest of the night.'

Sadie laughed. 'Helen's dating tips, number 157! Could be your next book!'

Then Abi chipped in. 'Remind me not to come to *you* for guidance when I begin seeing Harry Styles when I'm sixteen.'

'Is he that lead singer from that pop-group from that TV show?' Helen asked in a little old woman voice.

'Yes, but he's going to date me, not Abi,' said Georgia.

'Now that's visualising,' Helen laughed.

'Oh my god, so many comments, so little time,' replied Sadie, smiling. 'And I shall resist them all. You keep at it, girls, and you're right, you never know. And preferably not till you're eighteen. At least.'

'Well Clara in geography has got a cousin who dates a guy in Bee Bee Duke's rap group. They went to junior school together and he never forgot her, and picked her out of the audience and now they're together

– it was a very romantic story, she told us at lunchtime. AND her cousin's only 17.' Abi said, with her chin in the air.

'That's nothing. I once dated one of East 19,' said Helen, proudly.

'Who?' asked both girls at once.

'The one who wore that hat in that video, you know, *"Stay another night…"'* she began singing, 'he signed the album sleeve for me.' Then she sang some more.

'No, not who did you date,' Abi shouted, above the caterwauling, 'who on earth were East NINEteen??'

'And what's an album sleeve?' added Georgia.

Helen stopped singing, dramatically folded her arms and pursed her lips in mock-anger. '19 – 17 – only the postman cares, it was some famous group. Be impressed!'

Sadie ignored them and finished picking up the remaining pile of laundry from the floor, shoving half of it into Helen's arms. 'Now, you've both got the homework for Monday with you as well, haven't you?' she asked her kids.

The girls nodded.

'Well, try and do it at Dad's, before you come home, then we'll have all of Sunday evening together. We can do some baking or something else fun.'

'You know it's not "Dad's", don't you? Where we're going? It's Yvette's. Dad just lives there. He's her lodger,' stated Abi with a 'he's a loser' look on her face. Abi waited for her mum's reply.

Sadie felt anxiety course through her body. She swallowed hard but despite everything, still couldn't bring herself to say *Yes he is a grade one toad* in front of his daughters. She remembered briefly discussing this with a pal whose husband had left her and their two young daughters for another woman; the girls had later told her they'd needed to hear it from her lips that it was ok to be angry – ok to hate him for it. Sadie opened her mouth to speak, but the loud beeping from outside restarted with an angry rhythm. *What the hell?* she thought, and opened the front door to look.

There parked in the road was Stuart, not in his Yaris, but in a flash BMW sports car. When he saw Sadie, he did a double-take, turned the engine off and got out of the car. *Oh no*, thought Sadie.

The girls pushed past her and ran down to greet their Dad as he came up the path, then rushed on past him to go inspect the car. *So much for not liking gas-guzzlers.*

Sadie was still holding six pairs of kids' knickers in her hand and one enormous pair which she looked at curiously before stuffing them in a nearby welly boot and swinging round to greet him.

'You're early. For once.'

'Yes,' he said looking mildly amused. 'Yvette got me to drop her at the supermarket whilst I came here in our new – her new car. Beauty isn't she?' he said.

'Stuart, if I find out you've used the money you should have given me to buy yourself a car, I'll…'

'You'll what, sweetie? Hmmm?' he stood looking her up and down – using that expression she remembered from the deep dark depths of their marriage – a look that conjured up the early days when he was her amusement and she was his muse. She'd held the power back then. His look disconcerted her and she didn't reply. He gazed around the hallway.

'Just look after them, give them lots of attention, and make sure you're back in time for that "chat" on Sunday night, OK?' she said, standing in front of the welly.

'Yes, indeed, Lady Sadie – when you look like that, how can I refuse? You know, you look quite sexy, quite sexy indeed. Boy Racer's going to have his work cut out tonight isn't he?' Sadie felt herself battling a mixture of being chuffed and being miffed. She decided on miffed.

'He's not a boy – he's only a few years younger than me and unlike you, I don't put out on the first night.'

'That might be a mistake,' he said, 'Guys like him don't like to be kept waiting.'

'Guys like…? Oh, shut up Stuart, he's not like that.'

'Isn't he? Are you sure?' Anyway, it's time to get my reprobates off to our place for the weekend – Yvette will be waiting at Waitrose – she'll be "waiting-rose", "waitrose-ing"... doesn't quite work, does it. Hahaha.' He didn't wait for Sadie to respond, just ruffled her hair, picked the big knickers out of the welly and shoved them in her hand, saying she might need them, then he strutted down to the girls at the car.

Helen was watching from the kitchen door. She saw her sister straighten out her skirt again, with a tell-tale posture that usually meant she was on the verge of exploding at her soon-to-be-ex-husband. Then she watched as Sadie took a deep breath – her shoulders raising and then falling slowly, breathing deeply, slow, controlled. And then she walked down to the car to kiss her kids goodbye. The way she protectively folded her arms around herself as they disappeared from view in the new BMW made Helen's heart break – Sadie was used to seeing them go but not for a whole weekend. She needed a bit of galvanising before leaving for Damian's, Helen thought. Maybe the news would help... 'Hey sis,' she called, 'want a quick cuppa before you go? I've got something to tell you!'

'So they'd want you to run this piece when?' Sadie was asking, standing in the kitchen, holding a comforting mug of something fragrant.

'In two weeks – to tie in with their new syndication. It's going to mean a quick trip across to New York. Final stage, if it goes well, it's mine.'

'That'll be nice for you.'

'The trip's for both of us.'

Sadie looked quizzical.

'You and me – they want to meet me for a final face to face, and fit in a quick photo shoot – a head shot of me for the column but if you come too, they can get one of both of us. They'll also want some of the shop – I can get those done.'

'Sounds promising. But I don't have any spare cash for a trip to New York.'

'It's their shout – two days in the Big Apple – expenses paid – isn't it great? You and me travelling again. We can hook up with Kate – it could be like the old days!'

'That's great for you, Hells, but mum's away and Crystal's off travelling and I'm really not sure I can shut the shop for a couple of days – not right now. But you sound really pleased – I guess if they're paying out that sort of money to get you out there they must have been impressed with your feature. Well done sis. I'm so pleased for you.' Sadie put her hand on Helen's shoulder. 'But exactly what did you say I'd done that was so inspirational to other women?'

'I told you – I'll email you a copy so you can read it another time – don't worry about it for now – just go off and have your date with Mister Hugh and his Merlot. I'll leave it till Monday then I'll convince you to come with me. You can be my good luck charm.'

'Hah! You might not find me so much of a push over now I'm all suited and booted and power-dressed!' laughed Sadie, standing with her hands on her hips and legs apart, shoulders squared in a Wonder-woman pose. 'It certainly made Stuart do a double-take.'

'Good – mission one accomplished. Now get yourself going, leave the rest of the tidying to me, and let's hope mission two is you getting laid by midnight.'

'Helen! It's not like that – I don't put out on the first...'

'Dressed like that, you might have no choice. Might be worth borrowing these fat-pants of mum's to put on underneath it all?' she said, lifting the offending garment draped across the chair back.

Sadie's look said it all and she snatched them and made an "I'll get you" face then started to chase around the table after Helen, who chased her back, and Sadie squealed and ran off up the hallway.

'And no boring him about macro-anti-biotics,' Helen called, 'whatever he cooks you tonight, just look impressed and compliment him on his prowess in the kitchen! With a bit of luck tonight's the night you'll experience his prowess in the bedroom as well! Or the stairs... or the bathroom...'

Helen watched with pride as her sister finally drove away up the road to her saucy sleepover. With a bit of luck it'd be more sauce than sleep. And as the sound of her car faded into the distance, Helen became aware of how quiet the house was. And how very, very alone she was. Maybe it's time to do something about it. And she went off to do something she'd been meaning to do for a very long time.

CHAPTER EIGHT

Sadie pulled up outside a big detached Victorian house and checked the address. Was this it? Somehow she imagined Damian living in some sort of modern bachelor pad. But it was the correct road number – the sign on the iron gate at the front confirmed it. She felt her heart flutter slightly, *she was here*. Sadie got out and collected her bag from the back seat of her car, locked it and turned to face the house.

'Sadie! You're just in time!' a voice called from the front door. Damian was dressed in a casual polo shirt, short sleeves showing off his tanned, muscled biceps, and jeans which made her notice for the first time how large his thighs were too. He came to meet her and looked a little warm. Maybe he'd been slaving over a hot stove – for her. *Just for her.*

'Hi Damian – nice place.'

'Yes, it's …inherited,' he replied. 'Here, let me take that,' he said as he reached for her weekend bag and kissed her – on the cheek.

'Oh,' said Sadie as he relieved her of her bag and guided her up the crazy-paved, slightly overgrown short pathway and inside the freshly painted white house.

The interior was equally bright, as well as welcoming and warm. Something spicy was cooking in the kitchen, and the walls were totally magnolia, with some large abstract artworks hung regularly around the place. He showed her into the lounge and took her smart black blazer, looking her up and down with an approving gaze.

'Nice outfit,' he commented.

'Nice place,' she said. Again. And instantly chastised herself for being unimaginative. 'I mean – I love the red on the paintings. Really cheerful – eye-catching. Are you into art?'

'Yes, totally, but I tend to look out for the up-and-coming designers, you know, catch them "on the up," then their early masterpieces can make you a fortune! Ahaaha!'

'Oh, haha, right,' she said.

'Actually, these are mine. I painted them.'

'You're kidding?'

'No, I take evening classes as well as teach them. This was a triptych inspired by some of Bacon's earlier works.'

'If only yours were worth as much as his, eh?' Sadie said, guessing he meant Francis Bacon, of whom she knew very little, but she guessed his paintings had to be costly.

'Yes, wouldn't that be nice!' he replied, rising to the subject. 'There's something squelchy about the flesh of his early 70's works that contrasts with the planes of raw canvas and jet black doorways. I prefer the ostentatious authority and the variety of his later works though, don't you?'

'Oh, definitely,' Sadie replied. *Time for a swift change of subject.* 'So was the decision to paint connected to your talent for advertising?'

'Funny you should say that,' he said, and took her through to the study room nearby, where a cabinet was filled with neatly-displayed trophies and awards which he began talking her through – some from many moons ago, and one quite recent. They weren't all for advertising, though, Sadie noted, peering at the inscriptions of the older ones at the bottom of the display.

'I see you played rugby,' she said, 'I thought you had a fly-half's physique.'

'Yes, but I was a full-back. Our team won most of the inter-college leagues.'

'Nice that you still have them all on display together.'

'Evidence of achievement – picked up the habit from the parents. It was very important to them – only child, see. They only had me to show off about, so I did my best to provide them with the fodder they needed so they could boast to the bridge club or the W.I or whatever else my mother attended. She ahhh... incentivized me, shall we say. Made me a very competitive person.'

'I guessed as much,' Sadie smiled. *Nothing wrong with competitive –* Helen had been that way her whole life, hadn't done her career much harm.

'Anyway, let me take you upstairs…'

Sadie snapped a look at him.

'… haha, to show you to your room – never fear, Mrs. Turner, you're in safe hands in this house – I told you before – I wouldn't take advantage of you so early into our friendship.'

No, what you said before was 'relationship'…

'Oh… Ok, I'll get my bag,' Sadie said.

'Allow me,' he replied, and picked up her bag as if it was a feather, then took her elbow. He made her walk in front of him up the narrow staircase and Sadie felt very aware he was watching her backside swaying in the tight skirt as she swaggered and swiveled her way towards the top. Half way up, she stopped, turned and smiled at him then just bent down to take off the high heels, holding them in her hand for the remaining steps.

The landing was decorated in much the same way – if the little glimpses inside each bedroom were anything to go by – only the colour scheme of the paintings on the walls varied. Apart from one room, which seemed very dark. Sadie craned her head forward a little to peep further in. Damian saw her looking and reached over to shut that door.

'Messy room,' he explained. Sadie stepped back.

'Glad you've got at least one! I was beginning to feel a little self-conscious about my messy house!'

'Well, you can't help it with all the people you share it with,' he said, smiling at her as he pulled the door closed, and ended up only a foot away from her. He was inside her comfort zone, where he hesitated a fraction longer, then extended his arm past her, almost touching her shoulder, pointing to the next room along.

'I thought you might like this next room Sadie,' he said, opening the door to a beautiful white-linen-bedecked bedroom with fresh peach flowers in a vase on the sideboard, and fresh peach towels laid out on the luxurious white bed. It was an ornate metal bed like the one in *Bedknobs and Broomsticks*, one of her favourite childhood films, with brass fittings and knobs on each corner.

'Oh, Damian, it's beautiful,' she replied, and smoothed the bedding down with one hand whilst putting her rucksack style handbag down on the bed with the other. He immediately took the handbag and placed it onto a small ottoman at the foot of the bed. Then he sat down and patted the space on the bed next to him. Sadie gulped, then sat down beside him. He turned towards her and looked into her eyes for a long moment.

'Sadie,' he said, 'I want you to feel at home here – in my house. I don't have that many people back here, let alone cook them dinner. It's usually just for me. Or my aunt when she comes. I just wanted you to know that from the get-go. Tonight is quite a special occasion for me.'

'Me too,' Sadie said, in a little whisper.

'You look very … different tonight,' he said, his eyes flicking up and down her body and around her face. 'I approve.'

'I'm glad you approve,' said Sadie, a little catch in her voice, 'it's the new me.'

'Well I liked the old you, but if these lips are anything to go by, I guess I'm going to like the new you just as much.' He touched her bottom lip with his finger, and leaned forward to place his mouth over hers, a gentle kiss, more of a meeting than an exploration. She breathed him in – freshly showered, a slight cooking odour on his clothes, a dash of cologne. He broke off and stood up.

'So, what are you making for us?' she asked, standing too.

'Aha, you'll have to wait and see! More importantly, what wine have you brought?' he replied, with a little tease in his voice. Sadie smiled and opened up her weekend bag, producing the Merlot.

'How about this? For "wine o'clock" later?'

Damian looked quizzical for an instant then grasped the wine. 'Well it's not 1999 Washington State Ciel du Cheval, but if you are up for "Wine o'Clock" then you're a woman after my own heart. This Merlot might be from Wine Rack but it looks fine by me!' He pecked a kiss – on the lips this time – and took her hand to lead her downstairs. *So he's into wine as well as art.* Sadie fought off her 'being in awe' innate reactions. He could teach her a lot.

'Come on, Sugarlips, got some stirring to do!' he said and Sadie followed him down the stairs, putting her shoes back on when she got to the bottom.

Dinner was super – a concoction of mild fragrant vegetarian curry with half a dozen extra dishes all cooked to perfection. If he was competitive, it showed in his culinary expertise too – Sadie guessed he practised the same dish over and over until it was perfect. She also surmised that he was probably the same with paintings – maybe why there were so many similar ones around the house. She wondered what else he was good at, as she looked at his big hands and watched his lips move, listening to his conversation. Rugby – clearly. He'd been regaling her for the last half hour about his league triumphs and university sports shenanigans. He didn't really ask her many questions about herself, but that was ok, there was plenty of time. Sadie was having a nice evening and the good food had calmed the jitters in her stomach.

After coffee, they retired to the lounge, Damian put some soft soul music on and the sports anecdotes turned to the topic of his injuries and 'rugby war wounds'. Damian showed her his cracked rib bumps, lifting his polo shirt and revealing a stomach that wasn't quite washboard but definitely wasn't the paunch Helen had hinted at the other day. No moobs in sight either. *Thank god.*

Or was it? Did that mean he'd have higher expectations of her own body, should they wind up in bed together later? Oh dear, maybe it did, Sadie realised, making up her mind to find a class she liked at the local gym and stick to it.

But her palpitations were beginning once more as his smooth, warm skin felt like finding an elusive treasure – one that had been forbidden for many, many years. *Comes of being completely faithful for so long,* she thought. Then, having touched his ribs, she found herself suddenly terrified, and asking if she could be excused to go to the bathroom. He looked slightly put-out but just shrugged and she retreated.

Inside the elegant mostly-white bathroom upstairs, with its freestanding ornate bathtub and perfectly coordinated navy accessories, Sadie looked at her makeup – still intact – apart from the lippy, which was soon put right with an extra application from Helen's expensive brand – a last minute addition to Sadie's weekend bag and only after protest. One day, though, Sadie thought, I'll have my own expensive makeup and designer clothes. *When I'm a grown up.*

When she got back downstairs, she found Damian in the kitchen, everything already in the dishwasher and the remaining pots left to soak.

'Ahh, Sadie,' he said, brightening, 'I wondered if you'd care for a nightcap. I have brandy and several choices of liqueur or another coffee if you like? Although I wouldn't want to keep you up too late tonight... so I've got decaf if you prefer?'

'Er – ok, decaf would be fine – thanks Damian. I'm sorry I was gone a bit long, I was a bit... I suppose I should own up,' she said, turning to face him and feeling a bit awkward. 'It's unusual for me – to go on a date.'

'I thought as much,' he said, and put down the tea towel he was drying his hands on and turned to face her. 'Tell you what – let's take the heat off and go relax for a bit in the lounge, shall we? I'm sure there's something we can find to do together in there – like watch a film or... do you ever play computer games by any chance? With the girls? Wii? X box? I've got both.'

'Er...' replied Sadie, slightly surprised, 'well sometimes Helen and I have a game with them but I'm not very good.'

'Oh ok, well it was just a thought,' he said, leading her through to the cream leather sofas and vivid red artwork again. 'Always good to bond with the youngsters. Tell you what, whilst we let our dinner go down, why don't we go over your thoughts on that competition entry again, just, you know, to unwind a bit? I meant to tell you that I'm quite impressed with some of those ideas of yours. Very, in fact.'

Sadie sat herself down. 'Really?'

'Very much. Almost good enough for that competition, but not quite. Actually I'd like to hear more about what inspired you. Most of the first year students I meet are nowhere near as advanced as you appear to be in your analytical approach and...' Damian stopped. Sadie was staring at him. 'What? Wrong call? Subject too business-like for a date night?'

Sadie hesitated. *Date night.* 'You said... you were impressed?'

'Yes, impressed – for someone like you. Who is in effect a novice to my field of study,' he added. She felt her shoulders relax and experienced a little buzz inside her belly. Someone like him, impressed. *Squeee* indeed.

'Yet you said that it wasn't worth me entering?'

'Well, no of *course* not, not yet. Your style has to develop.'

The *squeee* squelched to a halt. It must have shown on her face.

'It's standard stuff, Sadie,' he explained, touching her arm. 'No-one wins the first time they enter, do they. Not even I did. Took me three goes, to be honest, before I won that first award out there in the cabinet – the top one, pride of place – hardest to win, you see? But,' he said, sliding a little closer on the sofa and reaching out to play with a tendril of her brunette locks splaying out over her white shirt, 'you will also win one – one day, when you're ready. And I can help you get there. Deal?'

'Deal,' Sadie replied. The way he was looking at her was some consolation. He thought she was good but not good enough.

Why are you really here Sadie? She asked herself. The reply wasn't forthcoming, as she jostled with the question. The answer was somewhere in between wanting him, and wanting to BE him. To have him. Or to have his knowledge. She felt a bit silly, as the dawning realisation hit her that she was caught in the middle of wanting him to be her rock, and a very hard place indeed.

'In the meantime,' he continued, 'tell me about what inspired the ideas that I saw. Sometimes,' he said, softly, leaning a little closer still, 'I think I learn as much from my students as they learn from me.'

Sadie felt a little better. She opened her mouth to speak but his lips were upon hers once again. Gentle, hardly moving, just experiencing the touch of her mouth. She kissed him back, but he drew away and smiled.

'Hey – I've got an idea. How about we go get into our comfy night clothes and then come back down so we can really relax together. I think we're both a bit tense to be honest and maybe it's a good idea not to… rush things. Do you agree?'

'Sure,' she said, and found herself glad of the reprieve. Upstairs she found herself glad she'd brought her fluffy pyjama set and opted for that, not the see-through negligee from Ann Summers which Helen had playfully stuffed into her bag. Ten minutes later they were both sitting on the rug in front of the wood-burner which occupied the small fireplace – Damian had lit up some kindling and the flames were flickering gently. As he carefully inserted some logs, Sadie relaxed back and leaned against the armchair, sipping at the drink Damian had brought in for her.

An hour of easy repartee followed. It wasn't the most fluid of conversations but it was comfortable enough. She'd explained her thought processes with her earliest concept sketches, talked him through the ones that hadn't made it to the final folder, and how the wording had come from a little online research about the product they were supposed to be designing the competition entry for. Damian's eyes were alight – he seemed to be fired up by discussions about his favourite topic and he was obviously very passionate about her ideas too. Sadie felt flattered. But she knew from his occasional raised eyebrow and chewed cheek that she was nowhere near the standard she needed to be for international competition. Especially with such a high entry fee at risk. She was hit with the sudden realisation that Helen's column might just be her best hope – if it really could work wonders and turn around the fortunes of the store.

'Penny for them?' she heard Damian say, as if miles away.

'Oh nothing. I was just thinking how kind you are to have humoured me by discussing my novice ideas. Tell me about yourself now, Damian. You never married?'

'Whoa! Straight in with the easy questions, eh? Not! "LOLL",'

Sadie cringed slightly, Georgia's voice ringing in her ears. 'Oh sorry, if you'd rather talk about something else…'

'No, I was teasing you,' he said. 'Nothing much to tell, really. Had a wife once, together seven years from uni, then one day she told me I had to get married to her or break up with her. And I chose marriage. Had a fabulous proposal as well, I got really creative. I made the newspapers 'cos of how I did it.'

Interesting, thought Sadie. He was obviously itching to tell all. 'Go on then, how did you do it?'

'Underwater,' he said.

'Do I really want to know any more about this?' she joked.

'I can show you if you like?'

'What?'

'Don't worry – I mean the clippings...'

'Oh, haha,' said Sadie, 'I had visions of you filling the bath up!'

'What? Oh er, no. Haha. It's in an album in the study, let me go get it for you.' He jumped up like a puppy and trotted to the door, then halted in his tracks. 'God, what am I thinking. What an idiot. Of *course* you don't want to see my marriage proposal to my ex-wife do you.'

Sadie heard the words but knew enough about body language to know what she had to say. 'Oh go on then, you've made me curious now. Go get it.' He bounded out of the room and was back again in an instant, like a dog with a new toy.

'See this one? It's where I put on my dinner jacket underneath the wet suit, and on a special board, here, I wrote 'Marry Me' so I could produce it when we were at the bottom of the sea – it was only a five metre dive but I was bloody freezing without the proper gear on underneath I can tell you!'

Sadie laughed politely.

'And here's the article in the paper – the dive master up on the boat had my SLR camera ready and took some pics and this was the clipping – it's just a few words but this photo they printed is the one on the boat, when I took my wet suit off to reveal the dinner jacket and dicky-bow underneath and pulled out the ring and... hey presto!' he said, turning the page to show a pic of his own face, beaming, and his ex-wife's face, bedraggled as apparently most people's faces are when they've just come up from a dive.

'Did she have any idea?' Sadie asked.

'None. None at all. It was a total surprise – she was gobsmacked, as they say "oop north". She was from Huddersfield, my wife. Said she'd have liked to have been able to put some make up on for the photos but she cried, and that was good enough for me,' he said, overflowing with pride and lost, for a moment, in his memories. Or his own innovation.

'Very good,' Sadie said, brimming with questions she decided not to ask. 'So what happened after? Why did you split up?'

'Not meant to be,' he said, curtly, snapping the album shut and coming back to the present abruptly. 'More coffee?'

'Yes, please.' He topped up her cup and she pondered whether to enquire further. Now she was really curious. 'Damian,'

'Yes, Sugarlips?'

'Were you married long?'

'Nope. Ironic really – cost a small fortune – I paid for the full McCoy – you know, a thirty grand "do" in a big medieval hall, extended family you haven't seen for decades, exactly the same number from both sides of course, plus a gazillion bridesmaids, white ponies and a master of ceremonies to make sure all the toasts were done the right way, honeymoon of a lifetime etcetera.'

Sadie blinked.

'Year later we'd split up.'

'Sorry to hear that,' she said. She meant it.

'So was I. Very sorry. If I'd known earlier that the woman in the office down the corridor had fancied me too, I might have proposed to her, instead.'

'You mean you…?'

'Had an affair, yep. Lasted two years. Older than me – proper cougar. Quite rich too, we had a whirlwind affair with tons of theatre trips and top restaurants and weekends away – that was when I found out all about wine actually. Then the day my divorce came through, *THE day*, I come back to find her gone off with a guy five years younger than me. From the office across the street. I've been a bit wary ever since, truth be known. Once bitten and all that.'

'Ironic,' said Sadie, but not for the reason he appeared to think.

'Yes very. And now the ex-wife is all sprogged up with my ex-best friend and I'm here in Surrey setting up a nice little life for myself. Burying myself in work, and the occasional bit of down-time,' he said, turning to her and raising his mug towards her.

'Gosh that's some story. Mine's… similar,' she said, and left it at that. Damian had gone off into his own little world again and Sadie felt sure he wasn't in the mood to listen to her own sob story about cheating husbands. Definitely not.

Sadie stared at the dying flames in the fire and suddenly felt overcome with a wave of tiredness. They both spoke at the same time.

'Listen Sadie I…'

'Damian I think… haha. Sorry. What were you going to say?'

'I was just going to say – you're obviously tired. All that lugging of boxes on your own in the store today no doubt,' he said, referring to their earlier chat during dinner. 'Next time, leave it till I'm nearby – I'll make light work of it, I'm very strong – feel…' and he held out his rather large bicep so she duly obliged and gave it a little squeeze, nodding. It *was* quite big and felt very hard. 'And I'd be only too glad to help you,' he added. 'I like you.'

She smiled.

'A lot.'

'That's nice,' said Sadie, 'I'll remember that. Now I'm guessing you're ready for… sleep then,' Sadie added, phrasing it carefully.

'Ahh, yes. Sleep. Up the apples and pears time, yes? Been a long day.'

He insisted they left everything as it was and saw Sadie up to her room. He bid her goodnight and gave her a tender kiss at the door to her bedroom. It was a long, gentle embrace, and she felt his arms wrap around her body and pull her towards him. Then it ended and she said goodnight and went to her en suite bathroom to clean her teeth.

Soon afterwards as she lay underneath the fresh white linen, she became aware of an unusual hum – a sound like a bass booming in the distance, and an occasional thudding noise. It was actually quite soporific and shortly after, Sadie was in dreamland, having a nightmare about being trapped under the ocean being attacked by a killer shark in a dicky-bow, with a wedding ring through its snout.

CHAPTER NINE

Helen felt jubilant. Her life was slowly coming back on track. After Sadie had left, she'd gone round the silent house tidying everything up and making it all spick and span for when her lovely, deserving sister got back. Sadie was due to return just before Abi and Georgia did on Sunday night, so Helen made it neat – just in case Turncoat Turner decided to poke his nose inside the house when he dropped the girls off. Even if Helen herself didn't give a damn about Stuart's opinion of how tidy the house was, it was important to Sadie. So until the day his opinion finally meant sod-all to her sister, Helen would toe the line.

She wondered what Sadie was doing right now. Leading question. Maybe getting some novelty nookie – her first since Stuart walked out. Or knowing Sadie, maybe not. But hopefully she was having fun. But if Sadie's weekend didn't turn out so good, and she left early, Helen had made her promise to text to say she was on her way back.

Not that she needed to – she could have just turned up. But Sadie always liked to have someone who cared about where she was. She'd always been the same. That's why, when her father had come back on the scene and filled the place that Helen used to dominate, it felt ok for Helen to spread her wings a bit, culminating in a year of studying abroad. After all when a girl's got her dad, she's 'in good hands', right? Helen wondered what that felt like.

Spotting another dusty surface, Helen finished her chores with a final flick of the duster and the house fell silent once more. It was midnight. In the years since her split, it would be Helen out burning the midnight oil and dancing till dawn. Now it was Sadie's turn. Maybe her younger sister was already in bed – and whatever she was doing in it, Helen knew she'd be happy. A good night's sleep or a good "seeing to" as their mother put it, either would be fine for Sadie. She needed both. Helen just hoped Sadie wasn't laying there on her own feeling rejected.

NO – as gorgeous and sexy as Sadie had looked this evening – surely not? Damian would be mad not to pounce on her at the earliest opportunity. Sadie's first experience of another man in… how many years? Well, the first of many, Helen hoped. Or until such times as she found herself one good one. Till they both found one, maybe? *No,* Helen sneered, after the last debacle she'd more or less given up hope. If only there was some way of properly moving on…

Before she knew it, Helen was pulling down her oldest suitcases which Sadie kept in storage for her in the rafters of the little garage. Something her pal Kate had said in her last Skype call about attic discoveries, had made Helen wonder if her own long lost memories were still up there somewhere covered in dust…

Pretty soon after, with a glass of wine in one hand and a host of photos in the other, Helen was sitting in her cobweb-covered track suit on an upside down crate in the garage, with a blow-heater warming her cold fingers as she picked through the remnants of her own years as a wife. Her own early incarnation looking back up at her with an early-twenties glaze of optimism in her eyes, totally besotted by the dark haired Mediterranean-looking guy next to her in all the photos.

'Why the hell have I still got all these?' she said aloud to herself – or rather, to an old, partly-clothed plastic doll with matted hair which she'd found in one of the suitcases. 'Eh, Susie?' she asked it. 'What did I think was going to happen? That maybe one day we'd reunite and I'd frame them all and put them back out on the mantelpiece of some bijou-terraced in Battersea and we'd live happily ever after? Eh Susie? Eh? Pah! Fat chance.'

Helen threw down the photos in the 'chuck' pile, and put the doll back in the suitcase. Then she hesitated, and picked up 'the' album. Her wedding. Now, this one *really* needed to go to the rubbish dump. She tossed it aside without opening it.

Men.

Maybe it was the embarrassment she'd endured as a result of the last break up, but she felt herself burning – burning with a mounting indignation that was overtaking the numbness she'd had for a decade or more. She held up a big faded sepia photo of herself and her ex-husband, dressed in *Olde Wilde West* outfits at Chessington World of Adventures when they were in their mid-twenties. Then slowly and deliberately, she ripped it in two, then tore *his* half into tiny, tiny pieces. Then she dragged a metal rubbish bin over, and shoved the fragments into it. Soon, they were joined by a dozen other photos, all decimated. The bin was full of a mish-mash of eyes and hair-styles and chins and noses. She felt better. Much better. *And this will be the icing on the wedding cake*, she thought, as she took it, her glass of wine, and a box of matches out into the garden.

Yes, it was time.

Time to finish a job she should have done years ago. Because it wasn't only Sadie whose whole new era had only just begun.

Sadie awoke the next morning to the sound of a shower-pump – throbbing through the wall next to her head. She glanced at the clock – six a.m. *God, was he mad?* Whatever happened to a Saturday lie-in? She put the pillow over her head and tried to go back to sleep, but to no avail. So she got up and had a luxuriously hot shower in the cute little en-suite to freshen up, then went to dress. She moved the hanger with last night's knock-em-dead clothing to one side, and picked up her usual 'uniform'. *What the hell.* At least jeans and a baggy t-shirt wouldn't evoke memories of any eighties pop videos.

She peered round the door of the bright kitchen to see Damian cooking up a storm – last night's dinner bombsite replaced with this morning's breakfast battleground - wrappers and refuse from veggie sausages, mushrooms, tomatoes and eggs, fresh toast and croissants and a lovely big pot of freshly brewed tea just waiting to be poured. She snuck up behind him and put her arm round his waist.

'Morning.'

'Oh! Morning, sleepyhead,' he said, kissing her on the lips briefly. 'Wasn't going to wake you – was going to bring you breakfast-a-la-Damian-in-bed... I mean, not "Damian in bed" I mean...'

'I know what you mean,' she said smiling, 'and that was a lovely thought. Thank you. Can I stay down here now? Or do you want me to go back up to get into the bed and wait for you? Er... I mean, not in *that* way, I mean...'

'I know what you mean. Stay here – you can pour the tea. I got the supermarket delivery man to bring us some almondy milky stuff so you can have proper tea with milk instead of herbal...' he said, watching her examining the label on the milk, '... but I've got herbal if you fancy that instead? Or I've got...'

'This is fine,' Sadie said. 'Thank you.' She sat herself down at the bench seat on the other side of the large high-ceilinged kitchen, and watched Damian at his wide range cooker. It was a lived-in kitchen – quite unlike the rest of the house, she decided, which still had an element of 'show-home' about it, almost unlived in. He looked happy and was humming to himself.

'Sleep well?' he said to her, over the sizzle of the frying pan.

'Very,' she replied, 'had an odd dream though. Can't remember it all now but something about an undersea predator...' she smiled at him and he turned around quizzically then seeing her face, broke into a broad smile.

'Ahh, that'd be me. I crept into your room last night and had my evil way with you whilst you were fast asleep.'

'Really, and did I enjoy it?'

'Yes. Haha. Actually the sleep usually happens *during* the sex. What can I say, my technique leaves a lot to be desired.'

'Well that surprises me, I'd have thought you'd have wanted to perfect that too...'

He turned and gave her a curious little look, then added 'Well, actually it's something I wanted to talk to you about.' He prodded a sausage with a fork and turned around to face her, forked food in hand. 'It's a bit delicate, you see. I wasn't going to say anything but when you turned up last night looking drop dead gorgeous...'

Sadie glowed just a little.

'...I found myself thinking improper thoughts and what with the promise I'd made to you and everything,' he stopped, as if waiting for confirmation that she knew what he was talking about. She nodded, and then picked up the tea pot to pour. 'Yes, well,' he continued, 'I know I said that, this early into things, it should be separate rooms, but, Sadie I – I have to admit I nearly knocked on your door last night. And it was all I could do to stop myself. There, I've said it. Ahh, that feels better.' And with that, he bit the end off the sausage and turned around to put the food onto the plates that were warming on the oven.

'Oh!' Sadie said, surprised, and stopped mid-pour.

'So is that an "oh, shit I'd better leave now" or an "oh damn, missed opportunity" kind of *oh*?' He graced her with his best innocent grin, as he stopped in front of the table, her plate in one hand, his fork and half-eaten-Cumberland in the other. 'And you'd better talk fast, 'cos this is pretty hot!'

'Ok, well it's an *Oh, I'm not leaving now – not with a sausage like that on offer*!' She laughed.

He chuckled, did a ceremonial final bite from his fork, then sat down at the table with a knowing look on his face.

'Here's yours – hope it fills the gap. Ooer missus!' he teased. 'Now, we've got a long day ahead of us and I'm planning on making it a weekend to remember!'

'Super... mmmm this is delicious, thanks so much,' she said, in between mouthfuls. 'I'm very honoured that you've done all this for me.'

'Yes,' he said, 'you should be.' They finished breakfast in easy camaraderie, and Sadie found herself looking at him in a slightly different way, now he'd confessed. He fancied her. Pure and simple. And she had a big sausage on her plate. She couldn't be happier.

Later that afternoon, they were on the way to Richmond Park, a place Damian loved to go jogging, as it was only half an hour from his house. But because they were taking a picnic, and the speed limit in London's biggest green space was only 20 miles an hour, plus deer weren't that font of Ferrari noise, he agreed to Sadie's suggestion that they go in her car.

Damian had packed a fabulous picnic hamper full of nibbles and spreads and dips and crudités, and they found a wonderful spot to sit in the warm spring afternoon sun, and get a little closer. In fact, they ended up getting so close, that she had to slap Damian's hand playfully a couple of times before they finally headed off home again.

'It's ages since I went on a picnic,' Sadie said as they unpacked the hamper in the kitchen. 'What a lovely trip, thank you.'

'My pleasure,' he said, tipping the last of the rubbish into the bin and taking the hamper out of Sadie's hand and putting it on the table. He leaned down and kissed her again, every bit as gently as before, a slow embrace, soft and intense. Even more intense now that she knew he wanted her. They kissed a little more passionately, but it was hardly the pinnacle of desire, and Sadie found herself making more of the moves than he did, now they were back indoors again. 'Everything ok?' she asked him, as she pulled away, conscious that things weren't exactly hotting up the way she'd anticipated they would as soon as they got behind closed doors.

'Yes, of course,' he replied, and then surprisingly began pouring himself a stiff drink from a cabinet in the corner of the kitchen. 'Want one?' he asked.

'No thanks I'll grab a bottle of water if that's ok.' She reached past him for it, and made sure she was extra close to his body. On the way back, she leaned towards his face and he sipped his drink swiftly, put it down and kissed her. But once again, it didn't last long. Sadie was confused. *If in doubt, ask…* 'I have a question. Are you,' she said, 'em… I just wondered if you were planning to… take me upstairs, at all?'

'Actually, yes,' he said, 'because I have a question for you.'

He took her by the hand, finished his drink and led the way up the staircase. Only this time they didn't go into her room, they went straight past it, by another locked door, past the room with the dark walls, and into his own bedroom at the far end of the landing. The curtains were still closed and they blocked out the fading early evening sunshine. It was neat, and tidy, with a faint smell of deodorant and sleep.

'Sadie – do you… Do you like to play games?' he asked. Sadie noticed a TV and a jumble of gaming boxes and cables by the wall.

'Er, we discussed this last night, didn't we?' she replied, disappointed. 'I'm not very good on the Wii but I quite like making the little people, what do you call them, avatars, and…'

'Yes, avatars,' he said. 'You know all about avatars? That's great. But I actually meant another type of game. Role play.'

'*Role* play?' Sadie swallowed hard.

'Role play,' he said, pulling a storage box away from the wall towards him just a couple of inches. You know, like, dressing up, using props, that sort of thing? Like people do… in the bedroom? There, I've just come out with it.'

'Oh!!' said Sadie, eyes wide.

'Oh dear,' he said, bowing his head. 'I don't need to ask what *that* "oh" means.' He was a little sad. 'Never mind, it was just an idea,' and he pushed the box back again and turned to leave.

'Wait,' said Sadie. 'Tell me – tell me more… about what you mean,' she found herself asking before she could think straight. Always having had a pretty conventional sex life with Stuart, she'd got used to normality and only two or three shades of grey. So she found herself more than a little curious about his intentions. Especially now she'd already spent yesterday dressed as an extra from a quasi-soft-porn music video. Complete with the lips and the heels.

'Well, I wouldn't have said anything, but when you arrived looking so totally different to what I'd been used to, it occurred to me that maybe you like to try different… looks.'

'Like what? What do you mean?' she asked again. He nodded briskly, like he thought he could share, and open up to her some more.

'Well, I actually have a – *fun* side – that I don't usually share with anyone on a first date, but with you, somehow, it feels like it's ok to talk about it.'

'Go on then,' Sadie replied, her mouth going slightly dry, 'talk.'

Half an hour later, Sadie was back downstairs with a blank look on her face. She'd been subjected to a display of outfits any good Madame would have been proud of. And none of them were hers. Damian came in the kitchen a moment later, face flushed with excitement.

'Thank you Sadie,' he said, kissing her more fervently this time, full on the lips and for the first time she felt his tongue. 'It's great to be able to share. Thanks for being so understanding. So later, I'll open the other chest and maybe you can try some of the female outfits on?'

'Oh,' she said again and grabbed the rest of his whisky and swigged it straight back. *'Why the hell not!'* She wondered just how far to take this whole 'new Sadie' thing, and just how much of it she'd be sharing with Helen when she got home tomorrow. Whatever happened, tonight looked like being unlike any other date night she'd ever been on, that's for sure.

Just then Damian's mobile rang. He said 'Business,' excused himself and went outside.

Business, thought Sadie, listening to the low thrum of his bassy voice, talking even lower. Wonder who's calling him for business on a Saturday evening? At least I've got Helen looking after my business today – the takings will probably just about cover the stock she'll eat, but at least it's better than a closed sign, Sadie thought.

Outside the door, Damian was talking in hushed tones – to ensure that Sadie couldn't hear him. 'I told you,' he was saying, 'not until tomorrow night... No, not this time... It's ready, virtually... Yes, she'll be gone... Talk tomorrow, bye.' And he went back in, to a completely unsuspecting Sadie.

Back at Sadie's place, Helen had had another one of her bright ideas. She was just arriving home from a busy day including a stint scouring the local shops, putting little postcards in every place that still advertised the old fashioned way. She'd placed the colourful postcards in every available window all over town – it had taken her hours. She dumped her expensive leather handbag on the kitchen table and rang Turner's Health Foods.

'Hello Turner's, can I *help you to healthy*?' Crystal answered.

'All ok, *sahib*?' asked Helen.

'Yes, no sign of her, you win the bet,' came the dulcet West Country tones.

'I told you – she's quite a long way away and with a hunky man – well *she* thinks he is – so the chances of her checking up on me were minimal.' Helen and Sadie had a deal in the old days – if a date was going well, you wouldn't hear anything. If it was going badly, you'd text each other little updates as often as you could get away with, for comedy value and for reassurance. 'And I haven't heard anything, so I don't expect to, for the rest of the weekend.'

'Hmmm…' said Crystal the other end of the phone.

'What! What do you mean, *hmmm*? Do you know something that I don't, Gypsy Lil?'

'Oi, don't diss my gran. It's in our bones, we know things,' Crystal replied making her voice go a little bit spooky. It didn't really work. 'Anyway, he's not the one, this guy Damian? Definitely not the one. But then *you* knew that too, really, didn't you.'

'Duh, yeah!' Helen responded, 'Don't need a crystal ball to know that!' She liked Crystal, having met her a couple of times on previous visits. Crystal was completely kooky, and Helen loved it. She'd jumped at Helen's request to pop over and help out, as she was saving up to go travelling. Helen had easily obtained her number from Grace who was away bowling all weekend so couldn't cover at the shop, but her mother was more than happy to have Crystal covering the store rather than Helen. And she'd told her so. *Whatever.* 'Anyway, you found your envelope under the till? All there?'

'Yeah,' Crystal said, 'thanks Helen – it'll come in handy. Anytime you need me, just shout.'

'No problem, hon. Actually… you know what? I *can* give you some more work – fancy a leafleting job? You know where to find the richer areas around here, don't you?'

'I think so. My pal's a postman.'

'Cool, I'll be in touch end of next week, if it all comes off. Bye till then.'

'Oo oo, Helen,' Crystal interjected quickly, 'You know that thing you're doing – the other one – the one that Sadie doesn't know about?' Silence from Helen at the end of the phone. '…be careful, ok? I don't think it's going to work out quite the way you expect.'

'Things never do, Crystal,' said Helen, 'things never do.'

Unbeknownst to Helen, her sister was thinking the very same thing.

CHAPTER TEN

That night Sadie was sat on the edge of Damian's bed with a camera in one hand and a whip in the other.

You've got to be kidding me, she thought. But he wasn't.

The ironic thing was that, after two hours of role play, which Sadie had found mildly erotic half the time and mildly amusing the rest, Damian still hadn't got "down to it". In fact, he was hardly getting "up" to it, either, so to speak.

And Sadie was just a little bit bored, and more than a little hungry.

There'd been some fancy leather gear, with strategically placed holes in, plus some maid's outfits – 'outfits', plural – which was kind of weird. That had really put her acting skills to the test, mainly in *not* giggling. There had also been some sort of space cadet's uniform, and an alien hat shaped like a weirdly deformed forehead with veins all over it and an eye in the middle. Now, Damian had reverted to 'dungeon slave' but it was when he'd produced the camera that Sadie started to wish it was time to stop for dinner. *Been there done that,* she thought, looking at the video buttons on the camera. So over it. Same with the dildos, same with the strap-ons – it had been fun back in her uni days, when it was all fresh and novel and daring. But having learnt what worked with Stuart in the bedroom over the years, and it wasn't the fancy stuff, Sadie had got to know herself – and what she liked. And it was good old fashioned, honest passion, between a man and a woman, vanilla style, as they called it now, rather than vanilla with hundreds and thousands and crushed nuts... and some weird 'voice-changing gadget to help you speak alien'. And a great big, fuck-off rubber flake.

Just then Damian's phone rang again, and he pressed a button and clicked it straight to voicemail. Then he looked down at the box and around him at the floor, both overflowing with paraphernalia. Then he focused on Sadie, looking 'pensive'. As opposed to looking like a 'penis', which is what he'd done for most of the last two hours. A prize one. A knob with knobs on. Actually, he'd role-played that too. She raised her eyebrows at him and he shrugged.

'Fancy a cuppa?' he said.

Downstairs, back in normal gear once more, Sadie found herself oddly unsatisfied. She'd not really thought about sex – that is, having sex – or more accurately, herself having sex – for such a long time that it had become automatic to dismiss it. But now Damian's shenanigans had aroused something in her which wouldn't calm down with a camomile tea, and began to needle her, *dammit.* She looked over at him – all big and butch, watching the kettle boil, deep in thought, back in his normal clothes. Sadie suppressed a grin as she recalled his attire not an hour ago, complete with feather duster. She rubbed her nose and scratched her cheek to disguise the smiles till the urge passed and she could trust herself to keep the image banished forever from her mind.

She had been very open minded in her day, had Sadie, and occasionally she'd been extremely adventurous, but to be honest, in the last few years a good book and a cup of tea, or a DVD night and a bag of special popcorn had thrilled her just as much.

Until tonight.

She found her focus strayed to Damian's backside in his jeans. His big thighs gave way to a solid muscular rear, or so she'd discovered. He'd asked her to slap it with a cat o'nine tails, through the gap at the back of some leather chaps during the 'cowboy/girl' game…

Annnnd there it was again – it was no good, the smile had defied her and crept back on her face.

Actually it was also true that the more she looked at his ass in jeans, the more it was a turn on – he had a good ass. He was actually quite well equipped, too, she thought, from what she'd seen of it, considering every time he'd emerged from the bathroom in a different outfit, he'd been mostly covered up.

Oooops, smiling again. Can't help it, thought Sadie, averting her gaze to the table in front of her hands.

'I'd say penny for them, but I'm not sure I want to know this time,' said Damian, placing the mug of tea in front of her.

'Oh, you know, just… reliving.'

'Sadie, be honest, were you into it? Only you did seem to be – some of the time. Or was I completely wrong and I've just ruined what could have been a lovely relationship with my self-indulgence?'

'No it's not ruined,' she said, truthfully, 'I'll never quite look at a feather duster the same way again though,' she added. Then she caught his eye, and they both burst out laughing.

'Sadie, I've got a confession to make,' he said.

'Oh, oh, this sounds serious,' Sadie replied, putting her mug down and waiting with baited breath.

'I'm… not very good, really. In the bedroom, I mean. I was serious earlier. On my own, without toys and stuff, I'm… I'm just not very confident in myself.' He waited for a response but she just sat there listening. He seemed really earnest and her heart went out to him. She'd felt the same way when she'd put on tons of weight after the kids, and Stuart had lost interest until she lost some of it again.

'Really?' she asked. 'A guy like you? Who doesn't stop until he's the best he can be – at almost everything? Really?'

'*Almost* being the key word. Yes, really.' He looked totally depressed for a second, then sighed and sat himself down opposite her. 'I've never told anyone that before. And to be honest, I haven't shared my dressing up box with another woman since Rosalee dumped me. It was her fault I got into it in the first place. Half of it's hers – literally,' he explained, and Sadie winced. 'I never gave it back when we split – thought it served her right that I kept it. She'd have to think of me using it with my next girlfriend, only, well, I haven't really had a real girlfriend since. At least…'

'Oh that's…' Sadie was about to say *oh that's sweet* but he finished his sentence.

'…who's been the same size.'

Sadie blinked. *So his ex was quite curvy too then eh. Fine.* 'Oh, right.'

'And considering how dramatic and amazing you looked when you arrived here yesterday – well, I played it by ear and asked you to give it a go – I hope you didn't mind? Playing games with me?' He blinked, swallowed and waited for her reply.

'If I'd minded, I'd have said so,' said Sadie. 'But Damian,' she reached out for his hand across the table. 'You still didn't seem… fulfilled – it was titillating – in more ways than one,' she said, and they both smiled, remembering the gaps in the bra section of a couple of the outfits. 'But – do you know what I'm trying to say, here?'

'Yes of course – it's obvious isn't it,' he admitted, with a shrug. 'Can't get my rocks off unless I'm being someone else. Unless – let's be frank – unless I'm NOT being me. And I'm always me.'

For the first time, Sadie saw him in a different light. She felt slightly sorry for him, and suddenly more than a little protective. She squeezed his hand.

'Tell you what, let's sleep together tonight,' she said, 'in the same bed, no garters, no leather, no clothes on. How about it. But you have to promise me one thing.'

'I'm not sure I can promise,' he said.

'You haven't heard it yet.'

'I can guess.'

'No you can't – you have to promise me that you *won't* make love to me. OK?'

'I'm not sure I can promise,' he said again, a smile spreading right across his face. 'But I'll do my best to give it a try.'

Sadie suddenly felt that old familiar surge of excitement swell up inside her and realised that she wasn't sure if she could promise, either.

That night, when they finally made it up to the bedroom, the first thing Damian did was turn out the light before he got fully undressed. Then he hopped into bed and began rubbing his legs over her side of the bed.

'Just warming it up for you,' he said.

Then Sadie slipped naked between the covers and moved down swiftly until only her shoulders were peeping out at the top.

'Oooh, it's quite cold isn't it!' she said.

'Still? Here, let me,' he said, and moved his leg across until it was touching hers.

'Gosh you're quite hot aren't you, that's lovely and warm.'

'So's my hand,' he said, 'Want me to put it anywhere?' His chuckle followed his question, showing he knew exactly what he was up to.

'No! You know what we promised. Now, stop being bad.'

'But my leg's ok there?'

'Your leg's ok. For now.'

'OK, g'night Sadie,' he said, and leaned across to kiss her lips. His mouth was hot and this time, for the first time, he opened his lips fully and she felt his warm tongue against hers.

'Ohhh,' she mumbled, which made him kiss her a little deeper, a little more insistently. Then his hand was rubbing her forearm gently, rising higher and higher towards her shoulder. Then his fingers were grazing her neck and face. Then they retreated, via the gap between her breasts, and he relaxed back as if he was going to go to sleep this time, his hand now holding hers. But then he slowly moved it towards his body – made her touch his hip, and he left her hand there whilst he began meandering across her body again. She felt his touch move back across to her waist, and curl a small circle around her navel, then down to her thigh, brushing her skin gently on the way to her knee before moving across and touching her all the way up the side of her other leg. By the time he reached her hip, then her stomach, then her ribs, and stopped short of touching her breast, Sadie realised she was so turned on, she was panting ever so slightly. She held her breath so she didn't let on – best not to, she thought, remembering that he didn't get turned on without all that paraphernalia so she'd better keep her desires in check.

Then suddenly with a swift move of his body, she felt him against her and knew, to her surprise, that may no longer be the case.

For the rest of the night, they continually broke their promise – several times before dawn and another few times when they woke up.

That evening, Helen was on 'welcome home' duty, waiting at the door of Sadie's house, feeling like the matron on the first day of term. She'd had the 'I'm on my way' text both from Sadie and from the girls – so who would be the first to arrive? Sadie was of course coming home in her own car, and Stuart was due back any minute with the girls – she listened out for the different car sounds coming up the quiet close. Nothing. It was a crisp spring evening – a bit cooler than it had been, but the setting sun shone a beautiful orange light over the pretty garden. And over Mr Wilson opposite, who seemed to believe that he was official street overseer, his beady eyes never missing an arrival or a departure. His, must be the most over-watered garden in town.

She waved at him as if to say 'I can see you too'. He just looked away and continued drenching his petunias. Helen decided to look busy. She had more big news for Sadie, but didn't want to look over-keen, so she decided to do be out doing a little trimming when Sadie got back, and went to the shed at the side of the house to fetch the secateurs and gardening gloves. Suddenly she heard a throaty roar from the street outside and rushed back to the front door just as the BMW parked a few cars down and Georgia and Abi got out laughing.

'Hey Auntie Helen,' they shouted, 'Dad says he's going to plant twelve trees to make up for all the pollution his new car is creating,' said Georgia, looking fresh-faced and happy, bounding up the path into her aunt's arms.

'Twelve – per month, more like,' added Abi, kissing Helen on the cheek.

'Yvette's car,' Stuart said, as he followed on, bringing both girls' bags in, 'not mine. It's not my car, hers, not mine.'

Helen just raised an eyebrow at him, and he poked his tongue out at her as he passed, walking straight by Helen into the house without being invited. 'I'll just clear some space so I can put the girls' bags down and... oh, it's all tidy in here,' he said in surprise.

Hah, thought Helen, and ignored him, standing near the front door with her hands on her hips and a haughty look on her face.

'No Sadie yet?' he asked, 'I'd have thought she'd have been desperate to see her daughters having been away all weekend. Shows how much she really cares, if she can't...'

'Don't try that with *me,* Stuarttt,' said Helen, virtually spitting out the consonant at the end of his name. 'This is *me* you're talking to. And the girls are out of ear-shot so don't bother trying to stir things up, ok? And it's YOU who's twenty minutes *early* as it happens. What's the matter, your woman unable to cope and sent the girls packing earlier than planned?'

Stuart looked at Helen's face and narrowed his eyes. Then he turned around and shouted. 'BYE GIRRRLS!' They both came running back out again, kissed him goodbye then went straight back in to the lounge where the TV was blaring out with the theme tune from one of those '*Get me Out of the Jungle'* programmes. 'The girls had a nice time, *actually,*' he snipped, through pursed lips, '*all* of them.'

'But did *you?*' Helen scowled. She had no time for him – now less than ever. And he knew it.

'Didn't even get to see my mountain bike crew, I was having *such* a great time,' he said, not meeting Helen's eye. 'Tell their mother that, right?'

'Bye Stuart, *don't* come again soon,' said Helen, indicating the door with her arm.

He didn't reply, just huffed a little and then left.

Sadie arrived home precisely ten minutes later, and was greeted with a raucous hello from her two youngsters who'd even put their favourite programme on pause, so keen were they, to rush out and greet their mum. Helen waited in the kitchen whilst Sadie spent time with them before leaving them to do their Sunday night 'thing' and joining her big sis at the kitchen table, where Helen was waiting with a little pile of postcards in front of her.

'Oh, oh, I know that serious look,' said Sadie, putting down an armful of washing.

Helen cocked her head to one side – *really?*

'What have you been doing and what are they?' Sadie asked. 'It's either really bad or really good.'

'The latter,' Helen replied, 'I hope.' *Fingers crossed this goes down well,* she thought.

'Oh?'

'Look at this,' Helen said and thrust a postcard in front of Sadie, placing it alongside a fresh cup of hot chocolate that was sitting waiting for Sadie on the table. 'I made it. And the hot chocolate.'

'So it appears,' replied Sadie, looking at the mess around the kitchen. 'The rest of the house looks lovely though, thanks.'

'Well, Turncoat's gone, so what the heck. So...' she indicated the postcard and Sadie picked it up and began reading from it.

'Coming soon – Launching Online – Sadie Turner's Anti-Ageing Secrets Revealed – mark STAAS, 'at' STAASRevealed'

'Good, eh?' beamed Helen. 'I told you it's a hashtag nowadays, not a 'mark' sign.'

'What, precisely, are my anti-ageing secrets? You forcing me to start using fat pants? And how will these secrets be revealed online?'

'I'm working on that,' Helen replied. 'Don't make that face at me, it'll be something brilliant, it always is.'

'Well if you're so talented, why don't you see if you can get more work in advertising when you're over in New York. You're so good at it.'

'No, I told you – bridges burnt – razed to the ground – still smoldering. There'll be a five mile exclusion zone around the Winston, Winston and Grant crew when we're out there, that's for sure.' Helen hoped Sadie wouldn't ask her any more about what had happened – she still wasn't quite ready to cough up the intricate details.

'So – what's this card then?' Sadie asked.

'It's a teaser campaign I'm initiating for you. In the run up to the big international feature online that will tie in with my new column – assuming all goes well in the Big Apple and it will indeed be *my* column.

These cards will pique people's interest and fulfill the cryptic requirement in advance of the full-blown hype we'll generate when... '

'Too much all at once, you're gabbling again,' Sadie said, giving in to temptation and sipping the syrupy hot drink covered in chocolate shavings. 'Ooooh, I shouldn't – but this tastes soooo good!' she muttered to herself.

'I knew you'd like it. You've got to give in sometimes,' Helen said. And from the look of Sadie that's not the first time she's given in this weekend, thought Helen. 'Look,' she went on, 'this is the way to get some interest, coupled with some leafleting I'm getting everyone to do – including the girls – and mum soon as she's able – and you and me too – over the next few days. Understand so far?'

'Ye-e-e-es,' Sadie said, sipping her drink and narrowing her eyes over the top of the mug.

Helen ignored her look. 'After that, there will be an ad in the local paper – their local-news picture-editor's mildly interested – I've been trying to warm him up a bit...'

'I'll bet you have,' interjected Sadie. Helen took no notice.

'...make him more curious to find out more. Newsdesk doesn't want to know, too small-fry. But that's pretty typical of self-important local paper hacks. A follow up feature about you being a survivor and an innovator will come out, later in the year, and all this will have built up the all-important buzz. All you have to do is follow the programme I'll design, and just... do what you do. Like make sure you've got some shit-hot offers on display in the store and sampling trays out the front and voila, quintuple whammy.'

'Mmmmm, this tastes so good. What?' Sadie teased. Helen grimaced. 'Only joking,' said Sadie. 'Well, I understood more that time, but you're still overlooking one thing.'

'What?'

'Who's paying for all that?'

'I am,' Helen replied, sitting tall, glowing like the Ready Brek kid. '*I am*, sister, Kate got me an advance on my expenses.'

'She managed to swing it?'

'Well she's got her finance guy wound round her little finger and she owes me, and she likes you,' Helen spoke in a drawl, 'She said it's about time someone *cut you a break*... so she got us upgraded to Club, which means more budget to play with if we only go *Ecwonomee*... Quite New York, eh? Did you like the accent?' and Helen said it again with a more pronounced twang, sounding a bit like Joey from *Friends*. *'How YOU doin','* she finished by saying.

But Sadie was silent. She sipped some more hot chocolate and closed her eyes. Helen looked from side to side at Sadie's face, to see if she could discern what Sadie was thinking – any little clue, any sound, any expression – nothing. Eventually Sadie spoke. 'Thank you,' she said, opening her eyes revealing a wetness in each corner.

Helen reached across and squeezed her sister's hand.

'It's very touching and you're very sweet. And I know what you're thinking – you hate taking my money 'cos you'd rather do it yourself but... this is all I'll be doing, promise. I won't keep bossing you around and taking over – unless you want me to. It's your shop, from now on. OK?'

'Er... I don't know if it's escaped your notice but it's been my shop for a while now. But... OK, I'll accept this little bit of help, but no more, right? And especially not the taking over bit.' Sadie looked thoughtful. 'Too bad that Hawaii competition's off my list. For this year anyway.'

'That's ok. It's what...' Helen was about to say 'what sisters are for', but Sadie butted in. It looked like something had just hit her.

'But I can't come to New York, I just can't. Economy or not. I'm sorry, Helen. There's too much at stake here and I can't afford to take more time off. Not a whole weekend. That CAP nerd Mr Percy could be back anytime and being away on a Friday and a Monday as well will fly in the face of what I promised the bank guy. And mum. Honestly. Please don't be too disappointed, and please don't try to change my mind. Not this time.'

Helen just put her drink down and shrugged. She could see her sister meant it. 'I won't.'

'See it's not just the money,' babbled Sadie, 'it's…' Then she stopped. 'What did you say?'

'I said I won't,' Helen said again. 'Try. To change. Your mind.'

Again Sadie was speechless, only this time her mouth hung open.

'Turns out the date's changed – got to leave Monday, not Friday so I guessed you'd duck out of it. In fact, I'd kind of counted on you saying no, 'cos I've done a bit of juggling. I used your part of the budget to pay for the extra adverts,' Helen explained. Sadie burst out laughing.

'Plus this trip's going to be one of the most important I've ever been on, sis and – it's really ok that I go alone. But I'll take you on the next one.'

'Am I really that much of a burden?' asked Sadie, looking perturbed.

'No, not terrible, well – Honestly? Ok, yes, you can be. Needing to plan everything out all the time and keep asking loads of questions I can't answer and insisting on your weird food and…' She stopped, as Sadie's bottom lip play-pouted. 'I'm just trying to make you feel better about not coming,' said Helen softly. 'But you know? It really is your time now – new era – isn't it? Time to reform. From now on you can do all that stuff for yourself, right? Even take over all this PR stuff if you want to…' she saw her sister's face drop. '…Apart from arranging the leafleting and the postcards and the ad in the paper and…'

'Ok, ok, you don't have to rub it in,' Sadie said, 'You can finish the job, I know you love it. Do your big plan for my shop. Knock yourself out.' She smiled half-heartedly, and Helen detected more than a little hurt in her sister's eyes and a certain thoughtfulness on her face as she buried her face in her hot chocolate mug and took another sip of her drink.

'And anyway,' said Helen, 'a certain Mister Hugh appears rather keen – you obviously had a good weekend judging from the way you strutted in here tonight. So tell me – what was the best bit and what was the worst bit? Go on, spill.'

'Er…. Where on earth do I begin,' said Sadie, 'You'd better get yourself comfortable, this could take some time.'

CHAPTER ELEVEN

The week sped by as Sadie and her family followed Helen's instructions and started delivering leaflets, all bearing the same message as the postcards, to hundreds of local posh letterboxes and relevant businesses. Abi tried her best to begin a viral campaign, and although limited in its success, she was rewarded with a lot of attention from her mum and auntie and a promise of a new computer as soon as they could afford it. As a result, Georgia became eager to also do something to get noticed, and out of nowhere, one day after school she produced a list of email addresses from all the mums in her class, most of whom were getting more and more curious about these 'anti-ageing secrets' that they kept seeing all about. If Anti-ageing secrets were on offer, none of them wanted to miss out.

It all helped. Sales figures started to improve a bit, but nothing astronomical. Maybe Helen's efforts had been more pep-talk for Sadie's benefit, than reality. A cast-iron guarantee of the store going into the black looked even further out of reach. Still, Helen coordinated the effort and kept track of all the progress. But as the week progressed, she was gearing up for her trip to the States and spending more and more time on Skype to Kate. A special delivery came midweek which she ran down to sign for, pushing Sadie out of the way to get there first, then disappearing straight upstairs with it.

Sadie was working flat out and despite several flirty texts, she didn't manage to see Damian until that week's class, when she rushed in almost late and out of breath. And she hated being late. She flumped herself down in a chair at the back and tried to set her stuff out on the desk quietly, whilst he paused briefly at her apologies then continued his introduction. By break time Damian still seemed very miffed. He held her back to *have a word*, whilst the others filed past to the tea room, and asked her for an explanation in a very loud voice – it was clearly less about her response and more about him being seen to be making his point in front of the others. But then, when the last student had filed out of the class and out of sight, he took Sadie by the hand, swung her round onto his lap and kissed her full on the mouth.

'Damian!' Sadie cried, laughing, and trying to get up again, but he just kept pulling her back again, once, twice, three times. Then suddenly he did let go and Sadie looked up. Delta was standing in the doorway with her arms folded, her jaw jutting forward, chewing her cheek as if assessing what reprimand to give.

Wait a minute, who's the teacher here? Sadie thought. She stood up, and brushed her tunic top down over her jeans, and defiantly held her head high.

'Is there anything the matter, Delta?' Sadie asked, arching her eyebrows as if to say *Go on, I dare you.* But Damian was at Sadie's side instantly, telling her to go ahead to the tea room and he'd join her shortly after he'd spoken to Delta – *about her assignment.* Reluctantly, Sadie left the room, passing a bristling Delta who ignored Sadie completely and walked into the room kicking the door shut behind her, arms still folded.

Damian didn't come to tea.

Sadie had to wait till the end of the class to ask him what Delta had wanted him for. By now, having established they were at least having some sort of relationship, and not having had the chance to ask him at the weekend, Sadie felt able to request an explanation as to why one of his students had needed to talk to him in private, whilst being quite rude to Sadie. *This new found confidence certainly does herald a new era for me, that's for sure,* thought Sadie. But it was short-lived.

'I'm sorry Sadie, but I – I can't say.'

'What do you mean, you *can't* or you *won't?'*

'Can't, won't, it's really the same thing – Delta's got... a special assignment – she has an issue with it. She's been getting extra-curricular help and since she's rather sensitive... well, I really can't give any of it away. She'd kill me.'

'Oh.' Sadie replied, and found herself turning round and packing up ready to leave without saying another word. *Not another word, Sadie, not another word.*

Like that was going to work.

'Are you having an affair with Delta?' The words were out of her mouth before she could stop them. *Dammit.*

'S-sorry?' he asked.

'Delta – are you sleeping with her?'

'Emphatically, no,' he said, firmly.

'*Were* you? Sleeping with her? Ever?'

'No,' he replied, looking Sadie straight in the eye. 'I can quite honestly say, no, absolutely not. If I looked like Brad Pitt with bigger muscles, maybe I would be. No, not even then. Not now I've got you.'

'Oh, right then. Ok then. It's just… oh it's just me being paranoid, I suppose. One day I'll believe that not every man is like my ex-husband,' she said, making a face.

'Your ex-husband-*to-be*,' corrected Damian, with a little dig in Sadie's ribs to lighten the mood. 'Won't be long now. Anyway, let's talk about this job you want us to do this weekend?' He lowered his voice. 'I know I said I'm into game-playing, but I don't believe that "Leaflet Delivery Dude" should be part of my collection.'

'Oh I don't know,' teased Sadie, brightening, 'I hear there are some quite big trees to hide ourselves behind, in the upper class area we're going this weekend…'

And by the end of Saturday, Damian had completely changed his beliefs and added a stack of leaflets, shorts and a baseball cap to his dressing up box in his room.

The girls were with Sadie all that weekend though, so it meant that once the leafleting was over, Damian actually came back to the house for the second time ever, and sat waiting for Sadie to cook them all some dinner. She'd banished him to the lounge to be with the others so that they could 'get to know' one another better. So there she left them – Damian in the middle seat of the sofa, Georgia on one end, and Abi in the armchair at the other end, both of them sitting staring at him, arms folded, looking far from amused.

Twenty minutes later when Sadie put her head round the lounge door to call them to dinner, she was greeted with the sight of her 'boyfriend' playing 'Call of Duty' with her daughters. And beating them hollow. So

Georgia suggested they change games and to his frustration, and Sadie's great amusement, he then had to spend another twenty minutes playing a 'make your own boy band' computer game which Georgia won, naturally. He left muttering something under his breath about getting Georgia an early birthday present of the latest version of 'BoyBand1.0' and making sure it was working ok by practising it himself at home before he gave it to her. Sadie just laughed and promised to see him again soon – after all, the leafleting work was all done, all the little jobs on the marketing plan were up to date, and Helen was leaving for New York on Monday.

Later when he'd gone and Sadie was tucking the girls up in bed, about to begin reading them one of her favourite classics, Northanger Abbey. But they both wanted to ask their mum about Damian. This time, however, they were genuinely interested. Perhaps more than a little bit due to his promise to hand over the 'cheats' for some of their favourite gaming titles. But Sadie didn't mind. Yes, Sadie's new 'boyfriend' was definitely a strategic 'game player', in more ways than one. And definitely a bit of a boy.

Early on Monday morning, Sadie was at the airport very early, seeing Helen off on her flight to New York. The whole family had wanted to come, but there wasn't enough room, or time to get back for school, so Sadie went alone. They stood at the passport control entrance and Helen gave Sadie a big hug.

'Look after yourself, Sade, and keep ringing that contact I gave you at the local paper ok? Hassle him. Send him cookies. But not the ones with seaweed in. Don't let the impetus slow down – we're on a roll now.'

'Sure will, boss-woman! Now get going and don't you and Kate get into too much trouble out in New York, I know what you two are like when you get together. And if you ever find *The Real Central Perk,* bring me home a souvenir mug.'

'Sadie – one more thing,' Helen said, 'if a big padded letter comes for someone called Sadie Helen Turner Parker, will you do me a favour and promise not to open it till I get home?'

'What have you been up to now?'

'Oh it was just a typo online – promise. I'm not up to anything – it's your turn – you've got to do things without me now, right?'

'Yeah, like that's going to happen,' Sadie said, 'You? Stop taking control of other people's lives? Ya-har!' she joked. But Helen wasn't laughing this time. This time, Sadie could see that Helen was deadly serious. She hesitated.

'You mean it, don't you?' Sadie said eventually, in a quiet voice.

'Yes I do. It's time, Sadie. I've been doing a lot of thinking over the last few weeks and seeing you get out there into the wide world again, dating again, studying to improve yours and the girls' lives, well it's really made me see how far you've come. A proper independent lady taking care of herself. No more telling you off for letting Stuart control you, eh?'

'I wondered when you'd realise.'

'Realise what?' asked Helen.

'That it wasn't just Stuart I was letting have control of me.' The reality of what Sadie had just said seemed to sink in.

'Oh my god. I've been just as bad as him, haven't I? Through the years? And you let me be. You let us both be,' Helen whispered.

Sadie was silent. She just blinked. Then nodded, and blinked some more.

'You pootled through life able to be so positive and optimistic 'cos there was always someone else focusing on the downside for you, and heading off the trouble at the pass. Well ok then, aside from what I've done recently, that's it. And it's time to turn the tables – I'll be taking a leaf out of your book as well. Writing that column really made me examine who you are, and what you do. And you know what? I want some of it. And you need some of what I've always done. Does that make sense?'

Sadie just nodded, smiling. The tannoy announced a final call for some other flight and Helen looked at her watch.

'So anyway, that's it, now. I'm setting you free, Sadie Samantha Turner, and you have to pick up from here, ok? You've got the suits, you've got the lipstick, you've got the heels. You've got the lot, and you can make your own way now. Apart from that list of things you need to do when I'm away.'

'What are you like?' Sadie replied, but her voice was soft and full of affection for the older sister who had helped shape her life to be the way it was – shaped her to be the person she was. She gave her the biggest, tightest hug and kissed her cheek.

'Bye sis,' Helen said. Now it was her turn to blink a little. 'See you in a few days. Wish me luck.'

'You make your own luck,' said Sadie, 'You're Helen Parker-Todd, remember?' Helen smiled back from the gate, and she was gone.

CHAPTER TWELVE

New York was every bit as bustling and frantic and fume-filled as Helen remembered and after the luxury of the fresh country air back home in Sadie's Surrey, it was a bit of a shock to be suddenly surrounded once again by the 24 hour commotion of the City That Never Sleeps.

First stop was the concierge at the apartment block where Helen used to stay on a company rent. It seemed like a lifetime ago but it had only been a few months since she'd left in a rush, humiliation hanging over her head like a cloud. She shook herself. *Focus on the positive.*

When she knew she wasn't coming back, she'd got the staff there to do the packing for her, with the help of Skype, to show them what to put where. Alfonso, the kindly guy on the front desk, had carefully stored a few boxes of valuables in his own place, and he'd put the rest in storage in their basement.

Helen went down and checked it all over, but found that she had no enthusiasm whatsoever to deal with it there and then. So she paid him a handsome tip to keep it for her and gave him the Harrods box of candy with a red London bus on the front, which she'd chosen for him specially. Alfonso was overjoyed and promised to keep a careful eye on her stuff 'until she came home again'. Helen smiled at his words and hopped in a cab.

Came home again? Where exactly was home?

She'd spent so many years flitting from one residence to the next – top floor penthouse apartment, little villa with pool, condo in a city centre, semi-detached with a white picket fence – that she'd always travelled light and never really put down any roots other than those which were permanently connected to Sadie's, and the little Clapham flat. *Wherever I lay my shoe-collection, that's my home.* Tonight, however, she would be at Kate's.

Well, Kate's mum's to be precise. Her mother Lorna was just in the process of packing up her own shoe-collection and everything else in her little bungalow, about to transfer to a new place in a nearby Home for Active Seniors. Lorna had had the whole house to herself after Kate's Dad had died but she was away overnight and they'd left the key with a neighbour, so Helen let herself in and made herself comfortable in the spare room surrounded by moving cartons and cardboard boxes and bubble wrap. Kate would be back from her business trip tomorrow and would be at Helen's all-important crunch meeting.

The residence was located way outside of New York itself, but Helen didn't mind taking the subway the next morning – she'd done it enough years when she was based there herself, and just like Kate, knew parts of it like the back of her hand. She also knew the stops to keep her head down, as they were close to her old offices – and potentially her old colleagues. And possibly, acute embarrassment. She buried her face in a magazine. But her heart pitter-pattered some more, as she made her way to a new part of town and to explore an opportunity which just might just be the start of her whole new life.

'So sorry my sister couldn't make it, Mr Adams; yes, she's getting the photos done in England this week. I told her what you need,' Helen said to the balding, slightly red-faced man sitting across the massive desk, which was so covered in paperwork and folders she could hardly see him over the top of it all. He gripped an 'E-cigarette' between his teeth and little puffs of vapour were seeping from the corners of his mouth as he flicked through her document on the flat computer screen in front of him. He wasn't listening.

'This has got a good pace, I like the tone of it. It rings sincere and very near succeeds. It's just the narrative – you say this sister of yours is totally up to speed? Ready to spill the beans on a national syndicated show?' He stopped looking at the screen and leaned forwards towards Helen. 'If we ask her to?'

Helen hesitated but only for a fraction of a second.

'Definitely,' she said, nodding her head enthusiastically. *Shit.*

'Well that's perfect. Nitty gritty. The online community likes a bit of nitty gritty. So – Helen – as Kate said to you earlier, it's a last minute vacancy, that's opened up because the last occupant dropped dead. Of stress. So – if we give it to you, you gotta promise me you won't drop dead until you've filed at least two more personality exposes.' He was looking at her now, and she had no idea if she should laugh or run.

Then he spoke again. 'Har-har-har. Ok, you got this column – for now. Contract needs to be signed today – visit Legal on the 27th floor, on your way to lunch with Kate. Photo on the 25th in an hour fifteen – the studio will be expecting you. Don't be late – there'll be a makeup artist waiting to airbrush you. And Helen – choose Parker OR Todd for the byline. Parker-Todd sounds like a firm of legislators. And Helen – just so you know – it was a close run thing – it went to the line. The first choice celeb wouldn't do it unless we guaranteed a mention of her fashion range, and I'm not being dictated to by anybody – least of all a B-list bimbo who's desperate for an A-list plug. Plus Kate bent my arm, so… Don't. Let. Me. Down. And Helen – get me a second piece synopsis as soon as you can. That means by tomorrow. Janiiiiiice!'

Having almost turned to go three times, Helen finally made it through the door, narrowly avoiding a harassed secretary rushing in with an i-Pad and closing the door behind her.

Helen didn't know what just hit her.

'I did warn you he was kind of hyper,' Kate said at lunchtime over a Caesar sub and a tall, skinny latte in the local coffee bar – which was sparse and stark and not at all like the one on *Friends.*

'Well you're lucky I'm able to talk 'cos he nearly bit my head off in there.'

'But you got it, right? He gave you the position?'

'Till tomorrow, when he hates my next pitch.'

'Hey! What were you telling me this morning – positivity all the way from now *awn.*' Kate's accent was light New York, but she still said 'awl' and 'maw-ning'. Helen smiled – she loved the rhythmic drawl and reassuring bite the native New Yorkers had when they spoke. You rarely heard one hesitate or stutter, not in Helen's experience anyway.

'Sorry,' said Helen, 'I should say *"when he loves"* my next pitch.' She bit into her own sub, oozing with salad and sauce dripped all over her fingers. She looked around but the mess was leaking everywhere. Kate reached over and dabbed her friend's chin with one napkin, then shoved several others at Helen.

'Good job you're not in your designer gear now – look at the state of you! So what's it going to be about? Your next pitch?' asked Kate.

'No idea. NO idea whatsoever.'

'Well, you got twenty four hours, and in this business, that's a long time. Now listen, you still coming out with me for a drink to celebrate?'

Helen just nodded, her mouth full.

'Well I've got this guy...'

'Kate!' Helen mumbled through her sourdough, swallowing it fast. 'I said no tricky stuff this visit. I've only just come back into the land of the living and it took a lot for me to come back. *Here,*' she said, gesticulating around her with her elbow, as her hands were holding together the 12 inch snack. 'It was a war zone!' she whispered. 'Painful territory – I'd rather lie low, why do you think I jumped at the key to your mum's place? You never know who you might meet around here and I'm still avoiding everyone from...'

'Now let me stop you there,' Kate responded, in between mouthfuls, 'it's like hair of the dog, right?' Kate waited for an answer but Helen just made a face – *no idea what you mean.* 'Falling off a horse – you get straight back on again after, so you don't lose your nerve. It's got to be the same with men.'

'Men and horses?' Helen said, 'is there a dating site for that now? Maybe that's what I can pitch tomorrow...' Her friend gave a look then just carried on.

'You remember I told you about that guy with the clever opening line? Well I asked him if he had a friend. For you. For tonight.'

Helen stopped mid-bite and just looked at Kate and pursed her lips, tipping her head to one side slightly. *Really?*

'So what do you say? Eight o'clock? O'Reilly's round the corner from here? Look at it like a trial run – maybe the next guy you meet will be your "Neo", but for now, just practise – practise being a woman again. Instead of a pity party. No man finds that attractive. Nor this,' she said, dabbing at another dribble on Helen's chin.

Helen looked thoughtful, smiled at the Keanu Reeves references then nodded. 'On one condition. If we need to abort, we use the code.'

O'Reilly's was a short cab ride from Kate's place, a stylish loft apartment in the Meatpacking Area – where they no longer packed meat. Except in a roll at the expensive Italian deli two doors down from Kate's complex. It was nowhere near Helen's old haunts so she relaxed a little. Kate had changed out of her trademark dungarees and was looking hot. Helen had borrowed one of Kate's red dresses, curled her hair, and put on full makeup for the first time in ages. Apart from a little bit of a paunch that had developed during her three month sabbatical from life, she almost felt like her old self. Confident, self-assured, and smart. Well, the last one anyway. And she could fake the rest. Together she and Kate cut quite a dash and made a tall, blonde and eye-catching entrance that garnered several head-turns. As well as an audible *'tut'* from a group of females at the first table just inside the door.

Kate jerked her head towards the bar, Helen nodded, and they both flicked their hair over their shoulders dramatically, then went and sat down facing the bartender, knowing they could survey the whole bar area by facing the mirrored wall behind him. *Old tactics, old habits, old routine.*

'Good evening ladies, what can I get you?' said the smartly dressed bartender, whose name tag made familiarity easy.

'Brad, good evening. We'll have two of those cocktails and some olives please,' said Helen, raising her voice slightly above the music. They both turned in unison on their high heels and leaned back on their elbows sipping the water he'd automatically poured them, whilst they waited for their drinks. Almost on the dot of eight o'clock the revolving doors span once more and in came a surprisingly presentable guy in classy business attire, followed by a shorter, stockier, less presentable friend. Guess which one was Helen's.

Before long, Kate was engrossed in conversation with 'her' internet wit, and Helen was listening to a summary of the New York Yankees merits versus the Brooklyn Dodgers – the guy didn't even consider, when she said she'd played football at school, that she didn't mean the American kind. After a while, he got the message – maybe it was her incessant yawning – and sidled off to 'tawk' to someone he knew in the group of first table women, who'd waved at him when he came in then scowled when he'd joined Kate and Helen. By now the women were getting pretty loud and had beckoned him several times before he'd eventually given in and dumped Helen for a more promising prospect.

Helen got out her mobile and sent a few texts, then chatted to Brad the bartender for a while who asked about her clothes and makeup and shoes before making her another Cosmopolitan. Two would suffice. She had a lot of work to do when she got back tonight. He prepared the drink cheerfully and pushed it across the bar.

'I'll get that,' said a voice next to her, and her heart skipped a beat.

It can't be.

She knew that bassy timbre, she knew that aftershave, and she knew that if someone didn't hold her back, she would be swinging for him in about five seconds flat. But instead, she plastered a grin on her face and thanked the lord it was still early, that cocktails came with a straw so her makeup was almost completely still intact. She took a deep breath then swung around on her stool to face him.

What she saw shocked her, and her smile faltered before she widened it again and greeted him.

'Hello Victor.'

His face was lined, gaunt. Still freshly shaven, still smartly dressed, but with an overriding air of something Helen had never seen on him before. Defeat. Still, he smiled meaningfully. So meaningfully, Helen feared she'd missed the meaning. It was like he was greeting a childhood friend – the one you loved so much, you gave them your best conker, so they could use it to beat the reigning champion in the playground.

'Helen,' he said, drawing out the first syllable. He just looked at her for a long moment as if searching for some clue as to whether he should reach to kiss her cheek or duck to avoid her fist. She made it clear it was the first one and he nodded. He bent down and she breathed him in. The aroma set off deeply entrenched memories and she wasn't surprised at how fast her heart started pitter-pattering. Nothing surprised her – it was all still the goddam same, dammit. Except how shockingly thin he'd got – she felt it when she hugged him.

'So… how…?'

'There was a rumour that you were in town,' he interrupted, anticipating her question. 'Kate's office said to try here.'

'Who started the rumour?' she asked, narrowing her eyes.

'Oh, you know, the usual suspects,' he replied, and she bristled slightly. He paid for the drink. The bartender gave Helen a concerned look but she nodded her head in reply. *He's ok.*

'I don't know what you expect me to say to you,' she said, crossing her long legs and making it clear she was in control of this one. Even if the jitters *had* started and she didn't know whether she could balance elegantly cross-legged on the stool for very long, *she* was in control.

'To hear you say *hi* was good enough,' he answered. His accent was well spoken American – it could have been from anywhere. No-one except those closest to him, knew how broad it used to be. He smiled again. 'To be honest, I was ready to duck.'

'So you should have been.' She almost spat the words out. Then recomposed herself. *This was hard.* 'After all you said to me, all you said to others. All you did. But no-one knows what really happened except you and me, do they? You made damn sure of that. Made it look like I was the fool. But, well, once bitten.' She paused meaningfully, and looked at him long and hard. He looked like a truly broken man. *What had happened to him since she last saw him?* She softened slightly. 'Victor, three months is a long time in my world, so – no hard feelings, eh?' Helen used all her self-control to hold out a steady hand towards him without shaking herself off the stool, her pulse was vibrating so much.

Again he looked surprised and practically snapped her hand off. 'No! Sure – no hard feelings. Ok. That's good,' he muttered.

She let go of his grip swiftly. What she'd just said and what she still felt were far removed. In Helen's book, what he had done was beyond reprehensible, and there was no going back. Not even for the sake of a light-hearted conversation for old times' sake. Unlike Sadie, who *had* to keep Turncoat Stuart in her life, Helen had no kids to create permanent ties. But Helen knew that her calm demeanor was the best revenge – it said '*you really don't matter to me now – in fact, you probably never did*'.

'Goodbye Victor, nice to see you again. Give my love to your other half,' she said, arching an eyebrow speciously. He accepted her snub, and nodded his head, jaded and downbeat.

Helen turned back round to continue her conversation with the lovely Brad, and Victor just inhaled deeply and bid her goodbye. She didn't even turn back round to face him, just gave him a half-glance, muttered a goodbye under her breath and heard him get up to go. Only when he was half way across the bar did she sneak a peek sideways at him as he left, ignoring the girls by the door who were elbowing each other and pointing to him. His shoulders were stooped, he was shuffling slightly, suddenly totally engrossed in checking his cell-phone. Nothing changes. *Damn ex-boss of mine probably checking up on him as usual – more than ever, nowadays, I'll bet,* Helen thought.

'So who was that guy? He was probably quite a dish in his heyday,' asked Brad.

'Yes,' said Helen, 'he probably was.'

Just then, Kate finally came over to find out who the weirdo in the trench coat was, and Helen told her. Kate had met Victor, and couldn't believe it was the same guy either.

'And you said what? Way to go Helen! Good for you, girl! Now maybe you can hold your head high round here again.'

'Oh I think it'll take more than me sending Victor packing for that to happen, Katski. Still, it felt good to get a bit of closure, that's for sure. Are we going then?' she asked her pal, who was putting on her faux-fur trimmed jacket.

'Yes, I've got a cab waiting outside,' Kate said, 'there's still time to go to our favourite Italian restaurant for dinner if we're quick. Come on, HellsBells, let's go. You can tell me all about it on the way.' Catching Helen gazing curiously back across the room, Kate added, 'No, it's just us. My date wasn't so quick-witted in person – he'd probably googled those chat up lines – always the problem with online meet-cutes. But all is not lost!' she added dramatically, 'he's got a pal he's going to introduce me to on Friday, so it wasn't a complete waste of time. Don't look at me like that, it's this new way of meeting a husband – I'll tell you about it in the cab, come on.'

'I'll see you outside,' Helen said, looking in her bag for her purse. Kate trotted off and Helen finished her drink, paid and said goodbye to Brad, informing him that should he ever discover a long-lost older brother just like him, to give her pal Kate Knight a ring.

'I *thought* that was her – Kate Knight – she's that presenter off the internet channel isn't she? That's three celebs today,' he said.

'Kate a celeb?' asked Helen? He nodded and Helen just rolled her eyes and smiled. *Dark horse.* There was obviously a lot they hadn't told each other over the last few months. Then Helen leaned across to give the cute bartender a little peck on the cheek, said goodbye and walked past the gaggle of girls on the first table. As she passed she heard one of them hiss to her friend,

'Fag-Hag, that's what she is,' and the others around her laughed.

If Kate wasn't waiting outside and if Helen didn't have a pitch to perfect for tomorrow... and if she hadn't just forgiven someone for doing the worst thing that had ever happened to her... well, those girls wouldn't have been laughing much longer.

But she *had* forgiven. She *did* shake his hand and take the high ground. And it had felt good. Helen felt strangely light and warm inside. Not purely because of the forgiveness, but because she knew she'd turned a corner in letting things go, and she wondered what else she could make herself let go of. She liked this new self-control. And suddenly she knew exactly what tomorrow's pitch was going to be all about.

Out in the street, Helen saw Kate waiting by the kerb inside a yellow taxi, stepped towards it and then froze.

Getting out of a cab on the pavement directly opposite were a couple of corporate suits... And her ex-boss. Helen squeaked, ducked down, and nearly tripped over a passer-by who jumped out of his skin at the crouching Helen. Then she waddled crab-like to the cab and hopped straight into the passenger seat next to the driver.

'Lady, what are you doin',' the driver said in a New York accent with an Indian twang. 'Get in the back with your friend. You are sitting on my poppadoms.'

'Just drive…' Helen hissed, shrinking down out of sight. 'Drive round the next block, and I'll change seats there. Just move!'

Kate was banging on the glass separating the front from the back, asking what on earth Helen was doing.

'Winston and Grant,' Helen was mouthing, pointing to the other side of the road, 'Winston and Grant.' But Kate couldn't hear, and Helen was sitting tight.

'You want to go to Winston and Grant?' he asked, pulling away from the curb.

'No!' screamed Helen, and Kate began to pound even louder. The poor confused driver roared away to the end of the block and turned right before stopping so he could retrieve his somewhat shattered bag of poppadoms from beneath Helen's *bottadom*, and she climbed flustered into the back seat with Kate.

The door slammed and the air filled with curses from the driver about a 'crazy English woman', then the cab drove on to the restaurant, but only because the girls had promised to tip him generously.

At the restaurant, when her heart rate had returned to normal and a couple of vodka shots were spreading a welcome warmth through her core, Helen spilled the beans. She told Kate for the first time the whole sorry tale – exactly why the events of three months ago had left Helen's career and reputation in ruins. For the first time, Kate fully understood.

'Well, we'll just have to make sure that your new career is even more successful than the last one,' she said, squeezing Helen's arm reassuringly, and Helen nodded gratefully. And ordered two more shots.

That night, in a phone call home which caught Sadie just before she left to open the store super-early, Helen told her sister all about the day's events, the night's Victor-shaped shock, and her plans for tomorrow. She left out the bit about the frantic taxi dash to avoid her ex-boss – it kind of spoiled the karma of the 'moving on' theme. Nor did she finally confess all to her sister the way she had done to her old friend. But Sadie sounded pleased anyway, pleased and in a rush.

'That's great news, Hells, really great. About bloody time is all I can say. Good luck tomorrow. Oh and I saw Crystal yesterday, and she said to tell you it's time to open yourself up to the universe, and that you can pay her the other half of what you owe her in cash next time she sees you so it doesn't have to go through the bank – what did she mean by that, Hmm?'

'Well I guess she means I've got to throw caution to the wind and focus on finding the right man now, and stop attracting nincompoops.'

'No, that's not what I was talking about, and you know it.'

'Oh, did that parcel arrive by the way?' Helen said, a big smile in her voice. 'Is it still intact?'

'Yes it did, and yes it is. For now,' said Sadie, 'but if you don't tell me what Crystal meant about what you owe her, it will stay unopened for about thirty seconds flat!'

'No, no don't open it! I want to open it first. I paid her… for doing some work for me.'

'For you? Doing what?'

'Er, more leaflets. Has it made much difference?'

'Tiny bit. But the *ladies who lunch brigade* were all coming in the store going on about hyaluronic acid tablets. I sincerely hope Mr Percy doesn't see it – he'll make me walk the plank. '

'But isn't it an anti-wrinkle secret? Has it got a *hashtag STAAS* by any chance?'

'Do what? Not a clue, didn't see it. Anyway you're not supposed to be paying for anything else, and who might I ask, did the leaflet?'

'Crystal.'

'Oh.'

'And Abi.'

'Helen! On my computer no doubt. Well in that case, I can't promise that parcel will last much past Thursday, the girls are dying to know why it's addressed to you and to me.'

'Tell them it's an early present for Georgia.'

'And what is it really?'

'It is a present, a gift. But it's not for Georgia.'

'Oh it's for mum then, is it?'

'Might be,' said Helen.

'Is it that photo album she's been banging on about? Of all her favourite snapshots through the years in chronological order...'

The next bit they both spoke together, '...Like the one Phyllis has got?' Both girls laughed.

'Stop guessing, all will be revealed soon enough. Sis,' Helen said. 'So are you ok?'

'Yes, yes, it's just really quite hard keeping up with everything at the moment – plus your long list of marketing jobs which you left us. If I hadn't transferred it into Excel and laminated it, we would have worn it away by now.'

'Trust you. Once a geek always a geek. Well at least you're getting it done. And how's Mister Hugh?'

'He's fine. Don't worry about me – we're all fine. Good luck tomorrow and let me know how it went, if you can. I know you're straight off to the airport afterwards but if you can text me that'd be great. Bye.'

Helen ended the call, and got back to preparing her pitch – but something was niggling her. There was a catch in her sister's voice. She'd known her enough years to recognise it and she wondered why she hadn't said anything during the phone call. Maybe she wasn't alone. Or maybe she was, and that was the trouble.

But at least she hadn't opened that parcel. Helen was going to have to blag it but she just might get away with it. As long as Sadie didn't open that parcel. Not yet. Not till Helen was ready. And not till she was sure Sadie was ready for what it contained.

CHAPTER THIRTEEN

Sadie was flushed and rushed and hassled. Again.

Helen's flight was late but she'd got safely home, and had taken the unusual step of going straight back to her flat in Clapham after collecting her things from Sadie's. She seemed a world away from the person who had arrived on Sadie's doorstep only a few weeks before and Sadie was relieved – and a little envious at the same time.

Helen had borrowed the Nissan despite moaning about it, saying that this car had one speed – *pootle*, and as soon as she got some money she'd get a big Red Ferrari like RacerBoy. Joking of course – because of Damian she now classified all such cars as *penis extensions* and all such drivers as *knob-heads*. She had a way with words did Helen.

She'd slept on the plane so she'd assured Sadie she was fine to drive after her long flight, and promised to leave the petrol tank full up this time. Well, now that she had a bit of spending money, now she *could* afford to refill it, Sadie didn't refuse – she needed all the help she could get at the moment. The takings were level – at least they weren't down. And ticking over was better than not ticking over.

But the rigmarole with Stuart about signing the divorce papers and re-doing the settlement had come to a head and had been very stressful, mainly because it meant dealing with Yvette on a regular basis, since Sadie was representing herself. She hadn't told anyone that she couldn't afford a solicitor and Damian had helped talk through some of the paperwork. She wasn't a charity case. Apart from her mum's help, of course – and that was different. That's what mums were for. And anyway maybe it was what her father had left her, you never knew with Grace.

Sadie had been kept busy replying to all the legal emails herself – sometimes a couple a day. Trust Stuart to insist on dragging it through the legal system. It was *'doing Sadie's sodding head in'* as Grace was apt to observe. And Sadie couldn't deny it. She just tried cheerily telling herself, and everyone else, that things were looking up, in the hope that the universe was listening. Plus Helen had come back on such a high, she hadn't wanted to go rain on her parade.

Helen's pitch had gone well apparently. The Editor had liked its 'refreshing honesty'. The second personality piece was to feature several high powered women who had been dumped and then got even by just forgiving their ex's and moving on graciously. With Helen's illustrations of mocked up scenes, rather than using actual photos. Mr Adams had liked the novelty of that. Meant no need to arrange expensive photo shoots with real people either. And although Helen did know a couple of contenders to be interviewed, she admitted she might have to secretly make up the others – hence the idea to do illustrations – she was good at those.

She was good at secretly making things up too. She'd had a lot of practice lately, she'd told Sadie, though Sadie didn't know why she'd said it so pointedly.

Helen told her the pitch was called 'Women In Control'. Which she'd also said pointedly. If she didn't know better, Sadie would have been certain that Helen was giving her a covert instruction that it was time to move on from Stuart. By forgiving him. Ya-Har!

Or maybe it wasn't anything to do with Stuart. Maybe more likely, it was just Sadie being paranoid thinking everything was all about Stuart all the time. Which really kind of implied that deep down she hadn't moved on yet. Unless… *STOPPPP!*

Time to get a grip, Sadie, me girl. If Helen could move on with her life, after the horrible humiliation she said she'd suffered, which she promised to tell Sadie all about 'sometime soon', then Sadie could move on from Stuart. And his grip on her, his overbearing influence and cynicism. It wasn't like she didn't have another boyfriend already.

So why now, when she was on her way to the weekly marketing class, did she have a sinking feeling – about tonight's class? About Damian? About life?

Sadie decided to be kind to herself and abort that evening's class altogether and go do some thinking. She got as far as the corridor outside the classroom, stood at a distance, watching them all file in, and hung back in the shadows. *What is it?* She thought. Damian was good company. And after the initial hiccup, absolutely fine in bed. But he was even better at teaching marketing. Sadie felt sure that if she didn't watch out, she'd end up having to leave the class she loved so much, when the relationship fell apart. *Dammit* – IF the relationship fell apart, not when.

But her gut told her it wouldn't last. The signs were already there – and let's face it, there was *being optimistic* and then there was just plain *kidding yourself*. Or maybe she'd have to stop the class to keep her relationship. What was more important? She felt a little bit sick. What would happen to the glossy marketing future she'd planned for herself when it all fell apart with Damian? ...*IF*...

From where she stood, it was looking more like 'when'. Bloody Stuart's fault for making her so suspicious of all men – but then she saw Damian talking confidentially yet again to Miss Delta friggin' Smartypants – leaning in a bit too close to him and touching his arm, showing him inside some big envelope she was carrying and both of them laughing and joking and...

But it wasn't the same as with Stuart.

All Sadie felt was annoyed. Not jealous, just annoyed. That counted for something.

But tonight, she just couldn't face sitting there feeling the tension in the classroom of madam looking daggers every time Damian came near or smiled. And suddenly Sadie felt exhausted. Perhaps she should quit the class and give herself a break.

It had been a long week.

The photo shoot for Helen's shiny new column hadn't helped make Sadie feel better – if anything it'd made her feel a little bit worse. The local paper's Pictures Editor guy had finally turned up at the store after many reminders from the bossy sister. But even if he *had* taken a shine to Sadie, and tried to make her feel like a model for an hour or so, it had still been stressful. She wasn't much good in front of camera, that's for sure. Give her people any day – a few at a time.

Still dressed up to the nines in the outfit she'd worn for the shoot, and another pair of Helen's shoes, more suitable for walking this time but still with 'shag-me' written all over them, Sadie still felt terribly uncomfortable. She absolutely didn't feel like sitting down in a warm classroom all evening. It hadn't helped being car-less, and being dropped off by Grace and the girls. Grace had taken great delight in reminding her daughter it was just like her schooldays, except without the packed lunchbox and apple for the teacher. *Helen better bring that car back soon.*

When Sadie had got out, the girls had shouted and waved out of the back window and she could have sworn she heard the words 'MacDonald's for a burger' as they disappeared out of ear shot.

Sadie turned her back on the classroom scene to adjust her uncomfortable clothing and looked out of the window behind her. The first floor view across the playing fields beyond, made her yearn for open spaces and the sunset made her think about a holiday. An exotic one. *A Hawaiian One.* Too late. And the last break she had gone on one with her pals – shortly after her split from Stuart – had been ages ago. Sadie watched a homeless man file into the classroom – oh, oops, it was one of the other students – and Damian shut the door behind him, without looking across to Sadie. No doubt he was still looking across to Delta. *Stop it Sadie.* Go home and rest, she thought to herself.

Then she heaved her bag, full of folders and text books, up onto her shoulder and turned around to leave.

'Sadie! How nice to see you,' said a voice. It was an old colleague from her last job, coming right up the stairs towards her.

'Oh, hi Nalintha, how are you?' Sadie replied, slapping on a happy face for her old workmate. 'How's the lab?' They'd spent many years together examining microbes and molecules under the microscope. The girl had never been a close friend but in that instant Sadie couldn't recall the reason why. 'What are you doing over in this building?'

'Fine, nothing changes. And I'm meeting a pal. Do you know, we were just talking about you the other day! Professor Johnson was saying you'd disappeared without a trace, just like he said you would, and all of a sudden, there was a leaflet through Sanjay's mum's door saying you were doing some sort of anti-ageing push at your new-age little health food store. Well, we all fell about! What a coincidence seeing you here now!'

And in *that* instant, Sadie could easily recall the reason why Nalintha was a workmate and never a friend.

After a brief – very brief – conversation, Sadie confidently declared that if Sanjay's mum came in for some hyaluronic acid she might soon look younger than Nalintha. She was going to add '*or at least have fewer bags under her eyes*' but she couldn't bring herself to quite become Helen – not yet. Then Sadie gave her regards to her old colleagues, and turned towards the stairs to leave. Then she stopped in her tracks.

'Well if it isn't Sadie Turner – better late than never,' said a booming voice behind her, from the classroom back across the hall.

'Oh, hi Damian,' she said meekly, swivelling back round again. 'Just saw a… er, ex-colleague.'

He walked over to her and lowered his voice a few decibels. 'Bit hot in here this evening, thought I'd prop open the door, get a bit of airflow going… You ok? You look a bit peaky.'

'I feel a bit peaky,' Sadie said, 'I think I'll give tonight's class a miss if that's ok with you. You've obviously got your hands full, helping Delta and everything,' she paused briefly to look for the slightest flicker in his eyes but he wasn't even paying attention, just nodding to another lecturer passing by. 'I'm going to go home for a rest – these past few days have taken their toll on my energy levels and what with collecting Helen from the airport early this morning and then that photo shoot, and new cash-flow projections it's really been a bit…'

'Yes, well, call me about it all later then,' he interrupted. 'Better get back inside.' He kissed her on the cheek and squeezed her arm. 'Safe journey back home – text me when you're safely there, ok? Oh and I wanted to check you're still ok to make that cake for my aunt's birthday on Saturday? It'd be good to impress her. Talk later? Yes?'

'Yes,' said Sadie, then the door slammed, and she moped off down the staircase, summoning her irritated mum back to collect her for a lift back to the house again. Or to the burger bar – right now she didn't really care. As she stood all alone at the front entrance to the complex, waiting, she felt tears prickle at the backs of her eyes without quite knowing why.

Sadie didn't text. But she did try to call – to no avail. It just kept going to his voicemail, so after the fourth attempt, she left a final message and just went to sleep. Not even Northanger Abbey and the Pump House Ball in Regency Bath could enthrall her, and that night, the girls read their mum to sleep instead of the other way round.

But the next day, everything changed. It was warm, Sadie got an unexpected large order of Hyaluronic Acid tablets from one of her regulars – paid up front – which lifted her spirits no end, and she had another gaggle of gold-bedecked, pink-rinsed, designer-clad older ladies come by to take advantage of one of the special offers Sadie was doing – maybe Helen's plan wasn't so bad after all. Or rather, Sadie's plan, inspired by Helen.

Then by early Friday evening, three things had happened.

First, Sadie finished the most impressive carrot cake she'd ever made. Damian's aunt shouldn't miss out, even though her nephew was incommunicado – and Sadie always kept her promises. Well nearly always. And making this cake was quite therapeutic, as she'd got up early after a good night's sleep and baked her blues away then iced it when she got back from work. So there it sat, waiting for Damian to arrange to come pick it up – whenever he decided to show his face. Otherwise she'd cut it into pieces and sell it in the shop.

The second thing that happened was that Stuart rang her to say he had some news. When he came to collect the girls that night, he would also be bringing the final divorce papers for her to sign. A family member couldn't witness her signature, so Sadie decided she'd pop across to ask Mr Wilson over the road. He witnessed pretty much everything else that happened in the street. And she was amazed to find herself completely uplifted – she figured it was because at last this might be the closure she needed – to put Stuart behind her and get on with the rest of her life.

The third thing that happened was that Sadie finally got through to the cynical hack from the local paper – finally – who said he just wanted to find out more about 'hashtag STAAS' as a few readers had left comments on his blog asking if he knew anything about the 'revolutionary new wrinkle treatments'. Plus the pics his photographer had taken had been on display in the office too, so he'd finally rung her, if only to 'cross it *off* the list of potential features'. Charming. But at least he was getting more curious. She'd crack him yet.

So by the time seven thirty came around, daughter pick up time, Sadie had recovered so well from last night's grumps that she was wandering around the house singing, alternately fixing dinner and playing computer games with the girls. Well, trying to. *If you can't beat 'em join 'em.* Or try to, even if you're rubbish.

When the knock came at the door, she'd just won her first ever round of Georgia's boy band game, much to Georgia's disgust, who blamed Abi for jogging her elbow when Harry and Louis were head to head in a sing-off. Sadie jumped straight up to see who it was without even tidying the hallway or checking her lipstick was still in place. She was still jubilant as she flung open the door.

It was Helen.

'Sis! You're just in time, come in, come in, I beat Georgia, I beat Georgia,' chanted Sadie, holding both hands together in a fist in front of her stomach and making a stirring motion.

'Oh God, mother, no one does *that* anymore,' cringed Abi, as she went past her and up the stairs. 'Hi Auntie Helen.'

'Auntie Helen?' came a little voice rushing out like a tornado to the front door. 'You're back!' shrieked Georgia, as she bounded into her aunt's arms and immediately whispered 'I let mum win, really, to cheer her up.'

'Yeah, yeah,' teased Sadie, as she unfolded Georgia from Helen's arms and packed her off upstairs to bring her bag down as their Dad would be there soon.

'What's that amazing smell, sis?' asked Helen, dumping a suitcase in the hallway and sniffing the air.

'Carrot cake, for Damian's aunt's birthday,' Sadie replied, looking suspiciously at Helen's luggage. 'What's with the bags – you back again?'

'Er... only for the weekend, anyway I had to bring your car back. I know I said I'm leaving you to it from now on, but I've written my second piece now, and done all the illustrations and I thought I'd pop by just in case you could help me with... something I need your help with.'

Sadie scrunched up her nose and opened her mouth to ask what on earth her sister was talking about then changed her mind and shrugged. 'Whatever,' Sadie laughed, 'you can help me get the next anti-ageing display ready tomorrow.' She hugged Helen and then stopped, as the door went once again.

'Don't touch that cake!' called Sadie, as Helen followed her nose down the hallway towards the kitchen. 'You're not our mother!'

This time it was Stuart at the door with an official looking envelope under his arm.

'Ahh, Sadie, sweetie,' he said, air-kissing her cheeks without quite touching. Sadie looked past him and saw Yvette sitting in the car drumming her fingers on the steering wheel. She saw Sadie looking and gave an awkward little wave.

'Why doesn't she want to come in?' Sadie asked. 'The more the merrier tonight – the gang's all here, it's a *cel-ebra-a-tion, come on,'* she sang, disappearing towards the kitchen as Stuart looked at her weirdly.

'Is your mother feeling ok, girls,' he asked as both his daughters came filing back down the stairs carrying their bags.

'Yes. She won one level at X-Box,' said Abi, reaching up to kiss him then disappearing into the lounge.

'My X-Box,' muttered Stuart begrudgingly.

'Do *you* want a game, Daddy?' asked Georgia, giving him his second hello kiss. 'Maybe I'll let you win a level too, if you like. Unless you know the cheats. Damian knows them and he's going to tell us. I still beat him at BoyBands, he's not as good as me,'

'But he thrashed you at Call of Duty,' Abi interjected, emerging from the lounge with her headphones in her hand.

'Your mother let that man play you at Call of Duty?' Stuart said, his nostrils flaring slightly.

'Ya-har!' said Georgia, 'Everyone at school plays it, Dad, don't be so old-fuddy-duddy. Hey Mum, can I take some carrot cake to Dad's house?' she called, and skipped towards the kitchen.

Sadie met her youngest with a plastic container in hand. '*Yes*, you can take some carrot cake, to *Yvette's* house, I made you all some small ones specially. *Yes*, I do let them play the computer games their peers all play, the same as you let Yvette watch reality TV with them and feed them takeaways. And *yes,* your father is a fuddy-duddy. Always has been and probably always will be.' And with that, Sadie shoved the plastic cake box into his arms, whipped away the envelope and made a big display of planting a very firm kiss on his cheek in clear view of both Yvette in the car and the man watering his plants across the road. 'Oh Mister Wilson, I'll be popping over to see you later, got something I want you to witness for me.' Sadie called so loudly that Stuart cringed. The old man looked around him, then reluctantly nodded and waved his hand in the air.

'But not,' Sadie said, holding the envelope full of documents up and pointing them at Stuart, 'until I've been through these with a fine tooth comb.'

Just then there was a huge roar from the other end of the street and a gleaming red Ferrari came into view.

'Oh God, not bloody Racer Boy,' muttered Stuart. 'Come on, girls, let's get going,'

'No, I want to see Damian!' cried Georgia and dumped her bag in her Dad's arms then rushed out straight past Yvette who was reaching to say hello, to where Damian was pulling up. He graciously got out and opened the door for Georgia so she could sit inside.

'What about you, Abi, aren't you going to rush out there too?' asked Stuart, resentfully.

'God, no,' she replied, screwing her nose up, 'I'm not eleven. Der!' And she kissed her mum goodbye, shouted bye to Helen, waved to Damian and stomped out to the BMW. Yvette had nipped out smartly, and also courteously opened the door, glancing down the street towards Damian, who waved at her. She looked embarrassed then waved back.

'Bye Stuart,' said Sadie, as he walked clumsily out of the house carrying all the stuff. 'Have a nice weekend.'

'I intend to – with our girls.'

'And I'm going to have a nice time too,' she said, with a deeper meaning in her voice, 'A *very* nice time.' And she winked at him.

After seeing her kids off, Sadie walked out to Damian who was just wiping some fingerprints off the car seat where Georgia had been sitting.

'Hello stranger,' Sadie said.

'Sadie, I'm so sorry – I've lost my phone and I was tied up till now...'

'Literally?' she asked. Then smiled.

'Haha, no, I mean I had back-to-back classes and meetings and my private tuition, plus I've just taken on some more consultancy work and I haven't had a moment to track down your number... sorry.'

'That's ok,' she replied airily. 'Have you come for your cake? I've made a belter.'

'Well, yes I was hoping you'd remembered. That's fantastic, my aunt will be thrilled,' he said, following her back into the house.

When they got to the kitchen he stopped short, spotting Helen at the table, quickly hiding some crumbs.

'Helen. Nice to meet you.'

'Damian, you too.'

They shook hands formally. The atmosphere was a little awkward.

'Well Sadie I won't keep you, if you're busy,' he said after a pause. 'It was just on the off chance, well, yes the cake, but also... if you fancied coming over – or tomorrow night, after work, that'd be nice. My aunt is popping by during the day but she never stays over. So I just thought... I wondered if you'd like to, then...'

'Thanks Damian,' said Sadie, and was about to accept when she hesitated. 'Not tonight, clearly. And tomorrow? Let me get back to you on that. I can email you, right? Or *twitter* you? Till you find your mobile. I'll let you know later on tonight. I may be a bit busy – I have something very important to do with my sister.' She looked over and Helen was beaming.

Sadie walked him to the door then handed over the container holding the pretty carrot cake complete with marzipan carrots and leaves on top.

'Sadie, I'm really sorry, I cocked up. I should have been in touch last night, after class, I know that, but I really was up to my eyes in it.' He stopped, put his free hand on her shoulder and lowered his voice. 'I'd be very happy to make it up to you if you'd care to join me tomorrow night.'

'Let's see, shall we?' she said, and bid him goodnight.

Back in the kitchen, Helen gave Sadie the biggest high five and they put the music on loud and both danced around the kitchen singing into make believe wooden-spoon-microphones, and taking turns to sing the lead, chanting the chorus together, something about wanting to dance with somebody who loves them. Then they flaked out in the lounge with two big envelopes lying conspicuously in front of them on the coffee table.

'My one's divorce papers, you can help me check them, if you would?' Sadie said, in between ragged breaths. 'I really must do that more often.'

'What get divorced?'

'No you nutter, dance round the house!'

'Oh,' Helen said, leaning forward and looking into her envelope. 'And mine is a little bit of er, freelance work I've taken on. I wanted to utilise your expert eye to help me come up with a new campaign for a product that's very similar to that water in the competition for that Hawaiian escape.'

'The one I never entered?'

'Yes that one.'

'Sadie, I want to buy your idea,' said Helen suddenly.

'What? With everything you've done for me? You don't have to buy it, you can borrow it.'

'No, silly, it's a copyrighted concept, you can't just lend it around – it needs to be an original idea if you're asking people to pay for it.'

Sadie just looked blank.

'Yes, that's the face I thought you'd make. Ok, so assuming it's been copyrighted then I want to buy it from you. How much would you charge me? For my client?'

'Oooh, bucketloads of wonga,' Sadie said, kicking off her shoes and putting her legs up on the sofa.

'Come on, seriously, how long did it take you?'

'About two days, start to finish.'

'With several earlier versions, presumably you've got all those sketches?'

'Yes I scanned them into a little Powerpoint so they were easy to compare. Then I just sketched the ones I thought were best. Though it's a subjective thing isn't it – 'cos they're not all that, are they? If Damian said not to bother, they weren't really original enough to win a big competition, don't you think your client would be a bit disappointed if you give them second rate stuff from an amateur?'

'No,' Helen said simply. 'How much?'

'Oh, I don't know. A few hundred quid?'

'What about if I could get you a few thousand?'

'Are you *serious?* That would take me through till the New Year. But surely that's not possible, is it?'

'Well you help me fill in all these templates and sign a couple of forms and we'll see. I've looked it all over so you don't have to. And give me the divorce papers and I'll help check those too, if you like, I can...'

'Sis,' Sadie said, her hand on Helen's. 'No.'

'No?'

'No – it's ok. After the fabulous day that I've had, I can take on the world. This time, I can handle the final ties to Stuart myself.'

And as she looked into her eyes, Helen knew that this time, her sister really could.

CHAPTER FOURTEEN

The tinkle of the doorbell came just as Sadie was about to shut up slightly early the next afternoon, and head off to see Damian unannounced. Or that was the plan. It was a cunning one. But it gave Sadie palpitations every time she pictured herself doing it. *What if he was with someone…?*

Helen had already left. They'd got a lot done today. Sadie looked up and couldn't have been more surprised to see who was standing at the counter.

'Delta! What brings you here?' she asked. Miss Delta Smartypants was standing there bold as brass and pointing to something she'd just put on the counter top.

'It's Damian's mobile. He left it in class. Are you going to see him? Or do you want to tell me where he lives?'

So she doesn't know his address. That's something I suppose, Sadie thought. Or she's lying.

'The battery died – same night. Forgot it was in my bag,' Delta added. 'And I found this charger – in case he hasn't got his, I don't need it. Maybe plug it in before you take it to him. Anyway, you going there later or what?'

'Yes, I'll be seeing him tonight. I'll take it to him. Thanks very much – he'll be pleased.'

'No problem. See you in class. If you turn up. We were taking bets on whether you'd dip out permanently.' And with that she was gone.

Cheeky little minx, thought Sadie. But she looked carefully at the phone on the table and chewed her cheek. She wasn't going to look – honesty and all that – but then she shrugged and plugged it in. Just in case there was, you know, like, a message or something which, possibly, Damian might need to be made aware of urgently. Or something.

Two minutes later there was enough charge to get the home screen up and running, but to Sadie's disappointment there was a lock code. She couldn't open it up to check what was on it – not that she was going to, of course.

Of course.

But what there were, clearly in view scrolling up and down the lock screen, were some of those little notifications which show up even when the phone is locked – a couple of tweets, some messages from apps, and the start of an email message from an email address with a star icon next to it – indicating that person was on his favourites list. Sadie knew that much from her girls' phones.

'NervadaQueen69,' Sadie read aloud. It was a hotmail address and the first line of the email sent some 12 hours ago. It read, *'Next rendezvous is set for 10pm Saturday. We're…'* but no matter how Sadie played around with the display or tapped the screen, she couldn't see any more of the message than that.

She decided to unplug it again straight away – probably better if she gave it back to him completely dead. But who the hell was NervadaQueen? And what was going to happen at ten pm? Whatever it was, Sadie was going to make damn sure she was at his house tonight at 9.55.

'No, nothing else on Google, only an advertising agency, and some Italian kitchen place. No idea what Nervada means apart from that,' Helen was shouting to Sadie through the closed bathroom door, 'unless it's a creature of the night from the ghostly goblins website. No, nothing.'

Sadie opened the door and came out with a towel round her head and a robe on. 'But it could be just a name of someone he works with, his new consultancy client, an old pal from uni, anyone.'

'Yes, you go ahead, focus on the positive, love,' Helen said. 'Or it could be someone he's been seeing behind your back the whole time, who's turning up there at ten 'cos he didn't hear from you.'

'Well he's going to hear from me, right now, in fact,' Sadie said, picking up her own mobile phone.

'Wait,' said Helen, 'are you sure you want to alert him? Give it another two hours, wait till you're nearly outside and *then* call him. In fact, do a Jack Reacher and wait till you're *sitting* outside then call him. That way you can say you're half an hour away, and you can watch who comes rushing out of the house! It's exciting! Just like a detective novel.'

'Listen, Miss Marple, I'm not sure I like the whole premise of setting him up for a fall – if he's guilty it'll all come out in the wash. And not make me look dishonest. I've still got classes to attend to, don't forget. We've got exams in a month's time,' protested Sadie. 'Not that I've revised enough. Maybe Delta was right…'

'What? Listen, you can still take your exams, you don't need him. You've done half the course work anyway. Then if you break up, next term you can transfer to a different marketing option – simple. Come onnnn! This is exciting, like catching a culprit red-handed – there's nothing more satisfying.'

'And you know this, how?' asked Sadie.

Helen just tapped the side of her nose. 'How do you think it all got messy with Victor in the end? Been there, done that. And tonight, you can do it too.'

Sadie stepped into her room and turned to close the door. 'Let me get ready, I'll think about it. See you in a bit.'

Pretty soon the sound of a hairdryer was blaring away and Helen's additional snippets of info could no longer be heard through Sadie's bedroom door. Helen gave up and went back downstairs.

That afternoon, Helen had done Sadie proud. She'd completely let her take the lead, and they had worked hard together on a huge new display called *'Sadie Turner's Anti-Ageing Specials'* complete with the little 'at's' and #STAAS clearly on view. It was far from trending, but consistency counts for a lot. Then Helen challenged Sadie – *'do whatever it takes,'* she had said, *'to make sure that the forthcoming appointment with the man from the local paper leads to a nice bit of editorial.'* It's always more impactful than a little paid-for advert, however carefully placed. Ok, Sadie had said, but not *whatever* it took. *Her and her ethics.*

Now Helen went into the back room to follow up with her new 'client' – deciding how many thousands to give Sadie for the 'use' of her concepts. Copyrighting had indeed been completed online, with only a little bit of help from Helen showing Sadie what to put where, so the concept was protected. *Therefore worth a bit more now*, Helen had told her.

Sadie had signed the forms Helen gave her without paying them much heed – she was in a hurry to scour through the divorce papers. Now Helen sat idly filling in some final missing info, stuff she'd left blank on purpose, knowing it would have caught Missus Fine-Tooth Comb's eye and made her query how Helen was doing it. Listening out for any sign of Sadie appearing, she finally filled in one last crucial line and everything was ready to go. And by the end of the month, the money would be safely transferred into Sadie's account, meaning a happy sister all summer and a full half a year's breather before the next watershed cropped up in her cash flow.

Who knows what would happen by then.

Helen put the envelope away and turned back to the laptop. The Google search for Nervada was still on display. It was probably nothing, but the devil in her liked to make sure Sadie was kept on her toes. Yes Sadie had finally agreed to sit outside his house for a while tonight, before announcing her arrival. It didn't take too much coercion. And anyway, Helen may have promised her sister she would back off and let her sort her *own* life out from now on, but it was more likely that that would start next month. Or maybe the month after... Maybe.

By the time a freshly made up, dressed up, perked up Sadie turned up outside Damian's, it was nine thirty. She'd decided not to call his home number until she was waiting outside. *Great news, Damian, I'm on my way – see you in twenty minutes.*

She parked in up the road a little way away from his well-lit house. Then she called. Exactly five minutes later, the door opened and a small shape in a big black hooded coat came out and Damian bent to kiss the person briefly – Sadie was too far away to see whether it was on the lips or the cheek – before walking the figure to a smart car Sadie hadn't seen before, and handing over some sort of parcel. Then he went back in the house as the car pulled up the street.

As it passed, Sadie looked round and saw clearly who was sitting inside, and the pit of her stomach fell away.

It was a glamorous older woman. Very glamorous. Maybe *that* was his ex, Rosalee? Maybe he was back with her after all. Or – be gracious here, Sadie – maybe she'd just come to collect her dressing up stuff, perhaps he'd given it all back now he didn't use it any more. At least with Sadie he didn't. Or maybe that woman was a new lover and he used *everything* with her. Eurgh.

By the time Sadie knocked on his door, she had wound herself up like a spring. She knew his first reaction would be most telling.

'Sadie!' he said. 'What a lovely surprise! I wish I'd known you were going to be early, you've just missed my aunt...'

'So how old was your mum when she had you?' Sadie asked fifteen minutes later over a pleasant cup of tea and tiny piece of her own cake.

'Thirty two, but she was the oldest of five siblings – my aunt's her youngest sister, she's only fifty five now. She loved her cake, by the way. Took a huge chunk of it away with her. Delicious – she wonders if you'd give her the recipe, as she'd like to do it for her WI fundraiser this summer.'

Sadie felt rather stupid. *Bloody Helen, winding me up.*

That was it, she wouldn't listen to Helen any more. Ever. Her gut instinct had been wrong all along, and she knew Damian wouldn't have anyone else on the go – he'd told her he wasn't having sex with anyone else and she believed him. At least... she *chose* to believe him. Innocent until proven guilty. With Helen it seemed that men were guilty until proven otherwise. All that talk about NervadaQueen... why *was* she called 69 anyway...? Sadie shook herself. Maybe she'd ask him later. But how could she say she knew?

'Oh, Damian, I've got some news for you,' she said. 'Where do you charge your phone?'

'In the kitchen, why?'

'Come with me,' said Sadie, and she hid the mobile in her jacket and led him out to the kitchen. Spying the charger in the corner of the room, she walked over and plugged in the phone. Almost immediately it bleeped and the screen lit up.

'Voila!' she said.

'What the hell? How did you get it?'

'Delta had it.'

'She did? Well why didn't she let me know?' he asked, scratching his chin and standing protectively next to the phone.

'Says she forgot and the battery was dead. It seems to be ok now, though,' Sadie said as the phone bleeped to life. 'Look, you've got – ooh, five or six messages, from…' And she reached her hand out to it.

But before she could touch it, Damian snatched the phone up off the counter and looked at the screen, then started pressing buttons. 'Ahahaa. Oh yes, so I have. And a dozen missed calls from my home number from when I was trying to find it.'

The phone began bleeping and new messages began coming through. Sure enough there were loads.

'Who are they all from?' asked Sadie, looking at the clock on the wall out of the corner of her eye. It was 9.55pm. 'Hope there wasn't anything too urgent. Nothing from your clients?'

He was distracted, looking at all the messages. Then he stopped – something important maybe – something that made him look up at the clock on the wall, then at his watch. Then at Sadie.

'Hmm? Er, no not really. Er, excuse me Sadie,' he said, 'I've just got to go send a quick reply to one of these messages, I won't be long. Make yourself another cup of something delicious. I've stocked up on nettleBerrywotsit. We can go back and get the fire in the lounge going – in fact,' he said, walking her back into the other room, 'you're better at getting it going than me. Why don't you do it for us? Make it lovely and warm in here. I won't be long.' And he kissed her tenderly, and left.

Sadie was confused. He certainly seemed genuine enough in the way he was responding – his actions and demeanour were not those of a guilty man. But... but... Sadie's gut instinct was nagging at her. And then she knew she had to find out why.

She quietly arose and crept into the study, expecting to see Damian at his computer, intending to go sit on his lap playfully and see if she could peep at who he was messaging on his computer screen. But he wasn't there.

Instead, there was a dull hum coming from upstairs and Sadie crept slowly up the staircase, step by step, gripping the bannister and putting her feet on the very edges of the wooden treads, to try to minimize the creaking from the old staircase. Her heart was pounding faster and faster. And as she got nearer and nearer, the strange humming sound got louder and louder. It was coming from a bedroom – the one with dark walls.

Sadie reached the closed door and took a deep breath, listening intently. The door was heavy and old and thick, and she couldn't really hear much more than a series of deep humming sounds punctuated by several bangs. Sadie tried the handle – it opened a crack, which surprised her, and she nervously peered around it into the room. She couldn't believe what she saw.

There in the middle of the fairly empty bedroom, Damian was standing with some sort of helmet over his head – it covered his entire scalp, and extended down to his nose at the front, but it had no eyeholes.

Then he spoke. His voice was altered – he sounded really metallic, kind of robotic. And deeper than normal – much deeper.

'Indeed we shall reconvene, on the morrow, NervadaQueen, and I promise our quest will continue. And this time,' he said dramatically, his voice rising in pitch, 'there will be NOOOO RESPIIIITE...' Then he shouted some sort of battle cry and a loud bang came from inside his helmet.

The sounds all stopped abruptly, as he clicked a button on the side of the helmet, which opened at the same time as the lights in the room got slightly brighter. Then he froze, looking directly at Sadie. 'Hello,' she said.

Sadie smiled and shrugged slightly. Damian smiled back, kind of. He didn't speak for the longest time. Then he grinned inanely.

'My, er... secret's out,' he said, meekly taking his helmet right off and carefully placing it in a foam case lying next to a big black cloth. The cloth swathed across one side of the room, covering a big bump about eight feet long and six feet high. 'Well? Where do I start? Ask me. Go on. You know you want to. What's the first question? You've always got a question. Fire away. Go on.'

'Ok,' said Sadie. 'First, sorry for being nosy, but I thought we were being invaded by Klingons. Had to come and investigate...'

'Understandable,' he said, standing awkwardly in his bare feet, then he began removing a kind of strappy body harness which was dotted with small yellow circles. She could see it clearly now the lights were up.

'So... What *were* you doing? You weren't replying to an urgent email. *Were* you.' It was a statement not a question.

'Well, kind of. I *was* online – rearranging a group meet,' he replied. Sadie was confused. 'I've got a confession, Sadie,' he said, sheepishly. 'I know it'll surprise you but,' he swallowed hard. 'Virtual reality gaming,' he stated simply. 'Next Gen technology. I play in a... league, in a *sort* of a league. You play with a – a partner, and have to accumulate points.' He drew the harness down over his hips and stepped out of it. 'Person with the most points wins that level. Best of three usually. Bit like X-Box.'

'Oh ok. I understand X-Box. That simple eh?' She asked.

'That simple,' he said, looking a bit more relaxed. *Relieved?* 'It's a kind of a... Tell you what, would you like to give it a go? I can put a beginners' programme into the control box if you like? I can turn the settings down – the first time can be a bit weird.'

EVERY time sounds like it's a bit weird, Sadie thought. This was a defining moment in their relationship. But she was in a new era. *Try it for the first time.* And anyway, she was safe enough, in a harmless bedroom in a run of the mill Victorian detached, wasn't she? So, *what the hell.*

'Sure,' she said. 'Why not. Beam me up, *spotty*. Haha. Sorry. Yes, sure.'

Damian suddenly looked really excited. He fiddled around with a control box situated at about waist height, close to the other wall. 'Just calibrating,' he said, moving to a small laptop and tapping some more buttons. Then he bent to retrieve his helmet from its box. He placed it carefully on Sadie's head, adjusted it, and stepped away. Sadie was left standing there holding her hands out blindly in front of her, swaying slightly from side to side.

'What are you doing?' he said.

'Acclimatizing – it feels like I'm under the ocean. Where have you gone?' she asked.

'I'm just over here adjusting the height of the sensors,' he said from the direction of the control box. Then suddenly there was a glaring light as the screens sprang to life and Sadie's eyes focused. A strange sight came into view. She found herself 'inside' a barren landscape with fire-breathing dragons in the distance, and a couple of weird dinosaur-like creatures flapping their giant wings high up in the sky above – if she looked up, the view changed to show a full sky above her head. If she looked behind her, there was no Damian, there was only a – *shit!* A vista stretching as far as the eye could see, with a huge ugly Tyrannosaurus Rex running fast towards her from a long way away. But it was getting closer by the second – and closer – and closer!

'Damian, it's... argggggh!' she cried, and grabbed the helmet trying to get it off but the chin strap was tightly fastened. 'Get it off me, get it off!'

'Wait a minute, here, here,' he said, chuckling slightly as he loosened the straps and eventually lifted the helmet off her head. 'There, you ok?'

'Oh... my... God. That is *so* realistic! Don't tell me – I'll bet you're one of the best players at this game, too.'

'Guilty as charged,' he said, puffing up his chest. 'It's my other guilty secret.'

'The only one?'

'Apart from my new sex dungeon in the cellar.'

'That's not even funny,' Sadie replied, smoothing down her hair, 'Considering what I've seen in the last few weeks that could be true.'

'Course it's not. This house hasn't got a cellar... Come on, let's go sit in front of the fire, I want to nuzzle your neck.'

'As long as you don't sink your talons into me, that'll be fine,' she said.

Helen waited for word from Sadie. She waited a long time. A text finally arrived just before midnight – an innocuous message which she'd obviously sent from the bathroom. *'All fine – it was just virtual reality games LOL – doing my teeth, then bed – knackered. See you tomoz night.'*

Hmmmph. Helen pouted her lips in thought. Maybe Sadie was more naive than she'd realised. Or maybe it *was* all completely innocent. Maybe Damian was indeed, completely honest. Or maybe pink virtual pigs with fluffy white virtual wings could fly right across a big blue virtual reality sky.

Men.

It had been a week or so since Helen had seen Victor again in O'Reilly's bar, and still the sting of it felt fresh in her heart – the stark reminder of what might have been – and the harsh reality of what *had* been. She took herself back to that humiliating time all those months back, and felt a pain that made her chest tight – made her feel like she might keel over if she didn't sit down. And reminded her of the very real possibility that she would never trust another man ever again. And there was nothing virtual about that.

Unbeknownst to Helen, however, destiny had other plans.

CHAPTER FIFTEEN

Sadie was back at home by six pm the next night, bringing a laughing Damian in through the front door with her, and they spent the next hour in the back room continuing a trip down memory lane which they'd started at his house, looking at his old photos.

They all giggled at the cute baby photos of the young Sadie and Helen, pics of Sadie when she was at school, as well as some quite risqué shots from their student days and all-girl holidays which Helen produced. Then she went off to make some afternoon tea and when she came back, she was appalled to find them surrounded by old albums and ancient storage boxes, poring over the Miss Combe Haven Camp Site contest, 1987.

'Nice pair of legs, Helen,' said Damian.

'That was back in the old days when the competition still had a swimming costume round,' added Sadie.

'That was back in the old days when I still had nice legs,' said Helen. Sadie went to protest but Helen added, 'it's all your fault – you and your irresistible flapjacks! Ok, that's enough of that, thank you! Leave my albums alone.' She tried to close them all up.

'Well, we've seen all of mine.' Sadie protested.

'Fancy joining us in a game of *Call of Duty* then?' Damian asked.

'No thanks,' Helen replied, 'I'm totally crap at that stuff. But you two knock yourselves out. Listen out for the girls though, Sade, whilst I stay here and made some calls? They're due home in half an hour but you know how Turncoat likes to bring them back earlier than he should.'

'Will do,' Sadie said.

'Hey, maybe we can all have a tournament tonight!' Damian suggested. 'Come on, Sadie, I'll show you the cheats.'

Oh joy, thought Helen, as Sadie and her man-child went through to the lounge to start playing games. She felt the odd one out, which was almost ok when there were three. But soon afterwards she was the odd one out amongst six – when Stuart brought the girls back, and stayed to see what was going on with 'his' old games machine. He'd walked in the house bold as brass as usual, then stopped when confronted by Damian, whose eye-line was a good five inches higher and a firm handshake that made Stuart wince. The slightly awkward moment passed quite swiftly. Then the games began and the new arrivals joined in.

Except Stuart. He 'oversaw' from the back of the room, beer in hand.

He grimaced as he watched his daughters arguing over who would play the first tournament with Damian, but only Helen noticed it. He glanced at her and she smiled smugly at him. He jerked his head towards the kitchen. *What the…? Does he want me to follow him out?* Then Helen nodded, overcome by curiosity.

'Tea anyone? No? Ok, I'll leave you to it then,' she announced, and followed him out of the lounge.

'Listen,' he said to her as he closed the big kitchen door behind him. 'What's the deal with this big guy? How old is he, exactly? Is he for real?'

'Oh he's for real, all right. Sadie's quite taken with him,' Helen lied. 'He told me confidentially he's thinking of taking the whole family away to Disneyland next year.' Stuart blinked, and looked alarmed.

'But they've only been together a few weeks,' he said.

'Well you know what it's like with true love,' Helen replied, enjoying the moment, 'You've found Yvette the secretary, and Sadie's found award-winning International Marketing Expert Damian Hugh with the Ferrari. Who's totally bowled over by Sadie. And her daughters.'

Stuart narrowed his eyes and opened his mouth to speak but just then a squeal of laughter came from said daughters, the speakers got louder, and a massive explosion sound came resounding round the house.

'Aww. Aren't they taken with him – lovely isn't it? How amazing that your Yvette is equally as entranced by the girls. Shame she doesn't want them at her Dad's timeshare in Cyprus though isn't it. Still, never mind. Perhaps one day when you earn as much as Damian does, *you'll* be able to afford to take them all away somewhere, too. Did you know his house is huge, apparently? With all sorts of expensive equipment inside it.

Makes a change for Sadie to have a guy who's well off. And capable. And not a prat.'

Before Stuart could reply, the kitchen door opened and an excited looking Georgia rushed in to get a glass of water.

'Abi's on level ten!' she squealed. 'Damian's catching up with her. It's brilliant!'

Helen watched Stuart's face as he appeared to make a decision. She caught his eye and smiled, but he looked away quickly and started taking off his jacket, then rolling up his sleeves.

'Come on, Georgia-Porgia,' he said, and without another word he exited the kitchen and strutted into the lounge with Georgia hot on his heels. Helen was going to follow them but she noticed a light flashing on her smartphone on the kitchen table.

Half an hour later, in the lounge, the competition was indeed hotting up. Sadie was 'helping' Georgia with her game, Damian was helping Abi.

'Mummmm!' shrieked Georgia, 'You're getting in my way! I've got Harry at the stage door and the roadies are trying to protect him from Marauding Fans! Mooooove!' There came a big crash sound effect, and a flashing sign came up on the screen. *Game over*. 'Awwww Muuummm! Next round you can be in *Abi's* team, not mine.'

'What!' said Sadie, feigning being hurt. 'You still got 135 points? What's up with that?'

'Nothing except I know how to increase it to 820 points,' whispered Damian under his breath to Abi as she slowly annihilated each remaining member of Sadie and Georgia's boy band and left them both reeling.

'Ok, bath time,' said Sadie. *Enough is enough,* she thought. They were about to throw in the towel and call it a night, when Damian produced a square package from his pocket. Stuart frowned.

'Not before I show them the big surprise, Sugarlips,' he said, and Sadie flashed another look at Stuart, whose eyebrow quivered slightly and he hid a grin behind his beer. *Shit,* must remind Damian not to call me that in front of certain people.

'OK, reward time,' Damian declared. 'Look what I've brought to give to the best player.'

'That's you,' said a disgruntled Georgia.

Sadie looked over at her youngest and made a *'now now'* face.

'Ok then, I mean the best team from round three, two levels ago. Who was it? Does anyone remember?'

No-one said a thing, just waited. Stuart was behind the sofa, sitting on a stool rolling his bottle of beer in his hand. He didn't look happy. His mobile bleeped from time to time and he just clicked it off. He was avidly watching the proceedings.

'You at the back. Do *you* remember, Stuart?' Damian asked him in a 'school teacher' voice, and Stuart nearly fell off his stool.

'Er… no idea, mate.'

'Well I do – it was Georgia and Abi – here you go girls,' Damian said, and held out the package. Both girls scrambled to open it and screamed when they saw that it was BoyBand2.0 – the latest import and not even available in the UK yet. They tore off the packaging and started putting it in the machine.

Sadie laughed at her two girls as she got up and walked over to the doorway, passing Stuart as she went.

'How the hell did he manage *that* one?' Stuart hissed.

'No idea – he's got international contacts, what can I say?' she replied. 'Last call for hot chocolate? No-one?' Sadie asked. 'Stuart?'

He just gestured at her with his beer – *'got this, ta'* – and raised it to his mouth, still watching the two girls fighting with the packaging, then handing the disc to Damian to undo for them. 'Might as well not be here,' Stuart muttered under his breath. Sadie heard it, did an about turn, leaned back in to him and whispered in his ear.

'Make more of an effort then, like Damian does? Or is this what you're like when the girls at yours… sorry, I mean at Yvette's? Hmm?' Sadie raised her eyebrows at him – *is it?* – Then marched off.

In the kitchen, Helen was typing frantically on her laptop.

'Turncoat still here?' she asked Sadie.

'Yes. His phone hasn't stopped bleeping – 'Er Indoors, probably – wondering where he's got to.'

'That relationship won't last,' said Helen. 'I'll give it a year. Listen, Sade, I've had some news about that thing I told you I was doing that I said I'd tell you about when it was time... well it's time. I need to talk to you about it.'

'What?' Sadie asked as she began getting the girls' packed lunches ready for school the next morning.

'We know your shop needs help. Like, *really* needs help, right?'

''Course. Don't rub it in. Go on.'

'You'd do anything to increase sales, yeah?'

'Almost anything,' said Sadie more slowly, suspicion creeping into her voice. *What is she up to...?*

'Well they want you to do an interview – on television.'

'OH no,' Sadie answered, 'You said it was an online column.' Sadie could feel her heart miss a beat, and not in a good way.

'Yes, well it's internet television. Part of the syndication I mentioned, remember? Y'see, the star of their lifestyle channel – a big face over there – does a weekly chat show. It's a big thing if they choose to feature this column and the people in it. And they want to feature you in a follow up to my column. They want to interview you. Next week.'

'Oh God.' Sadie plonked herself down at the table, going slightly white.

'Come on Sade! Think of the publicity! I know my column hasn't hit its full circulation yet so you won't have felt the benefit of that coverage. But imagine how much more powerful it'd be if you do this too?' Helen was on a roll. 'Their YouTube channel gets millions of hits a week – that local paper man will pee his pants once he finds out you're appearing on it! He'll be falling over himself to come interview you. The demographic for that channel is exactly right for your customer base – well, almost – and there are bound to be some viewers living near here. And you're being interviewed, not selling stuff – it's editorial not advertising. So as an expert you can say what you like - be honest about how things work and what they do – just don't mention the shop during the interview, it'll be in the sub-titles, and don't throw in too many scientific studies or they'll get bored.' Helen was rising to her theme. 'Sadie! Think of the extra business – think of the interest it'll generate in your anti-ageing display – it's working out perfectly! Come onnnnn!'

'I'll think about it,' Sadie said. Then immediately added, 'No, I'd be terrified. I might not be able to… form… form… you know, actual – words. They just might not come out.'

'Rubbish. You'll be great! Just treat it as though you're doing one of your little talks in the village hall – you've mastered those now, haven't you? You'll breeze it.'

'And what if I say no? Eh? What would you do then, Missus 'Helen *I'm leaving you to it, YOU run your own life from now on* Parker-Todd'? What if I turn you down flat? Maybe I should.'

'You won't,' she said. 'You know *I know* what's best for you.' Helen tried a broad beam. Sadie wasn't buying it.

'No! Honestly, no,' she said firmly. 'The village hall with half a dozen old age pensioners and some yummy mummies is one thing, but I really don't think I can do a live TV interview. Let alone with a celebrity.'

Helen batted her eyes at her sister. 'She's only a B-List. Come on, sis – you know I'll talk you round in the end!'

'Don't push it. New era. It'll make me less likely to do it,' Sadie threatened.

'No, it makes you *more* likely to do it – you know how this works – I keep nagging you and eventually you cave,' replied Helen.

Sadie looked at her sister long and hard. 'Well in that case, it's definitely a massive, whopping, unadulterated *NO.*' *That felt good. Really good. I should try this more often,* Sadie thought.

Helen stood looking at Sadie in surprise. 'You're kidding me, right?'

'No, sister, I'm actually not,' said Sadie, she stood there with her hands on her hips, then aggressively bit off the end of a carrot she was about to put in a lunchbox.

'*Well!*' Helen breathed. 'As Damian would say – *O.M.Gee*. How the worm turns.'

'Yes well, I'm fed up being the worm. You're always the early bird. Well now it's my turn. To turn. You started this "new era" so don't get any ideas about cancelling it, or getting me to back down. Not this time. You go do your thing, I'll go do mine.'

Helen looked crestfallen. 'You're serious aren't you? Well at least think it over, sis?' She made a little-girl-lost face and pouted a little. 'Please...? And if it helps, *pretty please?*'

Sadie shook her head and smiled jubilantly, threw the rest of the carrot at Helen and stopped munching. 'Tell you what – email me the info – all business-like, mind – in a proper proposal. You know, like professionals do, and I'll have my people call your people in the morning with an answer.'

'Ooh harsh,' said Helen, biting the carrot and munching it. She was silent for a moment looking strangely at Sadie. No-one spoke. They both knew what was being said, here.

Sadie finished her mouthful of carrot and spoke more softly. 'It's time. It'll be for the best.'

Helen just shrugged. There was a pounding noise coming from the hallway. She perked herself up. 'Well, it sounds like "your people" have had enough of playing BoyBands with a 30 year old man. Here they come! Quick, shut the kitchen door, keep them out... *no, no!*' Helen play-acted, pretending to shove the girls back out the door and trying to close it on them, as they came traipsing in from the lounge.

'Dad gone?' said a laughing Sadie.

'No,' both girls said at once.

'No?' both adults said at once.

'You mean he's in there with...' asked Helen.

'Come on Helen,' said Sadie, winking at her, 'come out here a minute, the girls can finish their own packed lunches.' But Helen just looked confused. *'Helen,'* Sadie urged, jerking her head towards the doorway, 'Come and talk to me about that *thing*.'

'You don't have to talk in code, mum,' Abi said in a chastising voice. 'Yes, Dad's in there with Damian. You know you just want to go and spy on them. We're not stupid. And I don't want a carrot. I'll do my own lunchbox.'

Giggling, Sadie poked Abi playfully then she and Helen quietly tiptoed up the hallway to peer round the doorway to the lounge.

'I don't believe it,' said Helen.

'Where's my camera? This sight isn't something you see very often,' added Sadie.

There, in front of the TV, Damian was playing Stuart at *BoyBand2.0*, both of them playing in total intense concentration, in silence, beads of sweat starting to form on their foreheads. The scene on the TV was filled with screaming fans, and lots of pink, and teen-pop music, whilst the scene in the lounge was two grown men, in shirtsleeves, on the edge of the sofa, jabbing manically at control pads and grunting, glancing sideways at each other every now and then.

'Boys, eh?' said Sadie.

'Weirdoes the pair of them.' said Helen.

The next morning being a school day, Helen went down after another long night on the computer. She'd waited till everyone had left the house and half-heartedly prodded buttons on the kettle – then stood staring straight at it the whole time it took to boil. Which was a long time. *Bloody eco-sodding-kettle.*

She didn't want to tell Sadie, but Mr Adams the Editor had sent an urgent email informing her that there was more news. For every column Helen submitted, an appearance on the TV channel was now going to be vital – obligatory, no less – to tie in with the *'cohesive whole and our new syndicated corporate international identity'*. Helen sighed – that was the sort of advice she used to give her clients. But what it actually meant was that Sadie *had* to say yes. And Helen was in trouble if Sadie said no.

If she couldn't get her own sister to agree to be interviewed, then what chance would she stand of keeping the column beyond feature number two. *Number two* – oh God. Half of it was with fake people – one's she'd illustrated instead of photographed, thinking she was clever. How the hell could *they* be interviewed on live TV? Her heart sank.

She collected the post, put it on the table, and sat warming her hands on her mug of tea. Then she noticed the note from Sadie on a bright purple note pad.

"I'm still thinking about it. But – don't push your luck with anything else in the future, ok? Yes, you probably know better than me about <u>some</u> things," – 'some' was underlined three times – *"but I want this next stage in my life to happen because of me, not other people. Just for once – all my own work, ok? Well apart from mum but she doesn't count 'cos, well, she's mum."*

Ouch, that hurt, Helen realised. That really hurt. *She'd* been like a mum to Sadie, a long time back. *Maybe if I hadn't gone off on my travels, hadn't left her…*

The note went on. *"I believe something will happen, to turn my business around, but you can't keep swooping back in to rescue me till the end of time, Helen. 'Cos I don't know if you realised it, but it's time to rescue yourself. I know you're still hurting. Go sort yourself out. Leave me to it. The girls and I will get along just fine, and anyway, Crystal says she's got a good feeling about what this next six months will bring. See you tonight, I'm doing Quorn and Kale Casserole. With chips – just for you."*

'Yummy,' said Helen out loud, with no enthusiasm. 'Hmmm. *Leave you to it*, eh. Unfortunately on this occasion, that might just be just a little bit impossible,' she said out loud.

She was pleased her sister was going to think about agreeing to be interviewed. But this new stronger Sadie might mean that Helen's next plan – Phase B as she was calling it in her mind – would be far more difficult to pull off. She'd intended to broach the subject with her this evening. Now it would have to wait. Till Sadie calmed down a little, or gave in a little or… But what if she didn't?

Whilst her coffee went cold, Helen thought of a strategy. She was good at strategies – at least she used to be. Before Victor had buggered it all up.

For half an hour, Helen tapped away on the laptop, looked thoughtful for a while, and then looked up the phone number for the shop. She'd go to see her with the news. Sadie just *had* to do this interview. And since Helen had a sneaky suspicion that this new feisty Sadie was here to stay, this was the most painless way to make it happen. A means to an end – and what Sadie didn't know, couldn't hurt her. Could it?

But Phase B was very complex. Very complex indeed. Helen knew that if her relationship with her sister was to avoid a little crisis, then the best tactics would be to say nothing – and for the first time in her life, to hope for the *worst*...

CHAPTER SIXTEEN

'Are you sure?' Sadie asked.

Helen was standing over the counter in the store, giving Sadie some unusual news.

'Yep, you can do it by Skype. Talk to a screen – easy.'

'But why would they be couriering me a new laptop?'

'I told them yours isn't reliable enough.'

'Well that's true.'

'Told you it was great news. It's the latest Mac.'

'I've always wanted a Mac. But why? How's that work?'

'Because it's cheaper than paying for you to go to *them*. Even though I could have gone with you which would have been fun. However, their nearest international studio facility is in Milan – but not the glamorous part, according to Kate.'

'Shame,' Sadie said wistfully, 'it would have been lovely to get away to Italy.'

'Not to a crappy industrial estate just outside the airport, it wouldn't. So that's why I said yes. The laptop's already on its way. Unless you say no, in which case I can get them to send it back...'

'How long do I get to keep it?' Sadie asked, narrowing her eyes thoughtfully. Helen took a deep breath.

'Well, the best bit is – it's yours for good – it's on "permanent loan", instead of expenses, and I guess it's in case they need you to be on video again about something else. I did rather big you up – being a scientist and health and nutrition expert and all.'

'You do exaggerate, Helen.'

'I'm in advertising, what do you expect?'

'Were.'

'Well anyway, don't sell yourself short. I don't know if you realise it, but you're one of the most knowledgeable experts in your field — especially the way you produced those ideas for that international marketing competition you never ended up bloody entering. They were superb. Your lateral thinking was pure genius.' Helen meant every word of it. Sadie's work had genuinely surprised her. Little sis was getting all *grow'ed up*.

Sadie was looking at Helen. 'Well Damian told me emphatically that I wasn't ready. And he might not be the most grown up boyfriend but at least he knows his stuff where business is concerned. Anyway, what are the chances I'd ever win? No, I'm glad I didn't give in to you. He's right — I wouldn't have even made the finals.'

'Wouldn't you?' Helen asked, miffed that Damian's opinion had been more important than hers. 'Wouldn't you have even liked to try?'

Sadie picked up a stack of health magazines and banged them together to align their edges, then placed them back perfectly in line with the edge of the countertop. She looked like she was thinking about the question.

'Well anyway,' she said, 'I missed the deadline. They were talking about it in class — a couple of the others were going to enter, but Damian put them off too.' Helen looked at Sadie's slumped shoulders. Clearly the shine had gone off Thursday night classes.

'Confident bugger, isn't he. Well, there's always next year,' said Helen, patting her sister's arm. 'What's the schedule again?'

'Winner announced at the annual European marketing trends conference in Tuscany next spring, then presented with the trophy by the makers of the product at the International Trends Summit in Hawaii a month or so later.'

'In Hawaii. Wow,' said Helen. 'Well you do this interview for me, and maybe I'll see if I can cadge some tickets to the Tuscany thing.'

'Yes, well, I'll think about it. Otherwise I'll just have to make myself into a millionaire by next year, Rodney, and then we'll all be able to go to Hawaii. I might even take mum too.'

'Well it'd be her or me – both would be a disaster. And one of us would have to stay here to mind the shop for you,' Helen paused. 'You know, whoever you most trust to look after it properly?' She stood waiting for Sadie to realise what she was asking, but her sister didn't respond. Helen was surprised to find herself disappointed. That was the second time.

Sadie and their mum were definitely becoming a tight little unit. No place for Helen – no permanent place anyway. Helen was lost in thought.

'You know she and Mr Rosebery are on the rocks?' Sadie added.

'When did she tell you that?' Helen asked.

'This morning – she's even coming back early from her bowls trip. They've had a tiff.'

'Oh god, that means she'll start bringing her waifs and strays into the house again. Time for me to decamp back to Clapham.'

'You're welcome anytime – and so is she,' Sadie said. 'Me *cassava-root* e su *cassava root*,'

'What?!'

'Mi casa es su casa – I was trying to be witty. Oh well it nearly worked.'

'No it didn't,' replied Helen, but she couldn't help laughing. 'Let's leave the languages to your daughters – you and I are both rubbish! If you're not going to be a millionaire anytime soon, you stick to running the shop, the home, being a fabulous mother and cooking... what exotic dish are we having again tonight?'

'Chips,' said Sadie. 'For you, anyway.'

'No thanks, sis. I have to shift these extra few pounds I've put on – made up entirely of your cookies and chips and carrot cake. I've got a lot of work ahead of me – I have to go find some real people – ones who are very good at forgiving ex's and I think I'll start looking in Clapham.'

Just then the store opened and a couple of smart looking ladies came tentatively in, holding what looked like a home-made leaflet with a big close-up picture of eye wrinkles. Sadie spied them and made a face.

'Looks like Abi will be in trouble again – she won't be getting any Quorn Casserole and Minky beans tonight if those leaflets are what I think they are,' teased Helen. 'not that I had *anything* to do with it you understand. I'm off now.'

'See you later sis, and keep in touch, ok?' Sadie said, and went to greet the ladies.

And with that, Helen left Sadie to it. She had an appointment to keep and a whole load of whoop-ass to sort out before her next column's deadline. But at least things were on the right track. And with a bit of luck, Tuscany could well be on the cards next spring.

'Helen wants to take you where for your birthday?' asked Grace, one February morning. The frost was crisp on the ground outside and Sadie had just come in from scraping off the car windscreen, completely bedecked in woolly gloves, hat, scarf, a huge coat and thick socks up over her boots.

'T-T-Tuscany,' she shivered, teeth still chattering.

'Come here,' said Grace, taking her grown up daughter's hands in her own and lifting them to her mouth.

'Wh-what are you doing?' Sadie asked.

'I'm going to "her" on them,' the older lady replied.

'*Mum?*' asked Sadie incredulously.

'Yes, let me show you,' and she filled her lungs and breathed out hard onto Sadie's frozen glove-covered fingertips. '*Herrrrrrrrr,*' she went.

'You're mad, mother,' said Sadie, laughing, 'Works though – a bit. Do the other one. Now only my thumbs are frost-bitten.' She could still see her breath in the chill morning air that had followed her in through the back door.

'About time you got that awful ex-husband of yours to fork out for a holiday for the girls as well, Sadie. Or at least contribute. He's barely giving you anything nowadays – your bank statements are starting to look like him – pale and pasty again.' Grace let go of Sadie's hands and bit hard into the slice of toast she'd been eating – it made a dramatic crunch. 'Make him pay more.'

'Mum, you know he's got to answer to Yvette nowadays, and as much as I'd love to "make" him, at least he's having the girls every other weekend.'

'*Nearly* every other weekend.'

'Anyway, I think the holidays will be down to me. It is years since we last went to Center Parcs though. Oo – tummy rumble – I'm hungry.'

Grace shoved the last bit of toast into Sadie's mouth – but Sadie just stood there with it half in, half out, as if she wanted to spit it out but couldn't grip it with the big gloves, then made a face and chomped into it anyway, whilst flicking her hands to remove the gloves. Grace then handed her a steaming hot mug of something muddy-looking, and Sadie cupped it gratefully.

'What about camping? That's not too costly, if they'd agree,' said Grace. 'I'd take them myself if you hadn't put them off for life – you didn't *have* to tell them that story about being gassed in a yurt. Ziggy only left the woodburner closed that one night, darling – the man at the A&E gave us all a clean bill of health the next morning. Said you and Helen were the fittest ten and five year olds he'd ever seen. It was all those outdoor activities, see?' Grace stopped when she saw Sadie's look. 'I thought we used to have fun! Didn't we? In the old days when you and Helen were little? When I was with Ziggy? Or was it Zen? And of course then there was that summer at Glastonbury with Earthman and his gypsy caravan – can you call them *gypsy* nowadays or is that too un-TCP...? Stop looking at that brochure and listen to me, Sadie. We had fun, didn't we? '

'Yes mother, we had fun. But a kids' holiday nowadays has very different demands. It involves wi-fi and satellite TV and room service type fun.' Sadie unwound her huge scarf from her neck, got tangled and had to be rescued by Grace.

'Look, let's see what happens once this money from my ISA comes through,' her mother continued. 'Assuming there's not something in the small print that prevents it. It won't last forever but I know you'll pay me back if you get it.'

'*When* I get it,' Sadie said, 'not *if*. This trip to Tuscany might inspire the marketing genius inside me.'

'I thought that was Mister Hugh? Haha... Oh don't look at me like that darling, it's not in front of the girls! Anyway, I thought we were all buying you some posh handbag for your birthday?'

'Helen said she's been given some freebie tickets by someone she knows who can't go – hotel included. All she's got to buy are the Simple-Jet flights. Might be inspirational, you know, all those keynote speakers – handy in case I can re-start evening classes again in September.'

'With a different tutor this time?'

'Yes. With a different tutor.'

'One you're not shagging on a regular basis?'

'Mum! And it's an *irregular* basis if you must know.'

'Sounds like *I've* had more sex than *you* have this year,' said Grace. *Eurgh.* Sadie made a mental note never to try to out-crude her mother, the older lady would always win. 'Anyway, where is Helen?' Grace asked. 'She never gets in touch much these days.'

'She's over in New York, again, Mum. And you're both as bad as each other – I keep telling you, you could contact *her*, you know that. Abi can teach you how to Skype one day, then you'll have no excuse.'

'Oh don't you start – it's bad enough with the girls forever playing games on that *Egg-Box* – it's as much as I can do to get them to watch the occasional Kardashians with me. Abi's been on that old computer of yours morning noon and night, and Georgia's just as bad. Whatever happened to a good old family evening together – with everyone ignoring each other in front of the *telly*, instead?'

Sadie just shook her head and smiled. Her mother continued. 'Thank goodness for Herb, Phyllis's ex, you know. He's been telling me about his time as a... Sadie, you're thinking about something else again are you?'

'Sorry mum, you reminded me of something I meant to tell you. I had that CAP man, Mr Percy in the store again yesterday – he lectured me for another hour and a half on the rudiments of advertising law and permissible claims procedures and smallprint font sizes and ...'

'Sweetie, I'm just hearing bleurgh-bleurgh-bleurgh now, just cut to the important bit.'

'Well, then he wondered if I was single.'

'He what?'

It had been the biggest surprise of the year so far, given how humdrum and routine her love life with Damian had become.

'So what did you say?' Grace asked. Sadie told her.

In her shock at Mr Percy's question, Sadie had actually said 'yes'. Then 'no'. Then *depends who's asking* – just trying to make light of it, but he hadn't laughed. Instead, he'd left with a firm 'no', a flea in his ear and a stony look on his face.

Grace rolled her eyes. 'Darling! Any port in a storm – why not try him out – maybe you could sample Mr Percy's wares, so to speak.'

Eurgh. 'No, mum. He's a bit creepy. Crystal used to call him 'Mr Pervy'.'

'Well, now I'm investing in your shop perhaps I'd better spend more time there, I'll soon keep an eye on him.' Grace narrowed her eyes at Sadie. *Oh-Oh... Sadie thought.* Then it came. 'So are you and Damian together now, then? Or what?' she asked. There it was, and off she went, like she'd been waiting for the right moment. 'He's got a proper job, and that big house. Lot to be said for a guy with his own big house like that. Mind you, I did think the writing was on the wall at Christmas time when he went away to his aunt's instead of being with you.'

Sadie just shrugged. She'd thought the same, actually. Sadie had spent most of Christmas being fed up and eating. But he'd come back in the New Year full of enthusiasm and for a while things had improved.

Obviously not improved enough to prevent Sadie unwittingly admitting to being single.

Just lately her supposed boyfriend had been spending more and more time in the room with dark walls. More and more time playing with NervadaQueen and co., she guessed. And afterwards, the very last thing he seemed to feel like was playing with Sadie. The last time her sex life had gone down the pan like this, exactly the same thing had happened – the pounds had gone up and the passion had gone down. Vicious circle. Too many curves can't have helped Stuart's ardour. All of Helen's borrowed designer gear had been consigned to the back of the wardrobes again. Not that Sadie was bothered – she'd still not quite mastered the art of not falling over every five minutes. Now, Sadie was full time back in jeans. Stretch jeans. With elasticated waists.

'I think I'm a bit jaded with men at the moment,' Sadie admitted, picking up her rucksack and looking for her keys. 'Me and Helen both. Sounds like she needs this Tuscany trip as much as I do. It's a nice birthday present – we can find some Italian men to sweep us off our feet.'

'Yes, well if you *do* go with her, try and make sure YOU find someone who lasts longer than five minutes – don't take a leaf out of your sister's books. That bald bloke at Christmas was a nightmare.'

'Oh Mum. She just needed company,' said Sadie, still searching for her keys. Although the Australian from Clapham whom Helen had invited over for Boxing Day was very short-lived. 'She's just had bad luck, choosing the wrong guys.'

'Bad luck? What happened to making your own luck?' Grace said, slyly. Sadie rolled her eyes. 'Well anyway, Tuscany trip or no Tuscany trip, more important will be what *Damian* does for your birthday. It's always a bit of a litmus thingy isn't it – how much will he spend, where will he take you. Indicates his commitment doesn't it. I remember being treated to a piece of a meteorite by one of my boyfriends in the early days – Gemini I think his name was.'

'That's quite impressive,'

'Not really, his brother was called Pod.'

'Not his name, I mean the present. Imaginative. Romantic.'

'Yes well, it really impressed me, until I found out it was a piece of tarmac from the motorway he was helping to build. No darling – let's hope this year you get treated the way you deserve to be treated,' Grace said with a flourish, spotting the keys and handing them to Sadie. 'And if not, kick him into touch,'

Kick them all into touch, thought Sadie.

She pondered the subject on her way to work through the frost and the bitter cold air. It had actually been quite nice without having to worry about being with Damian as often, over the last month or so – she'd spent some quality time with the kids, which they'd appreciated. Georgia had taken to keeping her room tidy, and Abi had done some fabulous online work for the shop, on health message boards and blogs – Grace was right, she was never off that old computer, now that Sadie had her new Mac. *And* she'd got it by biting the bullet and doing that interview, which she was very proud of. And the article in the local press had followed. And the extra attention had worked for a while. If only there was some way of getting another big PR lift. And with all this, no time to worry about Damian.

So it was time. Now Sadie needed to think about Sadie – she'd been working long hours and felt really tired. She was looking forward to the trip to Italy. She might have to travel there on a cheapo flight, but looking at the brochures for the hotel, the conference centre and the tourist attractions, Tuscany was gorgeous. There was even an old ruins nearby to explore, and a vineyard to visit, run by a local family who'd been in the area for centuries. She could sightsee a bit, drink wine a bit, and be a geek for a bit. Maybe this trip was just what she needed.

Meanwhile Stateside, Helen's trip to New York was precisely what she *didn't* need. The TV show was going to be live that afternoon, and Helen's latest interviewee had got last minute nerves, had thrown up in the toilet and wouldn't come out. Even Sadie's faltering debut last year would have been preferable to this. The boss, Mr Adams, was stomping about breathing fire, making all kinds of threats, puffing manically on his electronic cigarillo and uttering unintelligible expletives under his breath. Helen was thinking it was about time she threw in the towel with this column-writing lark. It was mayhem.

'Anyone,' Kate was saying on Helen's mobile, 'Just book anyone. Find someone, fast. Seriously, we only get the studio time till four o'clock and if your guest isn't here by two forty five, Kim will throw a tantrum.'

'Bloody Kim,' Helen whispered back. No-one could hear her but she still whispered. *God forbid* she should be caught slagging off the company's biggest money-spinner, Kim Kardigan. Since last summer when Helen had started the column, the B-Lister had become more and more A-List, with spin-offs and merchandising deals coming out of her ears. She struck lucky with one unhinged guest's live breakdown, which had gone viral. And now one complete channel was dedicated entirely to her infomercials, selling her endorsed products – from fashion to jewellery to cutesy collectable dolls. The viewers thought she was lovely, a girl-next-door. But once the red light was off, she was a Grade A Bitch.

Helen was standing in the foyer of the huge skyscraper. The studio complex was housed on the twenty-fifth floor. Behind her stood a life-size cut-out of *KiKa* as she was 'affectionately' known. Around the cut-out, a gaggle of oversized American ladies wearing oversized identical KiKa necklaces, earrings and rings, were all taking photos of themselves, dwarfing the diminutive star's cardboard image.

'Helen, honey, this is serious,' Kate continued. 'Mr A will have your head on a plate and I'll look stupid 'cos this is the second time this year. And Shirelle in bookings says your next week's guest has just cancelled, and Promo's had just finished cutting the trailer. Why didn't you tell me that Ashton hadn't signed the consent forms before you filed the piece with the editorial desk?'

'Because I thought I could fix it.' Kate looked at her watch and shook her head, peering out towards the pavement through the huge, rain-soaked glass window panes – just in case her absentee guest had had a sudden change of heart. She was becoming nothing more than a glorified guest-booker in the shadow of KiKa's rising star. 'I wanted to fix it myself.'

'Babe, one day, you have to realise it's ok to ask for help,' Kate said. 'Oops, gotta go – my next piece to camera is about to roll. Bye.'

'Bye,' said Helen to a dead phone line.

Ask for help. Helen shuddered. She'd rather kiss KiKa's pert little tushy. The last time she'd asked for help, look what had happened. Nope, apart from Sadie, she'd rather go it alone. Like she always had. And even her sister hadn't quite needed her the same way these past months, so she'd reciprocated, giving her the space she'd demanded, going home less and less. *So where exactly is home now?*

Outside, the grey dismal New York February was filling the world with a desolate haze, everyone shuffling around miserably, everyone in shades of grey – a light grey day in a dark grey city. The hot-dog stand outside was doing a roaring trade with those unable to resist, as his sizzling food and steaming coffee heated their hands and filled their bellies, and his banter warmed their hearts – for some lonely New Yorkers, his greeting was the only non-work-related conversation they had all day.

Helen suddenly felt very tired. She remembered a time when a showery day had been an excuse to don wellies and run through the New York rain laughing, sharing an umbrella with the man she'd loved. A man who betrayed her – in more ways than one. She sighed as the 'KiKa-Klan' pushed past her to squeeze through the revolving doors, overjoyed to have been photographed with their idol. *If only they knew that the cut-out is probably more three-dimensional than the real thing*, thought Helen.

As the doors revolved, and the large, jolly ladies went out one way, a familiar figure entered the foyer the other way, and came face to face with Helen.

Oh my god.

'Well if it isn't Helen Todd,' said the man, tall, impressive and incredibly well-dressed – Italian gear all the way, with leather wherever it was possible to have it, including his designer jacket and pointed European shoes.

'Day! Damian Grant! My old friend! It's you, isn't it! As I live and breathe!' she said, running over to him and hugging him.

'How the devil are you?' he asked, beaming at her. 'I haven't seen you since… it all happened. With Victor.'

'Yes well, I'll be fine, if… if you can possibly do me a favour,' said Helen, talking quickly and thinking even faster. 'And it'll only take half an hour – can you help me? You owe me after all.'

Two hours later, Helen had successfully averted a crisis of the nuclear kind with her boss, who suddenly became very impressed that the subject of Helen's next column, and the live interviewee on that afternoon's KiKa show, was none other than one of the most eligible men on the New York circuit, and one of the chief partners at Winston, Winston and Grant.

Damian Grant had then asked – no, he'd insisted – on whisking Helen off to a lovely little coffee bar he'd found, having cancelled his afternoon appointments, telling them all – within Helen's earshot – that it was because he *'had something far, far more important to attend to with someone very dear.'* She glowed – he'd been one of her best friends when they'd risen through the ranks of the marketing industry many years before. They'd lost touch, and she hadn't seen him for ages, until he'd tracked her down three years ago and offered her a job in his brother's department, within Winston, Winston and Grant.

But as a Director, Damian travelled a lot, and hadn't been around when the shit had hit the fan early last year.

'Well I, for one, would re-employ you on the spot. I'd have argued with the board, why didn't you contact me?'

'I was ashamed,' she said, honestly. 'I felt I'd let you down. Plus I didn't think your brother would be so keen,' Helen replied. 'I tried to fix it myself. Boy did I try. Called him loads to reason with him afterwards – but you know what he's like. I was continually told he was busy – he was in one long meeting from about the end of April till the middle of May as far as I could tell. Can't blame him really.'

'Well, I can. My brother's a fool.'

'I wish everyone else thought like you. They all think *I* was the fool.'

'Well you were! A bit – you knew what you were getting yourself into, yet you still did it. Typical Helen.'

'Yes,' Helen admitted, 'I suppose in retrospect ignoring all their advice and declaring to the world that Victor had changed was a bit rash. He'd been the same all his life, it turned out, so what difference could I make.'

'Well if it helps any, Victor's not had an easy time of it since. If you think your boss was always a micro-manager to all you staff – well you should see what's been happening in their home – 24/7.' He paused and stared at her. 'I hear they've even got a camera in the *john*.'

Helen laughed and he beamed at her.

'That's better. You're still beautiful, HellsBells,' he said, 'and smart – you were always smart. Apart from this one time, where you were pretty dim. Pretty much like a dim light bulb in dim city on Annual Dim Night.'

'Ok, ok,' she laughed, 'I get the point! And you're not clever – or witty – or funny. So there.' Helen looked at her old friend pensively. 'Shame you and I never worked out, you know. You'd have been my perfect match. If you'd been straight.'

'Or you'd been male.'

'We'd have been happily married with the picket fence, two kids and a Beagle.'

'A Labradoodle,' Damian Grant said.

'No, a Beagle – like Snoopy,' Helen said. 'We'd have been the perfect American family.'

'We would,' he agreed, and reached across for her hand and squeezed it. He didn't let go. 'And what about that family of yours back in *Surreh*?'

'Your accent's still rubbish,' she said, and told him all about her sister's latest update, the confusion over Damian Hugh last summer and the upcoming trip to Tuscany.

'Ahh yes, the European conference – that Tuscany event was on the agenda I was sent for the last board meeting – I didn't make that one either. We'll be sending over a scout or something I guess. Always keen on new talent. Especially when we've lost one of the best we ever had.' He smiled at Helen and she leaned her head against his shoulder briefly.

'Thanks Day.'

'It's true. Anyway, sounds like you're looking after your little sis, as ever, Helen. What would she do without you?'

'Actually, she's already doing it. And the most exciting bit's about to happen. She doesn't know it yet, but there's a little surprise for our Sadie when we reach sunny Tuscany next month. And if it goes as I suspect, it'll either be the best thing, or the worst thing – or the last thing – she'll ever let me do.'

They finished catching up, drank the last of the delicious coffees, and Helen gave her old pal a big, big hug.

'Goodbye, *old bean,*' Damian Grant said.

'No-one says that anymore! I'm going to get you an English phrase book!'

'And I'm going to get you one that will help you translate Gay-Straight/Straight-Gay... 'Cos let's face it – you need one! In fact, let's walk back via the bookshop – and maybe you can get yourself an Italian one in there too. Or maybe you could get an Italian. Preferably tall, dark and able to speak *"Helen".*'

Helen laughed.

'See? That's better? New York isn't so bad. All you needed was a little down-time with your old friend. And Hells?' he asked. 'Have you seen where we are?'

She looked up and saw for the first time, the sign on the door which she'd missed as they came in. The coffee shop was called '*The Real Central Perk*'.

'You finally found it!' she said, beaming.

'I finally found it. Now it's your turn. Get out there and find whatever it is that's missing. If anyone can do it, Helen Parker-Todd can.'

CHAPTER SEVENTEEN

The air was warm as the doors to the cabin opened, and Sadie and Helen stepped out onto the staircase leading down from their plane onto the runway at Pisa airport. The plane had parked a long way from the terminal and it was a fair old walk. Sadie sniffed the wonderful aroma of foreign air and followed Helen down the steps to the waiting bus, for the short trip across to the terminal.

Within an hour they were on their way to the International Trends Conference, Europe, and within three hours, they were registered, checked in, and dressed up to the nines ready for the first night Gala Reception. Their hotel was too far to walk, so they arrived in a taxi and as they pulled up outside the venue, Sadie looked around at the super-glamorous people – hundreds of them – and felt so nervous she could hardly speak. She practically tripped out of the cab, so Helen gave her an arm to hold on to, to walk up the few steps to the foyer of the luxurious conference centre for the start of their three day event.

'What did Damian say, by the way, when you told him about this early birthday treat from me?' asked Helen, as she waited in line, holding their tickets and her sister's arm.

'I, er, didn't,' Sadie replied. 'He was too busy telling me he couldn't see me 'cos he was going to be away this weekend, with his...'

'Don't tell me – with his aunt?' Helen interjected.

'Yes,' Sadie said, shaking her head. 'All weekend – he's helping her with some sort of project or other.'

'What type of project?' asked Helen. 'He can't mend things, I've never heard of him doing any gardening, he's not exactly a Mister Fixit. He's no Kate. So unless his aunt wants to travel to the Wilderness of Vagrabor, he's obviously lying. Or just baking her yet another veggie curry.'

'How did you know about the Wilderness of Vagrabor?'

'I didn't – I just made it up. Does it exist?' Helen said.

'No – hah! Got you!' Sadie joked, gripping her sister's arm as she almost tripped again bursting out laughing at her own joke. 'It's probably the veggie curry, you're right. The only thing he ever cooks me. Even if it is the best.' They both exchanged glances, then shuffled along another few feet. Sadie huffed a little, stopped, and took off one shoe. Helen didn't even bother asking about it.

'But,' she went on, 'what if he rings you, and hears the foreign ring tone?'

'He won't – he's a texter. And I'm turning off my mobile for the majority of this trip. Mum's got all she needs, and Crystal's come back from travelling so in case of emergency she can break... *crystal* – as opposed to break gla...'

'Not funny. I know what you meant, and it's still not funny,' said Helen. 'Hey – don't look now but – over by the far wall – the tall one – he's looking this way, oh my god he's gorgeous!' Helen was doing little jerking motions with her head and eyes indicating the two Italian guys off to her right. Sadie's jaw dropped. And then so did her shoe. Right onto her other foot. Both the Italian guys nudged each other and smiled. They were in another queue, heading in the opposite direction, but their eyes didn't leave the two girls as they slowly moved bit by bit further away.

'*Bagsy* yours is the slightly stocky one,' said Helen, harkening back to the terminology they'd used a couple of decades before. 'Hey, it's like old times – both out on the pull!'

'Well it would be, but I'm not single, so I'm not technically out on the pull,' said Sadie.

'Aw Sade, come onnnn,' said Helen, 'What stays in Tuscany and all that?'

'No! Honesty is the best policy.'

'Yeah, maybe I should have got *that* tattooed on your backside instead of the Chinese symbol for "available",' Helen said begrudgingly.

Sadie laughed. '*Quick Crispy Duck*, you mean? Serve me right for going to a Cockney-Chinese tattooist!'

'See, now you've lost me completely. There's no point trying to crack clever jokes that not even Einstein would get, because...'

'*Scusi,*' came a voice.

Both girls glanced up sharply. Sadie found herself looking into the deepest brown eyes she'd ever seen. Out of the corner of her eye, she glimpsed Helen's jaw hitting the floor – her gaze fixed on the taller guy who was standing next to the stocky one who was mesmerising Sadie.

Neither of the sisters replied.

'I am so sorry to bother you, but we wondered if you are also here for the Paleo-Astronomy conference – are you fellow academics?' Brown Eyes said.

And with that one line, Sadie was hooked.

She looked at Helen and tried to catch her eye, but gave up since Helen was grinning at the guys like a Cheshire cat.

'The... Paleo-what-now?' asked Helen.

'Ah, that means you aren't. Well that is a shame, as Francesco and I, we would have been honoured to have you join us at our table,' the taller guy said. 'To practise our English.' He paused. 'Maybe we can meet up again after the dinner – you are at another event here, this weekend?'

'Yes,' Helen said, 'it's the Marketing one – the big one – lots of people. International. We're in marketing.'

'And we're in paleo-astronomy,' said the stocky guy, Francesco.

'Is that a thing?' asked Helen.

'Yes,' said Francesco, 'it's a thing.'

Sadie spoke up for the first time, a flush creeping up her neck. 'Isn't that all about the identification of ancient prehistoric constellations that have never been identified as such before, by science?'

Sadie became aware that both men were now open-mouthed, and Helen's eyebrows were raised so high they almost met her hairline.

'Well, now, how rare to find someone who knows. Yes, it is indeed. We are lecturers,' Francesco replied, stepping slightly closer to Sadie. But then the taller guy spoke. 'Pardon but, we must go,' he said, noticing that another man was waving to them to re-join their line before it turned the corner. 'Maybe we will see you in the bar later? It is on the rooftop.' His gaze lingered on Helen, who was clearly besotted. Francesco elbowed him.

'Come Alessandro. See you this evening, we hope, ladies, when we can discuss more, *the ancient stars*,' he was looking right at Sadie, who was looking right back. 'Ciao.'

'Ciao,' both girls said together, grinning inanely.

Then the two men walked away and disappeared round the corner.

'I shouldn't be surprised really, should I,' Helen said. 'Don't tell me, you memorised the brochure for the venue.'

'Yes, I googled it. They're probably from the uni in Milan which offers the courses in paleo...'

'It's ok, stop now. So – Francesco, you. And Alessandro, me – that's all the info I need,' interrupted Helen.

Sadie sighed, looking longingly over to where the men had disappeared. 'But I can't. You have them both, Hells. I've already got a man. My one's back in the UK. With his aunt.'

Sadie expected some quick retort, but nothing came. Helen was staring at something. Sadie followed her gaze and then gasped.

'I think you'll find that "your" man is most definitely *not* in the UK. And THAT is most definitely NOT his aunt,' said Helen.

There, across the cavernous hallway, some distance away and dressed to kill, in a dicky bow and dinner suit, was Damian.

And there, in a purple cocktail dress, facing away, laughing with the couple standing on the other side of her, but holding Damian's arm, was Delta bloody Smartypants.

Damian's gaze met Sadie's, and he did a double take and stopped dead in his tracks. He was holding a ticket the same as theirs, which he nearly dropped. He looked dapper. Sadie had never seen him look so smart. She'd also never seen him go so pale.

Sadie's reality fell apart in that instant and her heart dropped through the floor like a stone.

Another liar.

Another liar, other liability, another let down.

She was rooted to the spot, unable to breathe. He moved first, bent down and whispered in Delta's ear, who appeared not to have seen Sadie and Helen yet. Then she nodded, and went the other way leaving him alone. He tugged a little at his dicky bow, and then started walking towards them.

Helen was building up for an explosion. 'Want me to handle him, Sade?' she fumed.

'No,' Sadie said calmly, surprised at her own icy self-control. 'Would you excuse us?'

Helen made a face. 'Are you bloody joking?'

'No, seriously – I lied to him as well, about where I was. I need to handle this my way. Alone.'

Helen went to protest.

'My way!' Sadie said, firmly. Helen made a motion, as if to say *well go right ahead* and folded her arms. Sadie walked towards Damian and met him half way. He nodded. She narrowed her eyes at him.

'Clearly you're not at home this weekend,' he said, a slight redness on his neck.

'Clearly you're not at your aunt's.'

'So, we both told a porky didn't we,' was all he could say.

'I didn't say where I was going actually, Damian. You just assumed it would be at home, and I didn't correct you. There's a difference.' He opened his mouth to talk but Sadie kept going. 'I just omitted to fill you in – and you didn't ask, so it's not technically lying. So now, here I am on an early birthday treat from my sister – whilst you're clearly NOT... what did you say? *"Helping your aunt with a project?"* Are you?' she said menacingly.

Sadie's voice was level, her breathing shallow and under control, hands on hips, feet slightly apart. *The danger stance.*

Echoes of a similar situation with Stuart four years ago hung like thunder above her head, and unfortunately for Damian, the incident had forged the radio-active neural pathways in her brain which were pinging away like crazy, ready for a fight. *Another betrayal.*

'What's *your* excuse?' she asked. 'For outright lying?'

The challenge was clear, and it hung in the air – she could almost see the cogs in his head whirring, clunking, working out the best response.

'Haven't got one,' he said. 'I lied. I'm sorry, Sadie, truly I am.'

Sadie wasn't prepared for that one. She felt a tear prickle at the back of her eyes but refused to let it materialise. Not this time.

'Well, at least you're being honest. So what *are* you actually doing here?'

'Delta entered the competition. She got through.'

Sadie felt a kick in the pit of her stomach. That hurt more than the lying. She felt as though a lead weight had plunged straight through her abdomen and out of her feet. *Delta's work had been good enough, it seemed – but Sadie's hadn't.* 'No wonder you put me off entering – for more reasons than one.'

'Yes, well, I didn't know back then that she'd get through, did I. Let alone invite me to be her plus-one. I guess *you're* Helen's.'

Silence.

He continued, 'Delta's very talented, she'll go far.'

'Not helping.'

'She wanted me here to continue my mentoring, in case she...'

'Mentoring?' Sadie interrupted. 'You're still claiming not to be having an affair then? At least do me the honour of not lying about that!'

'I'm *not* sleeping with Delta. Really I'm not. I know how important honesty is to you, Sadie, that's why I didn't lie just now. If I had been shagging Delta, I'd have owned up – for the very same reason. But I haven't been. Honest.'

'Well lately, you haven't even been "shagging" me, as you so eloquently put it. So it wouldn't surprise me if you *are* telling the truth.'

'I am being honest, Sadie. In any case if you really want to know, whilst we're talking home truths – you haven't seemed comfortable with yourself since you put on weight and...' he stopped, looking warily at Sadie's fist which was clenching and unclenching at her side. 'Er... Not helping?' he asked.

She just glared and shook her head slowly, murder in her eyes.

Then he carried on. 'And anyway, Delta got here all off her own back – completely under her own steam – she entered, she got through. I gave her some advice, but that was all. Plus, we're in a twin bedded room not a double and...'

'You're sharing a *bedroom*?' Sadie said. 'How on earth does *that* work?'

'I had to – to be the plus one. Otherwise it'd have been too expensive and I couldn't have come. I didn't have the cash to pay for another hotel room – have you seen the places they put you up in? They're extortionate.'

This from the guy with the big house and the Ferrari. Something didn't compute.

'See, I was saving up – to take you to Rome for your birthday...' He blurted the last bit out.

Sadie felt the tears come like a flood now. *What a mess.*

'Oh rubbish. Sod off Damian,' she cried, 'Just sod off!' And she turned and ran towards the Ladies' Bathroom, acknowledging her sister with a look as she passed her by. Helen had a face like thunder and looked fit to burst.

'Sadie,' Damian called out, 'I'm sorry... let's have a drink later for old times' sake...!'

But the words had no impact – they were hollow, they were meaningless.

Just like men were, thought Sadie, as she buried herself in a wad of tissues in a cubicle, and fought back the sobs that were desperate to escape, holding on to them tightly until she'd regained her composure.

So he'd lied about this weekend. Was it possible he was also really lying about Delta? They *were* sharing a room, after all – perhaps they didn't have twin beds. Maybe he was lying about that too.

And maybe – more importantly – he'd lied from the start about Sadie's ability. Perhaps that's what all that whispering in the classroom had been about – before Sadie had left his course, postponing it till next year when maybe it wouldn't feel so awkward – postponing it so she could focus on saving her shop.

Perhaps Sadie's work really *was* good – just like Helen had said. Damian must have been scared that Sadie would beat Delta, that's why he said she wasn't good enough.

A cold wash of realisation hit Sadie like a wake-up call.

Helen had been right all along.

Sadie felt so guilty for brushing off her sister's encouragement in favour of a man who didn't care. In fact, right now he looked like he couldn't give a rat's ass about Sadie's ability – or her future.

But Helen could. She'd always looked out for Sadie and now Sadie was going to look out for Helen. No longer would Sadie be the weaker one in need of help. From now on, she'd share the burden. And if that meant swallowing her pride and not running away – remaining here for the whole weekend – then if Helen wanted her to do it, she'd do it.

Even if it meant having to suffer the ignominy of seeing Delta-friggin'-Bitch-face carry off the coveted award she herself had wanted so desperately. The trip to Hawaii. The award which, if she'd won it, would have had the potential to change her life and provide the escape she so badly needed... Was she strong enough? *Could she stay and watch? Hold her head high?*

Sadie walked out of the cubicle to find a curious attendant and a worried Helen standing nearby. Sadie nodded to Helen, who looked relieved. Then Sadie walked to the mirror and looked at her reflection as if she was seeing herself for the very first time.

And suddenly, she quite liked what she saw.

She felt a fire start burning inside her heart, a fire she knew would take her forward into the future – a future which the universe would decide. A future which she was now finally equipped to face – on her own. An independent woman taking care of herself. And her family. Alone. Who needed to rely on a bloody man, anyway?

Sadie touched up her makeup and zipped up her smart red handbag then turned to Helen, who was just observing, at her side.

'Ready sis?' Sadie asked. Helen brightened. It was like she knew. She could tell. Helen grinned.

'Let's go,' said Sadie, smiling full beam at the attendant and leaving her some coins in the little tray on a ledge.

'This Gala Reception can't be over soon enough. What floor did those guys say the bar was on?' Sadie asked as she and Helen headed towards the Gala Reception.

'Rooftop. All the way,' said Helen, still smiling.

CHAPTER EIGHTEEN

Helen was glowing with pride. The Gala Reception had indeed gone by quite quickly and Sadie raced her to the rooftop. Not only did Helen have the bravest sister in the whole world, she now also had one of the most handsome men in the whole world, like, *ever* – paying her close attention. He was her very own Diet Coke Break. Plus they were in a picturesque rooftop bar on a warm evening, in one of the most beautiful places she had ever been in her whole life.

And Helen had been to some fabulous places.

'And what did you do once you realised there was no turning back,' Alessandro was asking Helen, seeming to be entranced by her stunning repartee and wit. At least it felt that way, even if the repartee had been more than a little influenced by the champagne they'd drunk earlier, to celebrate Sadie's new found chustzpa...chushtpa... chuzztpah... balls.

Helen had balls once. Would she ever have them again? She was actually quite enjoying being every inch a woman, at the moment. It was a weird old world.

'To be honest...' said Helen, continuing her story about Victor but holding the crucial bit back. She was never truly honest – with anyone – including her sister Sadie. But with a bit of luck, this wasn't the weekend when Sadie would find that bit out... Was it?

Sadie meanwhile, was nearby, looking quite intense, listening to Francesco as he gesticulated wildly and pointed to the stars. Every so often, she would lean in and angle her ear as if to hear more clearly, and then laugh out loud, both she and her companion seeming very happy in each other's company on this wonderful night.

A certain Mister Hugh, however, was very much unhappy about it. He'd strolled by their table several times, not once accompanied by Delta. Each time he'd lingered in Sadie's eye line. He'd lingered just a little too long – under the pretext of talking to some acquaintance or waiter. But, like a good girl, so far she'd successfully managed to completely ignore him.

Helen meanwhile was having the evening of her dreams. Alessandro was so handsome. He was totally delicious, and very intelligent, with an earnest manner that was almost exhausting, on his quest to glimpse her innermost feelings. But her innermost bits were innermost for a reason – and some of them had to stay secret. So she filled him in on the New York Fiasco, as she called it, with the same version she told everybody, whenever they asked.

Thought he would change, blah blah… shouted out of the office… never show her face again… couldn't possibly go back after that, etc etc.

He took it all in, then took her hand and looked deeply into her eyes.

'Helen,' he said, a curious lift to the word, as if he was very slightly reprimanding her. 'I hear your story, and I share your view,' he said, 'but I feel that you are not being totally honest with me, even though you say the words.' Helen swallowed. There was something about the way in which he was looking at her, almost as though he could read her thoughts, know her past, feel her pain.

'When you say "to be honest" it is but a phrase, a – how you say – *throw away?*' His command of English was more impressive than her Italian would ever be, the little she knew. Still working through the phrase book she'd got in New York. 'One day, if you want to tell me the full story,' he said tenderly, 'offload the burden you still carry, I would be only too glad to have the honour of receiving that gift.'

His eyes were so dark, so deep, so enticing, Helen thought she would topple into them, and for once in her life, she didn't know what to say.

'Caught me,' she said, sipping the last drops of her champagne and changing the subject. 'Shall we get another bottle?'

'Not for me – I am driving – Francesco likes the luxury of a hotel, but my family have a vineyard not too far from here. There is a wonderful ruined abbey on the hillside nearby – can you see it?' and he leaned his head closer to hers to point out where he meant, in the distance in the setting sun. 'It is full of legend and romance. A very beautiful place. Very beautiful…' he said, turning to her, his face close now.

Helen felt as though with those words he was serenading her, even though there was no music, his lilting accent carried its own tune and she was transfixed, staring at his mouth.

'…if you are not doing anything tomorrow evening,' he continued, 'I would like to drive you there. Would you care to accompany me? After the day's activities?' he asked her. 'I can have the kitchen prepare a picnic, by moonlight – what do you say?'

'I'm not sure – my sister…' she said, looking over. But then she saw how animated Sadie was, attentively listening to Francesco's stories, being watched by Damian standing ten feet away. *She knows he's there.* Helen remembered the fire burning brightly in Sadie's eyes – the fire of independence. *Let me do it my way…*

Kicking off her heels, Helen leaned back to admire the view, and signalled the waiter for some more champagne. Lots more.

'That sounds lovely, Alessandro,' Helen replied. 'Yes please. You can take me anywhere you like.'

The next day Sadie dressed more simply and didn't trip up once on their way back to the venue. Helen seemed far away. But then so did half the people standing in the coffee area as they all filed in for the start of the day's activities. There was a distinct morning-after feeling around the conference room as blurry-eyed delegates took their places in the re-organised main hall, this time with all the chairs facing forwards instead of arranged around individual tables.

Sadie made sure she and Helen chose seats as far away from Damian and Delta as possible, but had already seen enough to deduce that he must have had a hell of a night. A bad one, if his bloodshot eyes were anything to go by. And if Sadie wasn't mistaken, Miss Smartypants looked like she was none too happy either.

'He must have told her we're here,' whispered Sadie.

'So?' asked Helen, still preoccupied. 'You're not bothered by her, are you? Who is she, anyway?'

'She's nobody,' Sadie said, with a raised eyebrow and a straight back and an energy to her voice that hadn't been there yesterday morning. 'Just some student I used to be in a class with.'

Helen noticed Sadie's demeanour. She looked at her sister enquiringly and Sadie caught her staring, just as the main address began. 'What!?' asked Sadie under her breath.

'You! All glowing. *Some*body had a good night last night with mister paleo-wotsit, did they?' Helen said in a sing song voice.

'I don't know – *did* you? You tell *me*,' Sadie replied, still under her breath. A woman in front of them trying to listen to the speaker, looked back over her shoulder at the source of the voices.

'I would,' said Helen, 'if I could remember all of it. Ok I've woken up now. How did we get home?'

'Well, I shared Francesco's cab back to the hotels,' Sadie answered. 'You? You fell asleep. Alessandro carried you to his car and took you home.'

'Took *me* home?' she asked. 'Why just me?'

'His car's only got two seats. It's a Ferrari.'

'Oh no – not another gas guzzler, I don't believe it!' hissed Helen, making the woman in front turn round and look daggers at her. 'Scusi, scusi,' Helen whispered to her, then leaned towards Sadie. 'I come all the way to Italy and I've copped off with a Boy Racer just like Damian!'

'I think you'll find he's *nothing* like Damian, and his car is a vintage Ferrari apparently – very classy. Might not be very green though.'

'Well, looks like I'll have to examine his carbon footprint at the earliest opportunity...'

The two girls giggled, three more people turned round, and a ginger-haired steward looked directly at them and made a face as if to say 'shush'. Helen shrugged back at him and mouthed '*scusi*'. 'Oh my god it's like being back at school,' she squeaked in the tiniest voice she could muster, which only made Sadie giggle more. They both sat there, shoulders shaking, until the steward walked over to them and bent down apologetically to request that they please remain silent for the opening address.

They turned their attention to the speaker who was finishing his outline of the weekend's events. Sadie didn't need to hear it – in true form she'd already committed most of it to memory.

She knew that, today, the first of two full days of keynote speakers, would be when she needed to focus the most. *Learn, take it all in.* Then next year, come back as a semi-finalist, not a 'plus-one'.

At the end of today, the announcer said, over drinks, there would be a fun marketing event. It was to be a 'blind entry' FlashContest, where you entered under a number instead of a name, to avoid prejudicing the judges. Open to all. Top three announced this evening, winner chosen tomorrow. Good kudos, Sadie imagined, for whoever won it. Also tomorrow – more fascinating insights from more industry experts. Then the grand finale at the end of the day – the eagerly awaited results of this year's International Marketing Magazine Competition – and the winner of the cash prize and the escape to Hawaii – would be announced.

So, no more important speakers after about 3pm.

Sadie calculated that she could probably leave early, and get a flight home which allowed her to get back for the girls' bedtime. Assuming she didn't want to spend the last already-paid-for night in the hotel with Helen. Or with someone else. Or alone, if Helen was with someone else. Or maybe they both would be with someone else. Or maybe they'd both be on the late afternoon flight back to Heathrow. Maybe…

'That's interesting,' Helen said, as the speaker finished talking and the applause began.

'What is?' asked Sadie.

'What he just said.'

'What did he just say?' asked Sadie.

'*O.M.Gee, Damian,*' Helen called her, teasing. 'The man on the stage just said they've got an extra prize for the main competition – some investment company has offered an in-depth business analysis as well as the Hawaii thing. BUT – listen to this – there's a bonus prize been donated for this FlashContest as well. And it's been donated by – you'll never guess – the New York agency "Winston, Winston and Grant".'

'Who you used to work for?' asked Sadie.

'Yes, come to think of it, when I was with my Damian – Damian Grant – in New York, he mentioned that his firm had been talking about this conference – it's not unusual for scouts to attend events like this looking for new raw talent they can harness early. Now they've donated a prize fund. And did you hear how much it is?'

'Nope.'

'Ten thousand euros. You've got to enter it!'

Sadie said nothing, lost in her thoughts. The early flight home tomorrow afternoon just got a whole lot less appealing.

Shortly after the day ended, Sadie was in the ladies' room washing her hands – they were covered in ink, as she'd been frantically scribbling away for an hour during the after-conference networking drinks session and had just about had time to submit her entry as the FlashContest closed.

The door opened, Sadie looked up, and she found herself face to face for the first time, with Delta. Her adversary almost turned around to go straight back out again, then changed her mind and stomped into a cubicle.

Sadie suddenly decided that her cuticles needed an extra long scrub and an extra long soak and she was still standing at the basin when Delta came back out again. She took a deep breath, as Sadie watched her in the mirror, and walked over to the sinks. The only one free was the one right next to Sadie.

'Well, hello, Delta,' Sadie said, again proud of the control and carefree lilt to her own voice. 'What brings you here?'

'You.' She bit the word out of the air, but again was surprisingly – and annoyingly, calm.

Sadie wasn't expecting that. 'Oh?' was all she could manage.

'Him showing off about your sketches in our classroom – made me think I could do that. I could do better than that. So I did. You didn't get through did you?'

'Well of course not, I didn't enter.'

'Are you sure?' Delta said, a smile curling over the corners of her mouth.

Sadie was dumbfounded. 'Er, yes, I didn't enter.'

'Why not?'

Sadie knew where this was leading and she wasn't happy about it, but had to reply. 'Because *Mister Damian Hugh*, in all his wisdom, decided I wasn't good enough – so I didn't bother.'

'Why? Why would you listen to him?'

Again Sadie was amazed. She opened her mouth to respond but nothing came out.

'Your work was excellent, bloody excellent, and he knew it. He told me as much. He said that next year, you'd be the best student in the class, and he'd be the one who tutored you.'

Sadie was hearing the words but they all seemed kind of surreal.

'So – so he thought I was g-good...?' Sadie stuttered.

'No,' said Delta, 'he thought you were great.'

Sadie just stood there, the water running over her hands, motionless, her brain going round and round at the meaning of the words she was hearing. 'So why...'

'Because he wanted the glory! Don't you see? You win next year, he can claim it's because of his tuition. I told you he was unreliable.' Delta looked around her to see who was listening, and lowered her voice. 'And did you have a look at his texts? The day I brought his mobile into your shop? Did you? I bet you bloody didn't, you silly woman. Too bloody trusting by half, you are.' Delta began to vigorously scrub her hands, which were also ink-stained.

'What texts? I only saw an email, from some weirdo virtual game person – character – thing...'

'Oh my GOD. Look, he's here supporting me now 'cos I had to invite him. For tutoring me extra. It was after you left. But I don't owe nothing to nobody – I look out for number one in this world. And so should you.' Delta finished washing her own hands, and turned off Sadie's taps for her. Sadie was just staring ahead. Delta passed her a hand towel. 'Here.'

'Thanks. I think.'

'Don't mention it,' she said, then stopped and grabbed Sadie's arm, looked intensely into her eyes and said, 'Seriously, *don't* mention it. What happens in the lav, stays in the lav.' She smiled. 'OK?'

'OK, Sadie said, making up her mind to throw away her rose-tinted spectacles whenever she dealt with men in the future. Any men.

Who'd have thought it. Delta – an ally. Of sorts. Or was this more trouble-making?

Sadie went back out into the conference area, where the chatter in the room was competing with the gentle beat of the background music and the bar seemed a little less well-stocked than earlier.

Helen signalled her over, just as some lady official began blowing into a microphone at the front of the stage.

'You'll never guess what...' Sadie began, loudly.

'Shhhh,' said Helen – and so did about half a dozen other people nearby – including That Woman who was in front of them earlier.

The official told everyone that the FlashContest results were about to be announced. There would be three finalists, with the grand prize being decided tomorrow afternoon, once all the judges arrived. The official then read out the first of the finalists, then the second, and Sadie didn't recognise the names, especially with the woman's thick Italian accent. And then everything went into slow motion. She felt Helen grab her and shake her and scream in a deep, slow motion sort of sound, and the people in front of her – with the exception of That Woman – all turned to congratulate her. This competition was obviously a big deal, within these walls.

'I thought it was only a little informal thing,' uttered Sadie, still shocked.

'Which idea did you enter by the way? Which concept?' asked Helen, still jubilant and patting Sadie on the back. It was open to all delegates, not just beginners, unlike the main competition. Anyway Sadie didn't think that being up against a room full of industry supremos and expert professionals in a FlashContest meant she'd have a cat in hell's chance.

'Oh, funnily enough it was just a variation on a theme, based on one of the sketches from my old folder,' Sadie replied.

'From which folder, when?' Helen said, her face changing slightly.

'From way back when – one of the ones I was going to use for the main competition.'

'Which one?' Helen asked – she'd stopped patting Sadie's back now.

'That one with the...'

'OK, Ladies and Gentlemen,' boomed the M.C. – he'd been handed the mike by the lady official. At least he was easier to understand, with his soft Italian accent but loud Italian voice. 'Now comes the fun part. We've had the FlashContest. Now for a surprise – the FlashPresentation!' Everybody cheered. Except Sadie. 'Each of our industry experts must step up on the stage and tell us how they arrived at their design. So – this is what we want to know – original concept, inspiration – and the critical path to their final design. First, Mrs Sadie Turner.'

Sadie's mind went blank. She flashed a panicked look at Helen who shrugged, and then looked back at the stage. Sadie's tongue went numb, her chest went cold and she thought for one second she was going to faint. Then she looked at her sister, so proud, clapping louder than anybody. And then saw Delta, over the other side of the room, clapping her hand against her kilt-clad thigh whilst holding a wine glass in the other hand, Damian five people away from her, hand in pocket, beer at his lips, shooting Delta daggers. And then Sadie thought of the ten thousand euros and made her way to the stage.

For all her nerves and fear of big audiences, she did a good job.

The aftermath, however, couldn't be more different.

Sadie had given her explanation, got her applause, then the jolly MC had congratulated her, wished her good luck and welcomed the next person to the stage. Before that FlashPresentation had even begun, however, two officials they hadn't seen before, dressed in grey, appeared from the back of the room. One hauled Sadie off in one direction and one hauled Helen off in the other. This was strange. This was very strange indeed.

CHAPTER NINETEEN

Helen was locked away in a back room, now, far from the roaring crowd and the free bar. And Alessandro. She still didn't know how it had ended with him yesterday nor if they would meet later. And now this. Helen was pacing, grimacing, and having a rant. A full blown, force ten, batten-down-the-hatches, take-no-prisoners, chianti-fuelled rant.

'No I WON'T calm down.'

'Look – it's just for the purpose of this statement, we have to know your part in this peculiar situation.' said the woman in the grey suit – with a grey face and a grey personality to match. 'We have to get the facts straight.' Helen hated grey. All shades.

The woman scowled at Helen over the top of her specs – tapping her fingers on the desk and looking haughty. 'Tell me – you are booked in with...' she consulted her notes, '...Mrs Sadie Turner. And now we are faced with a baffling situation, Mrs Parker-Todd. How *did* this happen?' she said in a light Italian accent that was getting stronger the more Helen protested, But protest Helen did. She needed to get out quickly. There was a beautiful picnic and a handsome man somewhere outside waiting. And a sister who was probably having kittens. And it was all Helen's fault. Probably.

Helen sneezed, and felt rising indignation at being stuck here in a bare back room with just a few filing cabinets and a dusty old faux flower arrangement that was more faux than flower. Helen scowled back.

The woman scowled back even more, over the top of her specs, which made Helen laugh.

The woman's face might be grey but the rest of her looked like one of those actresses in a porn film who suddenly changes personality and lets her hair down, whips off her glasses and says *'would you like me to take down anything else, Mr Biddle, sir?'*

Helen couldn't help but smile – full beam. The woman looked irritated, still waiting for her reply. *Don't, Helen, don't – you know it gets you into trouble, don't...* But Helen did. She shrugged, guessing it would wind Grey Woman up – it was a *'Not a clue, what are you asking ME for?'* kind of teenage shrug.

It worked. The woman stopped her little recording gadget with an impatient jab, then started texting someone on her mobile. Helen looked at the clock on the wall – half an hour, she'd been there. And where was Sadie, anyway? Probably in a separate room, so they couldn't collude on their 'story' – not that Sadie would *have* a 'story' – she'd be in there telling the bloody truth as usual – and anyway, if Helen could wangle it, pretty soon they'd realise this whole fiasco was just one whopping oversight. Happily for Helen. And unfortunately for this sadistic woman, who'd soon find out that this off the cuff interrogation by the organisers' team was all a complete waste of time. Yes, that's what would happen – *focus on the positive...* that's what Sadie would do. Although Helen wasn't Sadie.

Sadie wouldn't have started mouthing off to all-and-sundry in broken Italian when they'd first brought her in. Gut reaction, she couldn't help it. *My bad.* And anyway how was she to know that in her attempt at speaking Italian she'd told the ginger steward who was trying to manhandle her that she intended to have sex. She'd meant go on strike. Damn phrase book. *Oh dear.* No more Chianti for you, Helen...

The woman's phone buzzed and the texting continued. She read something, looked up at Helen, back down at the phone and began texting again. Helen sighed, checked her own, but found her mobile had no signal. She had no choice but to wait politely and try to be Sadie. For once.

It didn't last long.

Helen took a deep breath and shot forward across the desk, making Grey Woman jump and lean back a little. Time was pressing, and if she could head this one off at the pass, she might just save the day.

'Right, I'll give you a "statement" – THEN will you get the head honcho in here. OK? No offence, but I don't trust minions. I want to talk to the top – or no deal. Capiche?' At least she knew *that* was the right word. *'Then* they'll see that this is one big accidental mistake!'

'What is a mistake if it is not accidental?' the woman said curtly. Then smiled and shrugged back. *Touché.* Or whatever that was in Italian. 'But these are serious allegations. Reputations are at stake here. And we don't take these things lightly. So, Mrs Parker-Todd, we need to know how there could be two almost identical designs.'

Helen swallowed.

Grey Woman glowered at Helen, checked her watch and then toyed with the little digital voice recorder sitting on the table.

Just then the door opened and another grey suit appeared. This time it belonged to a smart-looking but much older man also with gingery silver hair, leathery skin and an aquiline nose. He was probably related to the ginger steward. He looked down his nose at Helen, like there was a bad smell in the room. Then he nodded at Grey Woman.

'Very well. Tell us your story,' she said to Helen, clicking on her recorder. 'And please be accurate – there's a lot riding on this. Reputations are at stake.'

'No shit, Sherlock,' said Helen. The woman ignored her, and glanced at her colleague, who grimaced.

'Is the information you're about to give us totally relevant?' the man snapped.

'I sure as hell hope so,' Helen replied, sitting herself back down again. 'And you didn't bring that water you said you were going to get me.' He glared at her and Helen glared right back. 'And whilst you're at it, can I please have some more of that delicious meat platter from earlier,' she said, attempting Italian again, to get one up on Grey Woman, and uttered the words 'carne un delitto' to emphasize her point. The man looked at her blankly, then at the woman, who made a *just humour her* face. So Helen tried another sentence, which sent him off in a huff.

'Right, let's begin,' said the woman. 'And by the way, I don't think the bar serves blow-job pasta with a whore sauce, but he'll bring you some nuts instead.' Then she started the recorder.

An hour later, Sadie and Helen were sitting outside the organiser's office finally free to go. Helen had made a promise which she had to keep by midday tomorrow. Not that Sadie knew that. They were side by side, stony faced.

'That was for nothing, then,' said Sadie, her flushed neck and chest just beginning to subside.

'Well, I guess someone just got the wrong end of the stick,' Helen said, shrugging her shoulders encouragingly.

'So if it was a misunderstanding, they've got a funny way of saying "you're free to go." Thirty minutes we've been waiting,' Sadie went on. Helen debated whether to tell her sister what the delay was, and decided against it – she didn't want to put her hopes up. 'I bet Francesco will have given up waiting.'

'He won't,' Helen said. 'He seems really nice.' Helen hoped desperately that her message had got through to Alessandro. She tried to reach out for Sadie's hand, but she moved it slightly away.

Dammit, it's all my fault, trying to interfere yet again. Seriously, after this is over, I keep my nose out, Helen thought.

A different steward this time – a rounder, more jolly looking, dark-haired woman appeared at a door on the other side of the little hall where they were sitting, and said, in an English accent,

'Is either of you Helen with the pain in the butt ex-boyfriend in New York?'

'Yes, that's me,' Helen replied, but how did you...'

'The handsome guy waiting outside the front entrance for you in his flashy car – he told me to say that to identify you. I think he was joking.'

'Maybe,' mumbled Helen, and her heart sank. *That's all he remembers about me, huh?* Maybe her memory of last night was completely different to his. Helen's heart sank a little bit more. But, when she turned to Sadie, and saw her shoulders stooped and her head bowed, she realised her sister's spirits were even lower.

'Sis,' Helen said. 'Do you want me to cancel going out with Alessandro tonight? 'Cos if you like, I can stay with you and...'

'Helen, just go!' snapped Sadie. 'I'll see you back at the hotel room later. Or maybe I won't. In fact, if our candlelit dinner goes well, I'm going to bloody-well ask Francesco if he'll let me stay with *him* tonight.'

'But sis,' the words were out before Helen could stop them, 'don't beg! Men don't like that, they run a mile. He seems so interested, don't put him off. Or talk about your kids on the first date, and don't go on and on about the science of nutrition and mumbo jumbo beans – it's not an attractive trait.'

Sadie bristled. 'And what is? Wearing your fuck-me shoes morning, noon and night and acting dumb?'

'I'm not acting.' There was a pause.

'I'll see you back here in the morning.' Sadie was clearly very angry. 'Now go. I'll sit here for a bit longer to gather my thoughts, if that's ok – plus, after this, I'll definitely find out if I can fly back earlier tomorrow.'

Helen said nothing, just got up to go, then turned around and walked back towards Sadie.

'There's nothing wrong with wearing fuck-me shoes, Sadie,' she said, 'it's when they become "fuck-you" shoes you've got a problem. Don't be that person. And besides, look on the bright side – you never know what tomorrow might bring.' And she stooped towards her sister. Sadie stopped her.

'Actually Helen,' she said, through gritted teeth, 'I've got a pretty good idea about tomorrow. And just so you know – I have never in all my life, been disqualified. From anything. Until now.'

Helen bent down and kissed her sister on the side of the head anyway and left with the jolly woman. 'Make sure she's ok will you?' she said to the woman, indicating back in Sadie's direction. The woman nodded and showed her the way back out via the staff entrance to the main hall, where Alessandro was thankfully waiting to 'whisk her away to prepare for their evening at his family vineyard together'. Perhaps he was a salesman. Helen wondered whether she'd need to dress to be wined and dined, or just to buy his wine. Then he asked her a very unusual question.

CHAPTER TWENTY

If Sadie had known that a last minute economy trip to Tuscany would lead to so many heart-stopping moments, would she have put herself through it? Even now, back in Francesco's hotel room, Sadie was still not sure. He'd been witty, attentive, gracious and kind. He'd listened to her moan about her weekend, he'd regaled her with stories of his maverick 'ancient star chasing' – making himself sound like the Indiana Jones of Paleo-Astronomy. And he'd invited her back to his place for the night – without needing to be asked.

She'd steered clear of conversations about the kids, and macrobiotics. And it had worked. She must remember that for the future. But now as things were starting to get heated, Sadie wondered if she'd be better off leaving whilst the going was good. What had Helen said – don't put out first night? The problem was, the fire inside Sadie which was slowly building to an inferno, very much needed putting out. And from the look of Francesco's hose, he might be the one to do it...

If Helen had known that a last minute Tuscany treat for her sister would lead to so many heart-stopping moments, would she have put Sadie through it?

Or herself?

Or would Helen have run away like she always did, when things started getting serious? The sight before her eyes made her blink. For this, she'd have stayed.

Alessandro stood naked before her, apart from the tiniest of towels, dominating the doorway like some Roman god, the light from the marbled bathroom silhouetting his outline as he waited for her reply. Helen sipped her champagne and swallowed hard. This was it, then.

The evening had turned unseasonably warm – stifling, close, like a storm was brewing – and his unusual request had seemed innocent enough – to take a quick shower in her room after bringing her back from the conference centre. Before their picnic at the vineyard ruin. Helen had popped to her hotel to change before he drove her back into the warm night, back up the winding Italian hillside, back to a life she would glimpse but as usual, would never be a permanent part of. Always moving on, don't stay too long, don't get too close. *Better that way.*

Just a shower, he'd said.

Perhaps she should have known better.

To be honest, a marketing conference with her sister in tow hadn't exactly had 'find a naked hot guy' at the top of the agenda. But here he was standing there in nothing more than a towel. A little towel.

'You can't guess, then?' he was saying. 'Ok, I will tell you – I think I should take you up on your challenge.'

What challenge?

Oh-oh.

All the way back to her hotel, the signals were there – he'd been paying more attention to her face than to the road ahead. His voice had been low, seductive. The way he'd helped her adjust the seat, leaning a little too close. The way he'd brushed his fingers against her leg several times as he changed gear. Even the way he'd opened the door for her and taken her hand as she stepped out of the low, luxurious car – it wasn't her usual experience of a ride home. But then he wasn't her usual experience of men.

But there was a problem. He was exactly her type. Well, the type she *would* have chosen if life hadn't got in the way – you know, the film-star type.

Tall – tick.

Brooding – tick.

Broad – oh *yeah*, big tick.

Tantalisingly sexy, with his thick, dark hair falling over his deep brown eyes, and that Mediterranean charm… the accent which had made her quiver when he'd introduced himself yesterday. A quiver that reached from her neatly manicured, scarlet fingernails right down to the tips of her toes inside the towering 'I'm making a statement' Manolo Blahnik's she'd just changed into.

She was resting on the edge of the plush hotel bed with all its crisp, white linen and dozens of designer cushions, with her shoes still on, even though her jacket was off, and her shirt was slightly open... Well, it *was* hot.

'Challenge?' she replied, hoping desperately she wasn't getting the signals wrong. It wouldn't be the first time.

'Yes,' he went on, walking towards her. His towel was so small, he had to hold it together with his fingers, and she could see the top of his thigh, slightly whiter than the rest of his tanned skin. His chest was pin-up perfect and still moist from the shower – it rippled slightly as he moved. She snapped her eyes back up to his face as he replied.

'You said to me last night, did you not, that no man was capable of breaking down the barrier in your... defences – and that right now you are too closed-down, too hurt...'

I did?

'...And I told *you* – have faith, because one day a *very* special man would open your mind again...*Tesoro mia*, what if that time has come?'

Helen was silent.

'I want you to think about it,' he added, then disappeared back into the bathroom.

So she did. Helen realised what Sadie's answer would be – *yes, send me a special man to love.* But they didn't exist, did they? And if they did, Helen would gladly let her sister have him. Maybe she was off with him right now.

Come to think of it, where was said Sister? After she'd got the hump earlier on, she'd sent little more than a holding-text – *'I'm ok. Have fun. With F.'* Did she mean with Francesco? Or did she mean 'fun with an F'- their old code meaning third base, *don't wait up.*

Well, even if Sadie had begged Francesco to let her stay with him tonight, it'd still be nice to be sure. And she hadn't answered Helen's calls when Alessandro was in the shower just now.

Helen knew now that Sadie meant it, when she'd declared that she wanted to do things her way – well, so be it.

Knowing Sadie, that also meant she wouldn't stop until she got to the bottom of the accusations about identical entries. *Whose?* She hadn't understood the organiser's explanation for the interrogation followed by the sudden dropping of the matter last night. And now it looked like Sadie might be ditching out early before the big results were announced tomorrow afternoon. Helen could hope for a miracle, couldn't she? *For one moment, she made herself visualize a big announcement...* Now it all depended upon the checks being done by midday tomorrow... If not, Sadie might not talk to Helen for a very long time. Well, whatever – she wasn't going to hear from her tonight. So Helen turned her mobile off. There were other more pressing matters at hand. And just what *was* Alessandro doing in the bathroom?

Back home in the UK, Grace was listening to a very curious message from her oldest daughter. This was unusual. Grace had shut up shop and hadn't realised there was a message until she'd got home, where her trusty old-fashioned answerphone still responded reliably with one press of one button. She listened, then made a quick phone call.

'Darling it's me. Can you do me a favour? You know your mum's old laptop? Well I need you to talk me through how to turn it on and send an email... Yes an email... And attach a file or folder or something. Is it hard...? Well, I can work the washing machine darling so it can't be that difficult can it...? Mouse? Er... Well you'll just have to tell your father that dinner will have to get cold – your Auntie Helen needs my help, and this is far more important than bloody Yvette's sodding nut-loaf and veggie chipolatas. Ok, then here we go...'

Alessandro came back out of Helen's hotel bathroom no longer dripping wet, a slightly bigger towel draped round his shoulders. Helen's thoughts were brought dramatically back to the present as she gazed wonderingly at his toned body, his big shoulders and his 'tiny towel...area'.

'So, do you recall,' he said, 'I gave you a prediction.'

'You did? I mean...you did.' Helen muttered, sipping her champagne again.

'Yes, it is often true of women who have been hurt in the way you have. When you least expect it, a special man suddenly appears and turns your life upside down. Turns YOU upside down, *amore mio*. Do you not remember what I said?'

Last night was still a bit of a blur, if she was honest. After all, it wasn't every day you see your sister get to do a speech in front of five hundred people. One neither of you were prepared for. Then immediately afterwards, get hauled into a small back room to explain yourself. Her heart missed a beat, remembering for a split second that the biggest confrontation could still happen tomorrow. She shook off the sick feeling in her gut.

Focus on the Now.

'Can you? Can you remember what you told me, when I dropped you off last night, my sweet?' he asked.

'Er...'

'Think about it – for I have been thinking of nothing else all day. All day in a stuffy hall filled with stuffy people, waiting for our journey back, together.' He raised an eyebrow and waited.

Nothing – a big fat blank. Think, think!

'What I said to you, when I turned down your invitation to come in to your room?'

He turned ME down? Ouch.

'I see your face,' he went on, 'but do not be concerned – there was a very good reason I resisted the urge to join you in your bed.' No reply. He continued. 'I promised you that *l'uomo giusto* would appear in your life just at the moment destiny needed him to...' he had stopped walking now, and stood just in front of her, 'maybe he is right beneath your nose.'

He lifted her chin with his finger and she looked up, their eyes met and she felt a spark between them. Then he dropped her chin again and reached for her champagne, gingerly took a sip then offered it to her. She took it. When she looked back at him he was rubbing his dripping hair luxuriantly. He looked every inch a model, like he was auditioning for a shower gel commercial. Even his damn toenails looked perfect.

'Tell me, what do you want from life?' he asked, seeing her watching him and stopping suddenly to fix her with a gaze that felt as though he was searching her soul with those intense brown eyes.

'I – don't know. I thought I knew, but now I'm not so sure. Yesterday didn't help. Right now, maybe all I want is to get to midday tomorrow unscathed – that'd be a start.'

Alessandro didn't move, waiting for more. She watched a drop of water from his neck run down the centre of his chest towards his navel.

'The prize you and Sadie have come here for – you want it so much?' he asked, 'Is it so *very* meaningful? The anguish it causes – I see it in your eyes. Is it not more important – for the soul – to have peace? Peace... and love?'

'You sound like one of the Beatles – Maharishi era,' she joked nervously, but it went completely over his head. 'But, well – yes *of course* the prize is *so very important*. It's life-changing, Alessandro. It's why Sadie came.'

'And why did *you* come, Helen, my dear?'

'Eurgh, only grandmas and maiden aunts use *"my dear"*,' she said, smiling. The corner of his mouth curled up. 'Don't try to be English,' she said, 'I much prefer the Italian, *mia Carogna*.'

'Carina, my darling, carina, not Carogna. That's not nice. Or I can say – *tesoro mia* – is that any better? *Tesoro mia*,' he asked, his voice seductive and soft. He sat down on the bed next to her.

She raised her glass to him. 'Tesoro mia,' she said, imitating him in an exaggerated Italian accent. She felt a little nervous around him – that was unusual. *What had happened to the Magic Confidence of the Shoes?*

'Much better,' he replied, and tapped the tip of her nose affectionately. 'Tesoro mia,' he repeated, imitating her accent.

'Yes much better,' she said, aware now of being so very close to him, his towel gaping slightly as it draped over powerful thighs. 'As long as that doesn't mean "my little donkey" or something. It wouldn't be the first time.'

'Haha, no, it means *my treasure*.' Then he took her hand, and moved a little closer on the bed. 'So listen to me – *tesoro mia* – you have side-stepped the question. I think that whatever the reason you claim to have made this trip, there is a much deeper one – one that even you do not know. But it is there. And maybe we can discover it – but you have to open up to me – completely...'

Helen looked doubtful. He touched her face and gazed deeply into her eyes, down to her mouth, then back up to her eyes. He went on, 'Yes, I am sure that, if you give me the chance, I can help you find out what is deep down inside. *Very* deep in fact.'

And in that moment, she did something very uncharacteristic. But if she didn't do it here – now – with him – she feared it would be a long time before anything like this happened again.

'Ok,' she said. 'You may be right. And you've got me intrigued now. Go on then, show me.'

And with that, Alessandro pushed her gently back on the bed, and let his towel fall to the floor.

(for full x-rated scene, search for 'Hawaiian Extra: Helen and Allesandro in Tuscany' on Amazon, December 2013. OR email me at Debbie@debbieflint.com for free copy, or download from my website Complete Steamy version on amazon from March 2014)

CHAPTER TWENTY-ONE

The next day, Helen awoke in the hotel room to find Alessandro gone, and the light streaming in through the window. The memory of last night came back to her and she grinned and stretched luxuriantly, touching her body and closing her eyes. She sat up and looked around. The bedding was still all over the floor, his belt still tied to the bedpost and her sexiest underwear still strewn across the room. The remains of last night's carpet picnic were by the bin – they'd brought it in to the room once they ran out of time to go see the ruins at the vineyard. Instead, Alessandro had been the ruin of *her*. Or the making of her. She hadn't decided which, yet. Helen smiled and stretched her arms above her head, recalling one of the most passionate nights of her life, at the hands of this skilled Italian, and was filled with an unusual wave of something... Being sated, complete? *Was this how a proper morning after was supposed to feel?* she thought.

But then reality hit. Like it had last night. Other memories came flooding back, and she got up and tidied the room. No sign of Sadie yet. Helen went to the bathroom to shower. She examined her face in the mirror.

'What shall we do, HellsBells?' she asked her own reflection, 'Considering what's happened.' And she watched as a darkness crossed her face, and in that instant she knew what she had to do. The tiniest sign of a tear prickled in her eye. She pulled on her dressing gown and walked back out into the bedroom, just as the door handle turned quietly and the door opened slowly.

It was Sadie, tip-toeing back into the room, holding her shoes in her hand.

Sadie was no longer angry with Helen. In fact, last night had been the icing on the cake of this journey of self-discovery which meant that nothing would ever be the same again.

Nothing.

But not in the way Helen might think. But her sister looked strange. They looked at each other for a moment, then Sadie held out her arms, and Helen came over and folded herself into them and did something she'd never done before. She started crying into her sister's shoulder. Helen, her great big, grown up, protective older sister needed protecting herself, and for the first time in years, she was openly showing it.

'Shhhhh,' comforted Sadie. 'You ok?' she asked, expecting a new tale of woe – 'he loved me then left me' instead of Helen's usual, 'I loved him then left him.'

'Tell me what happened,' asked Sadie, 'did he hurt you? Woke up and he was gone? What?'

'No,' said Helen, sobbing a little still. 'Well yes, I woke up and he was gone and...'

'The bastard,' snapped Sadie, 'never trust a bloody man with a bloody Ferrari, that's what I say, I...'

'Wait, Sadie, listen,' interrupted Helen, and there was something in her voice that stopped Sadie short.

'You couldn't be more wrong. It was nothing like that. He... he...'

Sadie's heart began to beat a little faster, suddenly fearing this new look in her sister's eyes. 'What? Tell me!'

'He was... amazing...'

Sadie's eyebrows rose.

'...Astounding...'

Sadie's eyes were wider.

'Pure magic,' Helen said finally and did a little spin, then threw herself backwards on the bed.

'And magic makes you cry because...' asked Sadie, making a *what the hell* face.

'Because it's never been like this before.'

'Not even with Victor?'

'Not even with Victor.'

'Blimey,' Sadie said, sitting herself down on the bed next to Helen. She went to speak, hesitated, and then said it anyway. 'Not even with Jason...?'

'He's asked me to go travelling with him,' Helen replied, as usual ignoring the topic.

'Travelling?' Sadie repeated.

'Yes, travelling. All summer. We had the most amazing chat last night whilst we ate supper and...' Tears were forming in her eyes once again. '...And he wants to show me the world. His world.'

'And that's bad, why?' Sadie asked.

'It's *not* bad, it's not bad at all. In fact, it's great. It's incredible. He said he wanted to show me another side of life – and that it could be the making of me. He's going on a sabbatical and if I went he said he would... what was it again... show me how to love myself. And how to achieve bliss and self-awareness and do meditation and...'

'Meditation? You? No wonder you're crying,' joked Sadie, relieved, reaching over to wipe a tiny tear from the corner of her sister's eye.

'Exactly. It's just not me, is it? Maybe years ago,' said Helen, staring into space. 'Before...' her voice was softer. 'But now – I just can't. It's not what I am – it's not what I do. I work, I'm on the treadmill, I'm in the rat race, I'm...'

'Are you though?' Sadie said, looking carefully at her sister and seeing signs of confusion in her eyes. 'It's who you *have* been, but it doesn't mean it's who you always *will* be. Can't you take the leap of a lifetime and try something you've never done before? Go for it? I'm the boring one, remember? You're the one who likes trying new things.'

'Yeah,' Helen said, sitting up on the edge of the bed and grabbing a bottle of water. '*Trying* them. Like, *once*.' She unscrewed the bottle and took a drink. 'Not twice. And after Victor, I made up my mind I'd never do "twice" again.'

'But Alessandro's not Victor,' Sadie said, putting her hand on Helen's arm.

'You can say that again. For a start he's not...' Helen stopped herself and looked away.

'What? What is Alessandro? And what happened with Victor – when will you tell me?'

Helen looked at her sister, drinking the rest of the bottle of water, then changed the subject. 'Now *you* tell *me* about your night – what happened with *your* Italiano stallian-o.'

'That's not even a word,' Sadie sighed, then looked away and smiled.

'Go on, spill!' Helen said, sitting herself up to face Sadie, expectantly. 'Did you have sex?!'

Sadie grinned, then looked at the floor, flushing slightly.

'Hah! You did!' said Helen. 'So *up yours* Mister Damian frickin' Hugh, eh? Sadie Turner doesn't hang around waiting for a reunion with a loser – she goes straight out and finds herself an Adonis to shag.'

'Helen!' Sadie said, laughing.

'Did he have an amazing body, like Alessandro's got?'

'Yes, Francesco's body was amazing, he even had a six pack, and he was very strong – he had to be, to lift me.'

'Lift you?' asked Helen, with a look of mischief creeping over her face. 'Was he all *Tarzan and Jane*, then?' she asked, digging her sister in the ribs.

Sadie flushed some more and smiled, but shook her head. One particular memory from last night flashed back into her mind and she made a face, bit her lip, then wrinkled her nose.

'Oh, oh,' Helen said, the mischievous look suddenly gone. 'What does that face mean?'

'This face means that it was a One Night Only,' Sadie replied.

'Oh dear,' said Helen. 'Dare I ask why?'

'Well let's just put it this way, whilst my sister was off encountering the passion of a lifetime, I was in a hotel room with a guy who liked to sniff his own armpits, like...'

'...Kevin Kline in A Fish Called Wanda,' Helen joined in and both girls spoke at once. 'Noooooo!' said Helen. 'He didn't?! I didn't know that was a real thing!'

'Yes,' said Sadie. 'Maybe it's an Italian thing...?'

'It's *not* an Italian thing,' said Helen firmly, smiling. 'Go on.'

'Well, we had a lovely dinner, he made me laugh. And he was quite a turn on, even though what he did with the ice-cream was a bit messy...'

'Yes...?' Helen said, smothering a giggle.

'Then we got back to the hotel and he decided to do a strip-tease. Without music. Which was quite nice.'

'Quite...nice?' said Helen, over-enunciating each syllable.

'And then he disappeared into the bathroom with all his clothes. And came back out with his just his pants on.'

'Back on? Why?'

'That's what I thought. So I asked him. "Why have you put your pants back on," I asked. And you know what he said?'

Helen shook her head, so Sadie told her.

'Well, he just stood there in a kind of a porn star pose and said "Because, my dear, I want you to *find* me",'

'*I want you to FIND me?*' Helen said, an incredulous look on her face, 'As in...' she added, indicating lower down her body.

Sadie nodded. 'Oh,' said Helen, then burst out laughing.

'*Oh*, indeed,' said Sadie. 'Let's just say it took some concentrating to overcome the "eurgh" factor.'

'*I want you to FIND me,*' mimicked Helen, posing and doing a little imitation of Francesco.

When they'd stopped giggling, Sadie spoke again. 'The rest of the night was... satisfactory, shall we say, complete with a fireman's lift onto the bed. But it was nothing to write home about.'

Helen was still laughing. 'Unless you're writing to Weirdo-sex Monthly. Tragic. You've really had some perverts lately haven't you?!'

'Don't judge. One person's *perv* is another one's normal. But, yep, I suppose I have. I'm not saying it wasn't fun, 'cos it was, but he's not Mr Right, that's all I can say.'

'He was Mr Shite by the sound of it.'

'Haha, not quite that bad – he still had some good moves in bed. And on it. And at the side of it. And at the bottom of it.' They laughed again, then Sadie added, 'but there won't be a return journey, that's for sure.'

'You sure?' Helen asked, playfully.

'I'm abso-friggin-lutely certain,' Sadie said, adding in an embarrassed whisper, 'He took ages to come, and when he did, the only way he could do it was on his knees with my legs in the air, so he could look at himself in the mirror. And his face was so weird,' Sadie made the face, quivering her bottom lip and rolling her eyes to the ceiling and Helen burst out laughing.

'Ooo, no! No return journeys there then. Shame – I had high hopes.'

'I didn't, not really.'

'And what about Mister Hugh? Is it over?'

'How can it not be? He knew how important honesty was to me, and he turns up here with Delta.' Sadie thought about her last 'flame' whilst Helen *tutted*, and made a face Sadie recognised. She spoke before Helen did. 'No, before you say it, I'm not going to go running back to him, even if he has got a big house and prospects, as mother keeps saying. It's been nice just being with the girls more again lately. No, I think it's time I forgot about men for the time being.'

'Glad to hear it.'

'Well, there's too much else to worry about. I've been ignoring Abi and Georgia too much lately.'

'No you haven't, you're a good mum, Sade. They love you.'

And they need me, thought Sadie, feeling excited about seeing her daughters again. 'So, talking of return journeys,' she said, 'I'm going to check in again to see if that earlier flight has become available.'

Helen made a disappointed face. Her sister continued,

'Well after yesterday is there really any point hanging around till the end? Do you want to come back earlier too?'

'No, I've promised I'll see Alessandro this evening at least, before he flies back to Milan to college tomorrow. He finishes this term, then that's it – he's off to Tibet.'

'Go with him, sis. Take the plunge. Step off the rat race and get to know *YOU*. Really learn to love yourself, like he said. Go on – try it for the first time. You might like the person you uncover.'

Helen was thoughtful for a moment, but shook her head. 'Listen, there's no doubt he rocked my world, but I have to get back to my contract – I've got another column to submit this week – I'm interviewing KiKa herself this time. She's insisting on it, since the column's started to do well, she wasn't to stamp her mark on it just like on everything else. It's just an excuse though – to talk about her next fashion range, *"perfect for fall".'*

Helen mimicked KiKa, in a nasal Californian drawl, making Sadie laugh.

Then she continued. 'And I've got to do a lot of prep for this one, even if it is out in New York. But at least it'll take my mind off... other things.' Helen looked at Sadie.

Sadie knew exactly what her sister meant. 'Honestly, sis,' Helen continued, 'you've no idea how much it's meant to me to have this job, after what happened at the agency – it's meant I can hold my head high again – even though I still have to hide from the occasional ex-colleague when I'm in New York. And even though it's beyond ridiculous the stressful way they all work there, it's kind of rescued me a bit, you know?'

'You mean it's meant you can buy things again?' Sadie teased.

'Yes – lots of lovely stuff.'

'You and your stuff,' said Sadie. 'Life isn't all about stuff. Are you sure you won't change your mind? A trip with someone like Alessandro could be a whole new chapter for you, too?'

Sadie saw her sister's eyes flicker and a look of resolution appear on her face. Admittedly she'd been a lot happier since this whole column thing, but there was still an emptiness in Helen that had been there since her first marriage fell apart all those years ago. 'Listen, Hells, let's bunk off today – let's go see those ruins – wouldn't it be fun?'

'I was supposed to see them yesterday, but they'll keep. Hey look at the time,' she said, glancing at the clock. 'Let's get cracking – better that we attend those last few sessions this morning – there's a surprise keynote speaker – you might miss something important!'

'Well, ok, but if I can get on the earlier flight I will. I don't want to hang around near Damian any longer than I have to.'

Helen picked up her mobile and turned it back on.

'You checking to see if your sex god has messaged you already this morning?' asked Sadie, going into the bathroom.

'No, er… yeah, haha,' Helen said. 'Tell you what, I'll phone the airline for you,' she said, just as her sister closed the door.

Helen walked over to the bathroom and spoke into her mobile loudly so Sadie could hear it in the bathroom. 'Yes, I'm enquiring about a flight change…'

She told Sadie through the door, that the airline still didn't have any cancellations and they doubted they would now. Then Helen sat back down on the bed and waited as the rest of the messages all came through. Work… work… a lovely one from Alessandro… Dame and Kate in New York… and another work one.

Nothing from home – yet. Dammit. But with what was at stake, considering how it could turn Sadie's life upside down and she didn't even know it, there damn well better be some news, and she only had till midday to get it.

CHAPTER TWENTY-TWO

Helen had been in and out of the conference room like a dog on heat, and Sadie kept looking at her watch. The airline had said there was nothing, apparently, when Helen had checked, so she was stuck there till tonight. But maybe she could go do some sightseeing – see the ruins. Now she was disqualified from yesterday's FlashContest there was even less point waiting around for the Awards Presentation at the end.

Sadie saw Helen, elbowing her way back towards Sadie's table through the lunchtime crush, and waved. Helen waved back – she had a weird look on her face.

'Here,' Sadie said, 'I saved you some pasta – the ginger steward said to tell you it has *un sapore divano*, and laughed his head off, though I don't quite know why. I guess you didn't impress him much with your Italian yesterday. Where have you been this time? Wasn't that the MC I saw you with over there? And why aren't you answering any of my questions? Why are you quiet?'

'Give me a chance. MC – yes it was, actually. I was just chatting with him about the Hawaiian trip – lovely prize for whoever wins the main competition. I wondered if... em, there'd be another one next year, and he said yes, but it wouldn't necessarily be Hawaii.'

'No, I don't suppose it would – it was only there because of that special water they were using as the subject for the ad. Shame, 'cos I loved doing all that research, it was really inspiring,' Sadie said wistfully.

'Yes, I noticed. Your designs had geek written all over them. In a good way. Anyway,' Helen said, changing the subject, 'What's done is done. Everything happens for a reason. You will remember that, won't you sis?'

What the...?

'Why? What are you leading up to?' Sadie said, 'What has he done? He's done something else, hasn't he?'

'Eh? Who? What?

'Damian,' said Sadie, 'Has he said something? What has he done? Has he stolen my idea and entered it himself? Is that why he and Delta are here? Has she nicked my sketches and that's why he was colluding with her and...'

'Sadie, Sadie, calm down love – it's only a commercial,' said Helen.

'Yes,' Sadie replied, stopping mid-flow, breathing out and relaxing a bit. I suppose it is. But if I'm staying till the end, I'll go and check her entry when they display them all later – then I'll see if he's lied about that as well.'

Just then she noticed her sister wasn't smiling any more. She'd gone white. White as a ghost.

She followed her gaze and over on the VIP table in the lunch hall, she saw a small group of people shaking hands. Helen had frozen. Sadie was shaking her arm but she wasn't budging. Then Sadie saw one of the men in the small group looking their way. 'Who's that?' Sadie asked, but Helen didn't speak – she just swallowed and looked furtively side to side. Then Sadie turned back to see the man leaning in to speak to a woman, and pointing over at Helen, then heading their way.

'Oh...my...God,' Helen said, 'I don't fucking believe it. I can't run can I? This time? I can't run. I've been spotted.'

'Run from who?'

'Victor's partner, my boss.'

'Where?' asked Sadie, looking past the tall guy who was making his way over to their table with a stern look on his face.

'There,' Helen said, nodding her head a little in the direction of the VIP table. But Sadie couldn't see who she meant, and suddenly the stern man was upon them. He was smartly dressed, his hair immaculate, his after-shave strong, and his jewellery quite elaborate. He was wearing shiny, pointy Italian style shoes, and when he spoke it was with a New York accent in a higher-than expected voice.

'Hello Helen, long time no see.'

His lapel had a little name tag on it and Sadie read it – 'Winston, Winston & Grant.' Underneath, it read, 'Andrew Grant'.

'Hello Andrew,' said Helen, her voice tiny, and strangulated. He held out a hand to shake hers, and she hesitated, then shook it.

'I've been waiting a long time for this moment,' he said, and didn't let go of her hand. She pulled it free.

'I bet you have,' said Helen, looking crushed.

'And who is this lovely lady?' he asked, looking at Sadie.

'I'm her sister, Sadie,' said Sadie, when Helen didn't immediately respond. 'I'm sorry, are you here with Helen's ex-boss?'

'No,' the man looked strangely at Helen, then back at Sadie. 'I *am* her ex-boss.'

Helen couldn't believe her bad luck. All this time. All these months of careful avoidance and he tracks her down here in Tuscany where she can't scream or make a scene − not with Sadie's future at stake. Not if he's the surprise guest speaker from the sponsors. Not if he's standing here being so goddam civil. Much as she'd like to swing for him. Much as she'd like to shout, *Thanks very much for ruining my life, you bastard. And Victor's.*

'I'm sorry,' Sadie was saying. '*You're* Helen's ex-boss?'

Andrew was nodding.

'So you're the brother of Damian Grant?'

'Yes,' he replied.

Sadie went on, 'And you're Victor's...'

'...husband.' Said Helen. 'Married in Vermont in 2009.'

'And, sweetie, soon to be divorced in New York in 2012,' he added with venom in his voice.

Sadie looked at her sister, who was stumped. Helen's mouth was slightly open and she looked shocked.

'Sadie it's been a pleasure to meet you. I can't say the same of your sister but since Victor's futile attempt to try a heterosexual relationship *'just to see if it could cure his mid-life crisis'* and I quote, she became the laughing stock of the industry. Got to feel sorry for her, right? All Victor's broken promises and he still came crawling back to me. I made sure no one wants to employ her anymore, so all I came over to say is, *good job, HellsBells, good job.* And for your information, Victor is still gay, always was gay, and despite his brief flirtation with the opposite sex, always will be gay. In fact, I think *you* made him even more gay.' He looked challengingly at Helen who kept her mouth firmly shut, even though her fists looked dangerous. Sadie wondered if he knew how close he was coming to getting a black eye from a woman.

'Well,' he continued. 'I'm off to enjoy my VIP lunch, and to present a prize. Do enjoy my keynote speech – from what I hear from my brother Damian, you're quite the little talent. Maybe I should send over one of our scouts to talk to you. Perhaps *you'll* succeed in our industry, even if your sister has failed so miserably.'

He turned to go. Then stopped and addressed Helen under his breath.

'I hope it hurt you, catching him with his rent boys. I'll never forgive you, Helen. Never. When you finished with him, and he decided to come snivelling back to me, I didn't want him. Knowing where he'd *been.* Poor Victor said he was sorry, and told me I was the only one he'd ever loved. Do you hear that? The only one.' Helen didn't reply, she just stood listening. Sadie craned in to hear better, as he continued.

'So I asked him to prove it – I wanted to make him pay. So prove it he did – by telling our friends that he only went with you because *you were more man than he was.*' He leaned even closer to Helen, spoke in even more confidential tones. 'Oh, and by the way, if you ever wondered how that little rumour started – you know, about – cover your ears, Sadie – about how Helen here likes to be taken *up the alley*, and can only have sex using a strap-on, well, I deny all knowledge! Haha! *No comment*, as they say. Haha-Haa!'

Helen swallowed, and opened her mouth to speak. Sadie was scared of what might come out, knowing what some of her tirades had been like in the past, knowing what vitriol she was capable of.

'I'm… sorry,' was all she said. *Forgiveness.*

Andrew looked at her strangely then waved his hand as if to brush her aside. 'It couldn't save our marriage. I hope you're pleased with yourself. Still, that's all water under the bridge. I'm so over him – and you. Goodbye. Have a nice day, Sadie. And Helen, have a nice life.' And he was gone.

Sadie at once fussed around her sister, who was just staring ahead, trying to control her breathing. Sadie could see the pulse pounding in her neck. 'Oh my god, Helen, I'm so sorry. Are you ok? Can I get you a drink of water?' she asked.

'Please.'

Sadie rushed off to get a fresh bottle of water. She fought through the queues and when she returned to Helen, the jolly round steward from yesterday was just leaving the table and Helen was… smiling. Then she looked at Sadie. Then she began to laugh.

'You're – you are OK, aren't you?' Sadie asked. Had she flipped?

'Yes I am. I really am,' Helen said. Long time coming, that's all.

'What on earth is it that's cheered you up after *that* little scene? Did the steward say something?'

'Let's go and sit near the front to hear horrible Andrew's keynote speech, to show him he hasn't upset me. That'll mean more than any smack in the mouth could have done,' Helen replied. 'I tell you what, sis, will you – will you stay with me now? Till the end? Don't leave me here now?'

Sadie looked at her sister and shook her head in wonderment. 'Blimey – you talked about a whole new era for *me*! Seems like *you're* the one who's reformed. Sure – 'course I will.'

'I'm just going to the bathroom – the steward is saving us some seats. You go get them, I'm going to the bathroom – I'll see you in there,' she said, and pointed towards the Ladies' Room, mouthing 'bathroom'.

Sadie watched her elegant sister, with the smart purple business suit and confident stride, disappear through a crowd of men, who moved aside to let her through, and turned to watch her rear as she passed by.

With her matching shiny purple heels, she was as tall as many of them. She definitely got the height, thought Sadie, and the natural blonde hair.

Not for the first time in her life, Sadie wished she could have a few more of the genes her sister was blessed with. Still, the blonde hair was easily solvable. Yes maybe it was time for a complete change, thought Sadie, seeing the impact the long blonde locks were having on the crowd, and looking down at her own brunette tresses. Maybe it's time for me to have more fun... and if it's true what they say about blondes...

'Hello Sadie,' said a voice. She looked up and saw Damian Hugh and Delta, making their way past her table. He was holding two red wine glasses.

'Eurgh, I wondered why you made us come all the way over here to get to the conference hall,' said Delta. 'So unreliable. So predictable. And you snore. I'll see you in the hall. Bye Sadie,' she huffed as she swept past Damian, pushing him ever so slightly to get by. He nearly overbalanced, then rescued the glasses without spilling any wine.

'Sadie,' he said again.

'Damian,' Sadie replied. And tilted her chin as if to say *'and what do you want?'*

'Look. Things haven't quite gone as planned. But when we get back, maybe we can talk. It looks like I'm the tutor who's going to be taking that class you want to do next term, and...'

'You know, Damian I'm not so sure that I want to carry on studying now. Seeing all these inspiring speakers, mixing with the "real thing". Seems like I should just get on with my life and actually DO the job. After all, you know what they say about those who *can,* and those who teach...'

'Ouch,' he said. 'Ok, I deserved that. But... well, it's just that I had a lovely surprise planned for your birthday and I...'

'Leave it, Damian. Please. I've had enough surprises for now. Safe journey back,' Sadie said, picked up her bag and brushed past him, and this time he *did* overbalance, sending spatters of red wine all down his clean white shirt.

The rest of the afternoon passed by just as Sadie expected. Helen was a star, psyching out Andrew Grant by sitting in the front row and staring at him the whole way through his talk. Sadie actually found it quite interesting. It was a shame he was such a knob-head, it might have been nice to be talent-spotted for his company. Not that she could have gone to live in New York. Sadie's mind wandered as the next speaker got up to explain about the current shift to *geotargeting*, mobile marketing and online reputation management, in a very monotone voice with a very boring Powerpoint presentation to illustrate his talk. Sadie found herself thinking how much better her accompanying graphics would have been – page turns, reveals, clever fonts.

God Sadie, stop being a geek.

You need a break, she thought. *OOPS, just had one.*

It was the girls that now had to take priority in Sadie's life, she thought. Yes, with the help of her mum, and those newly-cashed in ISA's, if that's what they were – you never knew with Mum – Sadie's shop might last a tiny bit longer. Use all this info – *think positive, think positive* – don't let the money-panic kick in. Although Sadie had to admit, it was getting pretty near again now. Yes, that prize money and a wonderful exotic trip to Hawaii would have been a godsend. But there's always next year. Maybe.

For now, she'd get back from Tuscany and work really, really hard to make her business succeed – she had to, for the girls' sake. And men can stay on the back burner for as long as it took. *Maybe forever.* Or maybe she'd end up still fooling around when she retired, just like her mum. No, not a chance – it was Helen who would end up like Grace. They were so alike – and that was their trouble, Sadie thought. Then a sharp jab in the ribs brought her back from her thoughts. Helen was elbowing Sadie and pushing at her to let her get by into the aisle.

'Oi, Dolly Daydream! They're about to announce the winner of the FlashContest after the break,' Helen whispered, looking at her mobile. 'Andrew bloody Grant is going to be announcing who's won his precious ten thousand euros no doubt, so I'm not staying to watch him preening. You wanna go get a breath of fresh air? Alessandro's waiting in the foyer to say hi. We can put your rucksack on the seats – no one will touch *that*.'

'I see you're back to normal,' said Sadie, smiling. 'No, it's ok, I'll stay here. I won't come in case Francesco comes swinging towards me from the chandeliers...'

Helen laughed and squeezed by, and Sadie watched her go, stopping at the exit to talk to the round jolly steward again, who looked over towards Sadie and waved, then carried on talking to Helen as they both walked out the door.

Sadie felt someone tap her on the shoulder.

'Sadie, I've just come to say, I might not see you later.' It was Delta, 'He's doing my head in. All he's done is talk about you, since yesterday. And he still thinks what he did was justified. So whatever he says, just so you know, I didn't agree. OK? See you sometime – don't give up, OK?' Delta looked almost as if she cared, Sadie thought, but before she could ask her to clarify, someone started talking again on the stage.

Then the room settled down and the final part of the afternoon's proceedings began.

A short while later, there had been much vigorous applause when the FlashContest winner had been announced. Sure enough, Andrew Grant had bored everyone for about ten minutes talking about when he'd won his first prize for early viral marketing years ago. Then he did another five minutes talking about his 'award-winning' firm. The MC hovered behind him, and indicated it was time to wind up and he got on with awarding the prize. It wasn't to poor disqualified Sadie, but instead to a flamboyant, older blonde lady wearing clashing orange and purple and green.

When the coast was clear, in the final break before the last part of the day, Helen came to sit back down in the chair next to Sadie. Then she got up again. Then sat down again, then got up again.

'Sadie, I'm really sorry, I'll be back, er, soon. I can't stay here for this, I've got... er, a jippy tummy. I'll be in the loo. Wait here for me to come back, OK? Don't move.'

'What? Are you all right? Let me come with you, I can...'

'NO!' said Helen, a bit more sharply than it appeared she meant to speak. 'No,' she said, having lowered her voice again a little. 'Honestly, I need you to just stay put. Stay there. Promise?'

'OK, but I hope you're going to be well enough for the plane tonight, or we'll have to go find 300mg of arsenicum remedy which might...'

'Bye Sade.'

Helen left.

Sadie watched her go just as the MC stepped on the stage one final time. Just as he was taking his place, the round jolly woman tapped Sadie on the shoulder.

'Excuse me,' she said, 'your sister said her name is Parker?'

'Yes that's right,' Sadie said. 'Parker-Todd.'

'Hmm. Well, ok. They told me to put this here at the break, but you were sitting here, so I just needed to make sure. Sorry they got the name wrong,' she said, and popped a card on the empty seat beside Sadie and left. The lights began to dim and a spotlight lit up the stage. But just before they dimmed, Sadie saw the words 'RESERVED' and underneath it 'SADIE T. PARKER.'

Helen was watching from the back of the hall. Her heart was doing the fandango against her chest only marginally faster than earlier, which was only a little bit slower than when she'd been run out of the office by the male banshee last spring. And now here she was, a whole year later, at a turning point. What happened in the next ten minutes would mean either absolutely nothing, or that her sister would quite probably pass out and never speak to Helen again.

CHAPTER TWENTY-THREE

Helen was glad it was the latter. Well, the passing out bit. Well, she was kind of glad. Obviously not glad her sister had nearly keeled over when the jolly round lady had virtually dragged her up on to the stage, both of them arguing over the name-card Sadie was waving as she frantically shook her head. She'd tripped on her way up onto the stage – she was always clumsy when she felt out of her comfort zone, bless her. Then she'd looked like a rabbit in the headlights as her winning entry – yes, the winning entry – was flashed up on the screen behind them, and a middle-aged distinguished guy called Simon something or other, had presented her with her extra prize of the letter offering in-depth business analysis – Sadie would love that – all Excel documents and Powerpoints. But the proper trophy would be awarded to Sadie when she took the trip to Hawaii next month.

Sadie was going to Hawaii.

Sadie was going to Hawaii.

Helen could see her looking behind her at the screen, totally bemused, and then scouring the crowd, shielding her eyes from the spotlight, then looking behind her again at the winning entry. It was a picture of a naked woman's body, with the small picture of the pure water product at the side of her. Above her was the word 'temple'. Beside her were the words 'wholly water.' Clever.

So much for avoiding religious connotations. Damian was an idiot.

This design was sadly, very similar – almost identical in fact, to the one Sadie had entered in the FlashContest yesterday for a different product but one that was still pure, so she'd just swapped it for the water bottle. But the one on the screen looked so much more professional. Well it would do, as Helen had drawn it, compared to Sadie's much-attempted sketch in yesterday's contest. Only one thing had made the difference, and convinced the organisers that Sadie Turner Parker was indeed the author of both, and the self-same person. And thank god their mum had been at home – Abi saved the day by helping her send what Helen needed to prove it from the old computer with all the copyright info and early sketches still on it. *Thank god.* Now for the showdown.

Eventually, the applause subsided, the event was wound up and a general hub-bub began, and Helen walked up to the stage. Sadie finished talking to the Simon guy, taking his card and looking overjoyed at whatever it was he was telling her. Then she went over to Helen at the front.

'Kiss me or kill me?' Helen asked, meekly. She actually felt quite nervous. Overjoyed, thrilled, proud as punch, but, yes, quite nervous. This could be tricky.

'Both,' said Sadie. Then she threw her arms around Helen and began to sob. 'Don't you ever do anything like that to me again! Ever!' Sadie said through the overjoyed gasps. 'You're too devious for your own good, Helen Parker-Todd. Honesty from now on – total honesty, ok?'

'I had to lie – you'd have stopped me.'

'Yes but, well, maybe, but – promise whatever it is in future, no more lies. OK? I never want to find out you're lying to me again. Tell me before I find out from someone else, and I'll deal with it. Anything's better than someone else knowing before I do – especially a man on a stage with a microphone!'

'Anything?' Helen looked thoughtful for a second. 'Congratulations, sis,' she said. And the two girls just stood looking at each other for a second, before Sadie sobbed and hugged her sister again. Then she wiped her eyes, and began looking at the presentation folder they'd given her with all the info about her prize. Pictures of Hawaii, the product, and the other runners up, all below her own design in pole position at the top.

'Oh my god,' said Helen, looking at the pictures below Sadie's winning entry. 'Looks like I wasn't the only one keeping things from you,' and she pointed to an entry marked '*Delta Dawn, North West finalist*'.

At first Sadie only remarked on the name. 'I didn't know her surname really *was* Dawn. And why did she enter in the North West heat?' But then Helen pointed to the actual design on the page and Sadie looked closer.

'That's not what I think it is, is it?' Sadie said, the joy suddenly gone from her face as she peered at Delta's design – it was a variation on the tag line "Water – but Faster" from one of Sadie's earliest sketches which he'd shown everyone in class. 'I can't believe the lying toe rag would have let her take my idea and enter it, yet told me not to take part. Why would he do that, Helen? Why? He was supposed to care about me? I don't understand.'

'Maybe it was all about the question mark...' Helen said.

Just then Grey Woman from yesterday came up, ignored Helen and whisked Sadie away for an official photograph for the industry magazine, with the MC, that Simon guy and a few other officials and industry experts. *Industry,* thought Helen. Not my industry any more.

It's Sadie's now.

But she was glad the organisers had agreed not to let on to Sadie about the second entry whilst they waited for the confirmation from home to prove she was indeed the originator of the concept.

Helen watched her younger sister standing there a little awkwardly in the limelight, and made up her mind to tell her everything else on the flight home that night – including all the other lies, even if it was risky. Now was as good a time as any to wipe the slate clean, even if it did turn Sadie into *Sis-zilla.*

She's asked for the whole truth and nothing but the truth, so that's what she'll get.

Helen would be leaving soon after for her next assignment – off to New York to interview the prize bee-yatch that was KiKa – so she'd confess then disappear for a while. Again. Plus ca change.

Then she looked around her and spied Alessandro waiting in the foyer, looking drop dead gorgeous. And he was waiting for her – waiting to take her out for one last date. Or if he had his way – waiting to take her away from all this. No, she thought, stick to the plan. Have one last night with Alessandro, then do what you do best, Helen, and say goodbye. Although... For one precious moment she pictured a summer spent in Tibet, with all the fabulous first time experiences that would entail. Then she got scared, and banished the thought from her mind.

She'd have enough on her plate dealing with a scary woman – and she didn't mean KiKa.

Two days later, Sadie was back behind the counter in the shop once more, finding it very easy now, to obtain an interview with the local paper. Helen had given her strict orders on what to do and when, to maximise her exposure. And Sadie was ignoring all of it.

Currently, she was ignoring Helen full stop.

Sadie was overjoyed at being off to Hawaii, sure, but Helen had finally crossed the line. With the bombshells on the flight back home, Sadie had finally had enough. Of everyone. And especially of Helen. And Damian. She didn't know who was worse.

Later that afternoon, Grace stopped by the store with some disappointing news about finances, but hopefully it would only be a temporary setback that she could fix with a visit to everyone's favourite banker, and it wasn't long before the conversation turned once again to Helen.

'I've *told* you why, mum,' said Sadie, slamming down the new delivery of health magazines on the countertop and slicing the wrapping apart viciously with a paper-opener.

'But I don't *understand* why, darling,' Grace replied. 'For once Helen wasn't thinking about Helen, was she? Don't you think that's a revelation?'

Sadie just ripped off the plastic wrap and launched it to the floor.

'I saw the invoice, you know, when I was looking for the certificate online – she paid a lot of money to get that copyright done in your name – well, in your maiden name.'

Sadie just shrugged.

Grace continued unabated. 'Do you know, it took a lot of effort for me to find that account information and your early sketches on the power presentation – took ages on that rubbishy old computer of yours. All to 'save your bacon' as Helen put it. But I can tell you now, if I'd known it'd cause this rift between you and her, well, maybe I wouldn't have done it.'

Sadie looked up at her mum and sighed. 'Yes, mother, you did well, mother. Thank you, mother.' Grace looked offended. Sadie gave in and changed her tone. 'Seriously, mum, thank you. And well done. I was a bit amazed that you managed to do it all by yourself on my old computer I must say.'

'So was I,' Grace said puffing up. Then she shook her head. 'But tell you the truth, Abi came back and helped me do it in the end. Although I was the one who found your birth certificate to prove your maiden name – Abi only scanned it.'

'Like I said, well done mother,'

'Yes, it was rather clever of one, wasn't it, sweetie. Abi told me I'd done really well and now she's trying to get me to learn how to do more than just buy things on the interweb. She says I should get a...' Grace waved her hand around and Sadie waited for her to finish. '...bullet or something. Says it's easier because you just rap it?'

'A tablet,' said Sadie, 'and you tap it?'

'Yes, that's what Abi said. But we'll see about all that – I'd rather save the money, in the light of this latest news.' Grace flicked her eyes over towards Sadie, and then continued. 'Maybe I can have that old laptop, now she's getting an i-Pad from her father.' The older lady waited for a reaction and got it.

'A what?? How is he managing to pay for that?' Sadie asked, her eyes wide.

'To tell you the truth I think it's Yvette's old one, she's just like Helen – always got to have the latest stuff that woman. All she talks about is new this, new that. New, new, new. Apart from Stuart of course.'

Sadie laughed.

'Seriously, Sadie, it's not a good example for the children. The sooner he finds himself someone more grounded, more his own age, the better. Someone more fitting for the girls to spend time with. You know the other night, whilst Abi helped me, and Georgia played Hex Box?'

Sadie looked up. 'Xbox, Mum, Xbox,'

'Well anyway, they sat outside in the car, and all she did was kiss him. Kiss, kiss, kiss, that's all they did. Mr Wilson opposite was on the point of rapping on their window. Either that or wiping off the steam so he could get a better look. I must go over there and give him a piece of my mind one of these days...'

'Mum,' said Sadie, a curious look on her face, and her hand on her chest, 'Say that again.'

'I said he deserves to be told to mind his own business, he's...'

'Not the bit about my neighbour. The bit about Stuart. Kissing Yvette.'

Grace looked at her daughter a bit taken aback. 'What? What happened to you out in Tuscany – you've come back in a very funny mood.'

'Say it.'

'Stuart and Yvette were snogging each other's faces off in the car outside the house. There, happy now?'

'Actually I am,' said Sadie and laughed.

'Want to elaborate?' asked Grace, looking bemused.

'I just realised that I think I'm truly over Stuart. I had not one pang of jealousy when you said that. Not one! Hah!' trilled Sadie, and practically skipped over to the rubbish bin dumping an armful of packaging with a theatrical flourish and a twist on the spot.

'Careful, you'll fall over! You couldn't have done that if you were still wearing those heels.'

'Nope, no more heels – only for important occasions from now on. Which I will be having soon – got a meeting pencilled in with the journalist, for when I come back from Hawaii next month. And got that business analyst guy coming by in the next few weeks, too.'

'I wonder if he's attractive. Is he old?'

'Too old for me,' Sadie said, and Grace raised an eyebrow. 'And too young for you! He's very well-spoken, you'll have to be on your best behaviour when he's around.'

'Well one finds oneself wondering why one's daughter isn't proud of one's vocab?' Grace said in a sing-song voice. Sadie looked up – *what?* 'That's how this new woman talks at bowls,' explained Grace. 'She's Scandinavian, or from Switzerland, or somewhere – actually it might have been Swindon. Do they talk posh in Swindon? Anyway, Greta does. Herb's taken a bit of a shine to her already – thinks she's charming, so I've decided to befriend her.'

'God help her,' said Sadie, under her breath.

Grace continued. 'So when are you going to call her?'

'Call who? Greta?' Sadie asked.

'No, silly sausage, your sister. You can Skype her more clearly on that new computer of yours now, so why don't you do that?'

'Mum – that was another one of Helen's lies! She makes me feel like a complete charity case – or just stupid. She told me I was being given it by the company so I could Skype their studio. I couldn't believe it when I found out she'd paid for it. *And* a courier to make it seem more realistic – to fool me. She even paid him to say it was from the agency. That's some kind of deceit.'

'Well you'd have just refused to accept it otherwise – same as when she paid the entry fee for the competition. And if she hadn't, where would you be? No, for once, I can see why she would be devious. Can't you?'

'Not really, mum, no,' Sadie said. They'd been over this several times already. 'Mind you, it makes a change having you side with Helen.'

'Well I didn't like it when things got ugly. No wonder poor Helen made herself scarce.'

Poor Helen – THAT makes a change, thought Sadie. 'Look, if it was just that, it wouldn't be so bad. But she tricked me into signing the second round forms when I got through the preliminaries. She lied to me about my having sold my copyright for one of my ideas for thousands of pounds – I was really proud thinking someone would pay that? Do you understand? It made me feel *this* big,' she ranted, holding up her thumb and forefinger almost touching. Sadie opened the till and started counting the pound coins.

'Yes but now you feel ten feet tall, don't you? And it *was* your own work that did it? She only did what you should have done yourself – if she hadn't, you *definitely* wouldn't be off to the other side of the world next month.'

Sadie just shrugged. 'And she lied about other things too, mum. She knew I wouldn't take the money she'd only just earned for her column. Yet she told me I was earning it – for being a nutrition expert – I actually felt quite proud, but it was Helen all along. And then just to blow my mind, she admits that the tickets for the Tuscany conference which she supposedly got from her mate in New York were actually genuinely mine – 'cos I'd made the semi-final. It was just a complete mess, mum. No, honesty's the best policy, and I *honestly* need to give Helen some space right now. That's all. I love her, but I can't be doing with her – not right now.'

'Hmmm,' Grace, said, rubbing her chin.

'What's "hmmm" – don't you start giving me a lecture on treating Helen better, mother, 'cos that's something *you* should have been doing for years,' said Sadie, slamming the till shut.

'See there you go again. I meant "Hmmm, my chin has got some grannies coming through" – do you still have any of that hair-growth retard cream?'

Sadie had to laugh. 'And it's "retardant" cream, mum. Over here next to the hair dye.'

Grace walked past her daughter and looked her in the eye – then she picked up one of Sadie's locks and examined it up close, then poked her parting slightly. 'Hmmm,' said Grace, thoughtfully.

'Get off mum,' Sadie said. 'Now get going – if you're not quick, you'll miss the bank. I'm glad you and Mr Rosebery have patched things up, if he's agreed to an appointment with you.'

'He's not Mr Rosebery, he's still Tom. And he doesn't know I'm coming. Actually, can I take some of this cream for him too?'

'I hate to think where you're going to put it,' Sadie said, shaking her head in wonderment. 'But it's partly your stock, so knock yourself out.'

Just before she went to sleep that night, Sadie checked her messages – nothing, anywhere. The bright shiny new computer was now her pride and joy – not that she'd admit it to Helen – and it would be really useful now for the task that was ahead of her. A big business analysis, and suggestions for a follow on campaign and international expansion. And they'd be all her own work. None of them would include Helen's input.

Yes, from now on, Sadie would ignore anyone who underestimated her, or told her what she could or couldn't do. And though Helen didn't know it, Sadie acknowledged that this had been the final push she needed.

New computer, new era, new Sadie.

New message.

Sadie opened it and saw it was an email. From someone she never would have expected to hear from in a million years. Ever, in fact. Asking her to meet at 6 o'clock the following night. Sadie typed a reply – one word – and went to sleep.

CHAPTER TWENTY-FOUR

Over in New York, Helen had just got the sack. Again.

'It's not exactly the *sack*, Hells, is it?' said Kate over a commiserating hot chocolate in the local coffee bar. The sofas were cosy, the air was warm, and the windows were all steamed up. And so was Helen.

'It might as well be! Bloody woman. Thinks she's as big as the other Kim but she's not. Nowhere near as big. Except her ass. But why does she have to commandeer my column and suck it up as part of her reality show? *Schloop*.' Helen made a sucking noise, and waved her hands in the air. 'Just like that – gone. Why Mr A. has to bow down to her I'll never know – surely he could run two columns?'

'Her latest sales have been astronomical – I guess leopard trimmed everything – and I mean everything – is "bang on trend" as KiKa keeps saying,' replied Kate. She looked past Helen and continued talking. 'Listen, I've been thinking, there may be another opportunity just cropping up...'

'Oh no! I told you, no marketing. No-one in marketing will touch me – Andrew sodding Grant has just started a new twitter campaign showing my head on KiKa's body on a mock-up of her selling dildos on our channel. I'm poison, no one wants me.'

'You don't know it was Andrew,' added Kate, hurriedly. 'Oh look it's Damian! Hello Day!'

Helen swung round to see her other oldest, *bestest* pal in America just about to join them. 'Damian Grant! What a sight for sore eyes you are!' Helen said. He kissed her on both cheeks.

'Actually, it WAS my brother,' he said. 'But don't tell him I told you.'

The girls laughed and Damian signalled to the waitress for a coffee, making some weird hand signals to indicate his preference. 'That means skinny, vente, no foam latte with space,' he explained.

'God I've missed this,' added Kate, patting both her pals' shoulders.

A short while later, Helen was looking slightly happier. Kate was positively beaming and Damian Grant looked very happy with himself.

'You, my darling, are my fairy godmother,' she said to him. 'And if you can pull off your part of it, Kate, I will love you both forever.'

A new venture! And one that didn't involve screw-loose, ego-filled celebrities. In fact, it couldn't be further from it.

Back in the UK, Sadie had done some careful thinking. The message she received out of the blue last night was nagging at her. But she made up her mind to stick to her guns and go with her first reaction.

Because after all, she already had plans.

The next evening, after work, Sadie was knocking on the door of a certain Victorian detached, with one thing in mind. It was her birthday tomorrow, and Damian Hugh wanted to see her. He was now 'the other Damian' – the one whom her sister had originally mistakenly raved about and recommended to Sadie, but now wanted to see dead. He'd called when she'd got back from Tuscany – incredibly – asking to see her to explain everything. He said he wanted to give her the present he'd already bought, because 'no-one else would want it.'

Grace had overheard the phone call and had convinced Sadie to go and 'extricate what you can from the bounder' – her mother was obviously still trying to impress Herb – and Sadie had decided to go hear him out. More than anything, she wondered if he was lying about everything else as well as the competition. He'd stolen her ideas – well, the basic concept – told her not to apply so his protégée could enter, just so he could get the kudos himself for having mentored her after Sadie dropped out of his class. He'd lied about where he was going for the weekend, and even when he was caught out, he still didn't have the decency to come and beg her forgiveness and make amends. Perhaps that was what his request to see her was all about. So Sadie had thought 'what the hell' and decided to meet.

More than anything, though, it was because she was feeling particularly in the mood for giving him a piece of her mind, and she hoped that once she saw him, in the house where they'd shared their closest moments, she wouldn't give in. If Helen had known she was going, her advice would probably have been to 'leave on a high and if you want, go get a post-split shag but only meet him if you leave *before* he's got his end away.' But Helen *hadn't* known. Because Sadie still wasn't talking to her.

Anyway, Sadie didn't think sex was remotely likely. Just like with Stuart, the attraction had finally waned. Tuscany had changed her in a lot of ways, and that was one of them. The bar was now raised.

But at least Damian Hugh had been faithful to her, whereas Stuart hadn't.

This morning, Sadie had woken up to find a note pushed under the door and the noise of a loud guttural exhaust pulling away up her street. The note was from Damian, asking her to come over tonight. 'We've been building up to this for ages. P*lease'*. Lost his mobile again no doubt. So she decided to go.

Come on Sadie, she said, giving herself a pep talk as she walked up the pathway to the front door. Feeling strong, she raised her hand to knock on the door, but as she lifted the big black cast iron lion's mouth, the door moved – it had been left open.

Inside, at the foot of the staircase, she found another note. Next to it was a virtual reality helmet. 'This is for you,' she read, 'I'm waiting upstairs.'

Sadie closed the door, and listened. Nothing. Then curiosity got the better of her, and she picked up the helmet and the note, then walked slowly and quietly up the edges of the stairs to the sound of a humming noise. From the room with the dark walls, she saw a dim glow, the occasional flashing light, and a low electronic hum. She listened for a second, then took the plunge, and popped her head round the door. What she saw was completely unexpected.

On the other side of the room, the long cloth – that had concealed a large object the last time she'd been there – was pulled back, and a very, very wide bed had been lowered to the ground – it was one of those fold up beds, but twice as wide as a normal one.

On one side of it, lying directly beneath a sensor which was attached to the ceiling, was Damian. He was wearing a virtual reality helmet, and the weird strappy contraption with lots of yellow dots all over it. But that was all he was wearing. He lay on his back. She would have laughed, but she wanted to play this out, see what was in store. The events in Tuscany had increased her confidence no end. Plus she'd come back and immediately started spinning classes again, so was feeling a bit more trim.

She read the note again, looked at the helmet and pressed a button. *Is he waiting for...?* But he spoke before she could finish that thought.

'Welcome, mistress. I can tell you are not yet ready for our coupling,' he said, in that low, robotic drawl she remembered from last time. 'Maaaake yourself reeeeaaaddyyyy,' he said, almost chanting the words, as he patted the other side of the big wide bed.

Sadie suddenly understood and knew what she had to do. So this was her birthday gift? A sodding virtual reality helmet? Well it wouldn't surprise her, knowing Damian. She wasn't about to let him off easily, and wondered if she'd be able to have a cyber-row, so as her curiosity increased ten-fold, she climbed up onto the other side of the bed. She picked up a diagram which had been left next to another strappy, yellow-dotted harness, which glowed in the light from the ceiling strobe which passed by every few seconds. Then slipped it on, following the picture in the diagram, then took a breath and put the helmet on.

A whirring started. A weird music began, accompanied by percussion sounds like a tribal drum beat. And what came into focus as her virtual reality helmet fired up made her want to giggle. She had to bite her lip, so she'd make no sounds. Not yet.

There inside the 'virtual world' was a sex dungeon. There, on his back – *underneath her* – was Damian's avatar – a gorgeous, god-like creature, with Thor-like proportions and long flowing black locks. 'His' eyes met hers and 'he' began to move against her. She felt a pulsing feeling from the front of the jacket, and from a strap she'd fastened between her legs, which made her jump – it tickled, but nothing more. The rest of it was purely visual – virtual – inside her head. Their heads.

Damian's avatar – gorgeous as he was – was having simulated virtual reality sex. It was a bit like watching a porn film – well, from what she could recall – she'd only seen a few back in her wild student days. And none with a stud quite like this. Sadie was tempted to stay there and watch, but she had a burning question. This avatar was Damian – and he was already having quite a time of it, but with ... who? Sadie couldn't tell – couldn't see who she was meant to be – because she couldn't see her virtual reality self.

He spoke to her again. 'So tonight you choose to watch, Mistress? That is allowed by the Rules of Agar. But then I will watch you. Agreed?'

Sadie's mind was going overtime. Partly because if she spoke she didn't know what her voice would sound like. And partly because Agar was a Japanese sea vegetable. She decided to take the plunge and took a breath, then spoke.

'Agreed,' she said. Then added, '...Master.'

'Very well. Now does my Mistress have any special requests for tonight?'

She thought for a second then spoke. 'Yes...can my...Master, call me by my name?'

'My Mistress does not want to be called *Mistress?* This is most unorthodox.'

Sadie decided to sound more commanding and put some bass into her voice, speaking from lower down in her chest. 'It is my desire, Master. The sound of my name on your tongue is very... *turn-on-acious...*' she cringed at herself. This really was a new era. After this, she'd be capable of playing any role. He stopped, seemed to look up at her, but then continued, in a voice that was a cross between his virtual character and his normal voice.

'Just so we are clear, you mean I should say your avatar name?' He was gesticulating in a very Damian-like way, which Sadie saw in her helmet as Thor suddenly becoming a virtual Damian complete with mannerisms. She nearly lost it altogether.

'Yessssss, Massssterrrrr. Now DO it!' she said, and she used her virtual arm to 'slap' his virtual thigh as if she was using a crop on a horse.

'Arrrrrgggghhh!' He shouted and slipped back into character. 'Very well then, my Lady... tonight we will make virtual love together and it will be better than ever befooorrrre!' he cried.

'And how many times have we DONE it befoooooooorrrre?' she joined in, rocking backwards and forwards on her hands and knees on the bed. In her helmet she saw the effect it was having via his avatar, who was tossing his head from side to side. Sadie could feel the bed moving.

'Er... dozens... I mean – Dozennnnns,' he said.

'And when was our firrsssst tiiiimmme – and was it not the besssst!' she asked.

'When we first made love in this world of Rumingard, the cherry blossom was on the trees,' he replied, getting more and more carried away and forgetting to 'do' the voice.

'Last spring,' she added, slowing down her rocking.

'Yesssss!' he said, as the rocking on his side of the bed intensified even more.

'Like thissss?' asked Sadie.

'No, for many moons you and I were synching our time and space by the method of remote gaminnnnng. But now you have come to my domain. And our union may at last be completed once and for alllllll!'

'And now,' she said. 'Say my naaaaaaammme!'

'I will, I will,' he said, rocking helplessly as the bed started making a banging noise against the wall. Sadie held on for dear life.

'Take me noooooow, NervadaQueeeeeeeeeen.'

Sadie stopped abruptly, and his avatar in her virtual reality world opened one eye and looked at 'her'.

'What you doin'?' 'it' asked her.

'Who is NervadaQueen,' Sadie asked, in her own voice.

'What are you talking about, don't stop, Delta I'm nearly...'

But Sadie had stopped. She reeled back, took off her helmet and looked at him.

Oh my god.

Delta. Delta was his lover. But a virtual one. So did that count or not?

Well he hadn't lied. She just hadn't qualified the question. But 'are you having an affair – virtual or otherwise' – isn't the first thing that springs to mind when you think your boyfriend's cheating.

And as for Delta – well she suddenly disappeared off Sadie's Christmas list, having only just gone on it back in Tuscany. But if he wasn't expecting her, he was expecting NervadaQueen, then how did Sadie get here…?

Just then, Sadie jumped as a figure appeared in the doorway. It was Delta. She gesticulated to Sadie to 'come here and shhhh!'

Delta? Was she a goodie or a baddie in all this?

Sadie didn't know whether Delta had brought her here to do Sadie one last favour, knowing Damian was trying to see her again. Or if Delta was just being plain wicked.

Probably a bit of both.

This was ridiculous and Sadie looked around at Damian – O.M.Gee, she thought. *OMG indeed.* Sadie felt the sudden urge to laugh. He looked completely pathetic. What a nut job. She held up a finger towards Delta – *one moment* – and started removing the harness but then realised that he had stopped moving too. He felt out to the side of him – a gauntlet feeling nearer and nearer. She whipped her helmet on again quickly.

'Stayyy theeeeere…' she said, in the deep voice, 'I have something I need to doooooo,' and she sprang off the bed.

She swiftly found it all in exactly the same place – in the chest inside his bedroom. Sadie had a quick word with Delta and then left her to it, knowing the trussed up Damian would be in 'safe' hands – very safe hands indeed.

Sadie drove home smiling to herself. She suddenly felt more free than she'd ever felt in her life. Not just because she knew it was over with the Dark Lord or whatever he called himself. But also because she was off to

Hawaii – excited about this new adventure, and the only person she had to rely on now, was herself. And she quite liked herself.

And that night, as she lay in bed, looking at an email she'd been sent, she quite liked Delta too.

Sadie opened the photo attachment and gasped, then giggled. There before her eyes was a photo of a handcuffed Damian, still flat on his front on the bed wearing his harness and helmet, with a feather duster sticking out from where the sun don't shine, which was surrounded by a mountain of whipped cream and a layer of white feathers. *Surrender?* When Sadie had stopped gazing at it, she read the email.

"Just thought you'd like to see what fixtures and fittings were on display this evening when Damian's aunt's potential buyers arrived at her house – you know, the house he pretends is his? The estate agent woman ran a mile, I heard. I hope he gets kicked out for good this time, rather than just for the odd weekend."

Ahh, Sadie said as she read it, smiling and nodding.

"Hope the resolution is clear – it was pretty dark in there. Probably not one for the family album, but it might just happen to find its way onto the student union pinboard next week. Good luck in Hawaii. Delta."

CHAPTER TWENTY-FIVE

The next night, Sadie and her little family all went out to celebrate at her favourite local restaurant. It was Sadie's birthday, and the best birthday present she could ever have was sitting here round the table with her. Her two lovely daughters – arguing and fighting over who got the last prawn cracker, and her mother, who'd just agreed to mind the shop and the girls and the nosy neighbour whilst Sadie was away in Hawaii. And the laptop was sitting beside her, just in case a certain person decided to Skype.

'Mum, when you come back from Hawaii can you please get me a laptop too?' asked Georgia. 'The webcam's gone kaput.'

'Mum, Dad's supposed to be getting her one when she's *older* too – I had to wait, even for your old one – make her wait till she's the same age I was when you got me one although it would be handy to get a working webcam specially 'cos now with what's happened, you know I won't be getting that i-Pad. And even if I did, Georgia shouldn't get one before she's 14 either and...'

'But that'll be yeeeears!' cried Georgia, and she whipped the final prawn cracker from Abi's hand and popped it in her own mouth with glee.

'Girls, girls, leave your mother alone – she's lost in thought – look at her pained expression – you can always tell. Sadie? Sadie! No wonder you want to go away for a break. Tell you what, can I come too and we'll leave this pair with Phyllis – that'd soon sort them out. Now here comes the chow mein – who wants the bits I pick out...?'

Sadie laughed but she was indeed only half-listening. She was thinking about everything she had to do in the run up to the big trip. It was going to be a busy time. She wasn't even sure if she'd get the chance before she left, to visit the hairdressers for her planned transformation. That'd surprise Helen when she next saw her.

When next Sadie felt ready to see her.

Which wasn't just yet, Sadie had decided – it was quite nice having a rest from Helen, too. And anyway, a bit of radio silence would probably teach her bossy sister a lesson.

Sadie's mobile buzzed and she read a text. *Uncanny.* Fifteen minutes – just perfect.

Sadie reached over to help herself to some stir-fry and she noticed a lone figure just outside the window of the restaurant, giving her a pathetic little wave and pointing to a little package in his hand.

Sighing and pulling a face, Sadie beckoned him in.

'Daddyyyy!' said the two girls at once. 'Have you come to celebrate Mum's birthday with us? Are you eating with us? Mum is he staying, Mum? Mum?'

'Hello darlings,' he said to his daughters. Then he nodded at Grace and stepped back away from her fork which she was holding menacingly close to him. 'Grace,' he said, in greeting.

'Stuart,' she replied, in the same wary tone. 'No Yvonne?'

'It's Yvette, and no, she's at... at her house.' Grace's eyes lit up and she raised her eyebrows at Sadie, who'd also understood the implications of that one sentence. Sadie shook her head at her mother – '*not now, Mum.*'

'I just came to drop this off,' he went on, 'I was going to post it but missed the date and decided to pop in – you weren't at home but neither were the family so I thought you'd be here,' and he plonked the box in front of Sadie on the table. 'Still the same old Sadie, still predictable as ever,' he said, brazenly roughing up her hair in a mock affectionate way. 'Here on your own, though, I see. No Racer Boy? Shame – didn't think that one would last though – he was a bit too... *racy* for you, wasn't he. Still, too bad you didn't keep a rich one – could have lived a life of luxury. But then I know that would only make you uncomfortable and places like this probably suit you better, I think. And anyway, you'll never find anyone to match what we had.'

She placed her cutlery down on the table as the girls and Grace sat wide-eyed, watching, munching in unison, and saying nothing.

'Stuart,' began Sadie.

'*Sugarlips?*' he replied. She took a breath and turned to him, ignoring his jibe. She sat herself up as tall as she could. *Confident. Do it.*

'I think you're mistaking me for someone who gives a damn about what you think,' she said, slowly and clearly.

'Well, you always do, don't you, and...'

'Not anymore,' said Sadie, standing up and taking his arm by the elbow. 'Say goodbye to your father, kids, he'll see you next weekend.'

'Bye Dad,' they said as one.

'Er... bye girls,' he said. Then as they reached the door, Sadie allowed him to shrug off her grip and he turned to her. 'Sadie, about next weekend, I meant to tell you, Yvonne and I, I mean Yvette and I are a bit, well...'

'Stuart?' she said, enquiringly.

'...yes Lady Sadie?'

'Sod off. I don't care about your women, I don't care about your problems, and quite frankly, I no longer care about you. And if you visit the shop again when I'm not there and take an incense burner to give to me for my birthday, I will personally come and hound you until you pay the shop what you owe. Which currently stands at twenty seven pounds and sixty pence. I have more important things to do than spend time with you so if you'll excuse me, I'm going back to our daughters, who still, for some lovely reason, like to spend time with you. But I don't. So go back to... wherever it is you're living now, and get used to the new me. Because from now on, things are going to be just a little bit different around here. OK?'

Sadie turned to go back into the main restaurant and realised that everything had gone silent there. Suddenly she was greeted with a small round of applause not only from her own table but also the couples on the nearby tables and four of the waiters. She smiled, did a funny little bow and headed back to her own table.

Almost as soon as she'd sat down, her laptop began to bleep – it was Helen calling from New York. Sadie decided to answer it.

'Sadie!' she began, then sang a very bad version of '*hippo birdie two ewes*'. Sadie let the girls and Grace say *hi* briefly then took the laptop out to the foyer of the restaurant, where the takeaway section was, and the wi-fi signal was good enough to get a clear picture on Skype. Helen began to tell Sadie what had happened in New York, and what her old pal Kate and Damian Grant had done for her.

'A book? Not a column?' Sadie asked.

'Can't rely on signal being good enough in the places I'll be going, to meet regular column deadlines,' Helen explained, the signal flickering a little and making her picture judder briefly before it became clear again. 'And some of the challenges will take weeks on end.'

'What did you say it's called again?'

'Try it For the First Time club!' Helen said, and laughed. 'TiFFT for short! Damian Grant's got such faith in me, it's amazing. He heard what happened with his brother and me in Tuscany – said he wanted to make amends. So he and Kate got an investor and now he's setting up an independent publishers. He's given me an advance, and a year to write it. So I'm off, sis. I'm doing what *you* told *me* to do for a change!'

'I'm so pleased! Really. This is just the break you need,' said Sadie. *And just the space WE need too,* she thought. 'So when do you go?'

'Well that's what I wanted to talk to you about,' Helen said.

'Oh, oh, I know that look,' Sadie grinned, wondering what on earth her errant sister was going to say now.

'You see, I've already gone. I'm here. It's begun,' and she turned the picture round so Sadie could see more clearly the background behind Helen. It was the ruins, in Tuscany. And there beside her, was Alessandro.

'Happy birthday, *Bella*,' he said, and blew a kiss. The screen then showed Helen again, making a cheeky face and giving a big thumbs up to Sadie.

'Oh Hells, I'm so pleased for you – you go for it girl!' The signal started to break up again. 'Did you want to speak to mum?'

Helen hesitated and then shook her head. 'Next time. Maybe. But before I go, just to let you know, I've rented out my flat and Crystal's putting some of my stuff in storage for me. But she'll be bringing you a couple of things I can't risk getting damp. Is that ok?'

'What are they?' asked Sadie.

'My best designer suits and the rest of my most precious shoes. Keep them under lock and key, ok? Apart from those ones I said you can use.'

'Oooo – well maybe as a penance, now I know where the expensive stuff is, I'll have to borrow them – once I lose a bit of weight.'

'Yeah, I won't be worried about that then,' said Helen, laughing. Then the sound went all metallic and they said their goodbyes.

'Good luck, sis, on your escape to Hawaii,' Helen said. 'You might not hear from me for a while, after Tuscany we're off to Alessandro's retreat in Tibet, but I'll check in every so often. And remember – no news means I'm having fun! I've got a year to come up with as many TiFFT's as I can!'

And the first one, thought Sadie, *is for the first time ever, letting a man into your heart. Properly.*

'Safe travels,' Sadie said, just before the signal froze and Helen was gone.

A new era indeed. For both of them.

THE END...?

To be continued....

THE ADVENTURE CONTINUES...

HAWAIIAN RETREAT – Part Three of the Trilogy – Helen's story continues.

Helen's year of self-discovery begins. Italian passion meets tantric sensuality in the luxurious retreat deep in the Himalayas. But with a deeper secret from the past suddenly catching up with her, how long can Helen continue on her quest to complete her new column, the Try it For the First Time Club?

COMING TO AMAZON SUMMER 2014

HAWAIIAN AFFAIR – Part Two of the Trilogy – Sadie's story continues

Feisty single mum and would-be businesswoman Sadie Turner needs an investor – and fast. Nothing can stand in her way. With a life-changing deal on the table, success is finally within reach, but she only has thirty days to sign the contract, so the race is on.

Mac is a playboy billionaire with an appetite for extreme sports and supermodels. But he never mixes business with pleasure. So where does curvy Sadie fit in? From the most incredible board room showdown, via passionate nights on board a luxury yacht in Monaco and in magical Hawaii, their exciting adventure takes them half way round the world. But can they seal the deal, and stay out of love?

– Available on Amazon since summer 2013

– PG or STEAMY (adult content) options

– Paperback or eBook for Kindle.

Click here or search Hawaiian Affair by Debbie Flint. On amazon.co.uk

Or search amazon.com